The Banneret's Blade

TROUBLE BREWING

—ᗰ—

A Novel set at the Start of the Hundred Years War between the
Kingdoms of England and France

Nicholas de Rothschild

ISBN: 1499293666
ISBN-13: 9781499293661
Library of Congress Control Number: 2014907981
CreateSpace Independent Publishing Platform
North Charleston, South Carolina

Dedication

To my beloved wife, Caroline, who has watched this epic grow.

Acknowledgments

My editor, Tara O'Sullivan and my good chum, Andrew Duncan, deserve special thanks and a mention. Tara, who made sure all the 't's' was crossed and every 'i' dotted, each comma, full stop and, above all, the whole thing made sense. Andrew, also, has advised throughout on matters publishing. Alex Catto read an earlier draft and enjoyed it. Otherwise my sources and inspirations, ranging from documentaries on TV and snippets picked up via Wikipedia and other Internet sites, have been many and varied and most are included in a bibliography at the end of the book.

The Vow Of The Heron.

I vow and promise to God in heaven and his sweet Mother, who nourished Him, that before this year is ended I will defy the king of St. Denis. And I will cross the sea, my subjects with me, and I will pass through the Cambrésis by way of Hainault, and in Vermandois I will take my lodging at will. I will set the country ablaze and there I will await my mortal enemy, Philip of Valois, who wears the fleur-de-lis; I will wait until a full month has passed. If he and his subjects attack me, I will fight him, he can be sure of that, even if I have only one man to his ten. Does he believe that he can take my land from me? If I once paid him homage, which confounds me now, I was young: that is not worth two ears of corn. I swear to him as king, by St. George and St. Denis, that since the time of Hector, Achilles, Paris or Alexander, who conquered many lands, neither youth nor noble ever exacted such tribute in France as I intend to do before the year forty-six if he does not attack me with his subjects. But I renounce him, you can be sure of that, for I will make war on him by word and deed. With my oath I have undertaken this vow.'

King Edward III

When Robert of Artois heard that, he laughed and said to himself, 'Now I have my wish, since, on this heron that I caught today, a great war will begin…..

Contents

Prologue

The Ambush

The Jew poked the dead dog with his stick and watched as a swarm of iridescent green flies rose and settled back on the congealing blood that oozed from a wound that had almost cut through the creature's throat. It was Salomon's dog and half an hour before it had been running happily up and down his convoy, begging for scraps and barking incessantly. Now it was laid dead beside the road about fifty yards ahead of his *caravanserai*. He had spotted the corpse by chance, half-hidden in a bushy thicket. It had been the buzzing insects that had caught his attention.

A bead of sweat formed under the rim of his conical hat. This was the hated symbol of religious identity that all Jews had to wear by French law. Force of habit made him twirl his long, copper-coloured ringlets. Isaac was deeply worried and, stroking his neatly clipped beard, he scanned the road and his surroundings, his penetrating, yellow-flecked blue eyes taking in every feature and nuance of the terrain. Ahead, a rutted track just wide enough for his wagons, climbed steeply towards a nameless plateau. On each side rocks jutted out like bloated fat men's bellies, with scrubby oaks protruding between cracks and tangled scrub cloaking their bases like pubic hair. The air was still, pregnant with hidden menace.

Isaac swiftly strode the length of his column to alert his companions to danger. It could be bandits - he was not *too* worried by local robbers - or it could be worse. For whoever or whatever he had a surprise in store. A hay wain and tinker's cart were towards the front of the column and a dozen dozy-looking armed men accompanied a commissary wagon at its rear.

He ordered six men forward to scout the track. He stopped by his own cart, a non-descript general goods conveyer, where his daughter, Sarah, had taken over at reins and tried to come up with a few reassuring words, a shadow of fear crossing his face. Their destination lay within an hour's march, but it could have been next year now that he felt that they had been discovered.

He called for silence as he strained to hear the slightest sound but was only rewarded with the buzzing of flies. Oppressive heat made the air so thick it could be cut with Isaac's famous scimitar; this wondrous weapon, he had heard, had an illustrious history and was supposedly a gift from the great Sultan Saladin to the English crusader king, Richard the Lionheart. A scholar friend in Toledo had deciphered the swirling Arabic inscription for him. The gilding on the blade had nearly worn away, leaving only the faintest outline. It apparently read: *'From one brave warrior to another'*. The hilt was inset with emeralds and rubies; its blade was forged from finest Damascus steel and was kept so razor-sharp that it could cut silk wafted through the air, or sever flesh and metal with equal facility. The weapon had been purloined during the chaos following King Richard's death at Châlus more than a century before and Isaac had acquired it from its previous owner, a French nobleman of dubious worth, as part-repayment for a loan.

Long ago, Isaac of Rouen had made a pact with his Maker that if he did not kill fellow Jews, He would forgive him a few Christian souls. It was this willingness to use his weapon in the service of his business that made him principal carrier of treasure and valuables for his people. They called him 'The Moneymover', and his services were used by traders of all faiths, far and wide. His success lay in his apparent invisibility. His convoy was disguised so that to casual observers it was composed of itinerant tinkers and poor Jews accompanying some farm carts full of fodder and cheap tat.

In these dangerous times, when the battle lines between French and English in this region were blurred at best, poor folk on the move gathered together for mutual protection from robbers. Thus it was common for more than a hundred people to travel together for protection. So there was nothing unusual about Isaac's column of soberly dressed men, women and children, with some even in rags and none flaunting any outward signs of wealth. They were defended, ostensibly, by some cheap guards on horseback armed with nothing more than rusty swords and spears. This elaborate charade was the column's first line of defence. Who would suspect poor Jews and itinerant tradesmen, innocent-looking men, women and children?

Isaac's secret lay in the tinker's cart and the hay wain. The former was covered with pots and pans for authenticity, but in reality concealed a fortress on wheels where six Genoese, armed with loaded crossbows, sat athwart a strongbox, ready to fire deadly bolts at attackers through concealed slits. The hay wain was his other surprise. In this hollow cart, another six men-at-arms sweated profusely on benches, in full battle kit, in the dark. The pair nearest the rear sat with swords drawn, ready for instant action, while the other four would reach up and seize razor sharp pikes hanging from a false ceiling. Only a sharp eye would spot that the wagons were not being pulled by broken-down nags but prime draft horses with a double set of reins, one of which disappeared into the vehicle. Many of his co-religionists took advantage of the security provided by two disguised wagons. Who could resist being defended by a dozen ferocious warriors, all of whom were over six feet tall?

It was a toss-up as to which vehicle was preferable. For those in the tinker's cart, the incessant clanking of kitchenware was amplified by the confined space and, even with wool earplugs, the sound was maddening. The hay wain could be stiflingly hot and dusty, which made throats dry. To cough at an inappropriate moment could reveal the deception, but in the mercenaries' opinion the heat of the hay wain was better than the incessant racket inside the tinker's cart.

Each morning, as opposed to being brushed, the horses would be made purposefully dusty. A sprinkling of alum was painted on to highlight ribs, augmenting an image of decrepitude. If flight were the only option, the horses were capable of prolonged bursts of speed. The secondary line of defence was more deadly. If attacked, the back of the hay wain would swing open on well-oiled hinges and a fluid mass of angry, well-armoured warriors would emerge.

Isaac had been unable to quell the frequent quarrels that often erupted at suppertime and, even though he had devised a rota, the argument about who should sit where had been particularly garrulous two nights previously. The summer's heat had frayed tempers to such an extent that his men-at-arms had a *fuck-the-Jew-let's-get-drunk* attitude that particular Friday, and decided to flout their master's instructions about refraining from imbibing excessive amounts of wine. They reckoned that, as was his habit, he would be off in the woods with his tribe wailing to their God from sunset on Friday to sunset on Saturday.

An obscure tavern, in the middle of fuck-nowhere, proved an irresistible temptation, and all they could think about was slaking their thirst. It was obviously a popular joint with buxom country girls happy to entertain for a few coppers. The merchants and the other guards also were happy to join the party, so nobody really noticed or cared about a scruffy young man in deep conversation with a companion, hidden in shadows at the tavern's rear. They were also wrong about their assumption that the Jew would do nothing. As they spilled, happily inebriated, onto the street, their paymaster upbraided them, waving his scimitar menacingly within a hairsbreadth of their noses.

'You disobeyed me,' he hissed. There was a savage glint in his yellow-flecked eyes; Jew or not, he was not a man to be trifled with. He darted into the tavern. It was empty. 'One of you is supposed to buy wine, and then you drink it somewhere discreet.' These bastards knew and exploited his weakness; that he was not prepared usually to break the sanctity of the Sabbath to enforce his no-drinking-while-transporting policy.

This time his Genoese had stretched his patience to breaking point. Their shouting could be heard from a hundred paces and could have compromised their security. He had travelled the route enough times to make sure that they spent the Sabbath far from the beaten track where there were few prying eyes, always avoiding towns, sticking to byways. However this tavern was new and therefore unexpected.

Saturday was the convoy's day of rest for Jew and Christian alike. His monsters did not worry about working on a Sunday and anyone else could pray while they trudged. Isaac observed that his Genoese seemed keener on breaking most of God's sacred Commandments than upholding them. It was a matter of policy that his men eat apart, setting up camp each night at some deserted spot. The sight of twelve extremely large men was bound to attract unwanted attention. He would joke with them that he was Jesus and they were his twelve disciples. They retorted that they would burn him at the stake if they did not get paid and eat his roasted liver to boot.

His fury had only just subsided when he got back to where his daughter was helping the other women prepare their evening meal. He sat down on a log and prodded at his plate of bread and cheese. Salomon's dog put its head on his lap and begged for some scraps. Isaac liked the dog, patting it on the head and giving it a scratch behind its ears; it was good at sensing the untoward and often alerted him to danger.

'How much are we carrying?' Sarah asked, knowing she shouldn't- but the preparations for this journey had been more rigorous than usual. At seventeen she was Isaac's only child and the apple of his eye. His wife, *God rest her soul*, had recently died of a bloody flux. To begin with he had been reluctant to allow Sarah to come along. She had begged and pleaded and he had let his sentimentality get the better of him. If all went well, she would have a handsome dowry, and he knew that there were many eligible young men in his community who were interested... It was time he had a grandchild.

'Enough money for the King to build a fine castle,' replied Isaac, acutely aware that this was the largest sum he had ever had to transport. It had taken several years to collect enough money, a tithe raised on every Jew across the whole of Provence, Gascony, Normandy and Navarre, and laboriously assembled in Carcassonne. They hoped, through this generosity, to be allowed to remain in Paris, from where the Jews had been expelled from the Kingdom of France only two decades earlier. They had been allowed back nine years later under much more stringent conditions and after a payment of over one hundred and twenty thousand *livres* for the privilege of returning. They also hoped that this payment would forestall further attacks on their communities, which they heard had been planned by their enemies. A pliant and compassionate ruler was their only protection from the forces arrayed against them. Dispossessed of their land for more than a thousand years, exiled from their homeland, forced forever to wander by the Romans and now accused of being the murderers of Christ, the Jews' lot was not a happy one.

It was thus paramount to keep on the right side of any king, and this one was no exception. They had heard that he was planning a crusade and no one could tell how sympathetic King Philippe Valois would be towards the Chosen Race on this adventure. It was the Christian year 1336 and the idea of the crusade had subsided, but still they felt it prudent to give this man a present of suitable magnitude. Kings, community leaders agreed, liked castles, so what better gift could they give him but a brand new one? They could not build it for him, as the Jews were forbidden most trades. So they were sending a treasure chest filled with gold and silver bullion, jewels and the like; so much that Isaac had to strengthen the axles of the tinker's cart to take the weight.

His convoy had forded the Dordogne in what was nominally French territory, but there were few places of strategic importance in the area and the *châtelaines* of the region's castles were content to back whichever kingdom paid more, England or France.

To add authenticity, Isaac had been delighted to attract a party of Franciscan Friars to join the column. It had taken all his powers of persuasion, and a hefty donation to their order, to get them to travel on a Sunday. He made the monks walk beside the hay wain and conduct their services on the march. 'God will forgive you not being on your knees if you praise him loudly enough,' he had told their leader. They were dreadful singers, so Isaac took pleasure in torturing his Genoese men-at-arms, confined in their hot box, with their incessant out-of-tune chanting.

Isaac wiped a bead of sweat from his forehead, as he tried to focus. *Who had killed the dog?* His nervousness was as catching as off-key plain-song, which to his great irritation started up again, echoing off the cliffs and through the canyon ahead. For the Jews the proximity of these proselytising monks, too, was purgatory. *Sometimes Isaac could take matters too far*, they murmured amongst themselves. They would have *words* with him, but they would have to wait till later. Now the walls of rock on either side were becoming more threatening. A blackbird started chinking the alarm - it could be a snake....

A covey of partridges exploded from the bluff above Isaac's head, chortling in a whirr of wing beats. Slowly he drew out his wicked curved blade, which glinted in the afternoon sun. He was halfway along the convoy when a shout from behind heralded an explosion of sounds. Dull twanging thunks were followed by swishing - the whole effect being like half-angry bees - and then a scream. It was the sound of archers in action on the cliff top. All was confusion as well-armed horsemen attacked the column's rear, rapidly shredding his remaining rear-guard.

This was no bandit attack; they were being assaulted by seasoned troops, disciplined, with pre-planned malice. Isaac watched in horror as a team of men-at-arms ran out from behind some rocks with planks of wood, hammers and nails, sealing the back of the hay wain before his Genoese could react, and then setting it alight. He had expected to watch his giants come out like angry scorpions. Instead they were being roasted alive.

He had, indeed, been discovered.

A spiked wooden barrier crashed out from behind a tree where it had been cunningly concealed, barring the road ahead. A knight with an old-fashioned cylindrical helm, dented and rusty, directed the ambush. His surcoat, decorated with a 'green boar rampant' motif, had seen better days; his shield was battered from constant use. The outline of his once proud heraldic device looked like a sow with crisscross cuts across its belly resembling teats.

However, first impressions were deceptive. The knight rode an expensive high-necked destrier; Isaac recognised quality in horseflesh having taken enough as surety for debts. This prancing charger was caparisoned in a dirty green padded covering that came down to its fetlocks, and its rider was armed with a morgenstern - a spiked ball on a chain that was, in skilled hands, a lethal weapon. From there the knight issued a stream of muffled instructions to a sergeant, a man was as large, if not larger, than the Jew's own guards, who stood beside him carrying a falchion, a sword-like weapon that closely resembled a butcher's single sided meat cleaver except this one was designed to cleave men not beasts. The sergeant, in turn, shouted to squads of men, archers and men-at-arms, in more guttural words.

English! Isaac had not heard any reports of English soldiers in the vicinity - his scouts would have seen them, but they, he presumed, must have met the same fate as the dog.

The trapped Genoese yelled, maddened by the heat, as they struggled to free themselves from their fiery coffin, finally bursting out of the wagon through flaming straw. The knight was waiting for this moment, sallying forward he dispatched the swordsmen with clinical efficiency, the sweeping blows from his morgenstern crushing their tight-fitting bascinet helmets like paper as they stooped forward to jump out of the wagon's back - their only moment of vulnerability - withdrawing with alacrity as the pike men reached up for their weapons. *So he knew what was coming next.* Isaac watched his tormentor stagger as a crossbow bolt fired from the tinker's cart struck a glancing blow to the knight's chest. To his chagrin, the spent quarrel spun harmlessly into the air, being deflected off a concealed breastplate. The force of the blow, though, made the knight slip from his saddle into his sergeant's arms. At least his crossbowmen with the money were holding firm - Isaac was aware of the well-aimed quarrels that continued to pick off attackers.

'Get the Pigman,' he shouted, alluding to the porcine heraldic motif on the knight's surcoat, as he ran past Sarah towards his adversary.

The four pikemen emerged, slashing and stabbing, jumping over their fallen comrades. The knight had been replaced by a phalanx of men-at-arms who struggled in a wild melee to contain their charge. The sergeant barked an order and, immediately to a man, the English lay down. In the split second of confusion the Genoese paused, and archers on nearby rocks fired a volley of arrows at close range. As quickly as the enemy was distracted the attackers were up, stabbing at groins and hacking at knees. Knight and sergeant moved in for the kill, overwhelming the arrow-peppered Genoese.

Trapped in the gully with nowhere to hide, the fight developed into a massacre; the men, women and children were killed without discrimination. Isaac's people fought back as best they could. Their crude weapons were designed to be easily hidden and frighten off the inquisitive. They were not equipped to withstand the thoroughness and brutality of this assault. Isaac stopped and watched with incredulity as ironclad killing machines raced up to his cash wagon with stout poles, forcing horses to bolt. As they did so, the logs were jammed through the wheels, splintering the spokes. His mobile fortress toppled over, rendering the crossbowmen harmless. The knight, now recovered, assaulted the crossbowmen along with his troop as they struggled to escape through a tangle of pots and pans.

More adrenalin coursed through Isaac's body. Filling his lungs he rushed forward, yelling and flailing his scimitar. *I will strike at the head of the snake that is strangling my little army.* Chopping, piercing, slashing, he downed five adversaries that stood between him and the Pigman. *I'll kill the swine myself.*

The knight tried to swat his attacker with the morgenstern as he ducked and dived. The Jew was as quick and slippery as a greased monkey, dodging deadly blows, and in a flash of glittering steel he cut through the morgenstern's chain, slicing metal like a warm knife through butter, making the spiked ball fly harmlessly away. The warhorse rose on its back legs, lashing out with hooves. Isaac sidestepped and lunged as he aimed a deadly thrust at his adversary's heart. In his single-minded desire for revenge he'd forgotten the sergeant who, with a sweep of his falchion, severed Isaac's hand at the wrist. He stared in disbelief as a fountain of blood spurted from his severed wrist. His hand, still clutching his scimitar, lay at the feet of the prancing warhorse. His world was only confusion as he whirled round in a fountain of blood. He could see his sword six feet away. He didn't see the blow that removed his head...

Chapter 1

Dunbar Must Fall

The cold grip of winter did nothing to dispel the general euphoria that William Montagu, the Earl of Salisbury, felt as the vanguard of his army topped the rise overlooking Dunbar Castle. From this viewpoint in the hills the castle looked like an inconsequential pimple on an insignificant promontory jutting out into a leaden North Sea. During the previous siege, five years before, it had been battered to pieces and rebuilt, at ruinous expense, by the Earl of March. Now the Earl had reneged on his oath of allegiance and William was tasked by King Edward to batter Dunbar back to ruins once again.

'Last time it took three weeks,' Salisbury told the knight riding next to him, 'and then we only had one siege engine. This time I have two.' The Earl sat back in his saddle and rubbed his empty eye-socket. He had good reason to hate the Scots, who had robbed him of his eye five years before.

The knight, Sir Roger de Bohun, nodded; he, too, had been here before, after the Battle of Hallidon Hill, where he had won his spurs. Last time there hadn't been a causeway with marsh on either side, and the walls weren't made of granite. It might have cost the Earl of March a small fortune but this time the lessons of the previous siege seemed to have been well learnt.

'I see our galleys have arrived,' Salisbury continued blithely, pointing at two sleek Genoese warships that made their way round the headland. 'They'll stop reinforcements coming by sea.'

'That's going to be our problem,' said Sir Roger. 'That wasn't there before.' Sir Roger had learnt his craft the hard way - always seeking a fight, being bold and aggressive - though he was not averse to using subtlety and cunning.

Salisbury described his oft-time drinking partner, and now divisional commander, as mercurial and fox-like. His bluff exterior hid many secrets, not least in the detail of the acquisition of his fortune. The story intrigued him and had been told and retold many times, but it never rang true. The cash, and there had been lots of it, had been split between the King and Sir Roger, but it couldn't have come as a ransom. The rules about ransoms were strictly adhered to - there had to be a person of consequence to buy back. Treasure of that magnitude had to have come from somewhere. William had quizzed the King, to whom he was also extremely close, and been stonewalled by that friend as well. Rumours were that some of the coins were Moorish and Sir Roger's scimitar suggested similar origins. *I'll find out one day I suppose*, and William put the thought out of his mind. He had enough on his plate with troublesome Scots.

He fervently hoped that the Lady Agnes would give up without much of a fight, and ordered that they should send a herald with terms of surrender. There would be no dishonour in admitting defeat after an honourable, if short, length of time. 'She's a feisty cow, though.' He'd met the redoubtable lady in more peaceful circumstances.

'Last time, we could get right up to the walls.' Sir Roger could make out new thickets of gorse and a causeway that had not been there before. This time, as he and his men rode down; they discovered these thickets hid ditches filled with spikes and traps. The Hairy Ones had prepared the ground well. Dunbar would be a far harder nut to crack...

'Hold out until I return with reinforcements' had been the Earl of March's last instructions to his wife. 'I'll be back with the Scottish army.' It had turned out to be an idle promise; his relief force was no match for the English and was defeated, slinking away without even sending word. 'If she has any sense she'll surrender, but she's got the obstinacy of a Banchory Mule,' March had said bitterly as he retreated through snow-covered hills back to Edinburgh. 'A mere handful of Scots against the full might of England! Mind you, I've made that place damn nigh impregnable... And she's got the Silent Killer.' He could never remember the name of the leader of the five French crossbowmen that were on loan from the French King. Her husband had left a scratch garrison, mostly older or sick men, led by the ineffable Laurence of Preston, to hold out as long as they were able.

Forty against four thousand.

Not good odds. Pasquale de Puyguilhem, the so-called Silent Killer because of his exceptional skill with his arbalest, contemplated his chances with a degree of stoicism as he watched the might of England fill the horizon with an endless column of men and carts. Next to him Lady Agnes, Countess of March, stood on the highest part of the battlements watching the arrival of the English army.

'See, we've got the company of two earls.' She pointed to their pennants. Frenchie looked at his mistress and wondered where she got her courage. Though everyone knew her by her nickname, 'Black' Agnes, few dared to call her this to her face without receiving a withering look. She was in her mid-thirties and the shock of frizzy black hair that inspired he nickname flying out in all directions from under very modest headgear, giving her a distinctive halo that was instantly recognisable even from as far away as the English camp.

'I'll never surrender while there's breath in my body,' she told the crossbowman as she sat down to compose a suitable reply to the terms on offer. 'There,' and she wrote it out on a piece of paper torn from the back of the castle's only book, a bible. 'I hold my house for Scotland's king, he pays me meat and fee. And I will keep my house, while my good old house keeps me.' 'You see, us Scots never give up without a fight. And,' she said, lowering her voice conspiratorially, 'I've got you.' She would lead by example. Pasquale offered her a quarrel with a blunt head and, after wrapping the message around its shaft, mounted it on his crossbow.

'And where would Milady like it placed, on his head or between his feet?'

'Feet will do.' Even with the message attached, the Silent Killer managed to land it plum on the herald's toes.

—ᴍ—

Two months later, Lady Agnes and Pasquale looked out over the network of ditches and enfilades that spread out like a spider's web, channelling the English into killing zones where he and his team would pick them off with alarming accuracy.

From their eyrie they watched feverish activity in the camp where the English had sat since January. The Frenchman marvelled at the chatelaine's resolve, like a mother hen defending her chicks.

The siege's opening month had seen a bombardment of limestone balls, laboriously hauled by cart from Berwick to be flung by two trebuchets, most shattering ineffectually against the massive granite walls. Lady Agnes had taunted the English, dressing up her maids in their prettiest dresses and wiping the dust off with towels. Also, as luck would have it, the bulk of the castle now was out of range. Her husband had seen to that.

A massive battering ram emerged slowly through wicker siege casements at the English end of the causeway. 'I see the English have a new plan. Pick off any heads.' Agnes had faith in her Silent Killer.

'I'm the finest marksman in all of France,' he had boasted. 'I'm worth one hundred men, you'll see.' It was time to put this faith to the test, but that was not all.

'Ready and waiting,' she said, well satisfied with the heavy spherical stones her men had retrieved. Using all their ingenuity, these were presently poised precariously above the gatehouse. 'This should give them an unpleasant surprise.'

—ᴍ—

The ram, a metal-tipped tree trunk on ropes, was slung under an awning of dried ox-hide the size of a peasant's cottage. It was rolled on eight sets of wagon wheels and took thirty men to push it at a slow walking pace. These contraptions were often called sows because men were crowded round the log like piglets round their mother. The plan was simplicity itself, if you want to get into a house, knock on the door; if you want get into a castle, smash down the gate.

Sir Roger, whose task it was to command the sow, took his final briefing from the Earl who, after reminding him of its great cost, wished him every success. 'If anyone can triumph, you can.'

A good-sized, muscular man, taller than most, Sir Roger flicked his long blond hair out of his eyes and twirled his moustache thoughtfully. *I must make confession - better safe than sorry.* So he sought out a priest. Then he gave his squire, Justin de Frage, final instructions in case he should not return.

'I've left all my documents and prayer book in the chest under my cot - here's the key. Tell Lady Alice that I love her and make sure Harry becomes a pious and noble knight.'

Sir Roger was not one for long speeches. Kneeling down one last time, he closed his eyes and could see his wife with her lustrous red hair and emerald green dress, a colour she loved. He knew his young son Harry less well, having been away on campaign so long he had trouble forming a picture of him. He also had a daughter, but had only seen her once as a babe in swaddling. He kept his sentimentality to a minimum before striding out to find his men.

His faithful sergeant, John Gwyn, had assembled them for inspection. Gwyn had served him through thick and thin for six years and was dependable. He was a man mountain, known simply as the Ox. It was he who had saved Sir Roger from the Jew's scimitar.

'Shall I put the banner on the sow?' The Ox asked, though Sir Roger could see this was an after-the-fact request. His *Green Boar Rampant* banner had already been nailed to its front. Most of the thirty men-at-arms had served under his command since Gascony and had been well rewarded for their efforts. They all wore chainmail vests of varying lengths and rustiness. Those that had fared well in battle had collected further bits of plate, knee and elbow protectors, a few had breastplates and all had aketons or hauberks, different types of thickly padded jackets with metal plates or *cuir-bouille*, hardened leather, sewn in. All had helmets and all were dented to a greater or lesser degree. Their aim was simple: cover the body's most vulnerable parts with as many layers as possible and pray that whatever charm they had bought or owned worked. Mostly, these were a motley collection of animal parts, with hare's feet, rabbit paws and scuts being favourites. Sir Roger considered them part of Saxon superstition, pagan not Christian. He preferred more tangible blessed protection and kissed the leather token that he had bought at Queen Eleanor's shrine in Northampton. Though the inscription had faded from numerous kissings, he knew it still invoked the protection of the Holy Trinity and reverentially rolled it up and stuck it into one of the small holes that had been drilled in his helm's side to improve his hearing in the heat of battle. *What better shield can a man have than God the Father, Son and Holy Ghost?* He crossed himself as his armourer settled the cumbersome metal tube over his head.

His vision was limited as he surveyed his troops through the narrow eye slit of his helm as they took up their stations under the raw-hide awning and started the long push down the narrow causeway. *After this I'm going to get a new helmet with a visor.* He was fed up with this cumbersome piece of headgear. It might be fine for jousting but was wholly unsatisfactory for this kind of work.

'Put your backs into it!' roared Ox. 'Today we will cover ourselves in glory.' *Or die in the attempt.* The sow picked up momentum.

'Only fifty yards to go,' shouted the front man.

Sir Roger pushed as hard as the rest of his men. He believed that leadership was something earned and not, as most of his aristocratic friends- but not all, felt was a God-given birthright. Decisive action on the battlefield was always imperative; to dither was to invite death. Sweat formed rivulets on his brow that coursed down his face. The salty water stung his eyes and he stood back for a second to readjust his trusty, battered, heavy metal helm, and in doing so poked his head out from under the protective leather awning.

Whap!

A stunning blow caught him just above his ear, knocking him clean off his feet. Black Agnes's Silent Killer had struck again. Her raven haired figure could be seen flitting along the battlements as she directed her meagre but deadly forces. More crossbow bolts started to find their range.

Sir Roger lay absolutely still, staring up at the sky while he recovered his composure and gathered his thoughts. *Play dead*, a little voice in his head whispered. He was dangerously exposed. Then, not obeying his own instructions, his ears still ringing, dazed and seeing stars, he sat up and, as he did so a second quarrel buried itself up to the stiff goose feather fletching in earth right by his thigh; still dizzy, he grabbed it. More arrows and bolts came arching off the battlements. *They're aimed at me!*

His lapse in concentration, though, proved to be his salvation. From the corner of his eye he could see the ram arrive at the gate. His men had not even knocked at the door when a succession of boulders rolled off the gatehouse top smashing through the leather awning, crushing it, and all beneath it, flat.

—⦂—

Agnes watched as some surviving piglets scurried out from the sow's wreckage before fleeing in all directions. Hurling abuse and heaping insults she screamed happily at the top of her lungs. 'Run, you lily-livered sons of whores, run to your mothers. There,' she turned to Pasquale with a note of great satisfaction in her voice, 'that's put an end to that little game. What next?'

—⦂—

Adrenalin surged through Sir Roger's veins and, galvanised into action, he sprinted back down the causeway to safety. An out-of-breath Ox sat down beside him.

'How many did we lose?' asked Sir Roger as he took off his helm and examined the deep furrow gouged in the metal - the bolt had struck by his leather token, chopping it in half. At least his sergeant had survived.

'Too many.' Gwyn looked around, taking a head count. 'We've only ten men left, and you and me.' Twenty would not be coming back. Sir Roger was devastated; he had grown fond of the men who had followed him from Gascony and in the blink of an eye they were gone, buried under Agnes's pile of stone.

The Earl came over and placed a hand of commiseration on Sir Roger's shoulder. 'We will hold a service for the dead,' he said quietly. 'I'll send a parlay body under a flag of truce to collect bodies.'

Sir Roger realised that for all this time he had been clutching the crossbow bolt in his clenched fist. On examination he could see that the stiff goose feather flights were slightly twisted to make it spin as it flew. This made the quarrels more accurate and was the trademark of Rouen Armoury. This meant there were Frenchmen with the garrison. This was also the second time he had been nearly killed by a crossbow bolt.

'They've got a mighty fine crossbowman up there,' he told Salisbury, holding up the bolt that he was still clutching in his hand, 'a damned sharp shooter, that's for sure.' He crossed himself and went down on one knee, reciting a short prayer of thanks for his deliverance.

'See,' he said, showing Gwyn a scrap of leather from inside his helm, 'saved by St. Eleanor.'

'And these are my saviours,' said the Ox stroking the desiccated collection of hares and rabbit paws that were sewn onto his sleeve.

Chapter 2

The Alchemist

A large crowd had gathered in Norwich market square, eager to witness the burning of the sorcerer. Some had camped there for several days in order to secure the best position, helping the Bishop's soldiers lay piles of faggots and cords of firewood around the stake. The unfortunate miscreant was Christopher of Malmsbury. He preferred the term alchemist to sorcerer. As he sat in his cell he fingered the rosary the Bishop had given him, viewing the next few hours with trepidation.

He had tried to express his innocence as best he could, but there was no denying that he had been experimenting with quicksilver, sulphur, alum, mandrake and cat bile. He was sure he had found the formula, though still uncertain exactly as to relative amounts, for his Elixir of Immortality. His undoing had been to succumb to the pain of torture; his old body was no longer capable of withstanding his tormentors' ministrations. He had admitted to heresy, denying the Blessed Virgin and Holy Trinity. Though his other, more heinous sin was that, after imbibing the mixture, the Bishop had suffered the most abominable abdominal pain, hovering at death's door for a week. For this, the vindictive Bishop concluded, *was* worthy of the sentence.

Christopher wondered whether Dan Digby would be in the crowd to watch his fiery demise. *The best things come in small packages.* He loved Dan like a son. They had been through many adventures together, travelling to the Holy Land in search of knowledge. Dan had been invaluable, a Jack-of-all-trades. Many times his diminutive companion, his bantam cock, had proved a lifesaver on their journeying, fighting off brigands and putting robbers to flight. His acrobatic skill was extraordinary, and he could juggle and do magic tricks. His sleight-of-hand had saved the day when Ibrahim the Unwilling, as Dan had 'christened' him, refused to part with his knowledge. However, Dan had convinced him by conjuring gold coins from the mouth of a fish. If only Ibrahim had known that they were his coins to begin with...

Perhaps he did. Ibrahim's secrets were the reason he now sat contemplating his fate. 'I'm as old as Methuselah,' Ibrahim had said, attributing his great age to the potency of the Elixir. Perhaps it had been the effects of hashish cakes that had muddled Christopher's recollection, or the fact that, during their swim ashore after being shipwrecked near Alexandria, the ink had run in his journal, leaving only the faintest scratching of nib on soggy vellum. He should have known better than try and persuade the Bishop of his ability to reproduce the formula. He had ignored the warnings and for that he was going to pay the ultimate price.

He knew everything about Dan, how he had been born in the remote Lincolnshire village of Digby on St. Alphege's Day in the year that the roof blew off St. Mary's Priory, and that, since he had never returned to the village, Dan had only a vague idea how old he was. Christopher knew. He had made it his life's mission to know everything there was to be known. Somehow the subject had never come up, and now it was too late. The time for conversation was over. They had parted and would never meet again in this life. The irony of this would not be lost on Dan. *If my calculations are correct, today is St. Alphege's Day - Dan's birthday.* Dan's parents had been travelling acrobats and it was from them he had learnt his acrobatic skills. His father had died when Dan was in his late childhood. He had fallen from a tightrope, sabotaged, the subsequent manorial enquiry had established, by a jealous rival. Christopher of Malmsbury had taken pity on his mother, taking her into service along with her boy. She became more than just his servant and Dan became like a son.

'It's time,' said the sergeant of the guard. The sergeant liked the old man, enjoying listening to his stories. 'Don't worry; I'll make sure your death is painless.' The sergeant knew that the Bishop took sadistic gratification in inflicting pain on others and was determined to deny him that pleasure.

The alchemist thanked him. He did not fear death itself, only the pain. He had been dreading the pain of the flames, even though his phial of poppy juice was working its magic. Already he was being transported across fields of daisies; already he could see angels welcoming him into heaven.

Dan was there, unable to fight back his tears. He watched as the sergeant kept his promise slipping his dagger between the old man's ribs, surreptitiously piercing his heart as the faggots were ignited.

The Bishop glowered from his throne, which had been placed on a dais outside the cathedral facing the pyre, his pleasure denied as the alchemist's head flopped forward without so much as a squeal.

There was nothing to keep Dan in Norwich, and he determined to find himself a new master. His meagre possessions were already in a canvas bag. He would go south in search of adventure.

Chapter 3

Neptune's Gift

The small crowd on the beach had been watching the skiff struggle into the teeth of an increasingly violent squall. All morning the fragile vessel had battled against wind and tide and now reached the most perilous part of its journey. Although the Isle of Wight was only a few miles away, the waters near Lepe, where they stood, were treacherous, and the watchers were amazed that anyone should risk their lives to cross the Solent on so bitter a day. Even the ferry that would normally attempt a daily crossing was still pulled up high and dry on the beach.

One of the onlookers, James Whytethorne, was the newly appointed Steward to Sir Roger de Bohun, for whom he was building a new castle at nearby Ipers Manor. Crossing himself, he said a prayer to St. Aegidius, his personal saint. The celebrations of New Year were over and the work dismantling the nearby ruins had begun again in earnest.

The Steward had been in awe of a mosaic floor they had found under a thick layer of topsoil. On his whim, a frieze of fishes and sea monsters had been carefully uncovered, a task of several days' work. He could not imagine who had created a thing of such beauty. Sadly, his workmen did not have the same appreciation of art and it had broken up as they laboured to extract the dressed stone that was their main prize. The castle was nothing grand, more of a walled and moated manor house than a bastion, as it had no central keep. Instead there was a high-ceilinged stone hall with two stories of timber frame rooms above it and a sturdy, high watchtower at the seaward end. It was, according to the architect, being constructed in the most modern manner, boasting Flemish brick chimneys and an elaborate kitchen.

For months, teams of labourers had filled wagon after wagon with stone blocks ripped up from the nearby remains of an ancient Roman fort. When he had inquired who had built the fort, he had been told that they had probably been giants, judging by the size of the stones. This had been a godsend, the foundations had yielded massive blocks of dressed limestone and there were even arches and columns. The walls, once concealed under grassy ridges, were being removed and re-used and the Steward had come down to check that no one was slacking.

'How high are the walls now,' enquired a fisherman who had sidled over, ever inquisitive about the building works. These had provided much needed employment amongst the impoverished coastal community. Though this was a mixed blessing as castles meant soldiery, which meant they would be subject to higher taxes and their wives and daughters would also suffer unwanted harassment from randy troopers against whom they had no defence.

'Taller than a man,' the Steward replied, stretching up with his arm as far as it would go, still gazing out over the choppy waters. He would have said more, except, at that moment, tragedy struck as the skiff plunged over a hidden sandbar and sank. Heads bobbed briefly in icy water but were dragged down by the undertow.

The burly fisherman pointed and started running towards frothing surf. 'One of them still lives and swims,' he shouted over his shoulder and without further thought for his own safety, plunged into the freezing Solent.

By the time they reached shore, the rescued man had stopped breathing. However, delivering a hefty punch to his belly and hauling him up by his heels had seawater pouring out of his mouth as he spluttered back to life.

Whytethorne was full of admiration. 'Give him something hot to drink.'

The half-drowned wretch could hardly move. His hands, which Whytethorne noted were delicate, were blue with cold; from his clothing it was obvious he was no ordinary soul. Thin fish gruel somewhat revived the shivering man but he still lacked the ability to speak.

'Throw him on a cart,' ordered the Steward. 'I'll take Neptune's gift back to the Castle.' *And see what her Ladyship thinks of him.*

His new mistress, Lady Alice, also intrigued him greatly. She was an aristocrat of the highest pedigree, daughter of one of Brittany's premier Earls, and was married by royal decree no less, to a seemingly impoverished knight. At the time of the marriage her husband was not capable of rubbing two pennies together, however, recently he seemed to have made good.

'I'm the King's Friend, before that I was his Whipping Boy,' Sir Roger had told him proudly when James had been appointed to the Steward's job. 'And she was the King's gift to me.'

She had been Lady-in-Waiting at the Court of Queen Philippa, Edward's wife, and at the time, a ravishing, and innocent, fourteen-year-old. The King had walked into his wife's chambers with Sir Roger and without so much as a by-your-leave told her that he had decided that she should marry his Friend. 'I've already written to your father' (which he had,) 'and he wishes me to tell you he's delighted.' (Which he wasn't, but *he* was King and that was that.)

Within days they were lovers, within a month they were married, and nine months later to the day she had produced a son and heir.

James had watched her arrive with three French ladies-in-waiting, her personal servants, and two small children, and had been on hand to comfort her when she had broken down into tears at the sight of the dilapidated hall he had been tasked to rebuild. 'That bastard husband of mine told me it was finished and all I had to do was decorate,' she had wailed as she surveyed the building site of mud and rubble, rather than the lovely manor with rose-filled gardens that she had been promised. But then she knew her husband was an accomplished liar when he needed or wanted to be.

Since then James had developed an admiration for this feisty woman. Her resilience and adaptability won his respect as she rapidly grasped household matters and soon had a working knowledge of the local language, becoming quite proficient in producing an unseemly stream of English profanity that made the most obdurate labourers pliant and obedient.

When her husband had suggested she help oversee the enlargement and aggrandisement of Ipers Manor into a castle she had not *quite* realised what she was letting herself in for. Not only were there hundreds of workmen and artisans in residence in shacks, wattle hovels, tents and lean-tos, there were also new members of their entourage crammed into what few rooms remained around the old hall.

And I'm bored of living on a building site. Lady Alice gently dabbed some rouge onto her fulsome lips, carefully examining her fine bone structure in a hand mirror. She had an aristocratic hauteur, and, at twenty-two, she considered herself in her prime. She was well-satisfied with her appearance, as befitted a woman of her importance. When her husband had airily announced that he was going to turn this run-down property into a castle she had thought that it would happen by waving a magic wand rather than the concerted effort of many sweaty men who needed feeding and clothing.

Now, after her second child, Lady Alice was pleased that her breasts had remained firm. No suckling of infants for her, though they were *slightly* larger than she would have liked. The fashion was for breasts to be small, firm and pert. Large breasts were for wet-nurses and milkmaids. *I have my standards,* she reminded herself. Her husband had *views*, maintaining that nipples should point heavenward so the angels could appreciate them otherwise, so he used to say, otherwise they were no better than cow's udders. She enjoyed the act of coupling with her husband, and though she could make no comparisons, (she had been, to date, completely faithful), she understood from her friends that she was lucky that her husband was an enthusiastic and considerate lover. It worried - no, it infuriated - her to think that some of these friends spoke from experience.

Her mother's death had taught her self-reliance. She could read, write and speak passable Latin; she was also mathematically endowed, being capable of adding and subtracting. She could embroider with skill and had a fine line in salacious stories, which had made her a popular figure at Court. She could not, however, sing. To her chagrin she was tone-deaf, and try as she might, and she had been forced frequently in those early years, she could not find a note.

Like most wives of fighting men, she had not spent a great deal of time in her husband's company, as he was forever off warring. When they were together, however, she found his company convivial and she relished in the confidence he had bestowed on her and the power it gave her.

Lady Alice had been delighted when her husband had told her, in somewhat vague terms, of his new fortune. She relished the idea of becoming a proper châtelaine, even though it meant uprooting herself from all that was familiar. As far as she knew it was a substantial fortune, and she was determined to spend what she considered her fair share of it. *Have I not borne him a son and heir and a lovely daughter?* She thought her marriage had been arranged slightly beneath her status. She had been expecting at least an earl, not the cousin of one. *My father holds a title that dates back five hundred years - but when his King commands, my father obeys.* It was the price of loyalty to the English Crown.

'Do you like it here in England, Clothilde?' she asked. The seventeen year old French girl was one of the three personal servants and with her high cheekbones, well-proportioned straight nose, a blemish-free face surrounded by honey-coloured hair and augmented with cupid-bow lips, by far the prettiest. And she knew it. With a flirtatious nature, trouble with men had followed her wherever she went.

'Not much. I'm homesick and these Saxons are so ugly. I still don't understand a word they say.' Poor Clothilde missed Brittany and the orchards around Eseux where Lady Alice's father still lived. 'I haven't found one man who takes my fancy.'

Lady Alice nodded her head. Her husband had been away since autumn and she, too, craved a man's firm touch.

An insistent knocking interrupted her *toilette*. An agitated servant indicated towards the courtyard where the Steward, Whytethorne, was standing. Behind him a couple of men were dragging a sopping wet, shivering body wrapped in a blanket.

'We rescued him from the sea,' Whytethorne told her, 'we don't know who he is; he hasn't spoken, but sings in his delirium.' He paused before adding, 'he's got a wonderful voice.'

—⟋⟍⟍⟋—

The mysterious stranger's power of speech returned three days later, and when it did Lady Alice learnt from Master John that he was called Michael and was a troubadour by trade, which explained the delicacy of his hands.

Master John was Manor Chaplain. He was the children's tutor and quasi-physician, and a cunning and dextrous manipulator of hidden truths. Short, with a spotty, sallow complexion, he was in his late twenties, and there was forever a drip on the end of his nose which he used to wipe with his sleeve. Seemingly sexless, taking no ostensible interest in women or men, he practiced self-flagellation with a leather whip, for that purpose hung above his bed next to his crucifix.

During Michael's recovery, Master John had learnt many of his secrets, the first of which was a partiality to wine which, when fortified with certain herbs and distillates, would loosen any tongue. Michael had told him how he suffered pangs of guilt for the men who had, for his last pennies, risked - and paid with - their lives to ferry him across the Solent. He wished to confess to a priest.

'I can hear your confession,' offered Master John disingenuously, once he had encouraged the minstrel to drink a more than liberal draft. 'I have taken holy orders.'

He learnt that the minstrel was a serial seducer, and that he been forced to undertake his perilous and nearly fatal journey on account of his escapades. An island as small as the Isle of Wight had no safe hiding place to escape the eyes, ears and wrath of Sir Hog, as Sir Hugh de Trenchard, the island's Seneschal, was called and Christmas at Sir Hog's manor at Shalfleet with three delightful, wayward, bounteous teenage daughters had proved Michael's undoing.

'Have you ever had three ripe young maidens in a bed all at once?' Michael asked, and, seriously under the influence of the chaplain's concoction, he went on to describe, in graphic detail, their antics. It was all too much; Master John had never heard a tale so salacious. Of course, he was guilty of encouragement, with a series of short, probing questions, something that he, as an ex-inquisitor, was expert in. The sanctity of the confessional would *of course* be respected but this story was too good to be true. From then on, many hours of Master John's time would be spent practising the Sin of Onan as he, too, imagined ravishing Sir Hog's no-longer virginal offspring.

Chapter 4

The Toad has a Plan

The Year of Our Lord 1338 had started well enough for King Philippe VI of France, as he dabbed a dribble of spittle from his fleshy, pendulous lips with the ermine-fringed corner of his sleeve. This ever-flowing saliva was a problem he had been unable to control since childhood when he had been stung in the mouth by a wasp. The only cure for his affliction was to eat, so he ate a lot. A boil just above his left buttock hurt, making him fidgety as he shifted his obese frame from side to side on his blue velvet throne. Beneath him his court, serried ranks of clergy and nobles, were arranged in all their splendour - stretching out from his dais like the wings of a fabulous bird. Closest to him sat the Cardinals, robed in red with wide-brimmed circular hats - 'keep those you distrust most nearest the throne,' had been Count Robert, Prince of Artois's counsel. How he now wished that he had followed that advice more fully and kept his brother-in-law close at hand.

Troubadours were already spreading Artois's heinous poison throughout Flanders and beyond. *The Vows of the Heron* were being told and retold in inns and taverns, courts and castles across the northern borders of his realm, inciting the rebellious Flemish scum that lapped against the northern fringes of his kingdom into open revolt. *I'll turn that scum from white to red; I'll slaughter them in their thousands and reduce their towns to ash.* Just the thought of it induced uncontrollable rage and loathing. He had punished them once, at Cassel, ten years ago and he would do it again.

A pounding on the Audience Chamber's door brought him back to reality and he steeled himself to receive the Embassy from the one he called the 'Upstart', King Edward III of England. They had been on good terms once and had even planned their crusade together, but his mother, his cousin, the She-Wolf Queen Isabella, had soured that relationship over the little matter of Aquitaine. *He had been such a sweet boy.* Now he and the Upstart were mortal enemies.

The Bishop of Lincoln had been on his knees all week, or so his spies had told him. *All week, he must have something important to impart, though I doubt it.* The war that Count Robert had engineered was becoming inevitable. The trouble was France's coffers were empty so Philippe had to stall and buy time; war was an expensive enterprise that he could ill-afford.

The doors were flung open and the bishop, frame bent with age and arthritis, barely able to walk, entered, flanked by monks clad in plain brown habits, and flattened himself on the flagstones. The bishop's mitre remained on the floor as the old man struggled to raise himself up from his prostrate position. His rheumy eyes locked with the King who continued to seek some comfort from the horsehair cushion, but it was not to be.

The Bishop's voice was barely audible, so Philippe had to lean forward to catch the fateful words. He almost wished he hadn't.

'My master, the Rightful King of France, wishes to abrogate any Oaths of Allegiance made to you in his minority as being false and intends to pursue his vow to claim his birthright. He says that you are only King by dint of Self-Proclamation and that he is supported in his lawful claim to the throne of France by all who are faithful to his Capetian forebears.' The Bishop paused, never letting his gaze break from the slobbering, writhing monarch, whose lank black locks were greasy and unkempt, before continuing, now loud enough for those closest to hear. 'He will contest his claim by feat of arms and challenges you to single combat.'

The French King grimaced; this was all wretched Count Robert's doing. How he loathed his erstwhile adviser. *The conniving bastard.* This was his revenge, he supposed, for him locking up Robert's wife and sons; revenge for denying him his birthright. *No, he had forged his father's Will.* Philippe had chased him out of France, then, when he sought sanctuary in Namur he sent an army to oust him, he did this again when he fled to Brabant, forcing him into exile in England.

It was there that the Count had spread his subtle poison. Had he still been his councillor Philippe would have had a sneaking admiration for the way Count Robert had twisted his gullible cousin into this unwarranted aggression. With consummate skill he had manipulated the English King's penchant for feasting with his coterie of knights, where his warrior elite were imbued with the spirit of chivalric enterprise and the quest for noble adventure. He had been so bold to use such an occasion to accuse young Edward of cowardice, likening him to a bird - a heron no less - and then making all his companions plunge their daggers into the roasted heron carcass and swear a sacred oath to join a thoroughly unwarranted war against his fair kingdom. Oh yes, he had heard it all, each and every vow a dagger plunged into the gentle flesh of France.

Philippe finally found a comfortable position to sit in, hovering on the edge of his throne. Count Robert, *Cunt Robert* - he had a penchant for nicknames. Robert had thrown it back at him, calling him 'The Valois Viper' during their acrimonious last meeting; he liked that, just like he liked calling Edward 'The Upstart'.

It was beyond him, though, to feel any regret even though it was his scheming that had created this debacle in the first place. Robert's aunt, Mahout, had bribed him to deny Robert's claim to the County of Artois, a fine, rich inheritance that probably should have been his. The King gave an involuntary shrug as he recalled the shenanigans. *My little Toad made me do it.* This was his pet name for his treasurer, Nicolas Béhuchet, on account of his ugly warty face. It was the Toad who had made Mahout promise that he should receive half the wealth of Artois, swaying his judgement in her favour. It had also been the

Toad's bright idea to suborn the lawyers to give the decision an air of legitimacy and thus deny Count Robert his rightful inheritance.

The Bishop of Lincoln got to his feet and, leaning close to the King, whispered intently into the royal ear. He did not finish his sentence when Philippe could not stand sitting any longer and arose, his face purple with fury. Only the venerable cleric's unquestionable piety, and he admitted later, his diplomatic status that saved him from the gallows. *All that goes on here will be reported back to the Pope,* Philippe thought as he glanced across the red hats whose necks were craning as those closest tried to catch the hoarse croaking whispers of the affront.

'Where is Béhuchet, summon him to our gathering,' he screamed, shocking the nobles who had been unable to hear any of the insults that had been heaped upon their monarch.

'Send for Béhuchet!' The cry echoed down the Castle of the Louvre's stone corridors to the anteroom where the squat admiral had been pacing up and down. His origins barred him from these assemblies. Protocol forbade his inclusion with the aristocrats and prelates, but he did not care. The Toad was a Grand Admiral, Master of the National Forests and Royal Treasurer. His power stemmed from the King whose ear he controlled, and from his bodyguard of thugs, who enforced his will on weak and vacillating nobles. As he approached the hall's impressive door, even he could hear an enraged Philippe ranting and raving.

'Just because his mother is a Capetian that Upstart Edward thinks he can call himself King of France over me.' Spittle flew everywhere. 'It's all the fault of those damned Flemings; they'll burn in hell.' The tirade grew louder. 'I'll show him, I'll show them all.'

'All is well with you?' the sergeant-at-arms nodded and smiled as he held open the door for the Toad, who straightened his clothing before flicking a stray piece of straw from his sleeve. The Admiral made sure that all the palace guards received extra money for snippets of information and gossip. He filed all this knowledge in his remarkable memory - he could remember every conversation he had ever had almost verbatim. He could hear a rising cacophony of shouts and insults and was just in time to see the Ambassador, who had fainted, carried out by his monks as they scurried away from the Audience Chamber. He knew little of the meeting, but could tell from the demeanour of those involved that it had not gone well. Béhuchet loathed official meetings with the King in front of the assembled Court; the haughty nobles would invariably find some way of insulting him. It would be subtle, to be sure, but the jibes were just as deadly. He'd been born of humble parentage and the noble lords would not let him forget it. He was clever; very, very clever, and had graduated from the University of Montpelier as a lawyer. He could remember his journey; he had walked the length of France from his home in Brittany to get there. *I'll prove to those self-satisfied, arrogant halfwits that I'm better than all of them. I triumphed against the English. I destroyed half of Portsmouth. I earned my full admiralty the hard way.*

But it was in his genius for mathematics that his talents really came to the fore; he could add, subtract, multiply and divide all manner of numbers, weights, measures, barrels, bales, volumes and money. Admiral Béhuchet could cost a war galley to the nearest sou; he knew the value of every rope, nail and brass rivet, every plank and beam. As a party trick he would add up three pages of figures in his head, in whatever currency, be it Venetian ducats or Imperial Marks of the Holy Roman Empire or their own *livres tournois,* and convert them into each other, with interest. He could outsmart and outthink any of the so-called Royal Dukes in charge of raising the armies. But despite this he had no way of becoming a real aristocrat - his blood was wrong. He had an explosive temper and ferocious intellect and, should anyone get on the wrong side of him, he could poison minds – or bodies - with the greatest of ease. His ubiquitous personal bodyguards, massive men armed with razor-sharp short pikes, added instant menace to his threats.

Time for my entrance, I believe. The Admiral, who was not the tallest of men, shimmied his shoulders as the great oak doors swung open. He bowed as low as his expanding girth allowed; taking off his velvet hat as he did so, he ostentatiously swept the flagstones.

'May God save your Majesty,' he said loudly, seeing the distress on his King's face. Whatever had been said had upset the King so deeply that there were tears of anger flowing down his puffy cheeks. Having kissed the proffered ring-laden hand and waited until it had been lifted from his forehead, he turned to face the Court. He could see from their faces that they, like him, were none the wiser as to what had passed between King and Ambassador. From now on, Béhuchet was in control - calming Philippe was a speciality of his, and from a few twitches of the royal fingers he knew exactly what he had to do.

'The audience is over,' he said brusquely to the disgruntled courtiers, who had been summoned from their estates the length and breadth of the realm to assemble in Paris for this meeting that had taken less than five minutes, the substance of which had gone unheard and unrecorded, then watched their King scream and rant. It did not fill them with encouragement.

The Toad was gratified to see that Cardinal Alberghini, one of Pope Benedict's private secretaries, had made the long journey from Avignon to attend. The Toad knew that the Upstart had been pleading his case to legitimise his claim to the French throne at the Papal See. The Pope must have sensed something important was in the air. Alberghini was touching effeminate, highly cultured and low-born like the Admiral, he, too, had climbed the greasy pole through dint of a shrewd brain. The ladder of Church was better at concealing the humbleness of a man's origins, and, because of his origins, unlike most prelates who came from rich or noble families; he had lacked the financial wherewithal to indulge in the luxuries that others of his standing could afford. This had been remedied by the generosity of the Admiral who paid handsomely for ecclesiastic intelligence that flowed between Paris and Avignon. The Cardinal hung back, watching for the pre-arranged signal that indicated one of many clandestine meeting places....

—∭—

Constable Bertrand was only other person in attendance. He, too, was a close advisor to the King. Bertrand de Corbeil was a straight-laced, bull-featured aristocrat of the old school. A redoubtable fighter in his youth, his scarred, beardless face told the story of many duels and battles fought and won, his close-cropped hair was iron-grey. He controlled the Royal Dukes and armies of France with a steely grip, was an able strategist, and while he disliked the Admiral he also understood his value. Without the Toad's organisational acumen there would be no navy, and without an effective navy he would not be able to realise his ambition of gifting the islands of Jersey and Guernsey, presently in the hands of the English, to his King.

They retired to an antechamber where a great log fire crackled with warmth. This was the Valois Viper's inner sanctum, safe from prying eyes and flapping ears. Taking his favourite chair, back to the fire, he started to talk freely.

'Do you know what he said? *Do you know what he said?*' the Viper repeated himself, shrieking so his voice echoed round the stone confines of his study. 'He wanted to thank me. *Thank me.*' The import of this had been lost to the assembled company; they had seen the insult delivered but not heard the whispered coda, the scorpion's sting.

Béhuchet shook his head. He could not imagine what could have been more offensive to his master.

'The Upstart wanted me to know that he has recently built a magnificent Hall at his Palace at Westminster. He felt it appropriate to decorate it with murals of scenes from the Old Testament to acknowledge that he - the *Rightful* King of France - had received his share of *my* gift from the Jews.' He looked directly into the Admiral's eyes.

'Well, at least we know that he was behind the theft.' Béhuchet rubbed his hands together. 'As good a reason as any for declaring war.'

The gift had stretched the financial resources of Jews, leaving nothing. Now impoverished, they had struggled to scrape together a meagre set of plates instead, which had already been sold off.

'I had thought the Jews had made up this story, trying to buy their way back into my favour with falsehoods. I don't want war, I want *revenge,*' the King whispered hoarsely. 'Vengeance. Make it bloody. Make the Upstart and his poxy little kingdom suffer.'

'Then, Sire,' the response came as smooth as silk from Béhuchet, 'I have a plan. We must delve deep into *his* pockets. We should attack his ports. I'll send my spies to make a report. From what I know of the English, they put too much faith in *La Manche.*'

The King stroked his chin. *Anything to confound my royal rival, anything that will hurt his exchequer.* A villainous smile spread across his face. 'Before that why don't we take Jersey and Guernsey? These English jewels would look good in the crown of France.' The Constable smiled, the seed he had planted was bearing fruit, for only the King could authorise such an expedition. Then another thought struck him.

'If he said *his* share, who has the rest of the money?'

'You're right; the thief will still have the lion's share. When your spies visit England,' the King continued, nodding in appreciation to the Constable, 'tell them to look out for any new castles being built.'

'Your Majesty read my thoughts.' The Admiral's brain was working furiously. He would have to find additional warships. 'I think a trip to Genoa will be in order. I'm sure that the Italians would not be adverse to a bit of pillage and larceny...'

Business concluded, the King found the company of the Toad refreshing. Not only was he turning France from a moribund naval power into a force to be reckoned with, but also he made him laugh. 'You must be hungry. How's Lady Aliénor?' He had sanctioned Béhuchet's wedding to a lady of noble birth, daughter of a viscount. She had been badly disfigured as a baby so that no other aristocrat took even a passing interest in her modest fortune. This had not deterred the Admiral from making three half-noble children.

Flunkies were summoned, a mountain of food ordered and the King, draping his arm over the plump Admiral's shoulder, led him away, animatedly discussing matters of state. Béhuchet's power base, the Clos de Galée at Rouen in Normandy, was where the French built warships and manufactured weapons and armour. He searched around in his calfskin leather portfolio - only the best for the Grand High Admiral of France - and took out a report.

'My spy should be back from England very soon, he's been learning about a magic powder that explodes like burning naphtha.' He had no other way to describe the effect of gunpowder. Knights who had been on crusade had told of the Byzantines and their Greek fire, which contained a substance called naphtha. A Scotsman had told him of tubes that 'spat' death and he had sent a most clever young fellow to find out more. This had been well over a year ago and he was getting worried. *No news is good news*, he kept saying to himself, it would be a shame to lose such a promising apprentice.

Later that evening, in a quiet corner of the Cathedral of Notre-Dame, Nicolas Béhuchet entered a confessional. Cardinal Alberghini was in a lather of excitement, but the Admiral was nonchalant. 'There was nothing new, the same threats and bombast, you can tell your master that war is likely, but his Majesty will decline the offer of combat. We have other plans.' As an afterthought he added, 'We now know who stole the Jews' gift, and *you* will help *me* get it back.'

Alberghini knew what this meant. The Admiral had snared him in a moment of weakness. He had been trapped. The weakness he'd fought so hard to sublimate had been discovered with subtle insidiousness. His predilection for the unblemished voices of castrati had been his ruin. Their high descant chants, in cadences as sweet as the nightingale's song, had aroused his sexual passions, leading him into Satan's snare.

Inexorably, Admiral Béhuchet had persuaded him to do his bidding. To begin with he had fought, like a fish feeling the hook in its mouth for the first time, but the barb was in too deep and he no longer had the energy to struggle. Alternatives were too ghastly to contemplate and he had acquiesced - accepting his fate for a continued life of pampered luxury. In a way he found it liberating to indulge in his hidden vices. Temporal rewards were *most* adequate, but his soul was irrevocably soiled.

Chapter 5

Agnes's Love Arrows

'When you collect the bodies, see if old Robbie is still gatekeeper,' said the Earl as Sir Roger prepared the flag of truce for the burial party. Robbie had survived the previous siege and the brief period when the English had used the castle as a barracks in order to humiliate the Scots further. It was well known that he accepted money in return for favours. 'Money has no smell,' was his favourite saying, and as far as anyone could ascertain, Robbie's sole loyalty was to drink.

'If he is, slip him this.' The Earl handed over a leather purse bulging with silver pennies. 'Tell him there'll be much more if he helps us when the time is right.'

Carrying his scimitar instead of his broadsword - he liked the novelty and finesse of this oriental weapon and a man of his standing was permitted a sword at all times - Sir Roger, without any armour, led the burial detail of surly local Scotsmen that his sergeant had rounded up for the purpose. 'I feel naked,' he told the Ox as they followed the team pulling an empty cart down the causeway.

The peasants were set-to manhandling boulders off the rawhide roof, revealing broken and crushed bodies.

'They were my friends,' said Gwyn, his voice tinged with sadness, unable to stop hot tears from rolling down his cheeks. As each battered body was heaved onto the cart he closed eyes that were still open. Some, though, were so mangled that they were recognisable only from items of clothing or badges.

'Leave their armour and weapons in a pile there.' It was a stern order. The voice belonged to a woman. Looking up Sir Roger could see that the service door concealed in the great gate had opened and several menacing crossbowmen had emerged, pointing loaded weapons in his direction through the grill of the portcullis. It was the first time Sir Roger had seen the redoubtable and infamous harridan Agnes close-up and she turned out to be much more petite than he had imagined from the tales that preceded her, and, for a start, her hair was neatly braided into buns, not running wild, though her lips were pinched and thin. He bowed courteously, doffing his hat. She said something in Gaelic to one of the peasants who reverentially touched his forelock before making a monosyllabic reply.

'He works for me on our farm,' she said, as if reading Sir Roger's mind, 'and I was asking him whether his wife had given birth yet.'

Sir Roger grunted, acknowledging that even though her castle was under siege, whatever the outcome, life goes on. Then he straightened. 'I want my banner back,' he said, noticing that the flag that had graced the sow's front was no longer there and rather arrogantly omitting a 'please'.

Lady Agnes spat on the ground. 'Your banner? That ugly green pig. It hangs in my hall. I've given it pride of place.' She smiled sweetly, sticking the tip of her tongue out flirtatiously. 'You can have it back when you manage to -' She stopped mid-sentence. '*If* you succeed in taking *my* castle from *me*.' She turned on her heels and disappeared, leaving her archers. Sir Roger saw Robbie and tried to edge closer, but the lead crossbowman was having none of it.

'How's your head,' he laughed as he tapped his ear. 'So you know - I'm Pasquale de Puyguilhem - the finest marksman in all France. And now Scotland! You may call me the Silent Killer - everyone else around here does.'

Cheeky sod. 'Well, I'm going to call you Frenchie, and when we starve you into submission the first thing you'll eat is your own arrow. That'll give you something to chew on when we string you up.'

The Frenchman laughed again. 'You mean *if* - we've got two hundred men-at-arms and enough stores to last a year.' He said, taking the opportunity to disseminate any falsehoods that would undermine the enemy's morale.

Sir Roger caught Robbie's eye and gave him a wave, surreptitiously revealing the leather purse. He went to the last of the corpses and, slipping the money into a helmet placed it casually on the pile of weapons and plate. Their task done, they prepared to leave. Sir Roger turned. 'How good are you?' he asked Pasquale.

'The best. Wait for my next shot and you'll see. *Au revoir.*'

The Scots waited until the party had cleared the causeway before lifting the portcullis to retrieve the weapons. Sir Roger saw Robbie pick up the helmet. The bait had been taken.

'I don't believe they've got more than fifty in there,' said the Earl when Sir Roger reported what he'd gleaned. 'And now, sadly, better armed.'

The Earl looked disconsolately out across the bleak moors surrounding the castle that had been their home for the last four months. Holy Week had come and gone, Easter had been early, the days were lengthening and there was, finally, some sunshine. A stiff east wind dried the quagmire that had surrounded the tents and marquees of the besiegers, and as servants stoked up braziers, a group of knights warmed their hands and listened to their commander who had received the latest news bulletin from the King.

He ran through several points of interest and made a digest of events. Supplies were slowly being assembled for the Flanders campaign in Great Yarmouth and the King made it clear that they were to try and bring the siege to a speedy conclusion. 'He wants us to be with him when he sails next month.'

He tried to sound cheery and was rewarded with an excited babble as the assembled knights digested this news - they were going to get a crack at the French. This meant ransoms galore, big fat chests of money dragged out of rich estates, not the meagre pickings of Scottish moors. Their mood became buoyant again. Since the debacle with the sow they had made no attempt to do anything except try and starve the defenders out.

'I want to scout the northern sector of walls again. You, William,' ordered the Earl, selecting Sir William of Spens from his entourage, 'get your kit on and come with me.'

Only the richest knights could afford full suits of armour. Salisbury's had been manufactured in Milan. It was the very latest innovation from the armourers of that city and had cost a serious fortune. He was being encased in burnished metal plate for which he had sent a body-double to ensure that it was a perfect fit. The breastplate had been polished to a mirror shine so that gleamed in the sunlight. Most of his knights, however, acquired their armour piecemeal, with bits and pieces won in a joust or inherited from a crusading ancestor.

'Be careful, not so tight,' said William irritably, as his squire strapped on his leg pieces, thigh and knee protectors made of beaten iron. The rest of his legs and shins had a moulded leather casing that buckled on and fitted tight to his calves, while neatly articulated sets of metal sheets covered his short riding boots, ending in sharp pointed toes.

The process of putting on armour was a lengthy one. Layer went upon layer, starting with the feet. It was a fine balance, have too few layers and be vulnerable to sword cuts and spear thrusts, have too many and wielding a weapon effectively was difficult. Over his shirt William had an aketon, a tight-fitting padded jacket with small iron rings sewn inside. He then grabbed the two broom handles proffered by his squire; these were slid through the arms of his ubiquitous mail hauberk, which he fed his over his aketon, letting it unfold down to his thighs.

'It's getting rusty,' he complained, surveying where the damp had turned once shiny rings brown. Some had parted and the tear was crudely repaired with wire. A mail coif went over his head and neck, and a coat-of-plates - a metal covered canvas poncho - added another layer of protection. He affixed his gorgères, throat defences, and, finally, a surcoat with the Spens coat of arms, proudly displayed.

'Hurry up,' shouted the Earl, eager to get a move on.

William's squire was all fingers and thumbs and renowned for his inability to put his master's armour on quickly. He was, therefore, always the last to get ready, finally pulling on whalebone gauntlets and donning a tight fitting round bascinet that went on top of a padded head protector. The irritated Earl, who had a reputation for impatience, signalled his men forward and, accompanied by thirty men-at-arms, Spens and Salisbury set out from camp.

'There, what did I tell you, my line,' crowed a triumphant Eguerand de Tolna as they watched a thin candle burn down, with each knight having placed a line in the wax as to how long they thought it would take Spens to get ready. Eguerand, or just the Egg to his friends on account of his ovate-shaped shaved pate, came from somewhere in Hungaria, though no one knew where that was. How he had drifted to England and to the siege was generally an unfathomable mystery, not least because when anyone asked they were simply stonewalled. Sir Roger, who had delved surreptitiously through the Egg's belongings, had found nothing. He liked the fellow enormously.

'I am as you see me, take me or leave me,' he had once said. What he was, was brave and reliable and just the sort of fellow a man needed beside him when it came to a fight.

—⁓—

The excitement of the morning over, Sir Roger went back to his tent, which was pitched in an orchard. Blossoms covered the trees and the breeze blew some petals through the entrance.

A scarred face appeared round the flap of the tent. 'Rog, be a good fellow and lend me a couple of shillings.' Instantly Sir Roger felt his hackles rise. It was Sir Eustace de Frage, his squire's odious father. 'You've got so much money,' Eustace said with more than a hint of envy in his voice. A livid welt ran down the left side of his face, giving him a permanent grimace, the result of a sword cut sustained in a duel that had been badly sewn up by the barber-surgeon.

'Why?' Sir Roger asked curtly not wishing to engage in anything but the barest minimum of conversation.

'Because I want to buy Justin a present, it's his birthday. Some Welsh sod has stolen my purse.' A lie, of course, Sir Eustace was prejudiced against all but pure Norman blood, spilling venom and bile on all those he considered inferior. He was always broke, gambling away what money he had inherited, leaving his land to go to ruin, his remaining serfs living in abject terror of his capricious whims.

It was said that they prayed daily for him to meet with Death. When he made his infrequent visits to his estates, which bordered onto Sir Roger's land, at least one of their numbers would subsequently be found hanging from a tree.

Biting his lip, Sir Roger flicked him a silver shilling, 'Mind you pay it back.' He loathed this boorish ogre but, struggling hard, for the sake of good neighbourly relations, maintained his *sangfroid*.

'Thanks, may God in heaven reward you,' Sir Eustace said, his voice redolent with sarcasm.

'And may you rot in hell,' replied Sir Roger as he shut the tent flap. If he went to heaven, and he piously hoped that he would, he wanted to get a place on the cliffs overlooking hell, from where he could piss on Sir Eustace's head. For the whole campaign that odious brute had wheedled away like an annoying mosquito. They had met a couple of times before this campaign; once when Eustace delivered Justin into Sir Roger's care, and then again when Sir Roger had returned from Gascony, coming as a 'neighbourly gesture' shortly after Lady Alice, Harry and Isabel had moved into old Ipers Manor. Sir Eustace saw his neighbour's wealth and coveted it. Eaten up with jealousy, he wanted it all, including his wife.

'Miserly sod gave me a shilling,' Sir Eustace said to the Welshman to whom he had just lost yet another game of dice. 'Double or quits.'

The scouting party had been away for about an hour when whooping, though faint, was clearly heard in the English camp. From the hurried way Salisbury and his companions returned they could see something was amiss. William of Spens was slumped over the pommel of his saddle, jerking about without control. He was clearly dead.

They laid the body reverentially on the ground. Just visible were twisted flight feathers of a crossbow bolt that had gone through plates, chain mail and aketon, piercing his heart.

Sir Roger recognised it immediately - Frenchie the Silent Killer had kept his promise.

'Two hundred yards at least!' lamented the Earl in exasperation; he was in tears at the loss of his right hand man. 'We thought we spotted a good place for a ladder assault and stopped for the briefest of moments, and out of nowhere, pffff- Agnes's love arrows go straight for the heart!'

Before closing the coffin, each knight placed his forefinger in the bloody wound, swearing an oath to avenge his death. Everyone had respected William and they buried him in the little cemetery in the Dunbar churchyard with due and solemn ceremony. Dinner was a gloomy affair, but all agreed they owed it to William to brave the marksman and assault Dunbar Castle again.

It took several weeks to make enough ladders, a simple enough task, except that all the carpenters who had come with the trebuchets had gone home again when they had proved useless. 'The lower orders have no sense of duty,' complained Salisbury. 'Money, money, money, that's all they want.'

—∿—

As the siege entered into its fifth month, so the English prepared themselves for a dawn attack. The men hated getting up and putting on their armour in the dark, but the Earl was adamant. 'That's when Caesar would have made his move,' he said, having studied *The Gallic Wars* and now trying to emulate his hero's tactics.

The morning was still, with pockets of mist hiding the base of the wall, filling the ditches and folds in the ground with cotton wool. Sounds of preparation for the assault were obvious for miles around, and in retrospect Sir Roger realised that this had been their undoing, for, as they approached the wall, they found the garrison ready and waiting. They had sneaked out in the gloaming and were hidden in the fog-shrouded gullies.

The first scaling parties were approaching the walls when out of the ditches came the screaming Scots, led by Lawrence of Preston.

Instantly recognisable, he had often joined the lists for tournaments in more peaceful times where he won the hearts of ladies with his handsome good looks and reckless valour. The unexpectedness and ferocity of the counterattack caught the English off guard; the men-at-arms took fright and fled, dropping their ladders. Fair Lawrence then made his fatal mistake, catching up with the fleeing English.

They recovered his body a few hours later - skewered through the brainpan by a spear.

'Just the excuse we need,' said Salisbury. 'Let's see if Robbie will let us in.'

That evening, under a flag of truce, the body was carried, with full military honours, up the causeway to the gate. Sir Roger led the pallbearers carrying another bag of money, which he secretly passed to the gatekeeper.

'There's much more where that came from,' he whispered. 'The Earl will come down the causeway tomorrow at sunset, all you have to do is let him in....'

Robbie accepted the money happily. 'I'll set a lantern on the gate when they're having supper,' he winked conspiratorially and then said loudly 'Frenchie wants a word with you.' The crossbowman slid from behind the gatekeeper.

'I told you I was the best,' Pasquale said with a Gallic sneer. 'I aimed for the heart - tell me if my aim was true.'

Sir Roger nodded bitterly. 'Through three layers of armour, too.'

When they got back, he reported that he had given Robbie the money and told him that they would be coming at dusk tomorrow.

'Never trust them,' declared Salisbury. 'We'll send John Copeland; he looks a bit like me, and with my tabard on, the Scots should think it *is* me.'

'John, do you understand what you have to do?' The Earl straightened the borrowed clothing, John nodded vacantly; he was close to being a simpleton, loyal and brave. The plot was uncomplicated, once through the gates the men-at-arms would hold them open long enough for mounted attackers to charge down the causeway and get in.

The whole plan was going swimmingly, a light flickered at the gate and so the phoney earl set off with five men-at-arms. Many had volunteered for such a glorious mission and in the half-light of dusk they approached cautiously down the causeway. The portcullis creaked up and the gate swung open.

The men were in.

The knights on their horses prepared for their gallop into immortality through the songs of troubadours, but before they even had time to unsheathe their swords the garrison, hidden and waiting, had jumped Copeland and party. The portcullis crashed down again.

'My Lord,' came the familiar shout from Black Agnes. 'I am sorely disappointed, for I had prepared a special dinner for you, and now I must make do with lesser companionship.'

Next morning, the heads of Copeland and his five companions graced the spikes above the gatehouse battlements.

Chapter 6

Voice of an Angel

It did not take the Minstrel long to realise that he had been plucked from the jaws of death and deposited, unceremoniously, in a close approximation of paradise. He had often dreamt of the Elysian Fields and this was it: decent food, drinkable wine and, above all, lots of women, and pretty to boot. The flame-haired Lady of the Manor, with a predilection for green, was an intriguing creature and he fancied what he saw. *She's as hot as a bitch on heat, I can see the signs.* Where the female of the species were concerned, he had a sixth sense. She was a lady who wasn't averse to flaunting herself in front of strapping young men, and, he noted with a hunter's keen sense of his prey, she seemed to get a thrill from the younger builders, who as the weather warmed up often stripped to the waist, exposing rippling muscles. It was in the way she glanced furtively at them as they laboured.

He had to exercise a great deal of self-discipline to avoid the temptations on offer from her ladies-in-waiting, who were openly flirtatious, as he feared they would mistake their seduction as a prelude to marriage. *Bigamy is a sin I shouldn't commit again.* He thought about his other wives - not that he knew whether either was still alive. He was, in the eyes of God, still married. He'd been young, foolish and impulsive, fathering three children with the first before abandoning his family to seek fame and fortune. His second wife, an aristocratic young trollop, had been pregnant when he left her as well, but then she had turned into a screaming harpy.

His over-riding ambition was to sing at Court, but with scandal chasing him with demon's wings, he felt it better to put *La Manche* between him and her vengeful brothers and thus he had arrived on the Isle of Wight on a smuggler's barque.

Michael set about establishing his credentials and it didn't take long to find out that his new mistress was from Brittany, and therefore very nearly French. Unlike in England, where minstrels were of lowly status, in France there was a tradition of aristocratic troubadours and *trouvères* who propounded *les chansons d'amour*. So he wove a tale of noble ancestry, of abandonment, wandering and hardship, but above all his message to her was simple - *the blood that flows in my veins is as good as yours*. It could have been true, he really didn't know, but with his long, delicate hands and fine, indeed noble features he looked the part. He had been born, orphaned and learned his trade at Anjou where he had been brought up in a convent and treated well. No one there, however, could or would tell him of his true parentage.

—⁂—

Lady Alice had tried to ignore her feelings but couldn't. The weather had turned warm and all around spring was burgeoning.

She tried prayer.

She tried immersing herself in the household accounts.

Nothing worked.

On a flimsy pretext she went to where the stonemasons were carving intricate window frames. The knowledge that, if their overseer caught them staring at her, they would probably get a beating sent a frisson of excitement up her spine. She longed for the embrace of her husband. It had been a long time.

'Your ladyship might wish to see this.' It was the Bailiff, Tom Handley. She had disliked and mistrusted this bull-featured man from the first moment she had set eyes on him. His obsequious tone drove her to distraction and his habit of leering down her cleavage did not endear him to her further. 'What would you like carved here?' He led her over to where a mason was chiselling on a chimneybreast.

'Our boar, naturally.' *How appropriate.* Her husband could sometimes behave in a most boorish way. 'And have an eagle ride on its back.' *Then my family is represented too. I've managed the work so it's only fitting.* 'Can you carve it with wings open?' The mason nodded.

Lady Alice examined Handley's jerkin with disgust. It was greasy, covered in old food and barely contained a bulging beer belly. *He's had his own way for too long, and he's always prowling around day or night.*

'Do you ever sleep?' she asked. He was about to answer when she stopped him. A whiff of his breath, which smelt frightful, had hit her full in the face. The Bailiff had a habit of speaking to those he wished to intimidate - or anybody - by getting really close.

'In future,' she said imperiously, 'I want you to stand at least two yards from me when you speak.'

He stalked off, muttering obscene curses, still smarting from the last tongue-lashing he had received from his new mistress. *That woman,* as he now referred to her, *is sticking her nose into my business.* He had had free reign over manorial affairs for many years and the fact that he was no longer the final arbiter of the estate accounts was galling.

'I've been here for twenty years and she treats me as if I were dog shit,' he complained vociferously at the weekly manorial staff meeting. Handley resented that *he* had not been promoted to Steward and suspected that *that woman* had something to do with it. The new Steward was the other thorn in his side. Before, when he had been in charge, Handley had been merrily milking the accounts, siphoning off a healthy income. Now he was trapped between a rock and a hard place and didn't like it in the least.

The Steward, an ex-military man and a lawyer to boot, was considered by Sir Roger to be better suited for the job. *And the old bastard's scrupulously honest.* Handley had tried, obliquely, to make Whytethorne party to one of his scams, but been rebuffed.

The principle bone of contention was the transference from Bailiff to Steward of the job of going to Southampton and drawing off funds to pay for the building work. With hundreds of workmen and artisans crawling over every inch of the property, a large quantity of cash would be to put temptation in the path of the sinner.

'How much money do you need?' asked Whytethorne, sensing the hostility.

'Six pounds worth of pennies and groats should suffice.' A groat was a relatively new four-penny coin that had first been issued by the present king's grandfather, Edward Longshanks. Until the castle was completed and a strongroom built, Sir Roger felt it prudent to keep the bulk of his fortune in the Peruzzi's Bank in the town, which was a veritable fortress in its own right. This was also safer because there were no proper soldiers, only a few old retainers who had once borne arms, to protect Ipers, as the younger ones were in Scotland with the master.

'I see the Minstrel's recovered,' Whytethorne noted. There was, in his humble opinion, something unsavoury in this character that, as yet, he couldn't put his finger on. Still, the smarmy singer had become a pet hate of his. He particularly disliked the way he had wormed his way into Lady Alice's affections with such unseemly rapidity.

On this, the Bailiff kept his own counsel, maintaining for the time being studious neutrality in this particular war zone of castle politics.

'He's up to no good,' he grumbled, pretending to take the Steward's side. 'Just like on the Isle of Wight. I've a good mind to contact Sir Hog.'

Whytethorne raised an eyebrow. Of all the staff, only he, the Chaplain, the Bailiff and the Clerk could read or write, and in the Bailiff's case his writing skills were rudimentary.

'Master John told me what happened over there,' Handley continued. He had cornered the chaplain and given him a working over. With his arm half way up his back and face crushed against the wall, Master John had blabbed. As he'd reminded him, forcibly, the sanctity of the confessional was between confessor and God, and at Ipers *he* was as good as God.

Later, after pay day, Handley made his rounds of the workmen and collected a farthing a man a week for the 'privilege' of working on the castle. He had already accumulated a tidy sum.

Today was no different. As he rode off across the Forest whistling to himself, he had another fish to fry. His latest devious scam was progressing apace. The Abbot of Bewley, old King John's monastery set up in that field of bees, was a man of fine theocratic intellect, to be sure, but without an ounce of understanding when it came to matters commercial. He was not exactly gullible, and it was not as if he was going to be a loser in the deal. Handley's plan was simplicity itself. The Abbey's sheep, which had come, at great expense, from Coxford Priory in Norfolk, produced fine-fibred wool that attracted a premium. His master's flocks - Sir Roger had invested a goodly sum into bog-standard sheep - only produced inferior-quality wool. It was a simple matter of taking the Abbey's better-quality fleece and placing it in a thin layer around their inferior product. Anyone who sampled the fibre would not bother to delve past the outer layer and pay top price.

It was a matter of persuasion. Handley needed to buy a couple of sacks of high grade wool without arousing suspicion. Like a fisherman tempting a fat carp with a worm, he told the perplexed abbot, 'I'll replace them with a lower grade and pay you the difference.'

It had been a casual conversation with the shepherd that alerted him to the opportunity, as he knew that the Abbot had a penchant for self-flagellation and mortification of the flesh and felt that his brethren should follow the same practices if they wished to lessen their time in Purgatory before reaching the Kingdom of Heaven.

'Coarser, you understand - and then you can weave hair shirts for your monks from cheaper stuff - the scratchier the habit, the holier the wearer.' Handley laughed; he always laughed at his own jokes. He was confident his master would never find out and he'd split a part of the uplift just in case.

As for Lady de Bohun, as far as he was concerned he was sure he would find a way to get the upper hand - *and I do like looking at her tits.*

—◊—

The Minstrel had been watching the Bailiff leave. The courtyard was quiet, the workman packed up and gone for the day. The place was deserted. Lady Alice emerged from her garden, where she had been admiring the pink buds on her roses. They kindled a desire of which, for Michael, the signs were plain enough - a fluttering of eyes, a blush, and a wiggle of the *derrière*. *She's ready.* He flashed his smile, the one the ladies of easy virtue would usually swoon for, hoping this one would too.

Lady Alice shoo-shooed her ladies-in-waiting away with a wave of her fingers. It was a beautiful spring evening.

'Not you.' She signalled Michael over. 'I have a gift for you,' she whispered. 'Shut your eyes.' She slipped over to the door and surreptitiously slid the bolt across; she did not want to be disturbed. 'You can open them now. Here, this is for you.'

It was a lute, beautifully crafted from cherry wood and ash. Michael was overjoyed; tears came to his eyes as he remembered the loss of his last one. It had drowned in the Solent with his dreams.

'How can I thank you?'

'Play me a love song.'

And he did. She could not hold back any longer - her desire to taste forbidden fruit was overwhelming. As he played, he felt her hand massage his neck, then reach down his chest, and without further hesitation she gave herself to him.

Chapter 7

A Matter of Honour

Admiral Nicolas Béhuchet stood back and eyed the young man who stood in front of him, rather like a buyer would a horse. He was definitely more of a man than the callow youth he had entrusted with so delicate a mission, but then he had every faith in Simon de Pressi, who had, to his great relief, after eighteen months finally made it safely back to France. His shoulders had broadened significantly and there was now an indefinable air of confidence and maturity that emanated from his erstwhile pretty-boy face. His pale russet hair was cut in fashionable pudding-bowl style. He had wide, innocent blue eyes, and a regular straight nose, and the peach-fluff on his cheeks had matured into a beard that had been neatly trimmed. He was only supposed to have been away for six months, and the Toad had feared that he had been murdered or, worse still, captured. The Admiral was keen to hear every detail of life on enemy shores. Most of all, he hoped that his protégé had found out the secret of fire powder. However, first, he aired his irritation. 'Why didn't you write?'

'Not safe. The English are great readers of other peoples' letters.' Simon leaned over the desk. 'You do it all the time, and the mission required patience. And,' he added casually, 'I enjoyed fucking the English girls. The great thing is that the peasants think anybody who speaks French is a nobleman, I just had to make sure my accent matched the bastard Norman their aristos speak and they bow and scrape.'

He explained that, at first, he had dressed simply, initially pretending to be on pilgrimage. Then he had enrolled as a student at Merton College at the university in Oxford and enjoyed it so much that he had stayed on, supporting himself by becoming a good and subtle gambler, using that innocence to best advantage. Knowledge was power, so he needed to acquire the tools to get it. That is what Nicolas Béhuchet had said when, aged just fourteen and green behind the ears, a simpler Simon had stood in the same solar as he stood now, six years later.

'I don't want to know how you dressed.' The Admiral could not contain his inquisitiveness. 'Were you successful?'

'The old fool told me everything. I got the formula, everything - he showed me how to make it and how it worked,' and he went on to describe in detail all he had learnt. 'We must get the bell makers to cast us a few trial tubes. You were right - it's deadly stuff.'

The Admiral Béhuchet was delighted, it sounded as if the mission had been a complete success. 'You deserve a reward,' he said. He was in an unusually magnanimous mood, but then this secret had eluded him since he had first heard about it, ever since the Scotsman had told him about the tube of death... *What had he called it? A gonne...*

'I'll order you some Augsburg armour as soon as we get to Paris,' promised Béhuchet.

Simon was thrilled. *My own Augsburg.* Only the richest knights could afford these suits of interlocking steel plates. He was not to know that the Admiral had, in fact, already acquired the armour as a small part of a large bribe, without checking if it would fit, only to find that it would not, even with a great deal of alteration. Luckily the donor was roughly the same size as his young protégé.

Travelling by coach was an ordeal at the best of times, and Simon had been cooped up with his master for nearly a week. During this time, Simon counted the number of times the Toad had picked and examined the contents of his nose, tugged his right earlobe and, most annoyingly, poked him in the ribs to wake him up. Simon would have preferred to ride but Nicolas was insistent.

The state of the road from Rouen to Paris was abominable and, even though they had well-stuffed horsehair seating and cushions, every rut and pothole sent a jolt through his body. For the last hour they had discussed the complex web of oaths that governed loyalty. For the most part, men gave their oaths to a liege lord, and through him swore fealty to a king, holding lands under their suzerainty. Simon should have sworn such an oath once, to his uncle, but shortly before the ceremony his liege lord-to-be had fallen foul of his neighbour, a strong and powerful duke, who had razed his castle to the ground.

Since then, everyone assumed he had. Whatever the Admiral's present status as his de-facto master, his lowly birth prevented Simon, who came from the aristocracy, albeit very minor, from giving his Oath of Fealty. The matter had thereafter been swept under the carpet. Simon often thought about it. *One day I'll find a master to respect. It's a matter of honour…*

Being footloose after his uncle's untimely demise, he decided he wanted to go to sea. He wanted to be an admiral, coming as he did from the same village as Eustace the Monk, the legendary admiral from a previous century - near mythical tales of his prowess were still very much alive. To become an admiral Simon needed to be apprenticed to one, and thus he had found his way into the orbit of the Master of the King's Forests and builder of warships. What passed for the navy was a service for chancers, rogues, adventurers, and for those with a piratical bent, riches. The sea also offered a way of advancement and Simon was determined to rise high up in its hierarchy.

The promise of armour had cheered him enormously. It meant that he could push on with his desire to become a fighting man and see action. If there was to be a war, the one true way to advancement was to prove himself brave in battle.

'So King Edward of England reneged on his oath?' Simon asked, still counting. *Today twelve tugs, three picks and only two pokes.* He found most things about his master repellent - his wide mouth, with teeth ground down to stumps, that had earned him his nickname, but especially the black bushy eyebrows that met in the centre of his fore-head and dominated his face. *The devil's mark*. He often compared the Toad's features with the depictions of Satan painted on the walls of churches and found many similarities.

The Admiral, too, had seen the navy as his way for advancement. His father had been clerk to a shipbuilder and Nicolas had shown his mathematical and financial abilities early. Being of less than aver-age height, he had also learnt to manipulate other boys for his own protection. By the time he was eight, he controlled the most vicious gang of youths in the port. At university he honed his intellectual skills to perfection. From then on it was just a matter of continually consolidating and expanding his power base, graduating from larceny to piracy and from there, through expediency, to legitimacy. Now he controlled the fleets of France, determined foreign policy and had the ear of the King. *Where else can greedy Philippe get his favourite truffles?* Béhuchet ensured that *he* had the monopoly on the supply of this delicacy to the royal kitchens.

'Yes. But it wasn't a liege-oath.' The Admiral tried to explain the circumstances of the English king's treasonous behaviour, but Simon's primary concern was merely to keep his master amused. That was the reason why he had to ride in the carriage rather than on horseback with the rest of the Admiral's bodyguard.

A line of corpses graced the roadside, testament to the increase in lawlessness and poverty that now troubled the realm. Each great Lord maintained a set of gallows at the boundary of their lands. Their carriage approached the last great tollgate before the city. Béhuchet pulled open the curtain flap and ordered his men to fetch whatever tolls had been levied on travellers and goods using the road. In his role as a Royal Treasurer he had the power to collect taxes. He looked into the chest with disgust. The coins barely covered its bot-tom. Trade must be bad. A herd of skinny cattle blocked the gate, slowing their progress through the narrow streets that lead to the palace. Noise assailed their wagon from every side - shouts of cos-termongers, cries of *gare a l'eau* as slops were thrown out of upstairs windows, and clanging bells. Above all was a stench that was universal

- though it varied, depending on which trade was being carried out in the part of the city they were traversing. To combat this, the Admiral had drawn all the canvas curtains tight shut and lit a brass incense burner that he had filched from a church in Portsmouth.

'Frankincense, the Magi's gift to baby Jesus,' said the Admiral, as he fanned sweet smelling smoke around his head, 'I get it from the Cathedral.'

Steal more like. Finally they crossed over the bridge to the Île de la Cité.

'Keep your mouth shut,' urged Béhuchet as they made their way into the palace. 'Watch and listen. You're a clever young man, you'll go far.' *And I need another set of ears...*

—◊◊◊—

The Toad reported success in his negotiations when they were finally ushered into the King's presence. He had managed to hire a fleet of Mediterranean war galleys.

'The Genoese will provide twenty vessels commanded by Ayton Doria. I also persuaded Carlo Grimaldi, who controls the Rock of Monaco, to come with a further seventeen. The King of Sicily has sponsored three vessels for that empty-headed windbag of a son of his, Prince John.' Béhuchet had crossed paths with the prince before and thought him a buffoon. 'They've promised to arrive in Normandy sometime soon, after the Feast of Assumption. We've got them for three months.'

He was particularly pleased to have the Grimaldis back on board. Carlo's grandfather, Rainier, had done sterling service for the French crown, winning the battle of Zierikzee when they had thumped to odious Flemings.

'I presume you've done a good deal.' The Viper was confident that his presently bankrupt Treasury would receive a handsome share of the booty from this piece of naval opportunism. 'What do you have in mind?'

'I propose a sweep of *La Manche*. We'll start with raids on Jersey and Guernsey.' He turned to Constable Bertrand. 'As it was your idea,

I hope you'll lead the expedition.' *Flatter his ego*, he decided, *and he'll be putty in your hands*. The Channel Islands were presently firmly under English control - a continual thorn in France's side. 'Then we'll regroup and sack Hantonne.'

The King nodded and was about to ask a question but thought better of it, so he let the Admiral continue.

'My spies tell me it's poorly defended and by the autumn it should have full warehouses.'

The wine fleet would have arrived from Bordeaux and the new harvest of wool fleeces would be awaiting shipment to Flanders. The Admiral felt pleased with his intelligence. Hantonne, or Southampton as it was called in England, was the richest port in England outside London. To capture and hold the town would need a large army. This would be a logistical nightmare, but a sack was quick, in and out, *just what Italians love*. They had no stomach for prolonged campaigns where losses might mount.

'Like a ripe plum, ready for plucking,' he said gleefully, raising his arm and snaffling a handful of air. 'That should wipe the smile off The Upstart's face.'

'Doria and Grimaldi are political opposites, how are you going to square that one?' asked the King, concerned by the enmity between the pair. 'They're just as likely to turn their fleets on each other.' Italian politics were a nightmare, with two parties - Ghibellines and Guelphs - forever at each other's throats. The blood feuds that festered between them could bring their whole enterprise crashing down in ruins. Ayton Doria and the Genoese under his command were Ghibellines. The Grimaldis and his Monegasques were Guelphs.

The Admiral gave a shrug. He had given it much thought and had a simple solution.

'They have agreed if they fight each other all contracts are void,' he told the King. 'They don't get paid a bean.' And the desire to make a great deal of money, Béhuchet knew from many years of experience, was a compelling motivation that transcended politics. *Make the pot attractive enough and the Devil will happily sup with the Archangels.* 'Also, I'm not putting the whole fleet together until the last moment. I had to promise those thieves half the booty, but the contracts are only valid once they reach Channel ports, so we don't pay them for rowing from the Mediterranean.'

The King nodded. He was right to put his faith in his Little Toad, not only for the revenue stream that would revitalise his exchequer, but also because few of his other nobles, with the exception of Hugh Quiéret, the other Grand Admiral, had any desire to fight on water. His nobility were readily motivated by promises of castles and land in Aquitaine - even though they would only become available once the tenacious English were dislodged. Fighting at sea was anathema to the French aristocracy.

He called for a scribe and started to dictate a solemn Declaration: 'Let it be known that I desire the destruction and elimination of the nation of England and its language.' He watched as the ink dried. 'And send it to my good cousin John in Normandy and let him know that I have every faith in my Admirals.'

'There's no chivalry on the high seas, only a cold watery grave,' the Constable was forever pointing out. 'Nothing worth capturing, no one worth ransoming. Give me a horse and a lance any day.'

The Toad smiled. *All the more for me*, he thought, and he let his dreams of avarice run riot.

'What about the Scots?' The King was keen to know the situation with their allies. 'I have entreaties from them for more money and arms. It's never ending. What can we afford?'

The men present fell silent, waiting for some sort of lead. By providing regular finance and arms, they could keep up the pressure on England's northern borders and were honour bound to send another shipment.

'We'll send a ship in the summer,' said the King.

The Constable cleared his throat. 'I don't think we should send them anything, it's a waste of resources,' he pleaded. 'I need reinforcements in the south. Gascony must be our priority.' But his assertions left the Viper unmoved. Shaking his head the King changed the subject; the other men were given their leave. *The Serpent and the Toad make poisonous bedfellows*. The Constable bowed and left the room.

'By the by, Sire,' Béhuchet added, 'there is a castle being built close to Hantonne. My informant says it is being built by a knight called Sir Roger de Bohun; he's cousin to the Earl of Northampton. The word is he went from being poor to being rich overnight. I am told he is spending money as if it is going out of fashion. I think he's our thief.' The King's face reddened, a cheerful glow spreading through his sallow cheeks. 'I was also told that he was once the Upstart's Whipping Boy.' The Admiral had saved the best bit of news till last. 'My spy also ascertained that he deposited most of the money with the Peruzzi bankers in that town.'

The King smiled. '*Bon*, Hantonne it will be.' Then, as if embarrassed about what he had to say next, he looked away. '*Malheureusement pour vous*, the expedition will be led by Lord Quiéret.'

This was an unexpected blow. Hugh was a proper aristocrat, Seneschal of Nimes, and the first Frenchman to hold the prestigious post of Admiral of France, a title that he now shared. Nicolas looked at his King and wanted to express his disappointment, but felt better of it. There would be other times to seek glory.

Chapter 8

The Last Throw of the Dice

Sir Alexander Ramsay sat warming his hands as he listened with interest to the deputation of loyal Scots who had made the dangerous journey across the wild country from Dunbar Town, dodging English patrols. He felt the gentle hand of destiny rest on his shoulder as he put another bough on the fire and watched in deep contemplation as a procession of sparks spiralled up towards the ceiling of Wallace's Cave. It was here that a previous hero of Scotland, William Wallace, had spent the night before the defeat of the English at the Battle of Rosslyn.

'Aye, we've been resupplying the castle at night,' the leading burgher told him. 'We slip past the galleys in our rowing boats. The garrison are in good spirits and her ladyship is determined to hang on.'

'Then I think we can help.' Sir Alexander looked at his men, instead of the thousands that Wallace had commanded; he had only forty battle-hardened highlanders, all of whom bore grudges against the English. The caves at Rosslyn made poor accommodation and it was agreed by a unanimous show of hands that they should go to relieve Lady Agnes.

As dawn crept over the moor so, with steel in their souls and their hands, the motley band of warriors set off to help the embattled chatelaine.

—᠁—

Sir Walter Mauney was concerned as he re-read the letter from the Earl of Salisbury; it had taken the best part of a fortnight to get from Dunbar to Harwich. Mauney was a Hainaulter with an all-abiding loathing for the French, who he considered to be cheating pederasts at the best of times. This hatred stemmed from his youth, when he had won his first tourney but had his prize denied him by the Compte de Lisle, who had said that 'a boy with bum-fluff on his face had no right to enter a tourney, let alone win it'. The ensuing fracas, in which young Mauney had been grievously assaulted in a most unseemly manner, had served to compound the insult.

Mauney came originally from the court of King Edward's wife's father and thus he had jumped at the chance to come to England as a squire to Queen Philippa some ten years previously. Since then he had risen effortlessly in the service of the King, first as Keeper of the Queen's greyhounds, and then Yeoman of the King's Chamber. He was presently the de facto Chief of Staff in his capacity as Admiral North of the Thames. A tall, good looking fellow who bore himself with an easy grace, he was the epitome of the chivalrous knight, a soldier of fortune who, in Edward, had found a monarch and a cause he could espouse to. In Mauney, Edward had a man he could trust, a warrior courageous and daring to the point of recklessness, astute and dependable.

The news the letter contained was disquieting to say the least. It was an update on the siege. The castle remained well stocked with food and it was Salisbury who was suffering. They'd stripped the area of livestock and grain, and couldn't get close to the castle without incurring great losses.

'He says they're stymied' reported Walter at his regular briefing with Edward, who was sitting at a briefing table piled high with papers and maps. 'It's not good. Here, read it.'

The King took the parchment and examined it, a frown growing across his forehead. His right foot stamped down repeatedly as he worked hard to quell his frustration, making the hound that had curled up on his feet leap away with a yelp.

'I need him and his army here, now. I despair, we're already well past our embarkation date,' he said as he flung the missive onto the pile already on the table.

Getting an army together was a Herculean task at the best of times - getting one across the North Sea to Flanders was proving much harder. He needed Salisbury and his men to bolster his limited resources for this expedition. Most of all he especially needed the archers.

Mauney had set the example in a raid on the island of Cadzand on the Flanders coast the previous November and shown just how valuable an asset longbowmen were: with two thousand archers and only five hundred men-at-arms they had comprehensively routed a much larger Franco-Flemish army, before brutally sacking the town. Before retiring to their ships the English had then herded the survivors into a church and burnt them alive as an object lesson – support the French at your peril.

The last thing Edward needed now was for his force to be considered puny. Not only that but his assembled fleet of trade cogs and barges was costing a fortune to hold and already their captains, fed up with waiting, were starting to slip away. He needed to act decisively. 'We'll send Moray to the Earl,' said the King, thumping the table with such force that a pot of quills went flying.

Walter's face lit up, and a wry smile crept across his face as he nodded his unquestioning agreement. Lord John Randolph, Earl of Moray, had been captured the previous autumn and was Black Agnes' brother. Anything that could be done to vexate this vile example of verminous humanity was alright with him. They both hoped that sending Moray would be their trump card.

So it was, under heavy escort, stinking, unkempt and unshaven, Moray arrived at Dunbar in the second week of June - in time for the Feast of St. Aquilina.

'You can do the honours.' Salisbury deputised Sir Roger and his sergeant to take the prisoner down the causeway.

'He's an odious turd, nearly as unpleasant as de Frage,' said Sir Roger to the Ox as they endured a barrage of insults and spitting from the hogtied Scotsman. 'If you don't shut up,' Sir Roger bent down and whispered in Moray's ear, 'I'll tell him to hack at you with the blunt side.'

Gwyn grinned and flourished his falchion- ideal for beheading. 'Ironic, isn't it, that St. Aquilina was also beheaded. Sharp side, blunt side, you choose,' he continued while Moray hissed vehemently, a stream of unending insults continuing unabated.

Salisbury followed a short distance behind, carrying aloft white flags of parlay. The perceived Rules of War prevented treachery, and he hoped that even Black Agnes would stay her marksman's hand to uphold the laws of Chivalry.

'Lady Agnes,' shouted Sir Roger, his voice carrying powerfully. 'We have your brother here and have orders to execute him unless you surrender.' Heads appeared above the battlements, only to disappear again until eventually Agnes's black tresses were seen, discernible as she opened a wooden shutter hinged between the crenellations.

'My brother is a pig. Slit his throat. Make him squeal.' Agnes was her usual vitriolic self. 'I have no love for my brother. I care not if you chop off his head, in fact do it right away!'

Moray flinched and Sir Roger leant over and whispered in his ear. 'That's not a very nice thing for your sister to say.' Although not really surprised, he wondered what the condemned man had done to deserve such harsh criticism.

'No love between siblings? Pray tell, what did the oaf do?' He shouted up to Lady Agnes.

She was quick to provide an answer. 'Not since you tortured and murdered my darling Hector,' she shouted.

'Darling Hector.' Sir Roger could help chuckling. 'And who, pray, was Hector? Her first paramour?'

'No, it was her pet lapdog,' growled Moray through gritted teeth as he stared up at the sky as if beseeching the Almighty. Of course, Sir Roger wanted to know more, and Moray obliged him, if only to buy time. The dog's death had been an accident, a gruesome but unfortunate one nonetheless. He told Sir Roger that, when they were children, he and some friends had rigged up a rope across a pond and tied the dog to a pulley. Unfortunately, the knots had slipped and the poor animal had strangled as it gyrated helplessly out of reach. 'The bitch gave me these.' He still bore scars where she had scratched his face, drawing blood.

'A pooch killer. Who'd have thought it!' Sir Roger would dine out on this story.

'She went mad.' Moray remembered her demented screams about her vengeance - so this was it. He shook his head in disbelief, trying to plead with her, but to no avail.

'Chop his head off, rid me of this louse,' she shouted down. 'Do it, it'll make me richer. I'll inherit all his lands and money.'

The falchion was raised, only awaiting the nod from Salisbury. It never came. 'What do you mean?' he shouted, his attention piqued by this last remark.

'He's my only kin, so I inherit all his lands, his castles, everything. I've always hated him. He's only fit for worm food.'

'Spare him,' spat Salisbury in a fury. 'I would hate it if the only outcome from his death was the Bitch's enrichment,' he muttered to Sir Roger. 'Send him back to the King.'

—◊◊◊—

Another tedious week passed. The men practised duelling with wooden swords and honing up on their jousting skills. A short night had given way to a perfect dawn, the sun rising over the grey waters of the North Sea. The air smelt sweet and was filled with the cries of gulls and waders as summer transformed the countryside with carpets of flowers.

'The feast of St. Barnabus, a fast more like,' said Gwyn as he handed his master his morning mug of wine. It was June the tenth. 'Another fine day in hell.'

Sir Roger asked if there was anything to report and the sergeant shook his head, glad that his turn at night watch was over and he could now snatch some sleep.

The whole camp stirred, preparing for another boring day. The Earl and his commanders would go hawking, as was their wont. They were very competitive and the vast numbers and many varieties of duck, geese and heron made tempting quarries. Sir Roger summoned his falconer, ordering him to prepare Ariel, his peregrine falcon. All his birds were named after Archangels and he had brought three birds on campaign with him. For the rest of the army the routine would be the same as always. There were games of dice and complaining about the food - and the Welsh mercenaries, the archers, a surly bunch, who no one could understand.

—⚏—

A cursory glance at the castle showed nothing amiss. The Scottish flag was raised on the roof, along with the standard of the Earls of March. Only the sharpest eyes would have seen a third flag, but no one had bothered to look for days, and without any wind to speak of, all the draped cloths hung limply. But it was there, and belonged to Sir Alexander Ramsay.

'Heard you were still holding out, and thought you might need some help,' he said with a chuckle.

'For which I am most grateful.' The feisty chatelaine had a wicked glint in her eyes. As much as she hated her brother, blood was blood. She wanted revenge for his humiliation by de Bohun, who had made Moray crawl all the way back down the causeway, howling like a dog while booting him up the backside, and, in her book, that was unacceptable.

'Off they go. Every day is the same.' Lady Agnes stood dwarfed by the Scottish noble who had braved a perilous journey through the night with his forty warriors, sneaking in through the hidden postern gate at the base of the cliffs. It was through this same entrance that the loyal citizens of Dunbar kept the castle resupplied throughout the siege, slipping past the prowling galleys on moonless nights in their fishing boats.

The whole garrison assembled behind the gate. Pasquale was armed and ready, an ill-fitting helmet balancing precariously on his head. He handed his crossbow to Lady Agnes. 'Just in case.' He winked, kissing her hand.

She, in return, kissed his cheek. 'Be safe, Eagle-eye.' It was her pet name for him.

He respected this woman. Against impossible odds she had kept her nerve. In turn all the men bowed to her, tightened their straps and formed a schiltron bristling with pikes, spears and swords. The castle lookouts waited until the hawking parties had left camp and were out of sight. Only then, did the great portcullis lift and the main gates swing open.

The arrival of a phalanx of eighty bellicose Scots (and a Frenchman), screaming and whooping, caught the English completely by surprise. The meagre guard at the barricades fled immediately. Within a short space of time the English camp was wrecked - tents set on fire, spare horses rounded up and herded down the causeway. An orgy of destruction ensued. Those not quick enough to escape were hacked limb from limb and left gutted on the ground. Only when a few Welsh archers turned and started to fire into the pack of howling Scots did they retreat back to the castle, cheering and hurling abuse at the shocked English, most of whom had fled as fast as their feet could carry them.

—⁊⁊—

The Earl, alerted by an exhausted, out of breath squire who had ridden bareback across the moors, returned to survey the damage.

'So that's it,' announced Salisbury, dejectedly looking at the remains of his marquee. It had been slashed to ribbons. His personal possessions were strewn across the ground, his fine clothes trampled in the mud. 'The bitch has won. We go south; let us hope we have better luck in Flanders with the King.' And so the English packed up what was left of their camp and, to hoots of derision from the Scots, started their weary march south. It had been an ignominious end to an inglorious siege. They had been outfought and outsmarted at every turn - by a woman.

Chapter 9

Trouble with Wool

The stain of the English humiliation at Dunbar spread across the country as fast as a man could ride. In taverns, manor houses, castles and palaces the stories from the siege had been embellished and bowdlerised, merging fact and fiction into song - and now the ballads had an end. The 'brawling boisterous Scottish Wench', as William Montagu called Lady Agnes, had won an infamous victory. Handley, the Ipers Manor Bailiff, had heard the song and took special note - his master would surely return soon. Whistling happily, he oversaw the loading of the adulterated woolsacks onto carts. These would be taken to the Monopoly Consortium's warehouse in the port of Southampton.

He had been irritated with Percy the Reeve for not getting fresh canvas for the sacks, making liberal use of his rawhide whip to chivvy along indolent serfs who had spent many laborious hours unwrapping, doctoring and rewrapping fleeces.

'I tried to get new stuff, but there ain't any anywhere,' said Percy. The Reeve and Bailiff were as thick as thieves. 'That's not *exactly* true, but I didn't think you'd want me going to the Steward - you know what a suspicious bastard he can be.'

Handley knew exactly what he meant. Neither man wanted Whytethorne to poke his nose into their business. If he found out what was going on, he most definitely would not approve. The Manorial account books would only show a perfectly legitimate, and expected, sale of low-grade wool, and Bailiff and Reeve would pocket the difference.

There was, though, a potential fly in the ointment. The Consortium's agent, Alfred of Eccles, could be a tricky customer; they had met before and developed a mutual dislike for each other. So it came as a pleasant surprise when the merchant welcomed him like a long-lost brother, for Alfred was hugely relieved when the convoy of carts from Ipers arrived at the warehouse. He had had a grim week. Where there should have been a steady stream of wool, instead there was a trickle. He cast an expert eye over the consignment and shook his head. The bonhomie didn't last long; Alfred had never trusted the de Bohun's Bailiff. There was something about the sacks that didn't look right.

'It's the best I could get,' said Handley as they discussed the poor quality of the canvas. 'I like your new mantle,' he added, deftly changing the subject, enviously eyeing up the merchant's sable-lined collar that attested to an income of over £100 a year.

Eccles smiled. He was keen to comply with new sumptuary laws, recently passed by Parliament that only persons of wealth be allowed to wear fur. Handley was less sure about the peacock feather that sprouted from a gold pin on a turban of expensive fabric - *too ostentatious for my tastes*. The Bailiff wore the ubiquitous hood that was the mark of the common man. Eccles was, reputedly, the richest merchant in town, though few had seen the several chests of gold coins he kept hidden away in his mansion.

'Ten sacks of top grade,' said Handley, hoping he had disguised any nervousness in his voice that would betray his duplicity. 'The Steward asks that we be paid now.' This was a lie - the Steward was not even aware that any Ipers wool had been shipped. 'Twenty-five pounds, three shillings and ten pence, please.' Handley had worked it all out. The difference in value, £6 18s 4d, would take a normal labourer more than three years to earn. Percy would get a quarter.

Eccles had rehearsed his reply. 'Sadly,' he said, trying to add gravitas to his delivery. 'The Consortium has instructions from the *King himself*,' - he emphasised the last two words so there could be no doubt under whose authority he was acting - 'that I can't pay you. I am to issue you with a receipt which you can get cashed when the Exchequer releases funds.'

Handley's jaw dropped. The carts had been unloaded and the drovers were already on their way back to the manor.

'We're supposed to ship all sacks to Dordrecht, then, *when* it's sold, the money *should* be sent,' said Eccles without much conviction in his voice as he watched a clerk write out a receipt. Dordrecht, a port in southern Holland, was where the King had declared the Staple - the official marketplace for wool - should be located. Parliament, in its wisdom, had voted his Majesty twenty thousand sacks of wool to pay for his war against France. To date, hardly any wool had reached Southampton, or any other port.

All this effort for nothing. The Bailiff's mind was racing, but each thought turned down a blind alley. He had to admit defeat and, searching his purse for a couple of pennies, went off to find a whore. He stopped briefly to watch a tread wheel crane, one of several that were dotted along crowded wharfs. Six men sweated profusely as it unloaded a net full of barrels from the hold of a Spanish trader.

'That's what they do to petty criminals, make 'em work like slaves,' said a voice behind him. 'I think I'd prefer a day in the stocks.'

Handley turned to see who had spoken but whoever it was had gone.

The cheap whores hung out near God's Tower, a strong defensive gate on the eastern corner of town. Handley was not fussy, venting all his anger and frustration on an unfortunate slattern, leaving her badly bruised.

With the Ipers wool, Eccles now had enough to consolidate a shipment.

'Be careful,' he shouted nervously at the stevedores as the Ipers bales were being loaded onto a cog bound for Great Yarmouth. He could see that the man at the top was distracted. The uppermost bale toppled to the deck, where it split. Its contents, once tightly packed, burst out in a fluffy cloud.

'I think you should see this.' It was Eccles's overseer. 'Someone has not been *entirely* honest.' Sure enough, the outer layer of wool was finest grade, as it should have been throughout, but when Eccles delved deeper into the sack he felt the coarse, inferior fibre.

'I bet they are all like that. Have a look, and then sew it up well; we don't want them bursting open again. Mix the sacks in with all the rest and no one will be the wiser,' Eccles told his foreman, deciding to pass the problem on down the line. He would mix this shipment in with all the rest, and by the time the wool got to Flanders it would be too late to do anything about it. He, however, would not honour the debt for the fraudulent consignment. 'Get this lot to Yarmouth quick as you can,' he told his foreman. 'And give me our half of the receipt.' He took the document and put it in his purse. 'I'd better visit Ipers.' And with that Eccles strode off home, from where he dealt in many luxury goods - spices, wine and olive oil.

—⚜—

Sir Roger had been insistent that work should continue throughout the winter and for months the labourers had struggled through a sea of mud, but now spring had turned to summer and Lady Alice had heard that her husband was soon to return. A messenger from the King had informed her on handing over a sealed pouch that the siege of Dunbar was over. 'If your ladyship would kindly give your husband these,' he asked, while eyeing her up and down. Her new dress was of the latest fashion, with a low cut front that enhanced her bosom - hers was most *décolleté*.

Once it had become generally known that her ladyship was in residence, an endless stream of merchants and tradesmen had come to call, and today was no exception. The merchant in front of her today, however, was a cut above the normal riff-raff that came to peddle their wares; his sable collar and peacock feather attested to that.

'Milady, I would like you to meet Alfred of Eccles. He buys all of your husband's wool.' Whytethorne introduced the richly dressed merchant. This was the first time they had met, however, Lady Alice knew of his reputation from the Steward.

She welcomed him with a flutter of her eyelids and an outstretched hand which he took with a bow, sweeping the courtyard flagstones with his peacock-feathered turban. 'I have heard so much about you,' she said. 'What brings you this far?'

'Your husband's imminent return,' said Eccles. He spoke in mangled French, Alice's native tongue, though with a distinctly northern twang. It was an easy assumption to make, since musicians and jongleurs the length and breadth of the country were singing about Lord Salisbury's humiliating defeat. 'I had also heard all about your great works here and came to see if there was anything you might want from me.' He snapped his fingers and a minion ran over carrying a small hessian sack. 'I thought you might like these - a gift of lemons, freshly arrived from Spain, and I've brought some other bits and pieces for your larder.'

A wagon full of merchandise trundled into view, accompanied by an armed escort. It was obvious that the cargo was of enormous value. It was piled high with barrels, wooden boxes and numerous wicker baskets of all sizes and shapes containing olive oil, dried figs, almonds, ginger roots and pickled lemons. There were dates, prunes, currants and raisins, cinnamon, cardamoms, even nutmegs still covered with mace. There were casks of finest Bordeaux wine and some of the boxes contained fashionable Santonge pottery - plates, beakers and jugs that were all the rage, all neatly packed in sawdust.

The merchant produced a small box from a pouch that hung on his belt. 'Smell this.' He opened the lid to reveal bright orange filaments of saffron, its pungent aroma instantly filling the air. 'Fit for the table of a lord and his pretty lady,' he said, without a trace of lechery, so she took it as a compliment.

The wagon and contents immediately attracted Max the Cook, or Maximilian Grossteste to give his full name, who came swaying out, huffing and puffing. Eccles had rarely seen a fatter man, the epitome of a glutton, and even though it was still before midday, one that was *definitely* drunk.

'Been trying a new batch of ale, milady,' Max blurted out guiltily as he wiped the back of a podgy hand across his bright red face, while shifting from leg to leg as he tried to relieve the pressure on his sphincter, hoping it would be a silent fart - but it was not to be, so he let rip anyway.

Lady Alice tried to suppress a giggle and had to look away. Max's arrival, pursued hotly by constables, had been after a week of endless rain some six months previously. The bedraggled balloon had waddled across the courtyard festooned with many wafer irons and a wooden spoon stuck in his belt like a sword and begged to be allowed to stay, throwing himself in a blubbering heap at her feet, craving a safe haven from where he could create his *nebula* - his 'clouds'. At first she had refused, letting him rest in the stables out of Christian charity, but after a day of pleading, followed by a couple of hours in the kitchen, Lady Alice had relented. She needed a cook well versed in proper culinary arts.

In truth it was his heavenly 'angel's bread', that had sealed the deal. She had lied for Max after tasting his wafers. Though the honey ones elicited praise as they melted on the tongue, it was an especially spicy gingery one that had won her heart. He was a true master.

'Mister Eccles, may I introduce Grossfart the Cook.' After such a windy entrance she could not resist using his nickname. She watched Max reach involuntarily for his wooden spoon then stop, realising that it was his mistress, and not a mosquito-like scullery boy buzzing around his cooking pots trying to steal morsels and calling him names behind his back.

'He hasn't poisoned me yet,' she revealed to Eccles conspiratorially, putting the back of her hand across her mouth, 'though he did manage to poison most of Exeter - if the constables were to be believed. They said he left a trail of crumbs that any half-starved mouse could follow. But for five shillings each they agreed the trail had gone cold.'

She had made Max work off his debt by cooking without pay for three months. It could have been six for all Max cared, so enthralled was he by her beauty, watching as she and her maids picked posies of wild flowers in the meadow by the river. All she had to do was say the word and he would happily lay down his life for her.

His previous employer, the Bishop of Exeter, had welcomed his departure, as the scandal of poisoning the city had not completely died down. Max had developed a thriving trade selling leftovers from the bishop's kitchen to local bakers who, in turn, used these for pie fillings. Such was demand for his kitchen waste that Max had become too greedy, scouring swill barrels. The last batch had been seriously mouldy, resulting in at least four deaths from Bloody Flux that the justices linked back to the Bishop's kitchen. He had fled rather than face a hangman's noose.

'You still owe me your life, Max,' she said with a smile, and as an afterthought she added, 'though I think you would be too fat for the gallows.' But Max couldn't care; he had found his way to his new mistress's heart with his wafers and knew it. And now, with a new kitchen completed, he looked forward to producing feasts and banquets, which were his all-abiding passion.

Eccles and Lady Alice watched intently as Max rummaged through the cart's contents, sniffing, sampling and prodding with fat, sausage-like fingers. 'Your ladyship, I could use everything that is here, except these,' he pointed to a barrel of cured herrings. 'These smell bad and I must be careful not to make anyone sick!' He laughed, his belly bouncing up and down. 'In fact tomorrow I shall make Mock Egg,' he offered, picking out an almond and popping it into his mouth.

'He can get the outside white and yellow in the centre. Not many cooks can do that,' Lady Alice noted with a hint of pride. It was one of Max's greatest skills, stuffing a blown eggshell with different coloured almond paste so that it looked just like a hard-boiled egg.

Seeing the glee on her children's faces at Easter had made Lady Alice happy about lying to his pursuers, though she instructed Handley to ensure that no leftovers from their kitchen were sold on to pie men. But Handley and Max were men of similar ilk, and soon a thriving trade in leftovers started all over again. This time, though, Max was more careful not to include food that was too spoiled even for pie fillings.

'I feel as if I'm in heaven,' said a delighted Max. His larder was full and for the first time in his life he had been able to have a kitchen built to his exacting specifications - it even had a tiled floor.

'You can have the herrings for free, a gift from me to your build-ers!' The merchant was in effusive mood. He had only put them there because his wife had complained that they were stinking out his ware-house - unsold leftovers from Lent. Eccles took out a tally stick and made a series of notches with a sharp penknife to record amounts owed. Splitting the stick in two, he gave half to Whytethorne and put its partner into his bulging purse - he would send round an itemised bill later. Sir Roger's credit was good. Eccles had been entertained to dinner at the Peruzzi Bank and heard, in fair detail, just how large a fortune it was.

He had a feeling he would get on well with Sir Roger, and contin-ued to ingratiate himself with Lady Alice, for here he could sense an independent woman with a taste for luxury and a husband unafraid of spending.

'There is one small matter,' said Eccles quietly, when Whytethorne had left. 'I am concerned that your Bailiff is up to no good.' And he told Lady Alice about the wool.

She found this most tiresome, principally because she hated her meetings with the Bailiff. Whenever he could, Handley would lean over, breathing his halitosis breath in her ear and surreptitiously ogle her breasts. Because of this she changed into a more severe outfit with a wimple from which only a single wisp of red hair was allowed to escape. She summoned Handley to the solar and told him what Eccles had said but the Bailiff just looked at her with venom-filled eyes.

'It was nothing,' he said dismissively, denying all knowledge of the fraud. 'He's just trying to get out of paying us - he has no proof.'

'I shall tell my husband. He'll find out the truth,' Lady Alice replied, ready to end the conversation. She was not expecting Handley to respond.

'I wouldn't do that, Milady.' There was a note of menace in the Bailiff's voice. 'Or he might hear more than a song from your fancy minstrel.'

Handley watched as blood drained from her face, and he knew then that he was right. He had suspected that the randy songster could not keep his penis in his pants, and he often wondered what happened when the lute playing ended. Once he had sneaked up and put his ear to the door - *Lady Alice is a moaner*. And now she would do anything to keep this secret away from her husband.

—ɯ—

'You must leave here immediately; my husband will be here any day,' Lady Alice whispered into Michael's ear. She had been unable to resist one last fuck. 'If he finds out he'll kill you.'

Michael understood. Fleeing the wrath of vengeful husbands and fathers was a serial seducer's lot. So, clutching his new lute, he disappeared into the night. He would go to London, where Lady Alice had given him a letter of introduction to her friends at Court.

Chapter 10

The Star of the Show

If there was one thing that could ruin Admiral Hugh Quiéret's day, it was meeting with his co-admiral, the Toad. Unfortunately, however much he wanted to, he could not ignore him as he strode across the courtyard of the Clos de Gallées. A new war galley, freshly calked and painted in yellow and black vaguely reminiscent of a hornet, was ready to be launched down the slipway into the Seine.

'Your flagship,' said Béhuchet proudly. 'All she needs now is a name.'

'*St. Guillaume*,' Quiéret said decisively as he ran his hand through a thick mane of salt and pepper hair. 'She's a fine vessel.'

His co-admiral smiled smugly. *She's the best we've built yet.* 'I'm sure you'll make good use of her.'

Simon watched as the two men stood side by side. Quiéret was a big man with a head that was very large in relation to the rest of his body and who towered over the Toad. They were like chalk and cheese. Quiéret was a pure-blooded Norman aristocrat - Lord of Turns in Vimeu and Hamicourt, Seneschal of Beaucare and Nisme, Captain of Tournay and Chamberlain of France - and he had extensive estates close to Rouen. He had, however, fallen into debt. He was an inveterate gambler with an uncanny predisposition for losing streaks and had been forced, though not exactly against his will, to enter the tight-knit community of salty sea-faring folk that was the French Navy. Somewhere in his family's dim and distant past they had been

Norsemen and, as luck would have it, he didn't suffer from seasickness. *I need to keep the slimy Toad happy,* thought Quiéret. *He's my ticket back to a life of luxury.* His mind turned to his mortgaged castle, now stripped bare of furnishings and falling into ruin. He wanted that back, for a start.

'So, Baldy.' he could never resist making jokes about his colleague's lack of hair, though he was careful not to go *too* far - his co-admiral had a nasty habit of extracting revenge when least expected. 'What's our plan?'

'The Italians have arrived,' said Béhuchet, choosing not to rise to the insult. 'We've got to keep them busy for the summer; otherwise they'll be at each other's throats.' There had already been a knifing. He could see that his co-admiral was itching to get his hands on his new toy, peering past him at the galley.

'If I can make a suggestion?' Simon had been primed. 'Let's postpone the attack on Southampton until autumn.'

Béhuchet had noticed that Quiéret almost invariably rejected his ideas out of sheer bloody mindedness and thus he now always used an intermediary to float a plan.

'Split the Italians up,' Simon continued. 'Why don't you take Doria and his squadron north - there should be some fat prizes in the English wool fleet and we'll let the Grimaldis transport the Constable Bertrand's forces to Guernsey - he's already at Brest and needs transport.'

'*Bon idée,*' said Béhuchet, smoothly taking over from his underling. 'Encourage the Dorias to patrol off the Scheldt. Let's see how they get on in our northern waters. There's your answer and, in the meantime I need time to sort out the practical arrangements for the attack on Southampton.'

The Toad knew that proper planning was essential to the success of amphibious operations, and, if - and it was a big if - they were going to mount a full-scale invasion of England, or even to raid inland, they would have to have sorted out the details, such as signalling, custody and distribution of booty, order of battle at sea and rear-guard actions. Southampton would be a good test. *I also need time for Cardinal Alberghini to complete his mission.* He had sown the seed and needed time for the harvest to ripen. The Cardinal had set off for Marseille over two months ago with a chest of money - *set a sprat to catch a mackerel...*

Béhuchet's spies had also reported rumours of Quiéret's jealousy and he needed to nip these in the bud. Being master of the Clos des Gallées gave him advantages over his co-admiral, not least his ability to skim money off construction budgets, and though he sometimes shared this with Quiéret, it was only a tiny fraction of sums he took. Now, worried that his colleague might try to engineer his downfall, Béhuchet took a spur-of-the-moment decision. 'I'd like it if you could take Simon along with you,' he said 'he can report back on your sea trials in the *St. Guillaume*. I also want him to try out our new guns. In fact, why doesn't he give you a demonstration of his *ribaud*?'

The following day, Béhuchet had managed to assemble an audience of Genoese, plus Prince John of Sicily and about twenty senior fighting men from the Franco-Italian fleet on windswept marshes outside the city's walls.

If I'm going to be the star of the show I'd better look the part. Simon selected a quartered yellow and blue tunic in the latest fashion, with long scalloped-edged sleeves and an excessively elaborate *chaperon* hat from his extensive wardrobe. He spent most of his money on clothes.

'What a dandy. Is he a lady's man, or is he like our mincing prince?' whispered Quiéret to his colleague, waving towards the Prince, who all knew indulged in unnatural vices. 'What other skills does he have, other than preening?'

'He's a good lad and fucks like a rabbit, so I've been reliably informed,' Béhuchet replied - and the Toad *had* been told, that was for sure. In fact, he was told everything. He knew when, where and with whom most of the French court fornicated, and those he did not know about, he soon would. His network of spies paid servants and maids well for learning the grubby details of their masters' and mistresses' bedroom antics.

'I've given him a suit of Augsburg armour. Felt a man of his status deserved to be well kitted-out if he went to war. He's turning out to be good with these guns.' Béhuchet looked Quiéret directly in the eye and lowered his voice. 'I hear Henriette is pregnant again, and with a husband who lost his bollocks…'He watched his colleague's cheeks redden - *touché*, he thought. *Call me 'baldy' one more time and I'll have you gelded like her husband.*

Simon was in his element and took centre stage. Chest puffed up like a peacock displaying its great fantail, he waved his hand over a curious contraption - a large metal tube with a bulbous end mounted horizontally on a wooden bracket. He asked if anyone knew what it was, but only one of the noblemen had seen such a weapon before.

'This is a *ribaud*,' Simon explained. 'It fires these.' He held up a heavy metal arrow about ten times the size of a regular crossbow bolt.

Simon had spent the last couple of months scouring the country for enough sulphur. The rest of the ingredients, saltpetre and charcoal had been easy. From these, he had made a supply of gunpowder, not much, but enough. It was ironic that the formula for this magical substance had come from England. '*Vien ici*. Watch and learn.' He could not resist adding: 'This is the future of war.'

He ostentatiously took a large scoop of black powder from a small tub and, with a long ladle carefully loaded the gun. Exaggerating all his movements he put rags into the tube and pushed the arrow down firmly, so only the tip protruded from the end of the tube. Taking a quill filled with gunpowder from his purse he stuck it into a small hole in the bulb. 'Gentlemen, I want you to watch that hatch.' About twenty paces away a sizeable, thick oak target had been placed in front of some weighted wicker baskets. Lighting a taper from a lantern, Simon held it to the quill. The *ribaud* leapt upwards with a loud bang, bucking like a horse. A lance of flame shot out, followed by a cloud of dense white smoke. The projectile moved so fast it was hard to see. Its effect, though, was obvious - it had gone clean through the panel, shattering it, and through the supporting baskets, finally sticking out of the ground fifty paces further on. The explosion sent a mass of birds shrieking into the air from the surrounding flood plain.

'*That* is how we will open the gates of Southampton Castle,' announced de Pressi. The stunned audience of admirals and captains looked at each other then, as one, started to clap.

'But will it open a bank vault?' asked Béhuchet, taking Simon aside. He knew the demonstration had most likely been a sham, designed to awe.

'The *ribaud* might work,' answered Simon cautiously. He knew the Admiral had the habit of asking loaded questions and the raised hairs on the back of his neck told Simon to advance with caution. 'If I know precisely what you have in mind...'

'What would I do without you, Simon?' Béhuchet was effusive in his praise. He was always impressed by his protégé's diligence – Simon had the perfect combination of braininess and ruthlessness needed to join disparate parts of the maritime empire together. If he had a weakness, it was pride.

'Aristobollocks is my main concern,' Béhuchet subtly pointed his thumb at Hugh and confided his worries to his lieutenant. There was nothing subtle about Quiéret, whose simple maxim was 'why use a stick when you can use a battering ram'. 'I've asked him if you can attach yourself to his staff - now he's managed to persuade the powers that be that he's in command for Southampton. Make him think that I have somehow offended you,' he instructed his protégé. 'He'll be more forthcoming with secrets if he thinks you've changed allegiance.' Béhuchet felt that to be forewarned was to be forearmed. 'I know you want to see action,' he winked, and Simon's eyes lit up. 'Here's your chance. Let's see if that *ribaud* really works.'

Chapter 11

An Offer He Could Not Refuse

As his carriage bumped relentlessly towards Marseille, Cardinal Alberghini had time to reflect on his predicament. He felt only fury and blind hatred for the Toad and he cursed the little Admiral. *I would gladly poke my eyes out with a red-hot knife.* He stared unhappily into the bloody disc of the setting sun. As he stared the sun turned from red to black. Such was the depth of his despair he did not blink and when he closed his eyes the afterimage remained burned into his retinas. He wished he could turn the clock back, but he couldn't. He was powerless, trapped in a vice of vice. All his life he had been diligent, hard-working and careful. He had been rewarded with a glittering career. Coming from obscure origins - his father had been a poor but pious knight - Alberghini had achieved prominence, rising through the Church hierarchy through dint of a ferocious intellect. This was no mean achievement. In his present position as one of the Pope's Private Secretaries, he was privy to the innermost secrets of the Holy See and Keeper of the Papal Seals.

'We have arrived, Your Eminence.' It was the captain of his guard. Hot and tired, the Cardinal took the briefest of refreshment at the Bishop's Residence before setting out down narrow cobbled streets in a palanquin to the port. Crowds parted as his escort of Papal Swiss Guards made their presence felt. Reaching the crammed wharves, he signalled to the nearest uniformed man and imperiously ordered that the Harbour Master be fetched immediately. Their man arrived with all haste, genuflecting as he kissed the proffered ring.

'I'm looking for a Captain Bandolini, is he still here?' Alberghini asked the sweating official.

'Over there.' The harassed port officer pointed. 'At the end jetty, he's preparing to set sail.'

Urging his palanquin carriers forward, Alberghini's bodyguards were none too careful with their pikes as they parted crowds of dockhands unloading fresh Egyptian grain from the deep cargo bellies of fat cogs.

Captain Niccolo Bandolini scanned the dock for a final time before ordering his first mate to cast off.

It is imperative you wait. His agent's voice echoed in his ears. He had been emphatic, indicating that this enforced sojourn in Marseille would be worth his while. But it had lasted for over a week and now he was losing money. His patience worn out, he prepared to slip away at nightfall. Still, the emphasis his agent had placed on the importance of him waiting made him hesitate. Watching stevedores scatter Bandolini rescinded his order - this just might be his passenger. The palanquin stopped at his gangplank.

'Captain Bandolini?'

He nodded.

'I thought I'd be too late. I'm sorry for the delay.' Cardinal Alberghini held out his ring, and touched the Captain briefly on his forehead, blessing him and then his ship. The *Swift* was a Venetian spice runner, one of the fastest ships afloat - sleek, beautiful and filled with precious cargo, which Bandolini, much to his annoyance, had not been allowed to unload.

'What I have to discuss is private,' said Alberghini, looking around nervously. 'Can we go to your cabin?' The Cardinal was followed by a guard who struggled with a non-descript, smallish metal-bound casket. It made a heavy clunk as the guard heaved it on the table. In the seclusion of the cabin, the box was opened with a key that hung on a chain concealed under Alberghini's crucifix. It was filled with gold coins. He watched the captain's eyes widen - he was offering enough to visit the Fourth Level of Satan's Realm.

'I want you to go to England,' announced the Cardinal, 'on Papal business.' He counted out the coins, two hundred and fifty shiny ducats, enough to buy a grand palazzo on the Grand Canal.

Bandolini bit one, just to make sure. The soft gold yielded to his canine tooth, leaving a small but visible mark. The Captain had been to England before, but never so late in the year. He was not worried about the journey there - summer was still young, but, making a quick calculation in his head, coming back would be much harder. By September the weather in the Bay of Biscay would change. His vessel was not suited for the Atlantic, being of shallow draft, and he would have to brave it in the stormy season. He crossed himself involuntarily and recited a 'Hail Mary' under his breath.

'We want you to sell your cargo in Southampton and deliver these messages to the Peruzzi Bank.' He handed over a sheaf of documents sealed with Papal crests. 'Be careful, hide your intentions well. If they ask you why you came, just lie - the Lord will be merciful and forgive.' The Cardinal rose and handed the key to Bandolini and then, without uttering another word, left the ship.

If I make it back to Venice it will be my most profitable trip ever. But Bandolini was never one to count his chickens before they hatched. First he would have to break the news to his crew; his sixty oarsmen had already raced from Aleppo in the Levant; to complete their journey they would have to pull the same distance again to get to England before even setting out for home - *I'll have to break it to them gently.*

Chapter 12

Home at Last

'You ain't coming to Flanders. Here, see for yourself,' said Salisbury handing Sir Roger his orders from the King. 'Your job is to go home and organise coastal defences against pirates.'

Béhuchet's raid on Portsmouth the previous year had been a salutary lesson - a squadron of French warships masquerading as the English fleet had entered the harbour unopposed and destroyed most of the town. Now any knight with lands less than twenty miles from the coast had been ordered to stay at home, ready to repel raiders.

At first Sir Roger was crestfallen. He had lost three fine horses, over half his personal troop had been killed and his campaign equipment was sorely depleted. Flanders could have offered opportunities for enrichment, catching French knights for ransom. *Mind you, I would like to see how my castle progresses.* The more he thought about it the happier he became. *I'm getting tired of campaigning. Then there's Alice...* He conjured up his image of her, red hair coming down to her waist, green eyes that sparkled vivaciously. He had been thrilled when his friend the King had, without warning, given her to him. He had thought she was far too grand and would be given to a much more elderly, senior magnate as a reward for loyalty. She was not frightened of expressing her opinion and her forthrightness was forever getting her into trouble.

'I'll give you sons, that's my duty,' she had told him, 'but first you must win my respect.'

The road south from Dunbar was passable, apart from dust. At least it was dry, which, as far as Sir Roger was concerned, was one less irritation. *Thank goodness my tent was one of the few left undamaged by those Scottish thugs and my hunting birds escaped unharmed.* Of all his possessions, he valued his Archangels highest. As he thought about it, the only real downside was he had to endure an endless stream of snide remarks from Sir Eustace de Frage, who had latched on to his contingent as they marched south. Their destinations being so close, there was no way to avoid becoming travelling companions.

Sir Eustace had become fixated by posters announcing rewards for capturing outlaws. They were often nailed to church doors and village noticeboards, where priests or scholars would read them out to the masses. These he collected and made Justin read them. It was a little game he liked to play; he could read perfectly well, but liked to give the impression of ignorance and illiteracy - it often gave him an advantage, secretly knowing what was written. Many a time he had caught out liars and cheats with this pretence. 'I'm going to chase them down and collect the rewards,' he announced grandly.

'He'll join them, more like,' observed Justin to Sir Roger, as they tried to encourage Sir Eustace to start this mission right away, but he did not rise to the bait.

'Must get home first to collect the rents.' Actually, Sir Eustace wanted to see his neighbour's new castle and, maybe, stir up trouble.

'You mean hang another peasant.' Justin could not resist the jibe. He hated his father, and had to spur his horse forward to avoid a slap.

'So, all your money - who did you ransom?' This was the third time Sir Eustace had brought the subject up in as many hours.

'It's none of your business.' Sir Roger could feel his gorge rising - some time ago, he had told de Frage that his money had come from a handsome ransom.

'You wouldn't be lying to me would you? Roj, come on, you can tell me.'

'The matter is personal, between me and the King.' At that point he knew he had said too much.

'Blackmailing him are you, I know you and he used to be best friends.' A tone of malice crept into Sir Eustace's voice; the implication was plain and unwarranted. 'I suppose you shared his bed. You were his Whipping Boy, after all.' Not content with that insult, he ploughed on. 'I bet he's a bugger like his father.'

Sir Roger was shocked. This was a slanderous defamation of the King's character. He wanted to hit Sir Eustace, but better judgement stayed his hand - Sir Eustace's tongue frequently ran away with him.

Indeed, Sir Roger had grown up in the Royal Household as Prince Edward's Whipping Boy and then teenage friend. His childhood had been turbulent. Being an orphan, Sir Roger was often shuttled between households, making him tough and self-reliant. Nor had he been beaten very often - the Prince was studious and rarely naughty, and, when he was, he was rarely caught.

The highlight, Sir Roger remembered, had been the trip to France when Edward was supposed to pay homage to the Valois Viper. *Do that and you're stuffed*, he had told his friend. *Do that and he'll get your kingdom.* It had been boyish advice, but an oath once made was inviolate - unless you wanted to spend eternity being tormented in hellfire, and it had happened before - with the Saxon king, Harold, and William the Conqueror.

The idea was simple enough. Pay homage to King Philippe for Aquitaine and prevent further incursions by the French into English-held territory. At a ceremony in Amiens Cathedral, the Prince baulked at the last moment at making *liege* homage – which involved placing his hands between those of Philippe and recognising him as his sovereign. He opted to pay simple homage instead, an act which solely recognised his cousin as landlord. Sir Roger, who had been standing behind his prince as his robe-bearer, saw the venom in the French King's eyes. Rarely had he seen such hatred, as Philippe sought to quell his anger, and pass off the insult as if it were a mere misunderstanding.

Afterwards the Bishop of Lincoln gave a short speech reserving his master's rights, rubbing salt into the wound. *No wonder we are going to war.* It was, Sir Roger realised, the metaphorical we - he was going home.

Sir Roger spurred his horse on - anything to escape his tormentor. He fell in with Gwyn, who was sharing a joke with Justin. Justin, too, was fed up with his father and his vile tongue. *At least now he can't take a strap to my bare backside - I'd kill him for sure if he did.* Justin recalled frequent beatings during his early childhood at Caxton Deverell.

Sir Roger was already concentrating on his next problem. 'We have to recruit more men,' he said to his sergeant. Their homecoming would be tinged with sadness - there were several widows to console in the village. Sir Roger had been given a stern lecture on the need for vigilance by Salisbury. *The French might control the sea, make sure you control the land.* His words had been emphasised by Salisbury wagging his finger pointedly under Sir Roger's nose. Gwyn interrupted his thoughts.

'Looking forward to the fair, Sir?' Gwyn always enjoyed their annual event where he was undisputed wrestling champion. In truth, Sir Roger had so much else on his mind that he had forgotten all about it.

Ten miles to go. Sir Roger was in a lather of anticipation, forcing his palfrey on as fast as he could, without blowing out its lungs. The crisp, salty smell of seawater was getting stronger as they rounded the top of Southampton Water and clattered across the wooden bridge at the mouth of the Test - an hour would see him to his gates. Only the Ox had kept up with his master. He wished they still possessed their Green Boar banner, but that graced the wall of Black Agnes's hall. Sir Roger wondered if they'd finished building, shouting to Gwyn as they galloped down an ancient oak avenue. The last update from his wife was now three months old. He was gladdened to see the boundary stones had been given a fresh coat of whitewash. He was on his own land again and spurred his palfrey on.

The Ox was as keen as his master to see home, having been campaigning against the Scots for nearly a year. With a brood of children - he thought it was eight at last count - he looked forward to embracing his plump wife. He weighed his purse. Nice and full from wrestling winnings, and the handsome sum Sir Eustace had slipped him for telling the story of the ambush. He had been very drunk at the time, and now had no recollection of how he had earned the money.

The sun was still shining when they reached the outskirts of Ipers village, which was spread along the eastern edge of the New Forest and contained, in all, eighty-two hearths. At its centre was a green, surrounded by cottages and hovels, with the occasional two-storey dwelling.

Sir Roger stopped near the church, staring in wonder: dominating the far end of the Green, on a low plateau, stood his castle, which now had a stone wall three times the height of a man with turrets at the corners and a gatehouse. When his troop had ridden north the previous year he had left an insubstantial, insignificant, run-down manor house hidden up a hill in the woods, with muddy outlines of foundations and scaffolding surrounding columns rising out of a cellar floor. He had been able to jump across his walls on his horse. Now trees had been cut down and turned into beams, and stumps had been cleared, ripped out of the ground by oxen, revealing his fortress surrounded by a shantytown of shacks and tents - *my castle, my dream palace. Home.*

It was a telling statement of power, and nearly finished. The surrounding area was cluttered with all the paraphernalia of construction - beams, stone, bricks and slates. The main building, though lacking a roof, was three storeys high. His architect, Francis the Mason, had promised him a castle strong enough to withstand rebellion and insurgency, and by all accounts this would. It was not a complicated building - that would have taken too long to build- nothing fancy, be speedy, those had been his instructions. Hundreds of builders had been assigned to the task and had been working since the previous spring. The new building stood surrounded by a half-dug moat, as yet dry. *I'll put carp in it.* Sir Roger looked down into the dried mud and thought of fish as he crossed the drawbridge, which had yet to receive its rope so could not be pulled up.

His arrival stirred lazing workmen, who had long since downed tools for the evening and were busy fussing over dinner pots.

'They're here.' Shouts echoed and grew in intensity. Cheering started, alerting the castle's inhabitants.

'Alice, Alice,' he shouted, standing in his stirrups and waving as he spurred forward into the courtyard. Threading his way past wagonloads of stone, his eye caught on the mantled chimneybreast - boar and eagle beautifully carved. His wife and their two children made a grand show of welcoming their great warrior home.

'We're still in the Old Hall,' she said, leading him by the hand.

Inside, newly cut sweet rush was strewn over beaten earth floors, its delicate scent wafting up. Sir Roger's eyes took a few moments to adjust to the gloom. A long table dominated the room, and threadbare tapestries still hung on walls.

'Only a few more days,' said Lady Alice excitedly, 'and Master Francis says we can move in.'

Sir Roger could see a couple of servants busying themselves searching for elusive cobwebs - Lady Alice abhorred spiders, though for the life of him he could not see the scariness of them. Harry was already on his case. Isabel hid behind her mother's emerald green skirt, peeking out with huge blue eyes.

'Papa, Papa, tell us about the siege. Did you really kill twenty-fifty hairy Scots?' Harry made slashing motions with a little wooden sword he was carrying. 'Did you, did you?'

'All in good time.' His mother patted his tousled hair. 'Now run along to Master John, your father will tuck you both up in bed.' Lady Alice ushered the children away.

'It's good to be home, my love. You look more beautiful than ever.' He presented her with a bunch of white dog roses he'd picked from a hedgerow as he neared home. 'I brought you these. I've missed you so much, tell me all that has happened.'

'You have a package from the King. It arrived last week.' She entwined her arms around his and kissed him, ever so gently, just behind his ear, before whispering: 'Our bed has been so cold and empty without you.' *As long as Handley keeps his trap shut.* The guilty memory of her recently departed lover weighed heavily and she hated the idea of being in the Bailiff's power.

'I'm ravenous, I haven't eaten all day,' was his reply. He felt a familiar stirring in his groin.

'Then I have a further treat for you,' revealed Lady Alice. 'I have found us a dream cook. His wafers are mouth-watering.'

Max had watched the arrival with the rest of the servants. *So this is the great Sir Roger. Looks bit too thin - needs fattening up.* And with that thought, he harried his kitchen staff back to work, wooden spoon swiping at elusive backsides. Only a short time to deliver a hearty feast, *worry, worry, hurry, hurry.*

Chapter 13

Money Doesn't Grow on Trees

It was St. Swithun's Day and, God be praised, it wasn't raining. In fact the weather was perfect, which boded well. The English fleet was a grand sight as it set out with only a light wind and a calm North Sea. Too calm for Walter Mauney; he had hoped for a brisk westerly breeze, but he couldn't complain. To assemble, then man 350 ships of all shapes and sizes, then load an army with all its paraphernalia, war horses, tents carts, armour, arrows and feed had been a mammoth task. Even Edward felt a pang of pride, though he didn't show it. This would be his first overseas adventure with a proper army. They had done it, albeit seven weeks later than they had hoped. On either side, stretching across the horizon, his great armada filled the sea with brightly coloured sails and flags.

'William has a lot to answer for,' remarked King Edward grumpily to his Admiral as they watched the shore of England recede. The army from Dunbar had been arriving in dribs and drabs. A sorry, dejected bunch of dispirited knights, most of whom had lost equipment and horses. It did not give any cause for celebration, as they had all submitted large bills for the reimbursement of their losses. He had hoped it would be worth it as he signed off a series of promissory notes - he was hoarding whatever cash he had for Flanders. He felt very alone, even though he was surrounded by a multitude of advisors, his earls, magnates, bishops and a seemingly endless string of black-gowned 'crows' as he called the physicians and lawyers who seemed to multiply whenever trouble was brewing.

He regretted sending his Friend, Sir Roger, back home. He could have done with some sympathetic company; too many fair-weather friends, too many agendas. Of everyone, and that included his wife, only Sir Roger knew his innermost secrets, and was the one person he could really trust. They had grown up together and had participated in many adventures. Now he was King, he alone was final arbiter of the destiny of his nation, and the responsibility weighed heavily on his mind. Above all, he wanted to be successful. He had proved himself ably against the Scots and they had proved no match against his swift-moving hobelars, these lightly armoured longbow-wielding horsemen who could harry and kill. *Dead men can't fight.* Most knights could see no merit in using such lowly and humble soldiery - for them, glory was to be found in the charge of heavy-armoured cavalry, in ransoms and chivalry. For Edward it was a simpler equation. To win, one needed to kill the enemy, and the mountain of Scottish dead at Dupplin Moor had been a salutary lesson. The size of an army was irrelevant. It was *how* forces were used that mattered. His archers had won the day and were cheap in comparison to a knight or man-at-arms. At least Mauney understood exactly how powerful the archers were on the battlefield. They had been his trump card. Edward stroked his beard, something he did when he was nervous or deep in thought. He wore it in a point topped by a droopy moustache that accentuated a doleful disposition.

Walter could only guess at his master's thoughts. This was Edward's first foreign adventure, and the first time an English army had crossed to continental Europe. The stakes were high - the throne of France the prize.

'I'm going to win,' Edward said emphatically, fixing Mauney with hard blue eyes. 'I must discharge my vow to Cousin Robert.' *If it's the last thing I do.* It brought back bitter memories. *He called me a coward for not claiming my birthright.*

The royal party had been hawking on marshes along the banks of the Thames near Windsor, and Count Robert's *muskadin* falcon, one that he had bred himself, had taken a heron. It had been a poor kill and he had called it 'the most cowardly of birds, because it is afraid of its own shadow'. That evening, the Count had had the bird roasted and placed between two silver platters carried by two scantily-clad maidens, and, to the accompaniment of his musicians, presented it at dinner. Most of the guests that evening were young and friends of the King. The Count, who was a much older and hard-bitten, bitter individual, had stood on the table, prancing up and down, all the while drunkenly shouting: 'The most timid of birds for the most cowardly of kings, deprived of his inheritance in noble France which is rightfully his.' It was a grotesque and frightening performance that had turned a light-hearted festivity into one that was cloaked in malice. Even though spoken *in vino veritas* his words were etched for all time in poor Edward's brain. The Count had then jumped off the table, enunciating in a loud stage whisper 'But for his cowardice, destined to be deprived of it until he dies.'

Everyone was quite taken aback, but Edward had taken its message to heart and determined to rise to the challenge. He renounced the homage he had paid to Philippe for Gascony. 'I was young of years,' he had said. 'So it is not worth two ears of corn.' He had made a vow: *I swear by all that is holy, by the blood of the Martyrs and on my Grandmother's grave, I will carry fire and death into France. I will make no truce or peace until the crown is in my possession.* All the knights present had then sworn an oath on the 'cowardly' heron, each stabbing the roast bird with their daggers, crying 'Death to the Usurper!' and 'fire and death into France!'

'And now,' Robert had continued, with an awful smirk 'I have my way, since through this heron I caught today a great war will begin!'

How right he had been, the war he wanted has begun.

The whole episode still rankled, though his claim was not completely spurious - the Capetans, his mother's family, had failed to produce a male heir for the throne of France and Edward had been too young when his uncle, his mother's brother, King Charles IV, had died. The French 'crows' - *more like ravening ravens* - of their legal establishment, who were true power in the land, hated the thought of an English-born King with a sodomite father. They had opted instead for his distant cousin Philippe, the Valois Viper, preferring to keep bloodlines through male heirs. Although Philippe was more distant a relation, he did not have the taint of Albion and Normandy.

My mother married a weakling. Edward's whole kingdom, his whole royal being, the whole institution of the monarchy, was in peril. He had made his vow and sworn his oath and oaths were the cornerstone of his power. To renege or abrogate his oath would mean that his men would think him weak. *Weak kings end up as pawns to powerful barons like my father.* The thought made him shudder. *I'm a strong King, anointed by God. I am the dispenser of Justice, I am the fountainhead and will cover myself in glory.* He wondered how his father fared. Everyone thought him dead, and it was best it remained so, but Edward suspected otherwise. His ambassador to the Papal See was on the case.

'History will be our judge,' Edward said to Mauney. 'Do you think the French will fight?'

Mauney couldn't answer; no one had tried to overthrow a kingdom as powerful as France with an army as small as theirs. They would be outnumbered and could easily be overwhelmed by the mass of French cavalry. But Mauney knew his master was a canny tactician. He had decisively beaten the Scottish horde on two occasions by integrating his archers and having his knights fight on foot.

It all depended on the Germans. Mauney hoped that the Emperor, who fortuitously happened to be Edward's brother-in-law, would keep his promise. *If that wily old bird does, then we stand a good chance.* Ever the optimist, he knew that Ludwig of Bavaria had been offered a vast fortune to side with the English and bring his army to Flanders. From there they would squeeze the Valois Viper in a deadly pincer movement.

'Fancy a game of chess?' The thoughts of kingship had passed and Edward needed a diversion to while away the time on the voyage. Chess was like war, and the King was a *very* good chess player.

The whole of Antwerp, in fact everyone from miles around, had gathered to watch the arrival of the English fleet. They had never witnessed such a splendid spectacle. Cog after flag-bedecked cog slipped into hastily cleared wharves and the King of England, most splendidly attired in scarlet and gold, crown on his head stepped regally down the gangplank to be greeted by ranks of his allies - Dukes, Counts, Margraves and all the civic dignitaries from the Flemish towns. After the nobility came the war-horses, mighty destriers that had been dressed in the holds of the ships in all their finery, and after them the archers and pikemen with their Cross of St. George white surplices.

That evening a parade of splendour wound its way through the narrow streets; everyone cheered the bold young monarch. The burghers of Antwerp put on a feast, minstrels sang, maidens danced; the English had come to give the hated French a bloody nose.

'We have a problem, Sire.' It was William Pole, his principal financier.

'Not one to spoil my day,' said Edward, flushed with the adulation of his rapturous welcome.

'One to spoil your week, I'm afraid.' Pole struggled and dithered; no time was a good time to deliver the sort of news he had. 'The wool that Parliament promised has not arrived. You don't have any money.'

'What? None! How many people know?' Edward's temper rose quickly.

'None of your allies. I told them you were bringing money with you.' Pole was no fool; he had made his fortune by being the smartest operator, owning warehouses, ships, mines and sheep. He also controlled the Monopoly Consortium.

'We'll deal with that tomorrow. In the meantime, tell no one.' The King was tired and needed time to think. *I have to buy some time. I wish money grew on trees.*

He continued to mull over the problem that night, tossing and turning as he drifted off into a fitful slumber that was not destined to last. It was shortly after midnight when his terrified servant shook him awake.

'Sire, Sire!' He was insistent. 'Get up! The house is on fire!'

Already Edward could smell smoke and he leapt from his bed. Grabbing a robe, he just got out in time to watch the upper storeys of the mansion burst into flame. He thanked the Lord for his deliverance and for the fact that his wardrobe still remained on board his ship.

Back on board he tried to gather his thoughts. Already the expedition was going horribly wrong. He had expected full warehouses. His anger was directed at Pole, who could only stand, head bowed low as the furious King raged to an embarrassed conclave of his ministers. 'No wool, no money, now no lodgings, nothing.'

Pole could only splutter excuses. A sudden and unexplained shortage of sacks had kept fleeces resolutely in barns and on farms. He did not dare say that the extended credit terms offered by the Consortium, and whole-heartedly agreed to by *His Furiousness*, were so unpopular with producers that warehouses were still almost empty.

'I'm told that a shipment should be ready to leave Yarmouth any day now.' Pole at least had one bit of good news. It was true; he had received word from Eccles that some fleeces had reached port and would be loaded when the fleet returned.

'Send my *Cog Edward*,' Edward ordered his magnate regally. 'Pole, we need money, lots of it. Soon!' For emphasis, he added: 'Or I'll have your head on Traitor's Gate. Take the Crown Jewels and see what you can borrow against them. Even borrow from Jews, I don't care how usurious their interest rates are, they'll roast in Hell anyway.' He would have to bluff it out. 'We'll put on lavish show. Let there be banquets and jousting,' the King said. 'Let them *think* we have cash.'

Mauney expressed his concern. 'We don't even know where the French army is. What if they are arrayed and ready for battle?' The English had yet to deploy spies.

'I can get forty thousand florins by the end of the week,' said Pole with a modicum of confidence. 'We won't need the Crown Jewels *just* yet.' When his agents had informed him that the Dordrecht warehouses were empty, he had anticipated this problem. As far as local bankers were concerned, Edward's credit was still good.

'It will keep your head on your shoulders a bit longer, too,' said the King, his mind racing. 'I think we should put out peace feelers again - indulge in some diplomacy. You,' he pointed to the Archbishops of Canterbury and Durham, 'go to Amiens, make it a *big* diplomatic mission, and pretend to make up with them. Now we'll see what King Philippe has up his sleeve.'

Edward sat back on his throne and thought hard. He knew exactly where the root of the problem lay - *this war started with the Vow of the Heron.*

'Send word to England that our noble cousin Count Robert should be allowed back to Court. Let him enjoy our hospitality at the Tower.'

There are two types of hospitality on offer at the Tower. I presume he means the nice kind...

Mauney laughed. 'You think that's wise?' he asked. He trusted neither the man nor his motives. He was loath to point out that it was Count Robert's hatred of the Valois Viper that has brought about Edward's claim to the throne of France. He was the puppet master who pulled the strings... His master might play down the Count's importance, but Mauney suspected that the Flemings would never have supported him so enthusiastically without connivance from Artois.

'We're here and we'll win,' said the King emphatically, 'and Cousin Robert has wandered the wilderness long enough.'

Chapter 14

His Sunday Best

I t had been his wife's reaction that had alerted Sir Roger to the fact that he had been wearing the same clothes without the benefit of a laundress since Scotland and stank, as Lady Alice had said disdainfully, as she wrinkled up her nose after their first embrace, of goat. Sir Roger was minded to dispute the goat part, but thought better of it, goat, horse, or pig - it made no difference; in retrospect he knew he was stinky. On campaign, most men smelt. Some revelled in their filth and called it a manly odour, though women of sensitivity and breeding tended to call it revolting and, it was true, he had neglected to have a proper wash for many months. He urgently needed and actually wanted a bath. In fact it was one of the first things he'd intended to do when he'd got home. It had, after all, been one of his specifications in his grand design for Ipers Castle that a bathhouse be built alongside the kitchens and furnished with a circular wooden tub large enough for two.

The tub had been specially made by a master cooper and was an oval masterpiece of his art. The problem was to fill it. This proved to be an arduous task taking several hours, needing a stream of servants with an endless succession of cauldrons of boiling water which needed heating in the kitchen before being lugged on a pole by two strong persons to the bathhouse. At first they had refused point blank to have anything to do with it and an ugly scene had developed, so Edgar the Pantler, as the most senior staff member, had come to Lady

Alice to negotiate increased wages for the extra work needed to fill the tub. They settled on a farthing per person per bath, which Sir Roger thought was well worth it as he scrubbed away months of grime with olive oil soap from Eccles' cart and let his cares float away as he luxuriated in the water's warmth. Few of his aristocratic friends bathed in such luxury, if at all. *They don't know what they are missing.*

Max appeared with a tray of mixed wafers and a beaker of wine and watched expectantly as his master wolfed them down. If he had been expecting a compliment he was to be sorely disappointed, for Sir Roger just looked him up and down, dismissing him with a wave of the hand. The cook was followed by the local barber, who had been summoned from the village. Together they agreed on a straight trimmed fringe and hair just above the collar line.

Sir Roger felt like a new man as he sat in his new leather-backed chair at his new elm wood desk in his new solar overlooking the courtyard to the gatehouse beyond, and listened impatiently to Handley's litany of woe. As was his habit when concentrating, he twiddled the ends of his long blonde moustache.

'Rents are down. The harvest will be poor.' His Bailiff looked hard at his master's face; Sir Roger's flinty stare was difficult to read.

Sir Roger knew that in a good year they expected to receive £300 income from eight thousand acres, made up of a mixture of arable land, meadow and hunting woodland. Most farmers were hereditary tenants - some free, others not. Indentured villeins cultivated the demesne, the land in the castle's immediate vicinity.

'The Steward says our account at Peruzzi Bank is nearly empty,' Handley continued. 'But at least the building works are nearing completion.'

Lady Alice had already told her husband about the problem with the wool, so now he waited to see what his Bailiff had to say on the subject, or if indeed he said anything about it. It was as Sir Roger suspected. There was a stream of complaints, but nothing on the subject of wool.

A long line of visitors, local supplicants with petitions and peasants with grievances had formed at the door, materialising as if from thin air when word spread that the Lord of the Manor was back in residence. Sir Roger was in no mood to see anyone.

'Tomorrow. I will see everyone then. Today I'll just see my Steward,' he barked.

He and Whytethorne had only communicated by letter, so this was the first time they had met face to face, although Whytethorne had worked for him since the previous spring. The knock on the door was firm, and Whytethorne waited to be invited in.

At least the man has manners. 'Come,' said Sir Roger, and stood to shake the proffered hand. Whytethorne's grip was firm and confident. He had an avuncular air and was in his late forties and was direct in his answers to Sir Roger's string of questions. He was by all accounts a clever fellow, well versed in law and all its intricacies, having latterly practiced in Southampton. With this sinecure had come enough money to acquire prime farmland befitting his status.

Whytethorne, likewise, looked to assess his new master. So what were his ambitions? Would he prove a benevolent lord or be cruel like de Frage? Sir Roger's neighbour had a reputation for arbitrary acts of barbarity.

'How was Scotland, Sire?' Whytethorne, too, had experience of fighting the northern savages, having fought there in his youth, and it was this military experience that had persuaded Sir Roger to appoint him as his Steward. As such Whytethorne had overall responsibility for castle security, guards, watchmen, porters and messengers.

'I'm glad to be back with most of the summer yet to come.'

The men sparred, gently probing back and forth as they drank some fine Gascony wine and munched on cheese straws. They covered a range of topics. The Steward felt it was not his place to mention the minstrel - that story could wait. Instead, he described finding the mosaic before tackling the tricky problem of the wool. Whytethorne admitted that he didn't know the whole story and took a deep breath, giving himself time to think about how to explain the situation.

Percy the Reeve had come and complained about something petty – something to do with geese - and oh, the Bailiff owed him money and that was why he couldn't pay his rent arrears as he had promised. The Steward hadn't seen what any of this had to do with him and had probed a little deeper, catching Percy out. Percy was not very clever or good at lying and had mentioned the dodgy bales of wool. Whytethorne's lawyer's training had teased out a few more details.

'It seems that the Bailiff managed the transaction. Something fishy went on. I'll get to the bottom of it,' he finished, thinking *I knew I couldn't trust Handley.* He told Sir Roger he would investigate further.

'I know about the wool. Alice told me she had a visit from Mister Eccles,' said Sir Roger. 'We'll wait. It could just be an excuse from Eccles. Word from Flanders is that no-one is going to get paid for wool.' He shrugged his shoulders in resignation.

'I'll sort it out tomorrow,' said Sir Roger, who had warmed to his new Steward, feeling gratified that he'd made the right appointment. The man displayed a firm sense of fair play tempered by deference, and there was a willingness to please.

With Whytethorne dismissed, Sir Roger opened the leather pouch that had recently arrived from the King. It contained a sheaf of documents in a sealed envelope. He examined the seal for tamper marks. It was pristine, without chipping and intact. He used his dagger tip to prise it carefully off. *It might come in useful.*

To his joy and relief, the package contained his Licence to Crenellate. This document was a necessity for all castle builders and had cost the proverbial arm and a leg. It also contained a letter from the King, written in code. Getting quill and some scrap parchment, he set about decipherment. It was a long document that took him most of the afternoon and it turned out to be a riveting read. It was a copy of a confidential report from the King's agents in Rouen and gave specifics about testing a new type of weapon called a *ribaud.* According to the report, it made use of exploding powder as a *gonne* and fired metal arrows that could penetrate thick planks of wood. *It's a whole new form of warfare.* Edward had brought three guns to Hallidon Hill and he'd seen them in action, although only from a distance. He wondered why his master had sent him this particular report, but felt sure all would become clear.

Sir Roger was about to toss the pouch into the corner of the room when he felt a rolled vellum document tube wedged awkwardly in the bottom. It had been the first one in and could easily have been mistaken for part of the pouch's base. As he eased it out, he realised what it was. A dream had come true, something he had been hoping for after Salisbury's recommendation. He fished out a Letter Patent announcing his promotion to rank of banneret. This was a signal honour, confirming his elevation to the highest echelons of the military establishment, though it carried heavy obligations. He would have to find and equip many more knights, men-at-arms, hobelars and archers, but this was a mere detail.

'Alice,' he shouted down the stairs. *This news is cause for celebration.* 'Look!' he said, showing her the Letter Patent as she entered. 'We must organise a feast at once. Tell that fat cook really to show us what he can do. But first...' he took her in his arms and, looking deeply into her emerald green eyes, kissed her.

'You smell like a rose,' she whispered. 'I have waited so long for your return.' A welter of emotions and regrets plagued her as she tried hard to forget her indiscretions with the Minstrel. Because of this, she threw herself into the act with an abandon that delighted her husband. An hour later, their pent up passions exhausted, they went downstairs to announce his promotion to the world.

Sir Roger strode impatiently into the castle's cluttered courtyard; he didn't want to be late for his first Sunday service. Clad in a red and green suit with fine hose of purest English wool, woven in Flanders, and wearing red *poulaine* shoes of soft imported Cordovan leather with extravagantly lengthened toes that curled up elegantly at the tips, he looked and felt every bit the aristocratic banneret. He had inspected several piles of stone with feigned interest before his wife appeared, shimmering in an emerald-green silk dress that was cut low, with a high waist that enhanced the shapeliness of her bosom. It had taken nearly an hour for her ladies to braid and plait her hair into an intricate headdress, a green silk-stuffed and rolled jewelled hennin with gold reticulated cauls. A sheer muslin veil covered her face - this alone had cost him five ducats, and had gold thread and stars woven into the fabric that sparkled as she moved her head.

He had forgotten how long it took for ladies to get ready.

He exclaimed his admiration as his wife took his proffered hand. They climbed into their canopied litter, which was slung between two draft horses. The curtains were drawn back so all could see them in their finery on the short ride down the hill to the church. It had been a long time since Sir Roger had seen such a well-dressed lady.

'Your artist has finished the murals,' said Lady Alice as their carriage drew up to St. Michael's. 'They're wonderful. People are making pilgrimage from miles around to admire them.'

He nodded; he had commissioned them as atonement for the shameful crime he'd committed when he'd acquired his fortune. It still gnawed his psyche, burning deep into his soul. He could never confess, for he would never be forgiven. For a year after the event he had avoided the confessional altogether. What would he tell the priest? *Father I have sinned, I ordered the beheading of ten innocent monks - chop, chop, chop.* Before he died he would beg to be shriven. *On my deathbed - if I'm lucky enough to die in my bed - that's when I'll do it, at the last moment before entering the Kingdom of Heaven.* He hadn't actually done the deed himself. The Ox had. Godless Gwyn had no qualms, so Sir Roger felt his hands were half-clean. He was guilty, however, of giving the order. The Ox, his most trusted sergeant, had saved his life.

After massacring the Jews, they had taken the monks to a secluded wood. *Come, brothers, help us dig some graves for our dead.* Their graves. They had bound their hands behind their backs before making them kneel in prayer, before committing foul murder. Just the two of them, he had been surprised that none tried to run, then he remembered, half of them had been blind. Now, sitting in St. Michael's Church in Ipers he looked up, forever reminded of his wickedness. His dreams, too, were troubled by the crossbow quarrel fired point-blank into his body. He had been completely winded by the force of the bolt striking his ribcage - *thank goodness Gwyn stopped me toppling from my horse.*

This was the first chance Sir Roger had to examine the Florentine's work. He had commissioned the same artist who had painted scenes from the Old Testament at Westminster. At the base of the mural a gargantuan, monstrous black Satan, with tusk-like teeth and breathing fire, reared up to devour sinners. *Will I be one of them? Will this be my fate in the hereafter? Are those the imps that will drive me into fiery vats of brimstone? Or will I be saved - carried up to worship at the feet of the Divine Being?* He didn't know. The ten slain monks, depicted as angels, floated around the Divine Throne on the Day of Judgement surrounded by a sea of white and red flowers. Sir Roger's instructions had been specific: red to represent spilled blood, white attesting to innocence. Though the artist had been unaware any of the significance of his commission, the spectacle was awe-inspiring and those who knew their liege-lord could recognise his flowing moustache on the Archangel Michael.

The spacious church had been started by Saxon ealdormen and extended by Sir Roger's grandfather at the turn of the century, who had added elegantly pointed windows in the latest style. His father had built the steeple, with several bells, and he had continued the family tradition by decorating it. It was the envy of clerics far and wide, only bettered by the Abbey church at Bewley.

John Fyscher was the parish priest and principal beneficiary ever since his church had become a place of pilgrimage. Folk now came from many miles around to worship and to listen to his firebrand sermons and he was growing fat from sales of pardons and indulgences.

'…there is nothing beyond a river of fire and a foul swamp.' His voice rose to a crescendo. He was in full flow, again. 'Angry devils live there, with hands like the dragon's heads. Eyes shoot out fiery arrows; their teeth stick out like the tusks of elephants.' He doubted that any of his congregation knew what an elephant was. He paused - and wiped a trickle of sweat off his tonsured brow. 'Wailing! Groaning! Bellowing!' he thundered, eyes rolling heavenward. 'Believe, sinners, there is no rest for sufferers.' His audience, rooted to their three-legged stools, hung on every word as the performance headed inexorably towards its climax. 'The life of man is perishable and transitory and the wickedness of man abounds in the world. Woe is me.' Face flushed scarlet, Fyscher was determined to put on a good show - for sitting on high-backed chairs, carried down from the castle and placed directly in front of the pulpit, were his benefactor, wife and children.

Lady Alice had thoughtfully made the servants position their seats so that, at some point, a shaft of sunlight, coloured by a stained glass window, would illuminate the family.

'Vanity is a sure sign of the Devil's handiwork,' Fyscher intoned, with perfect timing as the sun came out from behind a cloud, a sunbeam falling directly on Sir Roger and Lady de Bohun - before launching into a tirade on the sartorial versus practical nature of the extra-long pointed-toed shoes that were now the height of fashion. It was his pet subject. For a man for whom soft Egyptian cotton was the preferred fabric for undergarments, this was hypocrisy indeed. But, he reasoned to himself, his congregation only saw a pious cleric in a poor Franciscan's brown habit. They weren't to know of his predilection for the luxuries of this life: good food, fine wine, and a horsehair mattress with feather pillows.

It was as if God wished to emphasise the point, Fyscher wanted to, but tactfully refrained from, pointing to where they sat, bedecked in all their finery. Sir Roger felt embarrassed and humiliated. He was not, by nature, prone to vanity; his wife had insisted on his outfit, saying that it matched hers.

Lady Alice noticed the angry scowl cross her husband's face. He would surely make the priest suffer for this insult. Overdressed she might be, but she had no illusions about her status. *It is* important *for aristocrats to show off their wealth.* She was inordinately proud of her husband and had not been paying any attention to the sermon, barely understanding what was being said. As far as she was concerned, they were the handsomest pair in Christendom and the splendour of their apparel was entirely appropriate. She had no qualms at all as the heaven-sent rays passed across them; the irony of the moment was entirely lost on her. *After all, it's not everyone's husband who has held a French Duke to ransom.* This, she believed, was how he had acquired the fortune. Her husband had told her that they had chanced upon the duke travelling the same road and nabbed him. She did not suspect her beloved husband had been lying through his teeth.

It had been a neat bit of thievery with no witnesses left alive. They had slaughtered everyone, Jew and Christian alike, raping the women first. He had taken the young red-haired Jewess and enjoyed it, although he hadn't killed her. He had left that task to others as he had found killing women and children distasteful.

It's going to rain. Sir Roger felt an involuntary spasm of pain lancing through his shoulder from a wound sustained years ago. Although listening dutifully, he was becoming more irritated by the minute with Fyscher's sermon. Idly shifting his weight from side to side; to try and stop his buttocks going numb, he silently cursed his servants for forgetting to bring cushions as he flicked through his illuminated *Book of Hours* – a treasured gift from the King's mother.

His reverie terminated abruptly as a scuffle at the entrance jolted him back to reality. A leper dressed in rags was trying to edge in, but was smartly ejected. Sir Roger watched with interest. *There is no place for these poor souls, even in God's house.* It scared him to think that Death could come in such a slow and ugly form. Leprosy was a hideous disease that robbed a man of his face, fingers and dignity. *I shall endow a hospice for these unfortunates*, he vowed.

Hand bells were being rung to alert the kneeling congregation that the service had come to an end. Sir Roger watched with relief as the Sacrament was held aloft behind the rood screen and was about to rise when the priest signalled to him to stay seated. Fyscher remounted his pulpit. With war looming, he launched into a diatribe against the French.

'Be warned, pirates are on the loose, so be vigilant.' His congregation did not really need reminding about French threats - most had family or acquaintants involved with the sea. 'This fate awaits those Godless heathens,' he declared, pointing to the tortured heads screaming in agony so graphically depicted on his walls. 'Those are the French and it's your job to send them to Hell. Now, go and practice.' He finished with a dramatic flourish, directing the congregation outside.

Men, eager and enthusiastic to plug a pirate for Christ, streamed out of the church to archery butts lining the Green's edge beyond the graveyard.

'Would you like to try, Sire' enquired a yeoman. Sir Roger drew gingerly on the stave. As he expected, pain shot through his shoulder, so he handed it back and contented himself with watching. The long-bow was not a knightly weapon. Targets were paced out at fifty, one hundred and two hundred yards - these were for real professionals. Groups of men waited patiently for their turn to loose off a dozen arrows from six-foot yew staves into each thick straw target. A skilled archer could pierce a heart at two hundred yards.

Against arrows, horses stand no chance. The thought terrified the knight as he watched fathers training their sons in the art of bowmanship. *They'll be the backbone of our army soon.* He had seen the blizzard of death the longbow could create. It was a battle winner, and his King knew it.

Thunder rumbled, heralding the arrival of a summer storm, as a column of black cloud was shot through with lightning. By the time their litter pulled into the castle courtyard, the first rain splattered onto the cobblestones. 'I hope this doesn't last,' said Sir Roger. A deluge of hailstones followed, leaving, as Isabel pointed out, what looked like a layer of white rabbit's droppings.

Chapter 15

Gwyn Meets His Match

The storm had passed, the hail transient, the damage negligible. The next morning was bright and clear with nary a fluffy cloud in sight.

'Foresight,' said Sir Roger emphatically as he got out of bed and stretched, arms reaching out, relieving tension. 'My ancestor must be thanked for that.' His annual Ash Fair was probably the most important fixture in the Ipers calendar.

'And thank the Lord for washerwomen,' Lady Alice added, joining him at the window. 'Thank God, weather's good, bodes well.'

With the Steward reporting a sizeable trade cog anchored at Lepe and three smaller cargo vessels berthed in the creek, auspices were favourable. Sir Roger's Fair should prove a lucrative event. His ancestor had noticed an abundance of glasswort growing in nearby salt marshes, and by happenstance knew, once burnt, that its ash was a vital ingredient in manufacturing quality soap. He had sought rights to sell soda ash. Empress Matilda had granted him a charter and so Ipers Ash Fair had been born. Over the centuries an industry had grown and now the whole district would harvest succulent stems at low tide, dry them, and burn tons in heaps to produce a fine white powder. The Empress felt it appropriate that the Fair should be held on St. Veronica's Day to celebrate the fact that she was patron saint of laundresses. Its only drawback was that it was held in mid-July, in the hungry gap, when food, especially bread, was in short supply.

The village green was filling nicely as merchants set out stalls ready to start trading as soon as Matins concluded. Many traders' carts and wagons made their way to the neighbourhood - testament to its popularity - all coming to buy this valuable commodity from marsh dwellers, or to sell useful goods to crowds who came from as far afield as Christchurch, Romsey, Southampton and the Isle of Wight. The occasion was a magnet for all, though not everyone attracted to the fair had come with honourable intentions. Undesirables, pickpockets, cutpurses, tricksters and charlatans found the draw of crowds irresistible, ready to fleece unwary folk by stealth or trickery.

Godfrey, from nearby Caxton Deverell, was one of these, in desperate need of money for food. Scouting near ale sellers, looking for fat purses, he had a razor sharp knife concealed in his palm. He spotted a tempting target, its owner already drunk. A casual bump, a muttered apology and a leather pouch left its owner's belt.

Unfortunately, as he discovered to his disgust, its contents had been used up on the ale that had brought on his victim's inebriation. He was rewarded with only a half-farthing, clipped and worn, stuck in the purse's seam - not enough to buy more than a mouthful. He threaded his way through food stalls offering mouth-watering grilled meats, spicy sausages and loaves of bread at exorbitant prices. If his thieving went well, he promised he would return and gorge himself.

Godfrey soon found what he was looking for. A barefoot girl dressed in rags was selling meagre brown buns from a wooden tray held by a string round her neck, the cheapest food at the fair. It was all he could afford. A scone baked from mouldy rye husk bulked out with ground pea and bean, and, usually, flavoured with darnel, poppy or hemp. She took his pathetic coin, looking at it disdainfully, thought hard and selected the smallest, meanest scone. It tasted like sawdust but Godfrey didn't care, nor did he worry that he might have mysterious visions or hysterical fits, as frequently happened to those who ate this lowly provender. At least his craving for food would be assuaged until a fatter prize could fall victim to his blade.

—ᴍᴍ—

Sir Roger was busy concentrating on finalising recruitment plans with the Steward. 'The church bell will be rung at ten, followed by a fanfare from the trumpeter, and then you'll read out a Summons to Arms,' he instructed Whytethorne as they went to where his men stood on parade. 'Good turn-out, John,' he said, giving his sergeant due praise as he inspected sundry men-at-arms and heralds wearing his green boar rampant coat of arms on freshly laundered surcoats. 'The saint will be happy.'

It had been at Lady Alice's insistence that all the castle's inhabitants were made to wear clean clothes in St. Veronica's honour, and Sir Roger was pleased to see her instructions had been obeyed.

'Round up as many young men as you can - fit and strong, no cripples or weaklings,' Sir Roger instructed his recruiters. 'We must be up to strength by Michaelmas,' he told Whytethorne, which was, by his reckoning, only ten weeks away. 'We'll hold the signing ceremony after morning service.'

'I don't foresee too much difficulty, Sire.'

'Let's hope we have a successful Fair,' said Sir Roger, mindful of his obligations as Banneret to raise and equip a substantial retinue. Even if his coffers were filled, it still meant he would need to petition the King for extra funds for equipment as the debacle at Dunbar had left him with a woeful quantity of weapons in his armoury.

Master John offered to say a quick prayer to St. Eulalia. 'She usually keeps rain away,' he said. If there was one thing Master John could be relied on for, it was for knowing which saint was responsible for what and, everyone concurred, a timely prayer was like a stitch in time - especially as it was only three days to St. Swithun's Day, and if it rained then they were all in for a long soaking. Sir Roger agreed as he rode out, his squire and Steward at his side; he didn't want a washout. Yesterday's thundershower had lasted into the evening, moistening and cooling the air, washing dust off leaves, making trees and grass greener. In the morning's freshness, whorls of evaporating moisture played above white and pink dog roses, their scent mingling with that of honeysuckle and cow parsley that filled the hedgerows of the winding village lanes.

Dan Digby had also arrived at Ipers Fair hungry; however, his multifarious skills had kept the wolf from the door. He had been contemplating catching a ship from Southampton, heading for sunnier climes. When he had heard about the Ash Fair he knew it was too good an opportunity to miss. This was his first fair since coming south and he could earn easy money for his passage from his acrobatic skills and tricks. A couple of smiley fisher girls had a laden stall offering tempting mackerel freshly grilled; he happily consumed two, letting the oily juices flow down his chin as he watched a long line of handcarts and wagons loaded with ash sacks waiting patiently for their turn to be unloaded into a stone storehouse by porters where they were weighed. A clerk wrote up a scroll with the name of each producer and value. Dan noticed this value depended on the size of sack, and that it was then then stencilled on with soot. A second clerk, abacus clicking at lightning speed, counted out payment, and the happy recipient then headed off to spend at the Fair. Dan asked a stripy-faced porter, white powder residue giving his face a deathly pallor cut through by rivulets of sweat, whose castle it was.

'Sir Roger de Bohun. That's him, with the fancy sword and yellow moustache.' The porter pointed towards the horsemen.

Intrigued, Dan peered through a scaffolding-clad gatehouse and admired the building within, before being shooed away by a giant of a sergeant with overdeveloped muscles. The building was immaculate, though still roofless, and more in keeping with a fine city mansion than defensive bastion. He had wondered what kind of man would commission such an elegant structure. *The kind of man who also owns an Arab's scimitar.* He knew it was a rare weapon of value with the distinctive jewelled scabbard. *Why would an English knight have a Saracen sword?* That was very unusual; normally Christian knights abhorred the weaponry of their foes.

Dan had already walked round the castle plateau, and visited Ipers mill and millpond in the valley. He had a good feeling about the place with its orderly demesne farms. A glimpse of emerald-green women had really captured his imagination. In the courtyard, before Sergeant Muscle had moved him on, he had spied three honeys. He deduced that they were French girls from their elegant upright posture, expansive hand gestures and singsong laughter. Like *houris* from a harem, they brought back memories of the time he had slipped into Ibrahim's private apartments while the alchemist and astrologer had been imbibing poppy juice and dreaming in the desert.

The horsemen stopped at the slope's edge, watching as swallows and house martins swooped and wove in pursuit of insects, skimming across ripening fields of corn nearby. Beneath them, the village green was covered with booths and a swelling crowd.

Sir Roger wondered how hungry they were. It was always the same: crops burgeoning in fields, vegetables growing in gardens- all promising bounty to come but not yet ready to eat. His harvest would start as soon as the Fair was over.

'I've had to tighten my belt by two holes,' said Justin jokingly, as they watched long lines form for whatever bread there was. Prices were exorbitant, so the majority had to content themselves with plentiful fresh fish and ale - it was half way into the hungry month.

'Looks like they've been eating crazy bread again,' said Whytethorne, as sounds of laughter and dancing drifted up from the valley - loaves made with mouldy flour invariably led to frenzied fits of mass hysteria.

'It's a shame our Fair is so early,' Sir Roger moaned. 'If only we could hold the Fair on Lammas Day we could provide fresh bread. I shall ask the King for a change of date. I'm sure St. Veronica will understand.'

'Twenty-seven stalls,' Handley announced, out of breath from climbing the hill. 'Better than last year, and the captain of that cog at Lepe has offered us a shilling a sack for about ten tons. We've been buying at an average of tuppence halfpenny each.' Sir Roger did some quick maths in his head; at a penny a stall, he would earn two shillings and thruppence. A broad smile broke across his face as he calculated he would earn a further nine pence per sack of soda after porterage.

Matins over, Fyscher came to complain about the drinking. 'They're like a pack of Godless heathens; they should have all been in church. I understand that the price of ash has risen,' he added. 'So I think we deserve a larger tithe.'

A tedious argument ensued over the Church's share - usually a penny out of ten per sack, but the priest felt he deserved an extra halfpenny.

Sir Roger exploded. 'Don't speak to me of avarice.' His voice dropped as he went for the jugular. 'I know full well that you withhold from paying any tax on sales of your indulgences,' he hissed, countering the fatuous notion that, since the priest was paid out of tithes, he would be only paying himself. 'You will give it to the poor as you are supposed to do,' he ordered. Then he remembered the unfortunate soul with leprosy. 'I'll grant you more if you promise here and now to use the money to build an alms-house for lepers.' With his conscience clear, he felt pleased with himself. The priest reluctantly agreed, but Sir Roger was not finished. He had been looking for an opportunity to express his irritation at being sartorially criticised from the pulpit. 'So the Church does not like my footwear, eh,' he whispered into Fyscher's ear. 'Next time, think before you speak,' he growled menacingly. 'You eat too much, my fat friend - you'll end up like my new cook.' He, too, had been impressed by Max's girth. 'I think our Holy Father in Avignon would advise you to manage our spiritual affairs and leave sumptuary matters to temporal law makers.'

Fyscher left muttering darkly; he was finding the return of the Lord of the Manor and his demands onerous.

The villagers watched apprehensively as a procession of liveried men-at-arms marched smartly over the drawbridge carrying a table and chairs, not sure what to expect. They hoped that their lord would look down with compassion upon them. The whole aspect of the village had changed since trees surrounding the old manor had been cleared away. It had been a tranquil, sleepy place before the castle walls had risen inexorably to loom menacingly over them. Opinion was divided. Some felt grateful for the protection they offered, others were more fearful, adding to their burdens and woes, for castles meant soldiers and these, more often than not, would abuse the common men of England.

All agreed, though, that the village was prospering. The influx of funds from building work and supplying needs of skilled craftsmen, who lived in the shantytown surrounding the gatehouse, had been a welcome addition to meagre incomes. Four village maidens had married well above their status. Three more had been cast out in shame, pregnant hussies dishonouring their families.

Business was brisk, with the villagers determined to spend their ash money as fast as they could. For them the advantage of an early fair was that they could spend cash before paying the tax that was due on Lammas Day - what they didn't have, they couldn't give to the collectors.

As instructed the church bell started to toll, causing heads to look toward the steeple. The trumpeter managed a couple of half-hearted blasts. As Sir Roger had hoped, it had drawn the attention of the crowd. Whytethorne started to read out the summons, but Sergeant Gwyn did not bother to wait for its end. 'Good wages in the service of Sir Roger de Bohun and the King!' he bellowed.

The recruiters were easily recognisable in their green boar rampant livery jackets. They mingled with the crowd, picking out young men.

Flicking a money spider gently from his sleeve, Sir Roger sought out Justin without success. *Where is my wretched squire and why does my wife always want new clothes? If I hear 'Gold trimmings are all the rage this year,' one more time I will...* his mind drifted back to the task at hand. He acknowledged the presence of Alfred of Eccles, who was overseeing his stall selling olive oil and wine, and approached the burgher. He thanked him for the palfrey he had bought last year. 'Done me proud, took me to Scotland and back with no complaints - but I lost three good horses to those blasted Scottish savages.' He would need to acquire more horses soon.

Eccles smiled ingratiatingly, pleased he had invested in a stud farm. The moment the Steward had read out his proclamation, the price of horseflesh had risen sharply. He stood observing the knight - *it will take me time to fathom this mix of bluff warrior and subtle aristocrat who has made a fortune.* Eccles suspected there were hidden depths to this character. According to his informant in the Peruzzi Bank, the initial deposit had been in high-value Mediterranean coinage, mostly minted in southern France or Spain. The merchant doffed his velvet cap deferentially.

Sir Roger couldn't help noticing the gold pin holding the peacock feather in the merchant's hat. *I need a feather in my cap too, but not that sort.* A number of his fellow knights sported ostrich feathers on their helms - expensive but noble - now *those* were the type of feathers he wanted. He would dye his bright green. *I'll be the Green Knight from the Arthurian legends.* The thought appealed to him - *a Banneret needs to be distinctive on the battlefield.*

—m—

Godfrey, meanwhile, was feeling the effects of the scone. *I've become invisible.* He stood stock still while his hallucinations grew more colourful. A beast somewhat like the one he had seen in the church, grew out of a cooking fire and disappeared in a cloud of stars as reality came and went. A harlequin was leading a brown bear on a chain, which snarled and swiped at worrisome dogs. These were shooed away as a circle of spectators formed. It was about to perform, raising itself onto its hind legs as bagpipes droned a reedy melody. Paws waving, it started to dance to the music. Reality returned again to Godfrey. He glimpsed a butcher wiping his hands on his blood-stained apron and leaving his stall, attracted by the nearby performance. The butcher had a fat purse beckoning at his belt. *I'll have that.* Godfrey sidled inconspicuously into the audience's periphery, blade ready.

—m—

'Go and remind Lady Alice that we'll need extra lanterns for our party guests,' said Sir Roger, finally spotting his squire, who had been happily chatting up the Hayward's demure daughter, making her blush at a lewd suggestion.

Justin blew a parting kiss; he would seek her out later. What had she said? *Fifth house along the lane towards Dibden…* His attention was caught by the glint of something metallic at the edge of the bear watchers. A scrawny fellow weaved purposefully behind the audience and Justin saw him deftly cut the purse from the fat butcher's belt. 'Stop, thief!'

he shouted, sprinting forward, making a flying tackle of the cutpurse before sitting firmly on his shoulders. The thief twisted, stabbing at Justin's arm with his blade, but the squire punched his head with all his strength. A dazed Godfrey was easily overpowered and dragged kicking and screaming to the stocks while the populace vented their anger with boots and spittle.

'I think this is yours,' said Justin, handing the heavy purse back to its rightful owner.

Sir Roger watched as the battered serf was secured in the head stocks. 'What's he done?'

'Caught in the act of stealing my money, Sire,' the butcher informed him.

Sir Roger listened to the story of Justin's quick thinking. 'Are you hurt?' he asked, seeing blood on his sleeve from the knife cut.

'It's only a scratch,' said Justin, relieved the wound was not worse. The Hayward's daughter came over to administer first aid and everyone called him a hero.

'Good lad,' said the butcher, effusive in his praise and generous with his reward when he saw whose squire he was. The recruiter's table was cleared as the lord of the manor took centre stage.

'I haven't eaten for two days,' wailed Godfrey, neck and hands firmly pinned by the wooden bar, eyeing his judges - reality was slipping again.

'Ale and capon.' The Steward signalled for a plate of meat. 'Well, hungry is what you shall remain,' he said with a masochistic smile, eating a chicken leg close to Godfrey's face while holding his head up by the hair. 'You can chew on this,' he said, as he stuffed the bone into Godfrey's mouth. The wretch was powerless to do anything. A cloud of black flies buzzed about the crust of dried blood that formed over a swollen eye.

'What is your name?' Sir Roger projected his voice so it boomed over the raucous mob. A hush settled over the crowd. What would the punishment be - a flogging, maybe even an amputation?

'Godfrey, sire,' came a squeaky, garbled reply as he spat out the bone.

'Speak up.' Sir Roger signalled for the crowd to hush. 'From where?'
'Caxton, sire.'

'Who's your Master?' It was Whytethorne's turn to cross-examine.
'I assume you are indentured?'

The crowd knew the answer before it was given; he was Sir
Eustace's serf, and a well-known scoundrel.

'You know Sir Eustace?' the Steward asked Sir Roger.

'I only left his company about a week ago.' Sir Roger nodded,
remembering their acrimonious parting. Distracted, he passed a lenient
sentence 'You shall spend the rest of the day in the stocks.' Immediately
he knew that this was inadequate.

'I would at least have had the scoundrel flogged,' grunted
Whytethorne.

'So be it. Twenty -' he paused. He had shown weakness once, which
had to be remedied immediately. 'No, fifty lashes. Let the punishment
begin.'

Gwyn stood forward, whip in hand, ready to administer the beating.

A low chanting started in the crowd. 'Ox, Ox, Ox...' They loved
their champion.

The flogging started. Godfrey passed out at the twentieth stroke,
was revived, and whipped some more, before being left hanging,
unconscious again, his back a bloody pulp. A wet clod of cow dung hit
was flung, hitting his ear. The crowd approved, and a hail of detritus
followed, attracting a pack of mangy curs that roamed the local rubbish heaps. Their leader, a large piebald dog, arrogantly cocked its leg,
producing a stream of yellow piss on the miscreant's foot. The crowd
went wild, hooting with laughter.

Dan watched from the platform's edge as the sergeant coiled up
his blood-soaked whip, stuffing it back into his belt. Sir Roger took
centre stage, holding up a purse of money - knowing he had everyone's
attention.

'I declare this the prize for a bout of wrestling - a winner-takes-
all contest.' He took out five silver pennies and gave Gwyn a broad
wink - this should be easy money for his sergeant. It would be a simple
contest: beat Gwyn and win. But in all the years he had known him,

no one ever had. A fight ring, hastily constructed from a few hurdles, attracted a line of hopefuls.

A flurry of activity heralded Lady Alice's arrival. Since the bear had ceased to dance, she had been inspecting merchandise and had ordered many local delicacies: samphire, elvers, fresh smoked mackerel and lampreys for delivery to the castle.

The priest felt it would be unseemly for a lady of her breeding to watch such a base spectacle with half-naked men and tried to assume a role as her moral guardian, but Lady Alice dismissed his concerns, brushing him aside.

'But they are bare-chested,' he spluttered.

'I know,' replied her ladyship haughtily. 'I like men's chests, thank you.' There had been many on display with the builders.

A space was cleared at the ringside and their chairs were brought out from the church. Women tittered as Gwyn stripped off his shirt and was ritually anointed with pungent goose grease. His muscles were astonishing. He had always been a big lad and, with his teenage years and early twenties spent behind an oar in the King's galley; he had developed, as well-fed rowers do, a massive upper body on tree trunk legs. The amusement increased as he pumped his biceps and flexed his pectorals. The more brazen women, of which there were quite a few who came to the Fair to sell their bodies for a few pennies, could not help speculating on whether the rest of him was so well-constructed.

'*Ça suffit*, that's enough,' whispered Lady Alice to her giggling entourage with a frown. 'Calm down!'

Dan, meanwhile, took the opportunity to view these ladies-in-green closely. His mind was made up; he would start with the one with sparkling, flirtatious eyes.

'I'll double the prize money,' shouted Whytethorne, getting into the spirit of the no-holds-barred contest. The rules were simple: no eye gouging, biting or kicking of testicles. The Steward acted as ringmaster, holding contestants back while he finished shouting out rules. 'Ground pin to a count of ten, thrown out of the ring or surrender. Now wrestle!'

The first contender was hurled over the front two rows of the audience; the second was flung to the ground and jumped on, a rib giving an audible crack as his breath was expelled violently. A third went back into the crowd. Five more were dispatched with equal alacrity.

'This is thirsty work. I need a drink!' Gwyn roared, gulping downing a full pitcher of ale in one go before wiping off remnants of foam from his upper lip. 'Come on, you scum! I want a *proper* fight.' He bellowed like a bull and went through his muscle routine again.

'I will take you down, I'm not frightened of you, you lardy-cake nancy-pudding!' The crowd looked round, shocked to see such insults from a wiry fellow half Gwyn's size, who strutted out, ducking under the rope.

'Come on - grease me up. He's greased, so I should be.' Dan took off his jacket and shirt and, with great deliberation, folded and placed them neatly on the lap of his chosen damsel. 'Look after these for me,' he asked Clothilde solicitously, giving her a broad wink and blowing her a kiss. Finally, he took off his felt hat, making sure that its pilgrim badge was clearly visible.

'He's been to Jerusalem!' whispered someone in awe to a neighbour, recognising the shiny token.

'Where's he from? Does anyone recognise him?' asked another.

'I need to warm up,' said Dan, shooing his opponent to a corner. He had watched Gwyn, looking for blind spots and signs of weakness. He had seen none, but suspected that, maybe, he was slow of mind - not stupid, just ponderous and deliberate and lazy through years of being unbeaten. *I've come across his type many times before.* Dan could read his opponents well thanks to his father. *God rest his soul, he taught me all the tricks of this trade* and he could read his opponents well.

Lesson one, put them off guard, and win the crowd. Dan enjoyed showing off, and executed a series of back flips, fast and fluid. *Then tease.* Surreptitiously taking a pig's ear from his pocket, he biffed Gwyn on the side of the head. 'I think you lost this,' he said patronizingly, tossing the ear into the air, creating much hilarity.

The crowd rapidly increased as the two men circled around, eyeing each other up. Dan was quick as lightning; in a flash of his foot the

Ox went tumbling down. Gwyn had been unprepared for the assault and found it surprisingly difficult to extricate himself before the count reached eight.

'A penny on the Shrimp!'

'Two on the Ox!'

Coins changed hands furiously as more bets were placed on the newcomer. Gwyn tried picking him up, but couldn't get a grip. The Shrimp, as he had been nicknamed, skilfully executed a head-butt, leaving a trickle of blood from his opponent's nose.

'No gouging!' the Ox bellowed with fury.

'That's not gouging.' The little man hissed in reply, jumping up and butting him again. *I've got him riled, now for a bit of showing off.*

Bellowing with rage, the Ox got his opponent over his head, ready for a throw. Like an eel, Dan translated this move into a handstand, before wrapping his legs round Gwyn's neck. 'Giddy up horsey,' he shouted gleefully, simulating a jockey whipping at a recalcitrant nag before jumping to the ground and making a lap of honour round the ring, chased all the while by an infuriated Gwyn.

'Shrimp, Shrimp, Shrimp!' The crowd were delighted. The two unequally sized, but surprisingly well-matched wrestlers circled each other, looking for an opening. The little man flipped onto his hands, kicked and rolled away. The fight went on, neither side prepared to yield nor gain advantage.

After a considerable time, and with no discernible outcome in sight, Sir Roger decided that enough was enough. 'I declare it a draw, share the purse.'

The crowd booed but Sir Roger was deaf to them; he had seen enough and knew he wanted to keep the newcomer honours even. The Steward was by his side as he strode into the ring.

'People of Ipers,' Sir Roger's booming voice silenced all and sundry. 'We have seen a contest of equals and it will remain as such.' He took Ox and Shrimp by the hands and raised them together. Then, in authoritarian tones, sergeant by his side, he reminded the crowd of their duty. 'As the summons read out in church confirms, you must ready yourselves to do service for your King. Those who owe mortmain fees must pay.' Standing next to his master, Whytethorne glared menacingly around the circle of faces, 'and those who are due to render service must present themselves on St. Margaret's day, seven day's hence.'

Gwyn was mortified. *I would have beaten this shithead shrimp eventually. I deserve better from the man whose life I saved.* He felt betrayed, as if his master had kicked him in the teeth. At the time, he had not expected greater pecuniary reward - the thought had never occurred to him, until now. The treasure chest had been brimming with gold and silver and all he had got was a *decent* whore - a real courtesan - and a barrel of wine. *Was my master's life only worth a mingy purse full of coins, a fuck and a drink?* The worm of resentment started to feed voraciously in John Gwyn's mind.

Turning to the combatants, Sir Roger handed each their purses, 'Well done Mr Shrimp, you are the first man to get even with my sergeant. Tell me, what is your real name and where are you from?'

'Dan, Sire, Daniel Digby. I hail from Norwich. I was on my way to Southampton.'

'Are you a free man?'

'I am, my Lord,' Dan replied nervously.

'Well, Master Daniel Digby, I shall double your purse again if you would consent to enter my service and serve under my banner.'

Dan had never spoken to, or even met, one of the ruling elite. He was impressed - everything about Sir Roger yelled class - his size, demeanour, clothing and bearing. For the first time in his life Dan was lost for words. He thanked goodness that Clothilde came and handed back the clothes she had been caring for, helping him lace his jerkin, whispering an offer he couldn't refuse. It was the breathing space he needed, and he made up his mind.

'I will accept your offer, Sire. It would be an honour to serve a great Lord such as you.' *But I'll have to be careful of Sergeant Muscle;* Dan glanced at his erstwhile opponent, who returned his look with venom in his narrowed eyes.

Sir Roger signalled to Fyscher. There was no time like the present for sealing a deal on oath. The priest took off the plain wooden crucifix that hung round his neck.

Such oaths had to be delivered publicly and before God, for hell-fire awaited those who broke such undertakings.

'Justin, get over here,' Sir Roger called to his squire. 'I want you to witness our new recruit swearing his Oath of Allegiance.'

Holding the crucifix, Sir Roger and Dan clasped hands; these were then placed under Sir Roger's mantle, near to his heart.

'I hereby swear by the Holy Trinity to serve King Edward and Sir Roger de Bohun as my fealte-lord,' intoned Dan.

Then, sealing the deal in prescribed manner, with suitable ceremony, the two men kissed. For the crowd, the sight of their lord bowing low, for Dan was at least a foot shorter - the top of his head not even reaching Sir Roger's chin - brought on loud cheering.

'That's done then. Make sure he has his new surcoat before sun up.' With that Sir Roger strode off to mount his waiting palfrey. As he walked his horse down the line of recruits, he drew his scimitar, flashing it in the sunlight. Shiny steel held high as if to make a point, Sir Roger turned and harangued the men once more. His recruiters had done their job: a line of eager young men, and a sprinkling of older ones, were paraded to the cheers of villagers.

'You men, at the Manor, after sun up, tomorrow.' It was a pre-emptory order. 'You need to have some practice if you are to fight the French.'

And I, Dan pictured Clothilde's lissom body, *will enjoy fucking one too.*

Chapter 16

St. Coloman's Rope

The heat was oppressive and thunder rumbled away in the distance. *Giants are rolling their dice across the heavens.* Sir Eustace scratched at a mosquito bite on his wrist, drawing blood. He sucked at the droplet, tasting salt as he watched his faithful lieutenant drag a struggling serf into the hall by his hair.

'This snivelling piece of shit was caught cutting purses at Ipers Fair.' Falke Walwyn pushed a dung-covered Godfrey onto the floor. 'Your friend de Bohun had him lashed and I retrieved him from the stocks for you.' Falke grinned, knowing his master's predilections.

'He's not my friend.' Sir Eustace snarled like a caged panther, hissing through ragged, chipped teeth. He had been sitting, forlorn and brooding, on a worm-eaten chair at the far end of his dilapidated hall. Now he rose and circled Godfrey, poking him, toying with him like a cat playing with a newly caught mouse. For good measure he kicked him in the guts. It felt good, so he kicked him again. His spirits started to rise - he enjoyed the sound of whimpering. 'Thieving was you? A cut purse?'

He kicked him again in the groin.

Godfrey tried desperately to cover his head with his hands, rolling into a ball, presenting only the bloody wreck of his back. Falke watched as his master danced around. He too found pleasure in other people's pain.

Their return from Scotland had been greeted by a total lack of serfs. Sir Eustace's fields had remained untilled, and instead of ripening corn there were just expanses of thistle and bramble. A few servants, who had nowhere better to go, had remained. 'The serfs fled after the last hanging,' explained his factotum. 'The day you rode north they upped sticks and ran.'

He should have been more upset, but in truth it served to stiffen his resolve to abandon Caxton. The de Frage family had owned the Manor, which was a miserable patch of stony, good-for-nothing fields, marsh and water meadow, since the Conquest, each generation continuing to impoverish the land and harass its inhabitants. And, like his ancestors, Sir Eustace existed on the dark margins of knighthood and was a stranger to ideas such as chivalry and charity. He worshipped Beelzebub, with necromancy and the black arts his true religion. He pretended to be a Christian, attending divine services, just as he pretended he couldn't read. But it was all a sham. *No one must know your true calling.* He remembered his induction into the cult, when he had plunged his dagger into a young boy's chest and pulled out his still-beating heart. *Couldn't blame that one on the Jews.* Satan worshippers always blamed their blood sacrifices on Jews, but now they had been banished from the kingdom, so they had tossed the body down a disused well instead.

The journey south with Sir Roger had sorely tried his patience. *King's friend, King's bum-buddy indeed, and a stuck-up, conceited prig, more like.* He had resented the way Sir Roger had lectured him, and now he harboured deep resentment for his neighbour. Envy gnawed at his malignant soul, for he had discovered how his neighbour had obtained his fortune.

'He's not my friend,' repeated Sir Eustace caustically, going to an ironbound strongbox. A hideous smile lit up his face. A plan was formulating in his mind and, in a flash of inspiration, he knew what to do. 'Our Master will be pleased and I needed something to cheer me up,' he chuckled as he opened the box, taking out a rope and a wooden bowl. 'This was the rope used to hang St. Coloman. I've been waiting for the chance to use it.' Sir Eustace examined the quaking Godfrey, who Falke had pulled back onto his knees. His eyes were tightly closed, as he prayed fervently for deliverance - he knew what fate awaited him.

'Let's take him to the boundary,' said Sir Eustace. 'The magic I have in mind will have more potency the closer we are to my intended quarry.'

As they dragged the struggling serf to an oak at the edge of the estate, Sir Eustace told Falke the rope's story and how his grandfather had stolen it from the saint's reliquary. 'The saint's body hung on this rope for eighteen months.' He smiled, his lopsided grin exaggerated by his scar. 'Incorrupt and untouched by animals,' he related as they heaved the struggling Godfrey up until his feet no longer touched the ground, watching as he slowly strangled. 'Now, cut away his undergarments,' he ordered. As he did at all his hangings, he collected Godfrey's semen in the wooden dish, as the serf ejaculated at the moment the spirit left his body.

'It's potent stuff,' he said, as he carefully drained the fluid into a glass vial and put it in his purse. 'Many sorcerers I know would pay dearly for this. But it's not for sale.'

Sir Eustace was even more cheerful when, on returning to the Manor, he found his gang of Norman malcontents had returned from rustling a herd of fat cattle. There would be full bellies this evening; a perfect start for the ceremony he would conduct in the dead of night.

'*Il y a aucun femmes ici,*' The Normans complained bitterly of having no women. 'Why can't you get us some?'

Sir Eustace had promised but, as yet, failed to deliver. *There's a castle full of women just waiting to be rustled...*

'I have an idea,' he told Falke, as he took his followers down to the vaulted cellars. 'We'll visit our neighbour - give him a surprise.' He lit black candles in front of an inverted crucifix. 'First we need to weave a net of power over him.' Placing the vial on the altar, which was a rickety table coated with grime from numerous blood sacrifices, he started a well-rehearsed mantra in a low voice. 'I command you, oh Demon King, in the name of the Lamb without blemish, who walks on the asp and the basilisk, and who has trampled the lion and the dragon; may you carry out quickly whatever I command.' His incantations rose until he was howling like a banshee. 'Tremble with fear when the name of God is invoked. Beelzebub arise and strike de Bohun, give me, your follower, possession over him and his chattels. Give me, your servant, his castle, his wife...' *The redhead.* The thought made him quiver, and for a moment he lost himself as he imagined her lying, legs wide apart, begging him for mercy. The Normans seemed suitably impressed and mollified by his promises.

'Are you going to his feast?' asked Falke, who, at his master's insistence, went on to describe the new castle and its defences. *No moat yet, drawbridge not in operation...*

'No.' Sir Eustace said, swatting at a fly that buzzed irritatingly around the corner of his mouth. 'We'll let him have *this* feast in peace.' *If I have anything to do with it, it will be his last.* 'We have preparations to make if we are to catch them unawares. First we need some wagons...'

Chapter 17

For You We Have Heronshewes

John Fyscher rolled his eyes heavenward and prayed as he watched his simpleton of a son Edwin chase butterflies through the church-yard. *Oh God what have I done to deserve this halfwit as offspring?* Edwin, who acted as the verger, thought, if he did really think at all, that he was a foundling, and was quite unaware that the priest was his father. The success of the Fair had put John in a good mood and he had decided to decorate the church with flowers, so he had asked Edwin to collect them for him. The verger stared back, deliberately making his face blank and uncomprehending, his mouth opening and closing without any words coming out, but the meaning was clear: do your own flowers.

The priest shook his head with disappointment. *What will become of him when I am gone?* He was tired to his bones, though the last few days had been most rewarding. His purse had swelled immeasurably, with his friend the Almoner they had sold at least two dozen indul-gences for minor sins, and fifteen scraps of St. Veronica's wimple. A quick visit to the nearby convent at Eccesbury had secured a genuine wimple, filched from a washing line, which had then been cut up and put into a tooled leather pouch for the purpose. The Almoner, who was a vellum maker by trade and thus had many off-cuts, had assured the purchasers - guaranteed in writing no less - that these were from the genuine article, and the recipients, all women of a certain age, accepted them as if they were parts of the True Shroud.

His attempt to secure a greater level of tithe from the Lord of the Manor, though, had left a sour taste in his mouth. Sir Roger was proving to be a tricky customer, much harder to fathom than the priest had been led to expect. Now John was looking for an excuse to get back to his bed and lie down.

'May I have a word with you?' The voice from behind startled him. It was the Ox. The priest only knew the sergeant by reputation and sight - Godless Gwyn was not known for his presence at divine services.

'My Son, feel free to tell me what is troubling you.' John knew from experience that when a man who had never before visited his confessional came to church, then *something* must be weighing on his soul. Nor did the Ox begin with the usual 'Father I have sinned' so he wasn't coming to make confession.

Instead, he pointed to the ten saints above the altar. 'Do you want to know who they were?'

Fyscher stared wide-eyed at the man-mountain. 'I killed them, took their heads off one by one. That's why they've got red flowers round their necks.'

The garlands had always troubled the priest. He could work out most of the symbolism in murals. Saints were usually remembered by the method of their martyrdom, like St. Catherine with her wheel, but these had remained a mystery. 'And who gave the order for their murder?'

The Ox nodded his head ever so slightly towards the castle. Fyscher knew exactly who he meant. That was it.

Gwyn smiled and left. *That'll teach you to make it 'Honours even'.* He returned to the gatehouse with a spring in his step.

Sir Roger looked up as he knelt in front of the plain wooden crucifix that adorned the wall above his bed. *Funds permitting, I will build myself a permanent chapel.* He prayed to St. Swithun to look favourably on him and his end-of-fair feast. It would be disastrous if the saint wept today.

He confessed it was a selfish thought, but his wife had sent out invitations the moment she heard of her husband's return from Scotland, without considering sleeping accommodation. She had assumed the castle would have its roof by then.

It was a quick-witted Francis, the Master Mason, who came up with a solution. Why not use ship's sails, he said, and make a series of tents, and he had set about scouring the harbour at Southampton, begging and borrowing from all the ships in the harbour. With Sir Roger generously agreeing to invite half-a-dozen ship's captains to his feast the gaily-coloured sails draped over roof beams did, he conceded afterwards, add to the party atmosphere.

Harry de Bohun had snuck into the solar with the intention of raiding the candle box for some stubs when his father found him. Being a bright child and wishing to hide his true intentions, he had quickly got to his knees and was pretending to recite his catechism. Sir Roger patted him lovingly on the head, and, mussing up his hair knelt beside him. He was pleased that Harry was already taking his duties to God seriously - *one can never be too young to become a true Christian knight*. It would soon be time for Harry to become a page. This was the first step on the road to knighthood.

'What shall I wear today?' Sir Roger asked as they got up off their knees.

'Blue, Father.'

'Good choice.' His wardrobe was extensive, courtesy of his wife. He chose dark blue suede riding boots, and a jerkin with green piping and elegantly long sleeves. His squire, Justin, and Bailiff Handley had preceded him to the hall and were guiltily tearing into a newly baked loaf of crusty white bread.

'That's for children.' Sir Roger shook his head in admonishment before sanctimoniously filling his usual mug of wine. But the temptation posed by Max's loaf proved irresistible and he, too, tore off a large chunk, dunking it in his wine. It was a guilty pleasure to indulge in a sop and, liquid dribbling into his moustache, he wolfed it down while inwardly chiding himself for not practising more self-restraint. It was unusual for him to eat before his dinner, which was a meal he liked to take mid-morning.

'It reminds me of a saying by the philosopher Diogenes,' he said to Justin. 'When asked what time was best for a man to dine, he answered, 'for a rich man when he will, but for a poor man when he may.''

His squire shot him a quizzical look.

Handley half- rose to his master, mouth still full as he reported the success of the fair. 'Only eight sacks of ash remains unsold. I'm sure it'll shift soon,' he garbled, and repeated once he had swallowed.

Justin added that their recruitment drive had raised forty would-be soldiers, though he had doubts that many would make the grade. 'A mixed bunch- we've got 'em lined up for inspection. Gwyn's going through their duties and boasting about his martial prowess.'

The sergeant viewed the recruits as a sorry bunch, a mix of yeomanry, erstwhile apprentice boys, some sons of villeins and a few disenfranchised serfs. He asked their names, listening intently, and promptly forgetting all but a few. He was no good at remembering names. There was only one name that stuck in his mind like a fish bone in his throat: *Dan Shrimp-Turd Digby*. He was quite surprised when five of the recruits turned out to be sons of gentry, eligible to become knights. 'Have any of you won your spurs?' he asked.

One of their number put up his hand. The rest were knight-aspirants, fresh-faced and eager. They all, at least, had their own horses - though Gwyn doubted whether any of these were trained for war. When word had spread through the district that a banneret was recruiting, enough had answered the call, all wanting a chance for glory.

Sir Roger recognised the one whose hand had been raised - Stephen, son of his neighbour John de Bokland. 'I believe we have the pleasure of your parents at our feast tonight,' he said, firmly shaking the young man's hand and winking. 'Make them proud.'

Gwyn brought the parade to order as Sir Roger came over to make his inspection, passing down the line and looking each man up and down.

'Stand forward, Dan Digby.' He did so, resplendent in his new surcoat, emblazoned with the Green Boar rampant. Gwyn prickled with hatred.

'Why were you going to Southampton?' asked Sir Roger, examining him in detail. The man had an air of confidence and looked his Lord straight in the eye - Sir Roger liked that, *no cringing subservience here.* He had been impressed by the wrestling and wanted to know more about his newest recruit. No one had matched up to his sergeant before.

'I was hoping to catch a ship to Bordeaux.'

'Are you well-travelled?' Sir Roger's interest was piqued, there was more to this fellow than met the eye.

'I have, Sire, with my erstwhile master - God rest his soul - we travelled to the Holy Land.' Dan showed him the pilgrim's badge pinned to his hat. 'We even got to Jerusalem.' There was a real pride in his voice, as few men braved the pilgrim way these days.

'You must tell me about it sometime,' said Sir Roger, feeling a pang of jealousy. He'd been tempted by calls to crusade, but those days were over. Ever since the last kingdoms of Christian Outremer had been overthrown by the Mamluks over sixty years before, there seemed no point.

Lady Alice appeared in the courtyard in conversation with Handley. Seeing her husband approach she finished abruptly. She was angry. 'That man is insufferable,' she told him, green eyes flashing. 'I ask him to do a simple task and he ignores me.' This was not the truth; the Bailiff had been reminding her about the minstrel.

Harry charged across the courtyard, wooden sword in hand, slashing air.

'Harry, go to your lessons at once,' she barked abruptly, venting her frustrations on her son.

'But Mother, do I have to?' The lad looked pleadingly at his father. '*He* said I could play soldiers today.'

'Master John is waiting for you in the school room,' said Lady Alice, shooting her husband a *meddle-at-your-peril* stare.

'Do as your mother says.' Sir Roger looked indulgently at his son; he was a fine lad, full of vigour. He knew how stuffy Master John could be, but felt it important that his heir should be able to read and write, as well as mastering the skills of sword and arrow. 'We'll do something special tomorrow.' He found he was always promising to do something special. *This time I mean to keep it.*

Edgar the Pantler emerged from the undercroft, followed by porters carrying wine barrels. Sir Roger took the opportunity to check on the arrangements for the feast. 'Did you get any heronshewes?' These were baby herons taken straight from the nest just before they could fly.

'Ralph could only manage to get a brace.' It took considerable tree-climbing skill to reach a heronry and bravery to avoid the jabbing beaks of the parent birds.

'Good, we'll give them to that fat priest as a special treat.' Sir Roger felt he had been a bit harsh on the priest; this would make amends.

The squad was practicing using blunted practice weapons; real ones were too lethal. The clang of metal on metal added to the din of masons and hubbub of the Castle. A steady stream of creaking carts disgorged heaps of stone as a mass of busy men removed them to dressing areas. From there, they went directly up by a series of buckets and pulleys to the Gatehouse top, where crenellations were finally taking shape. *Shortly I'll have a fortress fit for an Earl.* Sir Roger was pleased with the progress, but he had more immediate concerns - the courtyard needed clearing. 'Guests will be arriving at the fifth hour,' he told a harassed Francis.

Towards mid-morning, just as Sir Roger was heading in for his dinner, a royal herald arrived with a packet of letters, asking for him. 'It's your summons to Parliament,' he said, accepting an offer of bread and cheese.

Sir Roger was instructed to be in Northampton in a fortnight's time. A quick calculation - Southampton to Northampton would take about five or six days if the roads were good - three if he really pushed it. His expression spoke volumes.

'That's short notice,' Sir Roger couldn't help letting his unhappiness creep into his voice; he had been hoping to spend more time at home.

'Don't blame me,' replied the exasperated messenger as he remounted and made ready to leave. 'I've not been out of my saddle for the last three weeks and I still have five more summonses to deliver.'

Almost reluctantly Sir Roger instructed Justin to tell the Marshal, who was tasked with organising travel arrangements and running the stables, to get everything ready for the journey. 'We'll take half my men-at-arms and ten new recruits. Tell him I aim to be back just after St. Bartholomew's.'

The Marshal was an old stalwart who had been a stable lad in his grandfather's days. He did his job with quiet efficiency and had been deputised by Sir Roger to deal with Eccles over replacement horses. His particular expertise lay in knowing a bargain when he saw one.

'I want them all kitted out and looking smart. We need to impress the stuff-shirts and white hairs. Square pennants shall rule!' It was not as large a retinue as he would like, but he had lost too many good men under the sow at Dunbar that had yet to be replaced.

Also in his pocket was a letter from the King requesting that he advise and act as enforcer for his son, the eight-year-old Duke of Cornwall. *I'm going to enjoy making my voice heard.* As the King's Friend, Sir Roger looked forward to throwing his weight around. He had always liked that title, and now he was officially a banneret - the position had additional teeth and was a definite rung up the social ladder from the average Lord of the Manor. In fact, he was close to the top of the tree, and there would also be much greater scope for amorous adventures, a favourite pastime. Power and a promotion would doubtless bring out the trollop in many fair and chaste maidens.

Justin cast his master a quizzical look and asked what the summons might be about.

'We have to look into royal finances,' Sir Roger told him, trying to be serious for a moment. 'I can see trouble brewing. It's going to cost us dear, of that I am sure. It'll be a rocky ride.' Sir Roger considered the circumstances. Even in Hampshire, rumours about the parlous state of the King's Exchequer were rife.

The problem was wool. The King needed the revenue generated by wool to fight his war and he had promised his entire kingdom's income to secure the presence of his allies. He had discovered, to his chagrin, that there was an embarrassing shortfall between promise and reality. Parliament, therefore, had to sort out this muddle - and pronto.

'You know, Justin, high finance gives me a headache,' Sir Roger said, mounting his horse. 'Sort out travel plans.'

One task left to go before the feast. Sir Roger looked for and found his Bailiff in the ash store. He had been worried that five tons of ash had sounded a great deal, but seeing the small number of sacks, he felt his Bailiff's optimism was justified.

That's a relief.

He decided to tackle another pressing issue. 'How soon can we get the Manor Court back in action?' he asked, having been troubled by a string of visitors pleading for this and that, mostly tiresome disputes over field boundaries or begging poverty, professing inability to pay rents.

Handley ran his finger down lists of those who had received ash money. 'Lying bastards, they're an ungrateful lot, if you ask me. I'll sort out jury summonses and get the court working again as soon as possible.'

The time was ripe to bring up the problem with Eccles. 'I hear we made a wool shipment to Southampton. Did you give the receipt to the Steward yet?' Sir Roger tried to sound as casual as he could, but in his heart knew full well that he hadn't.

Handley gulped involuntarily and beads of sweat erupted from his forehead.

'Well, Sire.' Handley busied himself with his tally board, unable to look his master in the eye. 'I thought I could make *you* some more money.' The Bailiff was forthright, admitting immediately to doctoring the shipment, before subtly shifting the blame onto Sir Roger, who he said had bought the wrong type of sheep. So he, *Handley the Innocent*, was trying his hardest, on his own initiative, to make sure the estate didn't suffer financially. He finished with: 'I think the Reeve was trying it on with *your* Steward.'

Another feud brewing. It made Sir Roger despair. *I got those sheep from Essex.* He remembered it had taken months for shepherds to herd them across four counties. He'd done the deal himself with Pole, buying them unseen and at a price that had, in retrospect, been too good to be true.

So that bastard stitched me up. He would have to put pressure on the merchant Eccles, and resolved to dump on him from a dizzy height. *That'll shake him up.* Also Handley needed punishing - he might have managed to wriggle off the hook this time, *but from now on he'd better be on his best behaviour or it's the stocks for him.*

When he got back to the castle, Whytethorne was looking harassed and nervous, as any master of ceremonies would. It was no easy task for a newcomer to co-ordinate the kitchen and ensure everything ran smoothly for his first feast. Sir Roger gave him a few words of encouragement.

The first guests arrived. *Good, let the festivities begin,* Sir Roger happily surveyed his courtyard as it filled with travel carriages. Those that were staying the night could be heard chattering away on the top of the castle. The afternoon was roasting hot, with just a hint of breeze. The prospect of a night under canvas should be perfect.

In his cart, Fyscher flicked his whip across his donkey's backside as he crossed the drawbridge, merrily whistling to himself and confident in the knowledge imparted by Gwyn. This added a whole new dimension. A knight's profession was to kill. In war they did it every day, enemies either died or surrendered for ransom, but *murder* was a 'thou shalt not' sin. And murder was the word the Ox had used. Sins had to be confessed and absolution given before a soul could enter the Kingdom of God. It would be his mission; he'd try and save this Lord of the Manor's soul. How to do it without revealing what he knew - that was a wholly different and knotty problem.

Sir Roger was all *bonhomie* as he helped Fyscher down from his donkey cart. 'We have a treat for you,' he said with a broad grin.

What could it be? Fyscher wondered, deciding to temporarily suspend his mission until after the feast. Aristocrats had to be handled carefully and he'd blotted his copybook once already. Maybe it would be porpoise meat in parsley sauce - *my favourite.* He licked his lips in anticipation, and hoped it might be the 'royal' fish. Porpoise and dolphins were supposed to be offered to the King first. Perhaps one had been caught without his knowledge, though Fyscher usually found out through gossip or via the confessional, as his congregants knew he would keep quiet if a slice of prime section, lovely dark red meat surrounded by a rich layer of creamy-coloured fat, came his way. The mere thought of it made him dribble.

Lady Alice joined her husband as he took up his position, standing at the entrance of their new dining hall. He even remembered to compliment her on her new dress, which had been specially made for the occasion: a brocaded scarlet mantle rested over a dress of saffron yellow with ivy leaves finely stitched around its hem. Her hair had been plaited into buns on either side of her head, and covered with cylindrical cauls woven with seed pearls that were elongated to form horns. She looked radiant.

'Sir John and Annette de Bokland,' their son, Stephen announced grandly, giving his mother a kiss. Their manor was across the Forest, near the little harbour of Lymington, a veritable nest of smugglers and pirates. Bokland was in his mid-thirties, of medium build with a quick and ready wit. He commanded the western end of Sir Roger's patch. The Steward had described him as a stalwart and Sir Roger, who was a good judge of character when it came to military men, came to the same opinion after a brief conversation.

His wife was petite and vivacious, though Lady Alice had to wonder how she had produced seven children and stayed so slim. They were all healthy boys, much to her husband's delight and Annette's chagrin. She had wanted at least one daughter, but, having managed to produce each one on a different day of the week, decided seven was enough. If God had made weeks eight days long it might have been a different matter.

Next to arrive were Sir William and Lady de Palton. With lands stretching up the Test Valley he controlled the central sector. His handshake firm, his best suit of clothes slightly threadbare, he was an aging, battle-scarred veteran. From his snow-white hair Sir Roger reckoned he must be well over sixty years old. Over his first beaker of wine he gave his host a rapid run-down on the state of his militia. Poor to nonexistent, he said, shaking his white locks vigorously. 'Farm boys with pitchforks, woodsmen with axes, poachers with bows, not a bloody soldier amongst them.'

'He's forever complaining about his aches and pains. What he needs is some action,' said his wife to Lady Alice as they chatted amiably. 'He's bored. Your husband should make him one of his knights, put him back into training. The old dog needs one more moment of glory before he finally retires.' *And keep him off my back,* she thought, as she joked with her hostess.

A trumpet, blown by his coach driver, announced the arrival of the redoubtable Sir Hugo de Trenchard. Of the many invited local dignitaries, he, as Seneschal of the Isle of Wight, was the Guest of Honour, and was Sir Roger's counterpart and responsible for the island's defence. It was from his clutches that the Minstrel had recently escaped.

'The name's Sir Hog,' announced the large, flamboyantly dressed individual loudly, not waiting on ceremony for a formal introduction.

Sir Roger stepped forward, introducing himself as his host. 'And you may call me Hog, everyone else does,' Sir Hugo said as he clasped Sir Roger's outstretched hand with his own, which was the size of a spade. Sir Hog was over six feet tall and as rotund as a barrel of wine, with a beaming smile and cheeks the colour of claret. He was followed meekly by his wife and daughters, who were demurely dressed in baggy, plain cloth dresses and tight fitting wimples. They stood in the shadows - he did not bother to introduce them by name. 'My mice,' he said, before producing a disparaging belly laugh that reverberated around the courtyard, echoing off the walls.

Sir Hugo ruled the Isle of Wight with a rod of iron - woe betides any pirate who operated from his harbours and did not pay him a share of their plunder. It was said that the crows and seagulls fed well from the flesh on offer on his gibbets. Sir Roger stood back and took in his guest. Though he hadn't met the famous Sir Hog before, he found his bluff and hearty manner instantly appealing.

The walls of the hall were freshly plastered and painted with whitewash, making the room light and airy, though sadly the fine new tapestries of hunting scenes, on order from Flanders, had yet to arrive. The top table was resplendently decked out with a white linen tablecloth and Sir Hog was seated in the place of honour next to Lady Alice. John the Chaplain said grace and Edgar the Pantler arrived with bread rolls covered by a napkin, placing them in front of Sir Roger along with his cutlery: two knives, a sharp pointed one for eating his food and a broad bladed one for cutting his bread, and a spoon for sauces and gravy.

A page proffered a hand basin and towel, going round the top table so everyone could wash their fingers. Sir Hog plunged both hands in, spilling water before turning his attention to the green Saintonge mugs, admiring the delicately painted vine leaves. Along with wine jugs decorated with hunting scenes, they had recently come from the merchant Eccles on a ship from Gascony and were all the rage.

For the first course, Max had created a strawberry soup as an *amuse-bouche*. The Pantler placed a small bowl of pink liquid in front of his master and mistress. Sir Roger dipped his spoon in and tasted it, trying not to slurp as he appreciated the delicious, subtle flavour. Sir Hog, whose palate was unrefined, and, preferring quantity to quality, simply gulped his soup down in one, before producing a loud belch. 'Better out than in my mother always used to say.' After that, Sir Hog regaled Lady Alice with every detail of his financial situation, before enquiring none-too-subtly how her husband had come about his wealth.

'He captured and ransomed a French Duke,' replied Lady Alice, and left it at that. She sort of knew this was not true, but she wanted to believe it was.

Sir Hog silently thanked the Lord above that the strawberry soup was a one-off as servants brought in mountains of food - course after course, each on fresh trenchers made from firm, four-day-old sliced crusts of hard brown bread. As was customary diners were served small amounts of each dish before they were removed. Sir Hog slipped Edgar a groat to ensure that he got a triple portion of each dish. Lady Alice watched with a mixture of horror and amusement, noticing how her guest would surreptitiously loosen his belt. *It's like inviting a horde of locusts to one's table* - not that Lady Alice had ever seen locusts, but the Bible was clear on their effects. A drum roll announced Max leading in the main course for the top table: two whole roast milk-fed lambs, garlanded with daisies, rested on a medley of seasonal leaves.

Fyscher looked at the juice-oozing meat longingly, weighing up his options, wondering whether he should adhere strictly to the Rule of St Benedict that forbade priests from eating the flesh of four legged beasts - or would he let the sin of gluttony get the better of him? He was on the point of spearing a stray kidney that had rolled temptingly his way when Edgar arrived, carrying in a napkin-covered trencher that he placed in front of the priest.

'For you we have *heronshewes*,' he said, removing the napkin covering with a flourish, presenting a brace of elaborately trussed roast birds, necks twisted back, points of beaks stuck into their rears. Fyscher's face lit up with delight, and he clapped his hands with glee. Sir Roger was *indeed* offering a rare treat, a delicacy like no other and renowned for flavour and succulence.

'You do me a great honour, Sire,' he said, tearing off an elongated leg. *If he continues to feed me this well, I'll support all sins.* He let the exquisite flavour of sweet flesh fill his mouth.

Peasants might go hungry in July, but not Ipers Castle that night. The tables groaned under the weight of an endless stream of dishes, washed down with copious amounts of spiced Bordeaux wine or, for lower orders, ale.

Sir Hog proved an entertaining raconteur of tall tales that almost exclusively featured himself. 'I like small dogs,' he confided, unable to resist feeding titbits to Horace and Eloise, Lady Alice's lapdogs.

'I don't know what you see in half dogs,' said Sir Roger, disparagingly, joining the conversation on topics that engaged him. He struggled to get more than a monosyllabic squeak out of mousy Lady Hog. 'Now *that's* what I call a dog!' he proclaimed, calling over his favourite *alaunt*. 'Here, Parceval.' A large shaggy, wolf-like brute lolloped over and placed its head on Sir Roger's lap, looking up with adoring eyes. 'Bred them myself from a prize bitch I won from Cousin William. Courage, stamina and obedience, that's what I look for,' Sir Roger said, rewarding Parceval with a chicken carcass.

Max watched with satisfaction as trenchers made their way down tables, being filled and refilled until everyone felt suitably bloated. His first feast had been a triumph.

'How shall we be amused tonight?' demanded Sir Roger, after giving a short speech of welcome to his guests. A few lewd suggestions came back from the benches, but overwhelmingly they wanted a song from Michael the Minstrel.

When he heard the name, Sir Hog, florid face by now wholly scarlet with drink, started snorting and bellowing like a bull. 'Who? Is he here? Where's that scoundrel?' His wife tried to calm him down but it was no good. 'I'll cut off his testicles and stuff them down his throat - that'll stop him singing. Then I'll rip him limb from limb and put the bits on my gibbet for the crows. Yes I will.'

'He's not here. He left some time ago,' said Whytethorne, smoothly pouring oil on troubled waters.

'Who's Michael?' asked a perplexed Sir Roger, as Lady Alice was taken with a sudden coughing fit. The Steward came to her rescue out of gentlemanly charity.

'He was a travelling minstrel,' he whispered to Sir Roger. 'Left just before you arrived home. He was a skilled lute player and had a voice that could charm nightingales from their trees.' And then he said in a much quieter voice, 'and girls of their virtue.' Whytethorne had heard about Sir Hog's daughters. 'We rescued him from the beach at Lepe.'

A hushed silence fell over the room, hopes of a song dashed. Justin stepped up to the plate, fancying himself as a songster.

'You sing, he juggles,' said Sir Roger. 'My new man Digby tells me that he used to be a juggler and acrobat - let's see if he speaks the truth.'

'Shrimp, Shrimp,' the room shouted in unison.

Lady Alice said nothing, looking on nervously as Dan took two, then three, then four expensive Saintonge beakers and had them flying high in the air - though it was the mention of the minstrel that worried her most. *What shall I tell my husband if he asks? And what am I going to do with Handley?* They were vexing questions and she knew that she would have to confront them one way or another.

Sir Roger sat back with a glow of satisfaction as he watched Dan's dazzling show of expertise - *this man will keep us amused for years.*

At the other end of the hall, Sergeant Gwyn watched with gritted teeth. *Call me a nancy-cake lardy-pudding. I'm going to kill the show-off fuckpig. Give me a dark night and I'm going to slit him from guts to gizzard.* But, hypocrite as he was, the sergeant cheered as loudly as the rest.

'What next?' Dan asked as Justin came to the end of a rendition of 'Pilgrim's Song'.

'Song of the Saxons,' came the reply from the lower benches. Soon everyone was thumping down their beakers and chanting. 'Saxons, Saxons.' It was a piece of romance and derring-do with a loud refrain that had everybody joining in. At the song's end, Lady Alice took her leave. She had been sitting quietly and surreptitiously signalled to her maids. Leaning over, she whispered something into Roger's ear, biting it playfully. Her departure signalled the festivities' end and the hall cleared as sated guests, villagers and soldiery went off to their sleeping quarters. Dan sidled up to Clothilde, and, in execrable French, suggested a liaison. She smiled coyly and indicated that she would await his suit in the orchard.

Intrigued by Sir Hog's outburst, Sir Roger collared Whytethorne. 'What was that all about?'

'Old Hog still hasn't recovered from the scandal.' The Steward told him what he had heard from the Bailiff, who had extracted the story, under painful circumstances, from the Chaplain, who had it from the horse's mouth.

'Sneaked into their bedroom and deflowered all three in the same bed on the same night, so the story goes. Sir Hog was all for consigning them to a nunnery but their nurse swore blind their hymens were still intact. Still, I wouldn't like to be in the minstrel's shoes if Sir Hog catches up with him.' The Steward looked at his new master and wondered what he would do if he caught his wife being unfaithful - he had heard the rumours. 'The local wags reckon that he was trying to avoid having to pay dowries.'

A procession of tittering ladies-in-waiting, carrying bedrolls, descended the stairs from the bedchamber. Sir Roger could guess at the meaning of this. Normally closer household members all slept in the same room, albeit divided by screens, but tonight it was warm enough for servants and others to be banished to a courtyard lean-to. Even the children were made to sleep downstairs.

His four-poster bed had crimson drapes embroidered with lilies and leaves and dominated the upstairs sleeping area. Numerous boxes and trunks were piled on the floor. Lady Alice's long red hair had been brushed so it glowed; dainty spots of rouge highlighted her cheek-bones and cherry red paint made her lips inviting. She wore a simple chemise whose drawstring was prominently tied in a bow at the front and held a single white rose.

'Who was Michael?' Sir Roger asked as he rapidly divested himself of his clothes, leaving them in an untidy pile. 'Whytethorne told me all about him. Said he was quite a ladies man.' Unfazed, Lady Alice ducked the question, realising from the eager state of her husband's manhood that he did not suspect her of infidelity.

'I have but one aim,' rasped a relieved Lady Alice huskily, 'and that is to drain you of all your lust so you have nothing left for those doxies in Northampton.' *Fat chance,* thought Sir Roger as he mounted his wife with his usual enthusiasm, but here would be fun in the draining.

Chapter 18

The Stamp of Authority

As expected, on the stroke of the terce bell, Eccles and his ubiquitous guards clattered over the drawbridge. Whytethorne and Sir Roger had spent a pleasant half hour chatting jovially about this and that, and, as the Steward noted, his master was ready to bargain with the slipperiest of eels. Sir Roger had told him about the conversation in the ash store.

'I don't believe a word of it,' the Steward said, shaking his head in disbelief. He was still in favour of putting the Bailiff in the stocks, even though Sir Roger had said no. *And you'll be off on campaign again, leaving me to clean up the mess. Then I'll put him in the stocks and throw the first rotten egg.* The thought of his foul-breathed adversary covered in smelly detritus cheered Whytethorne up immeasurably.

'We have sherbet and sweetmeats,' the Steward said welcoming the merchant and leading him to the quiet spot where Sir Roger was waiting. He was lounging on cushions in an open-sided tent with soft furnishings in Saracen manner - his friend, Eguerand, had introduced him to the luxuries of the orient when they were at Dunbar. A servant was dispatched to fetch refreshments.

Sir Roger gestured to the merchant to sit beside him. 'They might be heathens but they know a thing or two about creature comforts.'

They made small talk while waiting for their lemon sherbet. *Lemons courtesy of me.* The merchant was proud of his lemons, and rightly so; but something about the Banneret made him feel nervous. Was it a distant look, a hint of hostility? *I must tread warily.* 'Let me, on behalf of the townsfolk of Southampton, congratulate you on being promoted Banneret.'

Sir Roger acknowledged the compliment.

'Did you visit Portsmouth and see what the French did?' Eccles enquired, feeling that military matters might be safe ground.

Sir Roger shook his head; he'd not had a chance or the desire to do so. A devastated town was a devastated town; he'd burnt several in Scotland.

'Teach us not to listen to our spies. Word has it that the Chancery knew this raid was coming months before it happened. They even got the date right as near as damn it!' said Eccles lamely. 'They were flying our flags from their masts - pretending to be the Winchelsea fleet. Destroyed the whole bloody town except for the Church and Hospital, and then ran off with their booty.'

'Lose much?' asked Sir Roger

'A salt shipment. Bastards sank one of my cogs.' Eccles took a long swig of sherbet. 'Thank the Lord it was insured. You would have thought that *someone* would have guessed that thirty ships *might* just be hostile?' The muster had failed to work even though there were elaborate plans - no one had bothered to implement them.

The whole system of defence was a complete shambles. The hilltop beacons that were supposed to be lit to forewarn of attack were next to useless. That was not *quite* right; they were used all the time, but inappropriately. The last time a host of ships was sighted off Cornwall, all fires had been lit, panicking the whole region. It turned out to be a false alarm: it was the wine convoy.

'What's supposed to happen?' Sir Roger tugged on his moustache. 'If I understand correctly, Wiltshire and Berkshire men are supposed to race down to the coast and help Hampshire men.'

The trouble was no one had been in charge and no one cared.

'I'm here now; I've been given control of coastal defence, with no orders or instructions of any sort.' Sir Roger shrugged; yet *another* task to be undertaken. 'I lost most of my trained men in Scotland and only have enough to defend this place.' Sir Roger had a habit of being self-deprecating. Humility was a Christian virtue to which he *occasionally* espoused and, realising he was being slightly too honest - *I don't want to send the wrong message* - he turned to Whytethorne 'No time like the present, get the smithy and woodcutters to build new beacons- one at Calshot and one on Farley Hill.'

'Trouble is, there have been so many invasion scares,' said Eccles, reminded of the popular fable. 'They've all been false alarms. Crying wolf too many times got the little boy eaten. The French have a navy, and what do we have? We have a load of merchantmen that get co-opted unwillingly and then don't get paid. We don't have any warships.' It was the old malaise - *react when it's too late and then fight like the devil.*

Sir Roger nodded. The French were alone in possessing a professional navy of a dozen galleys built and based in Rouen. 'Mind you, all this talk of war is pushing up prices,' he declared, starting to steer the conversation away from military to commercial matters, advocating larger convoys.

'Those wretched pirates captured two ships on the last sailing alone. I understand that you're going to the Great Council at Northampton,' said the merchant, deftly changing the subject.

Sir Roger nodded.

'Good. I hope you'll support re-opening the wool trade - granges are bursting with the stuff, quite a lot of it yours, and we haven't been able to sell any, officially that is, for over a year.' He smiled disingenuously, trying innocuously to hide a lie. He had actually cleared a good proportion of stock to Yarmouth but he wanted to act hard pressed.

But Sir Roger was not buying the line. *Perhaps this is the reason Eccles isn't paying for his fleeces.* It worried him. He still had a barn half full of wool and they'd be riddled with moths if a method of payment weren't sorted out soon. This was the downside to the Consortium's scheme. It wasn't so easy to turn fleeces into cash - only those in the King's inner circle could achieve that.

'All I can get are Promissory Notes from the Exchequer and they're as valuable as stones,' moaned Eccles derisorily. 'I tried discounting some with the Peruzzi but they offered only thirty hundredths of face value, so no deal.'

The conversation drifted on to Flanders and coastal defence and castle building before Sir Roger paused, judging that the time was right to bring up the subject of *his* wool. Standing up abruptly, towering over the merchant, who was still relaxed on the cushions, in a swift movement he placed his foot on Eccles's chest, making sure he felt his weight. 'Where's the receipt for my wool?' he said in a low, menacing tone. Eccles was trapped.

'I'll pay you the full amount when Pole pays,' he gasped, struggling to recover his composure. *And when the King pays Pole. Hell will probably freeze over first.*

'No,' said Sir Roger pressing more firmly, widening his eyes and flashing his eyebrows as a warning. 'You'll subtract the amount owed as payment for the goods my wife bought.' Again he paused. 'Nice soap, by the way.' Then he went for the jugular, even though his wife's bill had been two pounds more than the value of his wool, finest grade. 'The whole bill.' He put on his executioner's smile and watched the merchant's face darken; the onus was on *him* to get the money from Pole.

The prostrate Eccles cleared his throat nervously, making rapid calculations in his head. It was simple: *don't fuck with this man.* 'It's a deal,' he whispered.

Eccles left, tail between his legs. Whytethorne, who had watched this negotiation unfold in silence, was impressed with the finesse and delicacy of the thuggery. His new master was a class act.

Sir Roger was happy and hungry, and sure his reception in Southampton would be respectful. Wandering back into the hall, he went in search of sustenance.

'Pottage and make sure it's *stondyng*!' he shouted at a servant. On this matter Sir Roger was fussy. He liked his thick vegetable porridge augmented with bits of beef and other meat, and to be '*stondyng*', it had to hold together on his plate and be properly gelatinous. He hated runny pottage.

Ever alert, Max heard his master's request and came steaming out of the kitchen. It was imperative to know his master's tastes. 'You like it more like a *mortrew*, Sire.' It was simple; Sir Roger liked his pottage cold and set. The cook made a mental note always to add lots of shinbones and pig's trotters to the stockpot. 'Milady likes to eat hers runny, with a spoon.'

'Well I like it thick enough so I can slice it.' It was the soldier's way. 'I'll have a slice of fine white bread, no butter.' He considered the consumption of butter past noon unwholesome for grown men. After his meal, which was nearly to his satisfaction, he spent the afternoon chivvying all and sundry, but he could not hide his impatience. His castle was so nearly finished, only the moat remained undug.

'I want this flooded as soon as possible. Bring in every man, ox, wagon, spade and basket,' he ordered Whytethorne, waving airily at where the moat should be, 'and finish this off. Go to town. Go to surrounding villages. Round up everyone able-bodied. I don't care if you have to use whips, get a hundred men and women, a penny a day and all the food they can eat. Get the miller to grind the remains of our corn.' It was last year's and going mouldy and was only fit for animals, but he didn't care. 'That should do it.'

The Ox and six men-at-arms were dispatched with instructions to herd them like cattle if need be.

'I want to go hunting tomorrow with Harry.' Sir Roger issued his last set of orders to Whytethorne. 'Get Alfred to prepare early, tell him to draw the north woods.' He left the Steward darting around like a demon, issuing a stream of instructions.

Dawn the following day came with an angry sky of low, scudding clouds. It would be a wet hunt. Alfred the Huntsman had sent beaters out at first light to drive deer towards a clearing about half a mile north of the castle. The sound of their horns could be heard drifting closer.

Lady Alice thought her husband and son looked a comical pair dressed in matching green. 'Now get along, we could do with fresh venison.'

Sir Roger picked his bay gelding when he got to the stables, preferring the steadiness of this mount when chasing buck; his son had a New Forest pony of similar colour. A steady drizzle started as they rode to a grassy clearing.

'There!' Sir Roger was alert, pointing to a movement behind some hollies. A fully-grown fallow buck sporting a fine set of antlers, just out of velvet, hurtled out of undergrowth. 'Let Parceval go,' he shouted, as handlers slipped dogs to race, yelping, after the stag. There was no time to loose off any arrows. Father and son galloped down a narrow grassy ride, followed by Alfred and his men. Wet leaves brushed their faces, soaking their clothing. Harry hung on gamely. Already a competent rider, his pony was remarkably nimble and surefooted.

The chase went on for several miles, through woodland and across fields. They lost the hart at the edge of a large clearing. A gruesome sight brought them to a skidding halt. Hanging from a branch of a large oak was a rain-sodden corpse. A pair of carrion crows rose off its shoulders; they had already pecked out its eyes. On closer inspection, Sir Roger could see writhing maggots already working on the exposed flesh and that the protruding tongue was a ghastly blue. He recognised the corpse as that of the thief, Godfrey, from his fair. He had to marvel at the speed at which agents of decay worked in humid air. It had only been three days since he had sentenced this poor wretch to the stocks. A wooden board, with big letters burnt in with a poker, had been attached to the corpse. Sir Eustace had wasted no time in meting out justice.

'What does the sign say, son?' asked Sir Roger.

'Th…, Th…, Thief.' Harry replied proudly.

Alfred realised they had strayed too far north. 'We've got to the edge of your lands, Sire. This is Sir Eustace's doing, soon he'll have no one left to work his land.'

Sir Roger shivered as if someone had walked over his grave. Harry, having never seen a corpse before, poked it with his bow. The rope creaked as the corpse, hose and braes down around its ankles, swung back and forth. He was intrigued by what he saw. There were many questions he wanted to ask about dead people. Sir Roger drew his scimitar and cut the body down, ordering his huntsmen to bury it.

Sir Roger took the pony's bridle and led Harry away. 'You must learn a knight's duties. Next year, you go to Cousin William and you'll become a page, then a squire, and then I hope you'll earn your spurs, like I did, and become a knight. You must understand what it is to be chivalrous. It is your sworn duty to use your sword in the service of justice, doing right, defending the Church from Satan's allies. You must help widows and orphans. Protect the oppressed.' He mustered his most serious expression. 'You must never, ever, break an oath.' He paused. 'My life belongs to my King. I will shed my blood for my fellow man in pursuit of honour, and, if needs must, I will lay down my life.' Crossing himself, Sir Roger thanked God that the acquisition of his new wealth had not transgressed any oaths. *Other than murdering monks. That was bad.* He had only a slightest niggle of worry that one day the truth would out and placed no significance on the fact that Godfrey's genitals were exposed.

'Father, when I am made a knight I'll go on many adventures, like you,' said Harry, shivering from the cold and damp. 'Please tell me some stories.' So, as they walked their horses back through dripping woods, father told son of jousts and combats. Soaking wet, and having no further enthusiasm for hunting, they returned home. *Finally I've been able to keep my promise to the boy.* Back at the castle, a large body of men and women dug and sweated in the moat.

Chapter 19

Duty Calls

S ir Roger was unhappy. The embroidered tusks on the green boar that graced his temporary banner were piddling little tusklets. He'd wanted great slashing scythes, like on the one that was presently was hanging on Black Agnes's wall. It still galled him. His wife did her best to reassure him that a new one, with ivories dripping with blood, would be done in time for his swearing in and wished her husband Godspeed and a safe journey. Justin made the last adjustments to the pack animals, swearing quietly under his breath. He had never known his master to make so much fuss over his clothes. There were three trunks full, with enough pairs of hose, his servant had said, to last a lifetime. Sir Roger had said many times that to be under-dressed for Parliament would not be right.

Trouble started amongst the troop two days later. The Ox started picking on Dan constantly behind the Banneret's back, treating him with particular harshness, and finding fault with everything he did. Sir Roger was so preoccupied with his forthcoming duties that he failed to notice his Sergeant's demeanour, lashing new recruits with a venomous tongue.

Dinner had been pleasant enough on the final leg of their journey. The lady of the manor where they were billeted was gracious, entertaining many guests en route to Parliament. Sir Roger happily sang for his supper, regaling all and sundry with tales of Dunbar. It was not every day that a Banneret graced their table. 'I must go and sort out my wardrobe for tomorrow,' he said, rising from the table and proffering his thanks to his hostess. He had just the outfit in mind for his entry into Northampton.

The evening was warm; as he paused by a low door to the servants' quarters, a nightjar whirred in a nearby copse. Inside a rowdy discussion was taking place about his decision to call the wrestling bout at the fair 'honours even'. This shocked Sir Roger, who stood unnoticed in the doorway, silently witnessing as simmering animosity prepared to erupt into full-blown violence.

'I won't bother to fight you, I'll just give you a mercifully quick death,' Gwyn jibed, making a menacing twisting motion with his hands. 'I bet a weasily fuck like you has a small dick too,' he continued taunting Dan, rubbing his little finger in an obscene manner. This was too much for Dan, who had jumped on the table, dagger drawn, when Sir Roger intervened.

The action froze; time stood still. With icy firmness Sir Roger made it quite clear that he would impose severe disciplinary measures. 'One more peep and the one who starts it will spend the duration in the dungeons, then I'll have him stripped and flogged and he can seek employment elsewhere,' he growled.

There was open-mouthed silence.

'Nor will I sanction a rematch.' Sir Roger had never seen his Sergeant so riled up. He took him outside. 'This graced the pommel of my father's sword before it had rusted away,' he said, and showed Gwyn St. Oswald's knucklebone, which hung on a gold chain under his shirt. 'Now swear on this that you will not harm Dan.'

The Ox looked hard into his master's eyes before reaching out for the bone. Somewhat reluctantly, he swore. 'Sometimes, Sire, I feel you take me too much for granted,' he half-whispered. At once, he half regretted that he had said it, but he couldn't help it. He'd needed to say it for a long time.

Sir Roger knew that it was true. His sergeant was not a clever man. It was his strength and dog-like devotion, not his brains that endeared him to his master.

'I know. I owe you my life,' said Sir Roger. Then, adopting a conciliatory tone, he praised Gwyn for his bravery in battle and courage in his service. 'I don't know what I would do without you.'

The Ox smiled. Sir Roger had taken him from being a lowly oarsman on a nameless ferry that plied the Medway for his teenage years, until he had been consigned to the gutter when he had dislocated his shoulder. With one deft, painful push Sir Roger had cured him and raised him up to what he considered giddy heights. He was the unbeaten judicial champion, a man of status and relative wealth, and his master had finally recognised his true worth.

By noon following day they were watering their horses in the river under the towering walls of Northampton's Norman keep. Justin wrinkled his nose up as an atrocious smell wafted downriver from a nearby tannery. Sir Roger was unfazed; nothing could smell as bad as a three day old battlefield in summer.

'Now that we're here, I'll get myself a new pair of riding boots. I'll get you a pair too. The town is famous for its boots. First we must go to Queen Eleanor's shrine and say a quick prayer.' Sir Roger made a point of always visiting her shrines to buy a good luck charm. One such holy token, placed in the lining of his helm exactly where the bolt had struck, had been his salvation at Dunbar.

But first, Dan insisted, they must visit the Church of the Holy Sepulchre in Sheep Street. Known as 'Soldier's Church', it was built by a previous earl to celebrate his safe return from the Crusades. 'You see, Master,' he pointed out once they were inside, 'this is just like the one in Jerusalem. It's been copied almost exactly.'

They paced around the octagonal building, praying at Stations of the Cross. Outside pedlars swarmed, selling cheap rabbit and hare paws and other gewgaws so beloved of common soldiery.

'I'll get another one,' announced Gwyn, like a sibling vying for a parent's attention. He had many animal feet adorning his *aketon*. 'I've one for each campaign I survive! That should keep me safe another year,' he continued, threading it onto his sleeve. 'I had one from here when we came through on our way to Dunbar, but I lost it.'

'Let me buy it for you,' said Sir Roger, reaching into his purse for a coin, hoping an act of generosity would help him win his Sergeant back.

'No, I have my own money, thank you,' replied Gwyn sulkily. 'You can buy *him* one.' He pointed his head at Dan.

Inside, the castle was like a madhouse. Every conceivable space was occupied by the principal lay and ecclesiastical magnates. Anybody who was anybody, all the great and powerful of the realm were there - with the exception, of course, of those presently serving in Flanders. Sir Roger's allocated lodgings were in the Sheriff's suite of rooms.

'Bannerets have superior rights to common knights,' he asserted, waving his royal authority under a harassed clerk's nose, slipping him a shilling for good measure and choosing the best space available. The space he chose was one which a minor knight from the Shires had thought he had already bagged by arriving a day early.

'But what about my master?' bleated the knight's servant as he watched his master's possessions being unceremoniously taken off the bed and dumped onto the floor.

'It's either a room for two, or he can bugger off,' answered Sir Roger dismissively, as he tried out the bed. 'This will do for me. Set up a cot for your master in the corner.' The knight, he had ascertained, was not a man of any real consequence, and therefore a screen and campaign cot would suffice.

Sir Roger orientated himself and found the garderobe, which hung out over the river at the castle's rear. He needed a good shit and a think. The incident at the church troubled him badly as he relieved himself into the moat far below. *I'll have to defuse this rift between John and Dan.* The Ox was his right hand, and now it felt as though that hand were suffering from palsy. *If thy hand offends thee, cut it off.* He could feel the scimitar prick his flesh under his ribcage before the blade fell to the ground, still clutched in the Jew's severed hand. *I owe him my life. Perhaps I should have given him more money.* But that did not seem to be the solution. *I'll be endlessly in his debt.* At the time the Ox had seemed to be so happy with just a decent tart and barrel of wine.

—⁓—

If asked, Sir Roger described being the 'King's Friend' as a unique position that most knew of - but few understood. He would tell that it was 'a sinecure without power, an inconsequential reward for being the king's whipping boy then, in his teenage years, his boon companion'. He would often play the buffoon, behaving like a shallow, self-centred show-off. An act, his wife had said sarcastically, that came naturally. But it worked, disguising his task to act secretly as his master's eyes and ears, reporting by coded letter gossip and detail that would otherwise be withheld from His Majesty, and Sir Roger was a diligent correspondent. He learnt of confidences and secrets, of alliances and traitorousness that would otherwise continue undetected. No one ever suspected that an evening's drinking with Sir Roger could lead to the scaffold; he was too subtle and clever for that. And the King always ensured that the trap would be sprung by others. Women, too, he had found were a wonderful source of information. Pillow talk went both ways.

Sir Roger surveyed the Great Hall with its rows of benches, specially constructed for the Parliament that lined either side of the stone vaulted chamber. Members were allocated a seat according to rank. Heralds and Wardrobe had been inundated with bickering delegates unhappy with their allocations - particularly those with seats behind columns. Bishops and powerful Magnates sat closest to the dais, facing lesser landowners - the squirearchy from the Shires and lawyers - who had to strain to hear all that was going on.

His ostensible job, on this occasion, was to chaperone the eight-year-old Regent, the Duke of Cornwall, who arrived to a fanfare of trumpets. For all his youthfulness, the boy was eager and intelligent, determined to get a handle on affairs of state. Acknowledging the assembly with a regal wave he mounted his throne where he sat, small, alert and attentive. Sir Roger took up his station behind the Prince's right shoulder from where he could lean over and whisper into his ear. The young Prince took a keen interest in proceedings, often turning to Sir Roger and asking the identity of various speakers.

The debate boiled down to a single point. The King had still not enough money for his war. The previous Parliament's promise to ship wool to pay for the war had been a fiasco, and the King had suffered extreme embarrassment as a consequence. However, the twelfth article of Magna Carta clearly stated that no tax could be levied without the agreement of the Common Council of the Realm, so the whole exercise had to be gone through again.

This time the event was masterfully orchestrated. Every so often Pole and his cronies, who had been sent by the King, encouraged an upwelling of enthusiasm for the 'Flanders Venture'. This resulted in cheering and shouting, and any negative voices of opposition to the campaign were drowned out. The outcome of deliberations was hardly surprising - there would be another wool levy.

'If the warehouses had been full with the twenty-thousand sacks of wool *you* promised in February,' de la Pole explained loudly and clearly, 'then all this would be unnecessary.'

So tax collectors would again be sent to every town and village to reassess amounts due. There was a simple mandate: everyone remotely connected with the wool trade, producer and merchant alike, had to pay the balance in full.

'Officials will be given draconian powers to confiscate oxen and livestock and, if that is not sufficient, then other goods or chattels are to be seized, at will, to make up shortcomings.' Pole concluded that these measures might be unpopular, but the parlous nature of the King's finances made such arbitrary actions necessary. The King was canny enough to realise Parliament's incipient power - he had already horse-traded a series of favours and acquiesced to several petitions, but in return he got law and order throughout the land, and taxes.

Sir Roger bit his lip. He was always careful to conceal the scale of his investment in sheep, but knew that he, too, would be asked for his share. He took comfort in the knowledge that he had friends in high places - the rich and powerful rarely paid in full.

Three days of talk, with lawyers always wanting their say, and the Council was over, its business done and its proclamations written. The young prince was solicitous in thanking Sir Roger as he signed the final decrees on behalf of his father. During the quiet times they had been hawking with merlins and the Prince had downed his first lark. Later,

Sir Roger cornered his cousin, who was in charge of seating arrangements for the feast.

'Who's *that*?' he asked, pointing to a grey-haired magnate he didn't recognise who was sporting a truly exquisite blonde on his arm. Aging knights, their military career over, would frequently seek out and arrange to marry eligible heiresses solely for their wealth - perhaps he was one of these. 'Get rid of him and sit me next to her at the feast, *please.*' As family and a Banneret, he made top table, where he would get his pick of delicacies both in food and females.

'Of course you can sit next to Lady Caroline de Burgh.' His cousin introduced them with a meaningful smile.

Sir Roger had heard of her, she was an acquaintance of his wife, who had been given to an elderly but influential magnate. A bishop intoned grace while Sir Roger eyed up his potential prey. She was not just pretty, she had real beauty: slim, of medium height with pert bosoms and lustrous, golden hair. Her eyes were a vivacious clear blue. She was his favourite kind of woman. As grace finished he watched as she piously crossed herself with almost unseemly vigour. Her hands were slim, her fingernails long and manicured.

'Did you hear the story of that girl in Chester?' she asked seriously, but Sir Roger wasn't concentrating; *she has the loveliest eyes I've ever seen.* 'The young lady,' she continued, 'omitted to do either before nibbling a lettuce leaf.'

'Do what?'

'Say grace and make the sign of our Lord, silly. Weren't you listening?' She lowered her voice. 'She couldn't see him, but a devil happened to be sitting on the leaf at the time. Once swallowed, he refused to come out again!' She took a mouthful of salad, and purposefully ate it, before continuing, 'I met the priest who conducted the exorcism. He told me that it was the strangest experience he had ever encountered. He arrived and the girl opened her mouth and he heard through the girl's lips an aggrieved little voice, complaining: "Alas, what have I done? I sat upon the lettuce and she came, took me up and bit me!"' They laughed, and for good measure all the listeners crossed themselves again. Lady Caroline patted her lips delicately with her napkin. Sir Roger wanted to lean over and kiss them.

He contemplated his next move. His script was well rehearsed, and he turned the conversation to literature. André the Chaplain's seminal work '*De Amore*' was a topic that never failed. He had read it in the old Queen's library when he was a teenager; it had been a time when he had read as many books as he could, and could quote long passages. 'It is most informative about women,' he told her. It was also the seducer's handbook.

He flirted.

She played coy.

She flattered him.

He demurred.

His foot strayed over to hers. She was not unwilling.

He slipped his hand along her thigh. She gently pushed it away and gave him a look that was half-disapproval and half come hither.

Courses came and went, and above their heads sweet music floated over a packed hall from the minstrels' gallery.

He was entranced, enchanted and consumed with lust. Beautiful women were his greatest temptation. It was time to reel his fish in.

'The question is, which should I be?' He whispered so as not to be overheard. 'He who seeks the delight of love in the upper or lower half of you?' He paused, drinking in her ethereal quality. 'There are those who contend that the upper part is superior.' Her dress was cut to hug her figure in the latest fashion. 'There are some who say that the delights of the lower part quickly palls, but *I* have to say it is the enjoyment of that which entices me more. I believe that the pleasure of the lower part fulfils the whole effect of love.' He let his words sink in before adding, casually, 'Shall we make an assignation later?'

She blushed at his shameless approach. He knew he had said enough; he had laid out his stall and would wait for the fruit to ripen. More often than not, it did.

'You flatter me more than I can say.' She fluttered her eyelids demurely. 'I will consider your advances in the light of my husband's activities. He might be old but he is *most* lusty. Next time he suffers from droop I will consider your offer carefully.' With that she changed the subject with a deftness that spoke of other suitors having tried the same path.

Ouch. The rejection cut him like a knife.

Slow down, slow down, you went too quick, old son. He chastised himself and switched the conversation to her husband. 'And what does the randy old goat do?' He glanced over to the man in question. He was a suave fellow in his mid-forties who looked like a bit of a pussy-hound. Lady Caroline told him that he was a diplomat and that he therefore travelled a lot on the King's missions. She also told him that she had recently been appointed to the Queen's Bedchamber. This was good news; their paths would no doubt cross again.

He would have to wait. *I'll ask her for a token at the tourney.* That would be his next move. *If she's interested, she'll tie her chiffon scarf to my lance.*

Not too disappointed, he prowled the hall until he found a lady of easier virtue; his dear cousin always made sure that there was much pretty local talent available. The seduction was brief; a handsome Banneret was a catch for any girl. He was far too over-excited from his dining encounter to bother with much foreplay, which did elicit some complaint from the recipient of his lustfulness. She was hoping for more than a furtive fuck in a dark corner up against a pillar, which is all she got before Sir Roger retired alone, sated but slightly unsatisfied, to bed.

The Ox, too, had been thinking about how he had offended his master and approached him next day to make amends. 'I'm sorry,' he said, head held low. 'I was out of order.' Sir Roger nodded, accepting his apology. 'Take the troop home and get on with training the remaining recruits. Leave Dan and the knights, we'll split up at Oxford.' This would give him a chance to get to know the new members of his retinue better, find out what sort of men they were. If he was going to lead them into battle, he needed to secure their absolute loyalty, and they needed motivating. He would begin by learning all their names.

The cobbler had not finished both pairs of new boots so Sir Roger wandered over to the tourney where he looked through the lists. The competition, he decided, was not up to much: local lads starting out, a few old knights with time on their hands. Sure, it might have been fun, but the prizes on offer were paltry. He glanced over to the grandstand and watched, with a brief pang of regret, as Lady Caroline placed her chiffon around the lance of a handsome young blade he didn't know. She saw him staring and gave him a cheery wave to come over. As formality dictated, and noticing her husband close by, he introduced himself formally with a bow and a low flourish of his hat. They chatted casually and she introduced him to Sir John. It was only with great difficulty that Sir Roger managed to concentrate on the conversation with her husband on his views on the forthcoming expeditionary force now recently arrived in Flanders, and not on the delightful derrière of his wife, who was now gleefully cheering on her chosen champion of the day.

Later, riding back through the Oxfordshire countryside, golden ears of corn waving gently in the breeze reminded Sir Roger of her hair. He conjured up an image of her sparkling blue eyes and sensuous smile, but knew that it could be some time before they met again. As they approached Oxford a thought passed through his head. He rode up to Dan Digby who, other than by the Ox, had become well-liked. 'Daniel,' Sir Roger asked, using his full name, 'tell me more about the alchemist you worked for. What was he like?'

'Well, Sire, he liked to call himself a mathematician.' Dan had been fond of his old master. 'He was forever counting things and trying to find out how everything worked and why certain processes happened. I mean, why does metal become molten when enough heat is applied, or why does air burn when farted from a cow's behind? I can remember we spent all night in a barn holding candles to cows' arses. Great blue flames shoot out whenever the wind of a fart hit the candle. You had to laugh; he got it wrong one time and singed all the hair off one side of his head. I suppose it was the Lord's way of telling him of things to come!' Those who heard the tale roared with laughter.

'By the way, Daniel, I liked your performance at the banquet.' Dan had been a hit, making a coin appear and disappear from Prince Edward's ear, juggling daggers, and then executing a series of back flips down a table without knocking over a single wine beaker, or putting either hand or foot in remnants of food.

'Thank you, Sire.' Dan had enjoyed performing in front of the assembly. He was forever showing off magic tricks and sleight of hand and telling stories of far off places.

Sir Roger also noted that he had taken a fancy to the contortionist. Everyone, ladies included, had watched this erotic *saltatrix* with amazement. Clad in see-through, plum-coloured harem pantaloons, her bosom naked, nipples rouged, she could bend double with wondrous flexibility, backwards and forwards. As a finale, she had put her head through her thighs from behind. Afterwards, Dan boasted happily to the rest of the troop, they had fucked, 'in many interesting positions'.

'Disgusting, like eels in a basket, all slippery and slimy,' hissed Gwyn darkly. Since his talking-to he had left Dan alone, burying his resentment deeper. *There will be a dark night and a quiet alley and I'll gut the Shrimp.* He contented himself with images of intestines spilling into the mud... 'I'll see you at Ipers,' he said, taking his leave.

Sir Roger ordered Dan and Justin to find rooms. His Marshal had only arranged accommodation on the way north, where he stayed at castles and manor houses as befitted his status. Now, unannounced, he had to make do like an ordinary traveller. 'And make sure the sheets are clean. Not covered in puke, shit or spunk... or fleas.' Sir Roger couldn't abide fleas and drew the line at sharing a bed unless the other occupant was an attractive female.

He had to find Magister Frakenham he told them as he set out to find his old tutor, by reputation Oxford's foremost alchemist. *I hope he remembers me, I haven't seen the old buffer for ten years.* Even then, the prince and he had joked about the old man being immortal. The Magister had been an oasis of knowledge in a desert of ignorance and it was he who had taught them about the finer art of using codes. In his line of work,

Sir Roger had found the Magister's dictum that observation was the key to understanding was the true route to knowledge.

The heat of the day lingered oppressively as he strode through Oxford's familiar alleyways. Memories of his first heady days of student freedom came flooding back. In those days, the Magister had rooms close to college above a wine shop, a vintner's sign hanging above the door. Knocking perfunctorily, Sir Roger ducked under a low door beam and entered a dark passage. 'Anyone in?' he shouted.

A serving girl, arms full of linen, bumped into him in the gloom, apologising profusely. 'Can I help, my Lord?' she asked, trying to curtsey.

'I hope so. I'm looking for Magister Frakenham.'

She indicated that he was in an upstairs room at the back. It was more cluttered than he remembered, with manuscripts and books strewn across a wooden table, and curious objects filling every nook and cranny. Little had changed except there were many more Venetian glass jars containing liquids and powders, and collecting dust.

'Magister!' he exclaimed. 'You look younger than ever.' Sir Roger always tried to humour his erstwhile tutor.

'And to what may I owe this honour, Boy?' Everyone was 'Boy' to the Magister, who was seated near a window, reading by the light of the setting sun, a pair of spectacles perched upon his nose. These he took off carefully as he stood up to greet his visitor.

'Who did you say you were?'

'Roger de Bohun.'

'Who?'

'The King's Friend, his Whipping Boy. You remember he and I spent three months with you in the first year of his reign.' The old man nodded - he felt it best to do so, though nowadays his memory for people was patchy. The King he could remember clearly, but his friend... *I'll pretend I do, maybe I will later on.* Age was steadily robbing him of his faculties but he was determined not to give up. Only now, with the accumulation of wisdom, was he starting to see the light.

Wiping his glasses carefully on his sleeve, he replaced them. 'A godsend these,' he confessed, removing them again and holding them up to the window, checking for specks of dust. 'I paid a fortune for them. From Florence, you know. Means I can still read. I'd be lost without them.' He cleaned the lenses again; his great mane of snow-white hair fell down to his shoulders.

Sir Roger calculated that he must be over seventy, a tremendous achievement - the oldest person he knew. 'I'm after your knowledge. I need to learn about exploding powder - you knew Roger Bacon, didn't you?'

'What did you say? You'll have to speak up, I'm going deaf as well as blind.'

Sir Roger repeated himself loudly. 'Ah, the great Roger, same name as you,' the Magister guffawed, and went off at a tangent. 'He had the first pair of spectacles in England. I visited him in prison the year of the plague of frogs in Malmsbury. That's over fifty years ago - I was still a student then.' He rummaged through an impressive pile of leather bound volumes. 'I've got two of his books. Here's one,' he noted, carefully removing a volume from the bottom of the pile and holding it up into the sun's rays so he could read the title. "*On the Multiplication of the Species*'. What a *thinker* he was.' He scratched his forehead and sighed. 'Thought too much for his own good. His dictum "Cease to be ruled by dogmas and authorities: look at the world' got him into trouble with the Church. They hate it if anyone questions the natural order.'

As Dan's former master found out, thought Sir Roger. Any deviation from the Scriptures was heresy, and for unrepentant heretics there was only one punishment - burning at the stake.

'I spent a year with him. Taught me how to look at the world.' The old man looked up and wiped away a tear that had formed in the corner of his eye. 'That's why I hide away in my garret. Keep my work secret. Gunpowder, that's what that explosive stuff is called,' confided the Magister. 'Bacon told me he found out about it from a Mongol sage who came to visit Rome when he was there. It's spectacular. Boom!' He gesticulated wildly with his arms, knocking over his wine beaker.

They talked on long into the night, the Magister telling him of fantastical things Bacon had told him about flying machines, steam-driven boats and magnifying lenses. By the end of it, Sir Roger thought his tutor quite mad. They agreed to meet again in the morning when the Magister promised to give him a demonstration.

The Blue Boar Inn provided a bed with clean linen but no totty. The landlady had been reluctant to change the sheets until Justin pointed out what a great lord his master was, and how vengeful he could be if bitten by bed bugs. When Sir Roger returned, his squire had a nameless girl on his knee - a plump trollop who promised to dally with him for a farthing.

'A farthing. I usually get it for free,' Justin said jokingly as he tipped her off his knee, smacking her behind for good measure. Justin had an insatiable appetite for serving girls.

I wonder how many little bastard de Frages are bawling for milk in inns up and down the land. At least he hasn't inherited his father's brains - or lack of them. Sir Roger felt relieved at that.

Flashes of lightning followed by a distant rumble of thunder presaged the arrival of a downpour. As he undressed and went to bed, Sir Roger's thoughts were of Lady Caroline. As he closed his eyes he remembered how daintily she had dabbed her lips with her napkin, how prettily she ate, with the delicacy of a butterfly sipping nectar from a flower. When she had lent over and deftly wiped a drip of gravy from his chin. That was the moment at which he knew that he was smitten. He must remember to send her a *billet doux* declaring his passion. Her rejection still hurt. *The mountain might be steep, but the climb will be worth my while.* With those thoughts in his mind, he drifted into a deep sleep.

—∞—

'I thought you didn't eat breakfast.' Dan and Justin found Sir Roger having a rapid meal of *stondyng* pottage, wine and bread.

'You should eat too,' he told them. 'You might not get anything later.'

The morning was fair and after reciting some quick prayers they returned together to the Magister's lodgings.

'I remember you now,' the Magister said, looking up from where he was working yellow, white and black powders with a pestle in a mortar. 'You were the spotty boy who came with the King.' It was true, there had been an eruption of pustules on his face. Sir Roger blushed; the old man had shown him his reflection in a polished disc.

'You have to mix sulphur, saltpetre and charcoal like this.' The Magister concentrated hard on his task, pushing and grinding. 'The proportions must be correct. After a short while you get this.' He showed off a handful of black powder. 'Hand me that feather.' He pointed to a bundle of goose feathers, old worn-out writing quills that were wedged in a leather holder. 'Watch carefully.'

He cut off the end of a worn-down nib and, stripping off the feathery barbs, carefully filled the tube with finely ground powder. He told them it was a fuse. 'The shorter the length, the quicker it burns. Now,' he scratched his head. 'What shall we use for the body?'

There was a small gourd hanging by a string on the wall. 'Perfect' he concluded, carefully cutting it open and filling it with powder. He made a stopper out of wax that he had been warming between his fingers to make it malleable and inserted the fuse. 'Come. We must go somewhere quiet - out of the way of prying eyes. This is not for everyone to see. Bring a candle and tinderbox.'

He strode out with the gourd to a secluded orchard with the others running to keep up with him. 'I had another fellow wanted to see this, I think he was a Frenchman - if he wasn't, he behaved like one.' The old man stopped dead in his tracks and stroked his beard. 'St. Lambert's Day.' He stood again for several moments. 'Nearly a year ago. He didn't want me to know he was French, but I could tell - they smell different.'

A pile of broken masonry was selected as a perfect platform for the experiment. 'Stand well back,' the old man ordered, placing the gourd on top. Lighting the candle, he touched the fuse's top. There was a whoosh and a loud bang. The fuse had been quicker than expected and the Magister had still been too close. He was knocked off his feet, his face covered in black blotches, and a drop of blood emerging from his nose. His glasses, blown askew, hung from one ear, and a bit of gourd stuck out from a nasty cut on his forehead. He sat stunned as a dense cloud of brownish-yellow sulphurous smoke gently dispersed through the orchard. Sir Roger was quick to react, picking the fallen man up. The glaze went from his eyes and, to Sir Roger's relief, he took a deep breath. 'I think I used too much powder,' he observed wryly, and promptly passed out.

Justin and Dan were equally shocked by the blast - even from twenty paces they had been showered with bits of gourd. They picked up the unconscious alchemist and carried him back to the wine shop, where they put him on a table and tended to his wounds. Luckily they were superficial and with some wine poured down his throat he soon recovered. 'I need to experiment more on fuses,' he muttered, getting up from the table and dusting off his robe.

So this is the magic powder. Sir Roger had seen a gun before - the King already had several - but he had not been privy to their workings. The explosion's loudness had been quite unexpected and he still had ringing in his ears.

To his annoyance, the blast had broken a lens of the Magister's glasses and he bemoaned the fact that it could take him months or even years to get replacements. 'So much work, so little time.' The old man fussed around, ignoring his visitors.

'Time to go home, I think,' declared Sir Roger, taking his leave. He had been impressed with the demonstration. *If a gourd full of gunpowder could cause so much havoc... And why would a Frenchman be interested?* He would include that snippet of information in his next digest to the King.

Chapter 20

An Unwelcome Guest

By the time Falke Walwyn led his lame horse back through the gates of the manor at Caxton Deverell he had cursed the devil, Jesus, several saints known and unknown, had brutalised three serfs, two dogs and a stray sheep. His mission, from Sir Eustace, had been to spy on Ipers Castle and report on the disposition of their enemy. So he had spent an uncomfortable week dressed as a mendicant monk begging outside the gates of Sir Roger's castle, where he had suffered a tirade of abuse from the village idiot, who, for some reason he could not fathom, had taken a strong dislike to him. When he had tried, in his view, gently, to ask him to desist, he had also been assaulted by the village's priest. As a fighting man he had wanted to kill both there and then, but because of his disguise, and because his master had stressed the importance of his task and he feared his master's wrath, he'd taken his beating and left. He would seek out his persecutors on his return and ensure they died a slow and painful death.

'De Bohun's gone north with most of his men. If we're quick, he'll still be at the Parliament. He's not expected back until the Feast of St. Bartholomew at the earliest. I asked the Marshal,' he told Sir Eustace. Marshals were usually the most reliable source of information when it came to travel plans.

Sir Eustace rubbed his scar; it always itched when he got excited. That should be time enough. Two of Sir Eustace's men were coopers before they had been outlawed for debt and their skills had been put to good use. A couple of stolen wagons with six barrels on each would conceal enough men to overwhelm the garrison. Falke had counted no more than a handful of men. It seemed as though the place was deserted other than by workmen and women.

Sir Eustace lined up all his men by height before allocating each a barrel to hide in. 'You, you, you and you - get in and make sure you piss first.'

Since the hanging, he had been preparing his ruffians for the raid on Ipers. They would kidnap Sir Roger's wife and the children and hold them for ransom while placing a curse on her husband. *Give him an Egyptian Day or two or three.* The plan was simple enough: get the wagons inside, and at the given signal his men would jump out. He'd then stuff her, the children and as many women as possible into the barrels and leave. No one outside the walls would be any the wiser. *And the redhead will be mine - he can buy back soiled goods.*

—⚍—

A refreshing rain had made the countryside smell sweet. Hips reddened on dog roses, and yellow fleabane mingled with pink willow herb, filling damp patches. Fat cattle lazed in lush meadows. Corn had ripened nicely. Peasants, hose rolled down below the knees, were harvesting, scythes swishing regularly. All looked peaceful and happy. Mud and puddles had dried, leaving roads rutted and rough. Hooves kicked up dust. The troop had made excellent time from Oxford.

'About the other day.' Sir Roger deliberately sidled his horse up next to Dan's. He had not brought the subject up before, but felt the situation needed resolution. 'John Gwyn saved my life in France. He's jealous and can be vindictive. With your talents, I think it better if we made you our new minstrel.' *Every castle needs an entertainer and he'll fit the bill perfectly.*

This thrilled Dan, for he had seriously been contemplating abrogating his oath and doing a runner, prepared to trade a future in hellfire for distance from his odious persecutor.

As they rounded the final bend to home, Sir Roger stopped and looked on open-mouthed. His moat was finished, stream diverted. Spurring his palfrey on, his excitement was plain for all to see as he galloped round the completed body of water.

The Steward emerged from the gatehouse. 'It's finished,' said Whytethorne, puffing his chest out with pride in a job well done. 'We rounded up every able-bodied man and woman in the district.'

The moat diggers had been pressed into completing the building using the clay they dug out from the moat to coat the wattle of the upstairs walls. The stone lookout tower that dominated the solar had been given a shingle roof, which, in case of dire emergency, could be fired to form a beacon. The upstairs living quarters on the building's eastern side, where the sail tents had been arranged for his feast, was swarming with tilers. The Old Hall sat square and severe and had been relegated to form the west wing. Sir Roger marvelled at his achievement.

Francis stood silently in the courtyard, admiring his handiwork. It had been two years of solid, hard graft. He had regrets - he would have liked the top floor to have been stone, but then again the wood-framed top floor gleamed in the sunshine. White painted plasterwork, radiant and unblemished, was framed between dark beams, and the very latest innovation in building, Flemish brick chimneys, poked out of a Cornish slate roof. It had cost the Jews' fortune.

'Consider it a job well done,' said Sir Roger, handing over a purse full of money. 'This covers everything. By the way,' he added, 'I had a word with the Clerk of Works at Winchester. They've got a job for you at the Cathedral if you want it. They've got a problem with subsidence. Your speciality, I believe.' Sir Roger remembered a conversation they had had when sinking the foundations.

The Master Mason smiled and thanked him; his engineering skills would be put to good use. 'We couldn't have done it without finding those ruins,' he said, 'the skill of those ancients who dressed all that stone…' He shook his head, still in awe. They had manhandled huge lumps of carved rock and a couple of pillars for foundations onto a specially built ox-pulled cart and employed hundreds of labourers. Now, with the builders gone and most of the scaffolding removed, the courtyard was virtually empty. Five round turrets, with garderobes hanging over the moat, graced each corner, with the west end wall forming a dogleg.

An experienced eye told Sir Roger that his defences were formidable enough. He'd surveyed many enemy fortresses while in France and his recent exploits at Dunbar had shown just how hard it was to assault a well-designed set of walls. To take Ipers, attackers would have to climb a slope, cross the moat and scale a wall that was over twice the height of a man. An imposing gatehouse, where Whytethorne had taken up residence, had twin towers with shingle roofs. A drawbridge was the only way in or out. Inside, the walls were lined with a series of ramshackle buildings - barracks, stables, armoury, a mews for hawks, workshops, two gaol cells with iron bars sunk deep into the ground, and a pigsty, where those leftovers not sold to pie men were thrown.

The three chimneys of the kitchen area were a marvel. There was one for a bread oven, one for the main cooking fire, which was large enough to roast a whole animal on a spit, and one for a smaller oven. The dairy, like the bakery, was housed in a room of its own and contained a collection of wide, shallow *panshions* for holding milk, with skimmers, ladles, brushes and jugs hanging on hooks on the wall. A butter churn, cheese press and dairymaid's pails completed the equipment.

A tribe of boys, mostly sons of maids and poorer villagers, had taken up residence under tables and in corners. They were tasked with cleaning, spit turning, preparing food and washing up. Max would beat or bugger these as the whim took him. Dirty, hot and sweaty places, kitchens were a man's domain. Max had been getting the smith to make a new spit when he spotted his master galloping round the moat. *I hadn't expected him back 'til next week.* That gave him only six hours to prepare a welcome home feast.

Handley, too, expressed the same thought, appearing by his master's side wearing an unusually lugubrious expression. 'Tax collectors came yesterday to assess and told me we had to pay more. We got rid of them,' he said with a beaming smile. This was an understatement.

Gwyn had driven them from the property using whips and the flat blades of swords.

But his master wasn't listening. 'Carp, Tom, I want carp,' he said. The moment he saw the water-filled moat his mind had turned to fish. *Fishing was my childhood's greatest pleasure.* He remembered the time he'd caught a mighty pike in the moat of the Tower of London, and how the prince had forced him to let him take over landing it.

'I'll get some.' The Bailiff knew of well-stocked stew ponds that would benefit from an evening's netting.

'We'll have to sort something out about tax,' said Sir Roger, returning to the subject of wool. 'Where's Lady Alice?'

'In her new garden.' The Bailiff's breath smelt even worse than usual. 'She's got company.' *I probably pong too.* Sir Roger decided against going straight to his wife, and he slipped into his living quarters to clean up and change first.

Lady Alice had created her garden next to the courtyard. There, with a coterie of women in attendance, she was absorbed in embroidery and chatter. 'We weren't expecting you back until tomorrow at the earliest, no jousting then?' she asked as her husband approached. It was rare for Sir Roger to pass up a tourney. 'How did it go?' she enquired, after rising and giving him a kiss on the lips, eliciting giggles from her companions. *My you look fine*, she thought, admiring his new shoes.

Sir Roger smiled. *She's noticed.* These were an extra pair he'd acquired along with his boots in Northampton.

'I also love *them*.' She pointed up to a pair of leaded glass windows that gave light to their newly built bedroom, which looked out across Southampton Water. 'I'm still in two minds as to where we should hold the Court. All those undesirables...' She hugged her husband. '*C'est magnifique.* I shall write to my father.' She looked at him, 'I'm proud of you. Look what you have achieved.'

'We,' he replied. 'Proud of what *we've* achieved.' *Give credit where credit is due.*

'This is Elizabeth of Rochester,' Lady Alice introduced him to a most alluring young woman in her early twenties, richly dressed. 'Her mother is my kinswoman. She's come to stay while her husband's away.'

'Well, Mistress Elizabeth, you are most welcome.' Sir Roger flashed his finest I-want-to-fuck-you smile and was gratified to see her blush and giggle coyly with a barely discernible, but definitely there, come hither raising of a fashionably plucked eyebrow. *She'll make a suitable quarry for 'La chasse d'amour'.* This explained his wife's overt show of affection. There was jealousy brewing. Elizabeth had the pale gold colouring of a newly minted Tower sovereign and, he noted, was as thin and supple as a weasel. Her body, almost as skinny as a boy's, was as close to perfection as he could desire. *I will have to get this sexy little minx on her own.* 'I will see you at supper I hope?' he said, and he strode off, eager to examine his completed gatehouse with its drawbridge. Saracens, he had read, kept many wives in something called a harem. It was a word he'd heard old crusaders use. *Blasted heathens, seems like a sound idea. Lots of women, all for me....*

'I've been doing accounts.' Whytethorne showed Sir Roger around his new quarters which consisted of his suite of rooms, twin towers, drawbridge and portcullis. 'This whole building, cost £45 6s 9d.'

My wife's new Vair cape cost £5. What made Sir Roger think of that, he didn't know. The cape was made up from five hundred Baltic squirrel pelts. *Five hundred!* The figure had boggled his imagination. The idea of catching one squirrel was hard enough.

Usually he kept quiet on the subject of his wife's spending on clothes but on that occasion he had berated her, as it had been *so* expensive. It got him nowhere.

'The Queen has one,' she had argued with finality. 'They are the *height* of fashion.'

At least this should last much longer than that ruddy cape. He banged his fist on the solid stonework as he climbed the stairs to the battlements. The sediment had started to settle in the moat and the reflection of the walls was broken here and there as swallows and house martins skimmed and dipped into its glassy surface, chasing insects. Another quite unrelated thought came into his head: *shall I shave off my moustache?*

He decided that he would ask Lady Elizabeth and he could not help lustful thoughts happily invading his mind.

It was the Steward who interrupted his reverie. 'Strangers approaching.' Whytethorne pointed to seven men that, without so much as a by-your-leave, were unceremoniously crossing the drawbridge.

Sir Roger's heart fell. It was Sir Eustace. 'What's this bastard doing here?' he hissed through gritted teeth to Whytethorne. 'Put the guard on alert.'

There was nothing friendly looking about the six Norman thugs, in chainmail, who now clattered menacingly round his yard.

'De Frage, how pleasant to see you,' Sir Roger greeted his visitors with *faux*-cordiality, honour-bound to be charitable. *I suppose giving travellers succour is a Christian virtue.* Dismounting from a white stallion, which snorted and pawed at the ground, Sir Eustace immediately went round and breathed gently in its nostrils to calm it down.

'I see you've got a new horse.' Justin ran over, greeting his father.

Sir Roger also admired the destrier, he had an eye for good horse-flesh and this one was of an unexpectedly superior class, and flashed his neighbour a quizzical look.

'Spent all my pay from Dunbar on it, it's my pride and joy,' the lie flowing out like water from a spring – and as clear. He'd sneaked north to a neighbouring county, ransacked three churches, robbed a wagon train, and stole the horse. He loved the beast, which he'd had for three weeks. It was the finest he had ever owned.

'It is a pleasure to see you home, Rog,' Sir Eustace sneered with no conviction at all. 'May we rest here tonight? I see you have made a fine *little* fortress here.' There was, as usual, a nasty undertone to his voice. Surreptitiously, he felt for the vial of Godfrey's semen hidden in his aketon; it was imperative he hide it where its magic effect could do most damage. *I hope my curse will still work.* His beady eyes were taking in the changes and concluded that his present plan was over-ambitious. To start with, he hadn't bargained on Sir Roger being home so soon

'You can sleep in the Hall after dinner is cleared away.' Sir Roger would not give anything more than basics and wanted to know what they were doing here anyway.

'Picked stuff up from the Isle of Wight. Supplies for the King, we knew you were here and thought we'd drop in on an old colleague,' replied de Frage vaguely. This time he purposefully avoided the word 'friend' as he knew he'd get a rebuke. It was plausible - a ferry operated across the Solent. The pair of carts carrying a dozen barrels rumbled across the drawbridge. Sir Roger made an expansive gesture, ushering him into the new hall.

'I hear you were at the Great Council,' said Sir Eustace, picking his nose and flicking the bogey onto the ground. He shot a glance at Falke. 'I thought you said he'd be back after St. Bartholomew's,' he whispered angrily.

'That's what I was told,' said Falke with a shrug. His men would have to stay in their barrels and get cramp and no women… At least he'd get a free meal.

'I've just got back this afternoon. I saw you hung that cutpurse.' The swinging corpse still troubled Sir Roger, and try as he might, he could not get rid of the image.

'It was kind of you to leave him for me. This is splendid,' Sir Eustace grinned as he admired the new carved mantelpiece. He'd found a perfect spot for his curse amulet to lurk unseen in the heart of his enemy's hall.

The Pantler emerged ringing a hand bell to announce that dinner was served. While his host's back was turned, Sir Eustace placed the vial into an insignificant gap behind the eagle's wing.

Sir Roger and Lady Alice surveyed their hall from ornate chairs. Max had muttered a few choice expletives on being told about the extra guests. Lady Alice steeled herself for an uncomfortable meal and hoped that at least Whytethorne would help her out.

'I *like* these,' cooed Lady Elizabeth to her host, admiring a pair of gold salt boats that Sir Roger had acquired in London, ordering them from Bernard the Goldsmith.

I paid £8 7s 4d and consider them a bargain. He had haggled hard, getting the price down from £10.

'These are new, too.' Lady Alice told him. A set of six pewter plates had been sent, compliments of the goldsmith.

'It seems a shame to cover them with trenchers.' Sir Roger examined his platter. 'I think he wants us to order some more stuff from him.'

The tablecloth was spotless. 'Please *try* and keep it clean,' begged Lady Alice wishfully, flicking off some crumbs. *Though not for long.* She watched with rising horror as Sir Eustace pushed back his seat sending page and fingerbowl flying.

'You can't keep the Saxons at bay unless you thrash 'em *and* hang 'em,' he propounded to Whytethorne as they argued about the fate of Godfrey. 'If you get soft they'll steal everything that isn't nailed down.' Sir Eustace slammed his hand down on the table, causing everyone close by to start.

The conversation moved on to the merits of swift, brutal punishments for trivial crimes and de Frage was warming to his theme when the first course, a fish pie, was brought in. This was followed by a diatribe against the Scots during the rabbit and almond stew. He quietened down in time for the boiled chicken with *powdor-douce*. This was a mixture of ground cinnamon, ginger, grated nutmeg and ground black pepper, all the most expensive products from Eccles's cart.

'I love this stuff,' chortled an increasingly intoxicated Sir Eustace, taking an excessively large pinch.

A salad of fresh leaves followed, dressed with oil and vinegar. Sir Roger toyed with a lettuce leaf. 'You have to be careful,' he remarked turning it over, examining it as if for slugs. 'Beelzebub has a nasty habit of sitting on these things.' And he told the story of the girl and lettuce. Lady Elizabeth picked up a leaf and blew on it, as if to unseat the Devil, before placing it suggestively in her mouth.

Falke Walwyn and the Normans were placed with lesser members of the household and men-at-arms. They had to wait till last before being served with coarse rye bread, boiled meat and onions. The top table's final course was broiled beefsteak with ginger and red wine sauce, sprinkled lightly with cinnamon and garnished with the last of Eccles's lemons. More vegetables, onions, celery, cabbage, and a novel, slightly bitter, root from Hainault called a carrot accompanied this dish.

Sir Roger was deep in conversation with Lady Elizabeth and the more he heard the happier he was.

'My husband is in Flanders,' she revealed, smiling, 'and he's so old. I fear he will drop dead at any moment, he's nearly forty-five.'

Same as Sir John de Burgh, Sir Roger also rapidly deduced from a few subtle hints that her husband was not interested in satisfying her carnal needs.

Lady Alice, on the other hand, was getting agitated. Her husband was being flirted with on one side, and the biggest boor in the world was on the other. 'Please curb your tongue,' she demanded tartly, as yet again Sir Eustace took the Lord's name in vain. As far as she was concerned such language was unacceptable, and she noticed that his was the only place at table where sauces had been spilt on her clean tablecloth. *Has he not been taught how to use a spoon?* Unwisely, she voiced this conjecture.

For Sir Eustace, too, the meal, though tasty, was hell on earth. Here he was, seated next to the woman of his Onanistic dreams, and he had to try and be nice. And she was lecturing him on table manners. The spoon was the final straw. The image of her spread-eagled, naked and writhing and begging him to take her filled his head. Involuntarily his hand reached down and grabbed between her thighs. She reacted violently, slapping him across the cheek. The shock made him round on her loudly in a most unchivalrous manner.

'I'll tell you something you don't know. Where did your husband get his money? He stole it. Your husband is nothing better than a common thief.'

Sir Roger stopped mid-mouthful, practically choking on the morsel of beef he had been chewing. The room fell silent, all eyes fixed firmly on the top table.

'You will retract your last statement.' Sir Roger glowered as he stood up. 'How dare you insult me in my own home?'

Sir Eustace reached over and nonchalantly helped himself to some mustard. With careful deliberation he pasted it onto a piece of steak; this he held up on the point of his knife and waggled it in Sir Roger's direction.

'Come on Rog, old chap, tell us the truth,' he goaded his host. 'Robbing Jews, wasn't it?'

Whytethorne watched with rising horror, quietly summoning a page. After a whispered word, the boy slipped out of the hall.

'My affairs are *nothing* to do with you. Leave right now!' Puce with rage, Sir Roger pointed to the door. 'Get out!'

Sir Eustace staggered to his feet smiling, reeling from alcohol. 'Scared someone will find out about your crime?' Sir Roger punched him on the nose, breaking it. Sir Eustace reeled back from the blow then, lurching forward, splattered droplets of blood onto the table-cloth. Lady Alice was appalled, cowering low in her chair while the men stood aggressively on either side of her.

'You'll regret this.' Sir Eustace muttered, the blow somewhat sobering him up. He wiped his bloody nose on a napkin and picked up a stoneware wine pitcher into which he dribbled a large gob of blood and spittle before handing it to a stunned Sir Roger. He turned his attention to Justin, who stood mouthing words that failed to come. 'If you stay with this crock of shit then I'll disown you.' Putting his foot up on the table, with a great heave he kicked it over. Whatever Sir Eustace said next went unheard as the Hall erupted.

Furious, Sir Roger smashed the ewer with all his might into his enemy's ear, rendering him unconscious. Outnumbered Falke and the Normans were made to carry Sir Eustace's prostrate body out into the courtyard, where horses and wagons were gathered in the advancing gloom of night.

Sir Roger found Justin and placed a reassuring hand on his shoulder. 'Remain here,' he commanded in a gentle voice. 'He will be the death of you before I.'

A page handed Sir Roger his scimitar.

'Revive him,' he ordered. Sir Eustace's arms were pinioned behind his back by Gwyn, a pail of water thrown in his face.

'This is what happens to those who abuse my hospitality,' Sir Roger growled and with a swift blow severed the stallion's tendon. The horse reared up, whinnying in agony before a lunge through its flank pierced its heart and it collapsed, quivering, in the courtyard. Foaming at the mouth, Sir Eustace watched his prized possession destroyed.

'I'll get you for this,' he shouted and then, uttering hideous curses, he was ejected from the castle. Sir Roger's retainers tried to keep the party together while ushering them out of the village beyond the moat; but more armed men sprang out of the wagons and, in the chaos, slipped away. Soon flames were seen licking up the sides of the mill. It took the rest of the night to restore order and put out the fires.

'I'm sorry you had to witness that.' Sir Roger had to quell flames of a different kind. In the privacy of his solar he recounted to his wife the true tale of the acquisition of his fortune. 'We had been harrying supply lines and spying. We were well off the beaten track when John and I found this small village.' He looked earnestly into his wife's bloodshot eyes. 'We were in a tavern when a dozen of the largest Genoese you have ever seen came in arguing loudly... I know there were twelve because we counted the bodies afterwards. We hid and watched... that's how we discovered the Jew's convoy. We got the better of the mercenaries. I'd peeked inside their wagons and knew what to expect.' They had still been tough opponents; one had nearly done-for Sir Roger with his crossbow. 'It's true - it *was* the Jews' money.' More specifically, it was the King of France's, he explained. The tale unfolded. 'Many, many thousands of gold ducats and *livres d'or*, jewels and other valuables were in that strong box and we took it all.'

He didn't tell her about killing women and children, or about raping the young Jewess. He made it sound noble, something hard fought between men. He never mentioned beheading the monks. 'If you hadn't have known, you'd have thought they didn't have a brass farthing to rub together,' he continued.

'I didn't think Jews were allowed to carry weapons?' Lady Alice interjected.

'You're right. Isaac of Rouen put up a good fight.' Sir Roger had subsequently found out his name, for armed Jews were rare. 'We lost some good men in the melee before John's lucky blow severed his hand.' Sir Roger remembered it as clearly as if it were yesterday, the hand still clutching the scimitar when it was presented to him. He described the curious dance of death the Jew had made, spraying blood all around as it spurted out of his severed wrist.

'I think I'm going to be sick,' said Lady Alice, gagging.

But he ploughed on. There had been enough treasure for a proper Duke's ransom, he had joked to the King. After taking the royal share, Edward decided to declare it as such, and so their lie was conceived.

'I'm sorry I lied,' he said, truthfully, to Lady Alice, who was still in tears from the evening's events, consoling her as he wrapped his arms around her shoulders. 'I love you,' he whispered in her ear. He wondered how Sir Eustace had found out. Everyone involved, other than members of his troop, had either died mysteriously or been bribed excessively. Perhaps, in a drunken moment, one of his men had been loose tongued. Sir Roger had an uneasy feeling. Someone must have spilt the beans on the journey south from Dunbar, and he thought he knew who it was.

Lady Alice understood. *It would have been unwise to publicise the true origins of the money. Easy come, easy go, some would say.* She did not know whether this put her husband up in her estimation or down. She had naively believed his tale of the duel on the road and the great single combat with a Duke of the Blood, while it had all been a tissue of lies... In retrospect it had surprised her that the ransom had been paid so quickly. *The truth is out now, and my husband has a mortal enemy.* They would have to be vigilant. Who could tell what form Sir Eustace's revenge would take.

The following morning revealed the scale of the destruction. 'The mill's been badly damaged,' Whytethorne reported. 'It'll take months to repair. They also went for your barn.' Sir Eustace's men had pillaged several buildings during their night of stealing and wrecking.

'They've vanished,' reported Gwyn, who had been sent to scout the vicinity. 'Gone, like early morning mist. We've found his wagons. Empty - the horses gone too. The Reeve's dead. They murdered him.'

Percy's body was carried into the courtyard and laid out. A solemn service followed in the graveyard. The whole village turned out to watch as a hastily constructed coffin was lowered in to the ground. The priest tried to conjure up words of comfort, but could find nothing adequate. With the family breadwinner gone, the Reeve's widow was inconsolable.

'How am I going to feed four small children?' she wailed, beating an ample chest. Sir Roger found ten shillings in his purse. She thanked him profusely.

'I want you to suggest they appoint Walt the Reedcutter as the new reeve,' Sir Roger told Whytethorne, who had come to watch the interment. 'Can you see to it and put in a good word?'

It was a village matter who became reeve. It was he who looked after their interests, and they had the right to choose. Walt would be a popular choice; he was a man who spoke his own mind, unafraid. With the backing of the Lord of the Manor, his election was secure. Sure enough later that day Walt was carrying the white stick of his new office.

Chapter 21
What a Prize

The Toad rubbed his hands with glee. His plans for the proposed raid on the fat, rich, joyously poorly fortified port of Southampton were advancing steadily, and money would soon be flowing into the Peruzzi Bank in Southampton.

'I've dispatched a Venetian spice runner with the documents,' he reported to the King, pleased with progress. 'The captain thinks he's on Papal business.'

A messenger from Alberghini said he had done the Admiral's bidding, which came as no surprise to the Toad - the poor Cardinal would do anything to prevent the Pontiff hearing of his indiscretions with the catamites.

'How will it work?' The Viper was intrigued.

'Letters say that the Pope wishes to inform all Florentines of the creation of a new saint. That one of their own was brutally martyred by heathens. To celebrate her beatification- I thought it should be a girl - they must place a wreath of flowers on their doors and leave them there to dry.' Thus, he said, the raiders would know what they were looking for.

'Tell Quiéret that the contents of those buildings are mine and mine alone,' said the King, taking a handful of sweetmeats from a tray. 'I don't want Italians stealing *my* money.'

'No. I've told them to avoid the houses with wreaths altogether. I've said that they're properties owned by our allies and we don't want to aggravate them. I'm sure there will be enough confusion to hide our real intentions, Majesty.' The Toad bowed low. He had decided that it was better not to tell the King that the papers to the Peruzzis were all immaculate forgeries. Although the Papal Seals were real enough, their contents were his ingenious fabrications. They purported to authorise, on the Holy Father's explicit instructions, the collection of monetary reserves from all nearby abbeys, priories and churches and ordered them to hold the funds for safekeeping in their vaults in the town to await further instructions, in preparation for a new crusade. The Toad wanted a bank full of money. He wanted enough for his master to be able to build that castle those wretched Jews had said they had wished to give him. The money the Upstart had been boasting about.

—∾—

Like wolves, French and Genoese war galleys prowled across a wide section of the Brabant coast, searching for fat prey. Ten vessels, four from Rouen and six belonging to Ayton Doria's Genoese, all packed with crossbowmen and men-at-arms maintaining vigilance, looking for easy pickings.

A fair breeze was rippling the surface - perfect conditions for the prey to risk the crossing. Admiral Hugh Quiéret preferred to say they were fishing and that the fish they sought were a steady stream of cogs, laden with wool and war supplies, heading out of Great Yarmouth for Antwerp and Dordrecht - each a prize worth having. The summer had been good to the Admiral, he reflected, as he scanned the horizon from his galley *St. Guillaume*.

As Simon de Pressi joined him on the deck, the Admiral looked with scepticism on this eager young man and wondered how good the Toad's pet lapdog really was. They had been arguing as to the usefulness of men-at-arms on navy vessels. The Toad did not favour them and felt that they were unsuitable for naval warfare. They were ideal as assault troops for raids, but at sea they only got in the way, consuming stores at a prodigious rate. Hugh, on the other hand, liked the presence of trained, armoured fighting marines.

'He has a point,' Simon tried to argue in his master's defence. 'For every hundred we need to provide a further supply vessel.'

'That's the accountant for you,' replied Quiéret caustically, 'always trying to save money.'

Simon nodded. He needed to ingratiate himself with Hugh Quiéret and pander to his soft spot. 'It amazes me how a man of such humble origins can curry so much favour.' He knew Quiéret was one of those who fervently believed in the superiority of the aristocracy, a fact he constantly rubbed in. 'I think that it's nothing to do with the money; he just won't have lordlings on his ships.' Quiéret guffawed - in Simon he was starting to find a man after his own heart.

Hugh was about to probe further when the masthead lookouts spotted the tops of masts tucked in behind Cadzand Island. If they were quick, they'd have the element of surprise. Within moments the oarsmen bent their backs to the task, while the men-at-arms donned armour and prepared their weapons. As they closed in, sure enough, there were five fine cogs, and they were the biggest they had ever encountered. These were a prize worth having.

'I'm still not convinced that these guns of yours will be of *any* use,' said the Admiral, 'Here's your chance to show me what they can do.'

Simon grinned; he was ready to show off his skill. He had mounted a pair of *pot-au-feus,* small calibre cast iron tubes about a yard long on a swivel which were capable of firing stone or lead balls, on the corners of the poop deck railings of the *St. Guillaume.* He'd invested much time persuading the Admiral that his new weapons were battle winners. He had spent a week casting his lead balls and had a keg full of them. He'd also been practising and could hit a floating target at two hundred paces.

As they rounded the headland, Hugh realised that, joy of joy, they'd caught the English napping; their sails were furled and they bobbed helplessly at anchor. 'We've got a pair of big ones. I'll be damned.'

As they closed in on the English ships, he knew they'd hit the jackpot. 'That's the *Cog Edward* and the tall one must be the *Christopher.*'

The *Edward* was the largest ship afloat and had cost the King of England £450 - it was one of those facts that all the French admirals knew - and they were low in the water, obviously still laden with victuals for the English army. Quiéret salivated at the thought of the riches and kudos to be had.

The approaching galleys caused panic on the English vessels. Men swarmed up from the hold, ready to repel boarders, and a rowing boat was lowered manned by three men desperately heading for the shore to get help.

The Admiral exhorted his men to pull with all their might; he was shouting and slapping the rail. They had to stop them. The French closed quickly on their victims. Simon, sensing an opportunity to show off his skills, loaded his guns with three balls in each as the *St. Guillaume* skimmed the flat waters of the bay, propelled by one hundred and twenty oarsmen.

When they had closed to within two hundred yards, Simon took careful aim and fired at the skiff. *I can do this!* His practice paid dividends; he got the trajectory just right, hitting the little craft amidships on the waterline. Running over to his other gun, he did it again, the balls bouncing over the water like skipping stones, finishing off the floundering vessel.

Distracted by the cogs, Quiéret had only been half watching. Now he was suitably amazed and impressed and congratulated Simon. 'You've booked your trip to Southampton.'

Simon was thrilled and bowed gracefully; he just hoped his new armour would be ready in time.

The men on the cogs put up a brave fight, but for nought. Having refused an offer to surrender and live, it took the rest of the day for the French to finally overwhelm the crew. The Admiral was furious - for this, the survivors would hang.

Chapter 22

A Grievous Loss

The English army was encamped near Antwerp and chaffing at the bit for action but King Edward was frustrated. His army was small and the Flemish contingent was ill-equipped and reluctant to join an untested force. For all his blandishments about the power of his archers on the battlefield, his principal ally, the Wise Brewer of Ghent, the Flemish Jacob van Artevelde, had been expecting plenty of knights if they were going to confront the French heavy cavalry.

It was his wife, Queen Philippa, who came up with a solution. 'My sister Margaret wrote the other day and says her husband is bored.'

Edward's ears pricked up. *Why hadn't I thought of him?* Margaret was only married to the most powerful man in Europe; 'Old Ludders', as his mother used to call him. The scary Ludwig - the Holy Roman Emperor.

The summer had been so busy and Edward had been over-generous with his pay chests. Now they were getting worryingly close to their bottoms. His Friend had written with a digest of the Northampton Parliament and he got some comfort that his subjects had bent to his wishes. He did not like the phrase that Sir Roger had used: it would take time for funds to flow. He needed funds now to buy a breathing space. The Earl of Salisbury was worried by a conversation he'd been having with the Margrave of Juliers, one of Edward's staunchest allies, and was the only one who had, to date, been paid even a part of what he had been promised.

'He thinks you should nip this in the bud.'

'Then we'll send him to arrange an interview with the Emperor,' Edward told the earl, 'and I want you to visit all our women and take their jewellery. We'll pawn it in Germany. Get the Great Crown and my full robes sent by barge. We'll ride ahead. We won't wait for a reply; we'll just turn up on his doorstep.'

—⁊⁊⁊—

Ludwig IV of Bavaria sat back, stroked his grizzled beard and read intently the letter that the Margrave had just delivered from Flanders. He had clawed his way up, battle by bloody battle, to become the principal power in Europe and had been for many years Holy Roman Emperor, holding sway over most of central Europe. There were a few thorns in his side, notably the Valois Viper in France and a belligerent Papacy, who had recently become more than usually prickly.

'What do you make of this?' He handed the letter to Baldwin, the Bishop of Triers and one of his closest friends and allies. 'I think the Pup has come to play.' A new piece had arrived on the chessboard of Europe; his young brother-in-law had arrived with a small army from England, intent on razzing up the French. Baldwin smiled: another player in the game of prosecuting the odious Viper was always to be applauded and supported.

'What does he want?'

'He wants to buy my army.' Ludwig's knights had been quiet of late. The Hapsburgs had long been put back into their box; the new Pope was a pain but ensconced out of reach, and it was true, he was getting bored. 'Let's test him out.'

'I hear he's short of money.' Baldwin's spies, too, had taken great interest in the goings-on at Antwerp. Triers was close. 'Still, I like the sound of him. Shake the tree and see where the apples fall...'

—⁊⁊⁊—

At dawn a week later, muffled in cloaks and laden with all the cash they could muster, Edward and Salisbury set out with a bodyguard of liveried archers for their make or break dash across Europe. Innkeepers were surprised by a personage as great as the King of England himself travelling without a magnificent retinue. Many were disbelieving and had to be mollified with a sizeable bag of silver before unceremoniously clearing their best rooms for so august a visitor. Half of the said bag of silver was then retrieved by the royal bodyguards with menaces and threats of arson shortly after the King had galloped away.

It took ten days of hard riding to reach Koblenz, where Edward found his brother-in-law the Emperor ensconced with the Imperial Diet in the Kastorkirche. To start with, the Emperor, he was told, would only speak German. To his great relief he also found an elderly English monk, William of Ockham, who could help with translations. Actually Ludwig was not unable to, but was loath to speak French. He could speak it quite fluently but proclaimed it to be the language of his enemies. 'Just a little game,' he told Baldwin later on. 'Tease the Pup, scratch at his skin, see what's underneath.'

The pious Ockham, the English King learnt, had been with the Emperor's court for ten years after the Papacy had moved to Avignon. Edward found him fascinating, reminiscent of Magister Frakenham. The subject that really caught his attention was the monk's view on the separation of the church from the state and his curious notion that people hankered for something called property rights. This was intriguing, before everything had been so clear cut in Edward's mind: he owned all the property. Why anyone else should want what belonged to him by divine right didn't make sense. A bell rang in his head over something his Friend had said in his letter about finding a compromise.

It was William's disarmingly honest approach to the divisions between the natural and spiritual worlds that appealed most, though the idea of Apostolic Poverty was a bridge too far; men had been burnt at the stake for less. Ockham found in the young English King a man whose heart was pure, and he could sympathise with his irritation at the negativity of the Papacy in denying his claim to the French throne.

Pleading poverty was not a line Edward was going to take; instead he determined to entertain magnificently, generosity abounding as if money had fallen like ripe fruit. The delighted Empress Margaret received two thousand four hundred florins, and Queen Philippa insisted he gave her secretary sixty florins as well. 'Make sure she knows it came from me', she had said when they'd bid farewell. A debt handsomely repaid.

He gave Ludwig six thousand pounds, which he received grumpily, waving it away dismissively. Edward was deflated; it was a bit like a beggar receiving a halfpenny when the sumptuousness of his clothing demanded a payment of at least a silver shilling for the good of his soul. He felt his mission was teetering. Self-doubt consumed him before Ockham found him again as he paced disconsolately round the cloisters. Ockham had good news: the Emperor was not angry, quite the opposite. He was suffering from an attack of gout, which had joyfully passed. He was most grateful for his gift and going to seal their official friendship with a singular honour: he would make his young brother-in-law Imperial Vicar-General of the Holy Roman Empire.

Thankfully, the barge with his robes and his crown had arrived. Edward, robed in scarlet and ermine, sat stony-faced on a throne at the Emperor's feet, feeling the weight of the Great Crown of England on his head. *Is this the last time I ever wear it?* He stared across at the Prince-Abbot of Mainz, to whom he had just pawned the crown, and wondered if he'd ever get it back. The Prince-Abbot produced a grin that spoke of malignancy, more a malevolent sneer than a smile of pleasure, and Edward knew he had been ensnared in a ploy within a plot - someone else's game, the rules of which he knew nothing. Baldwin had witnessed the transaction with horror; Edward had been sorely misadvised, but if Ludwig had his reason, so be it.

The ceremony began. 'I declare my cousin's wars to be our war. They are to defend the integrity of the Empire against the usurpations of France. Let all present know that any disobedience to him,' the Emperor pointed to Edward with the sceptre, 'is tantamount to treason.' *So far so good… now all I have to do is persuade them to get their army to Flanders.* And that would cost a lot more.

'You'll have the rest soon,' Edward had promised, relying on the next shipment of money and wool from England. It should be awaiting his return, delivered by the *Cog Edward*, when he got back to Antwerp…

—ɯ—

It was a pleasant enough trip back down the Rhine on Ludwig's royal barge, with the finest wines from the Moselle, fresh venison, fish and ducks, until it was spoilt by Mauney, who brought the grievous news of the loss of the *Edward* and the *Christopher*.

'Too late, we got there too late. I led a contingent of household archers to try and rescue the ships. From all accounts your sailors put up a good fight, but ran out of arrows,' he related details of the fighting. 'It lasted all day. We were just in time to watch that bastard Quiéret hang the survivors.' They knew it was he from his banners, which flew brazenly above the corpses. Walter had been shocked by the French Admiral's brutality and had tried to get to the stricken ships from Antwerp in a couple of old barges, but the tide had been against them. This had made the journey agonisingly slow, and they only arrived as the last of the prizes weighed anchor and was towed away by the jubilant French.

'Will *anything* go right?' The King went through his usual routine: towering rage followed by deep depression. 'We need galleys to fight, they've got fifty or more, I've only got four.'

'We picked up one survivor; you might be interested to hear what he has to say.'

A sailor was led into the King's presence. He dared not lift his head from the floor and Mauney had to haul him to his feet. 'We were rowing for shore to summon help when the skiff was hit by God's thunderbolt.' The poor man was quaking with fear.

The King rose. 'Take a deep breath and start again.'

'Like I said, your Majesty, I could see the French galley two bow-shot away when they come at us, then I saw a flash and a plume of white smoke and then a bang come from a stick on the poop deck. Next thing a sledgehammer smashed a hole in our waterline. It happened again shortly afterwards, it was the Devil's hand, Sire, it plucked off my friend's head and then we sank.'

Edward admired the sailor's clarity. 'What do you make of that, Mauney? They must be using guns.' The King knew that was what had happened, as he had several of these weapons in his armoury. 'Thank you.'

The shaking sailor was given a gold sovereign as he was ushered out of the royal presence.

What did de Bohun's letter say? He found the report and reread the passage. 'Last year a Frenchman visited our old tutor to discover the formula for gunpowder.' *So that's where the bastards got it.* It would be a good discipline to tighten up security against spies, and he told Mauney to increase the number of agents being sent into France. 'I want to know each time the Viper farts, and how smelly it is.'

Chapter 23

A Truly Egyptian Day

Whytethorne finished running through his agenda, ending with a warning that the roads would be busy. Sir Roger was by now only half paying attention. He nodded as if listening, but his brain was miles away. The problems caused by Sir Eustace remained uppermost in his thoughts, unresolved and rankling. He drank his breakfast wine, indulging in dunking a sop for good measure.

'Hope to stay at Winchester Castle tonight. I shall ask if Sir Hugh will help me sort out that bastard de Frage.' He hoped Sir Hugh de Lacey, who was Sheriff of Hampshire, would lend him a sympathetic ear.

Trouble started early. As he was mounting Theseus his stirrup strap broke, sending him onto his backside, into fresh dog shit. This required a change of clothes.

'I'll say a prayer to St. Eligius,' said Lady Alice, trying to be helpful. She held her nose between thumb and forefinger and gave it a tug, mimicking the tongs with which the Saint pulled on the devil.

'Well, it is an Egyptian Day,' added Master John, unhelpfully. 'I've been working on astrological charts and it shows Aries in conjunction with Mars - and that thunderstorm,' he shook his head, 'not good, not good at all. Portents have all been bad. A chick was born with four legs. Max gave it to me.' The tutor had paid a groat for it and laid it carefully on his table. *Turned my back for a second and the fucking cat grabbed it and ate it. Definitely a bad omen.* 'Sadly, Sire, it will last all week,' added Master John gloomily.

Whytethorne was right; the lane was clogged with cattle going to market.

Sir Roger felt his dander rise.

The highway, too, was blocked. A haywain had tipped over; its axel was shattered, its load strewn across the narrowest imaginable section and an inevitable snarl-up had developed. For some reason every farm in South England had decided to deliver all their wool at once. At least two hundred laden pack animals had bunched up to form an impenetrable plug. Tempers flared and a brawl erupted as angry drovers lashed stubborn animals and then each other.

Letting impatience get the better of him, the vein on his temple throbbing with irritation, Sir Roger drew his scimitar. His men did likewise as he ordered them to cut their way through.

Like Moses parting the Red Sea. Dan was impressed with speed at which cursing men parted. Mules, goaded on by sword points jabbed in backsides, brayed wildly and tried clambering up steep, bramble-covered slopes or slid, thrashing wildly, into the marsh on the other side. The lead muleteer dared complain and lost an earlobe for his troubles, neatly sliced off with a deft flick of Sir Roger's wrist.

'Woodworms are the scourge of humanity,' muttered Sir Roger darkly as they finally threaded their way past the worm-eaten wreck, leaving behind even worse chaos. 'It's the effects of the war, I suppose.'

Their destination, Winchester Castle, sprawled long and thin across the top of a ridge. It was surrounded by dilapidated walls that were, in places, reduced to the height of a man, with shrubs growing out of broken, ivy covered stonework. They entered the courtyard, which was dominated by the sheriff's suite in the Old Hall. Sir Roger admired its patterned brick and flint wall. He had wanted to copy it for Ipers but it would have been too expensive, so he had to make do with the much cheaper recycled Roman stone, which, in retrospect, had proved much better.

Uniformed men-at-arms at his side, he barged into the administration building, pushing aside all and sundry. Inside, porters were unpacking boxes filled with sheets of vellum while lines of clerks and scribes were busy writing up rolls, recording transactions, registering deeds, wills, land claims and fines. As it was nearing close of business, tempers were beginning to flare as jostling citizens of all classes strove to reach harassed bureaucrats.

'Make way,' bellowed the Ox in a voice that wags said could be heard two counties away. After a few initial complaints, the crowd hushed and parted deferentially for the Banneret, all recognising him as their superior.

'Where's Sir Hugh?' he demanded.

'He's away on important business and won't be back for several days,' said the Under-Sheriff, sporting a vivid black eye, sitting in his place. He listened impatiently as Sir Roger recounted the tale of Sir Eustace.

'I want him declared an outlaw, and I'm willing to put up a reward.'

'I'm sorry, you've not given me enough evidence,' the Under-Sheriff said dismissively.

'What more do you need?' Sir Roger's patience was wearing thin with this surly individual. 'I've a good man in his grave. I can't let this crime go unpunished.'

'That's as may be, but you've got no proof that he was the murderer. I can't issue a warrant. It sounds to me,' he scratched at a straggly beard, 'that Sir Eustace has a better claim against *you* for assault and killing his horse.'

Sir Roger spluttered with fury.

'Where is there any proof that Sir Eustace intended to do you harm?' The conversation took a nastier turn. 'I think you're making all this up to avoid paying your Wool Levy. Your bloody bailiff gave me this,' he said, pointing to his shiner. 'He assaulted me.'

Sir Roger hated grovelling, but the man had a point, so he apologised. *Trouble follows Handley wherever he goes.* He signalled to Whytethorne to hand over most of his cash, from which the Under-Sheriff took a generous cut. 'As damages,' he said when Sir Roger complained. The presence of half a dozen of the Under-Sheriff's henchmen and a sniggering crowd dissuaded him from making further protestations.

'You still owe seven pounds,' said the clerk as he wrote out a receipt.

Ouch. Sir Roger felt humiliated. Having hoped to spend a convivial evening with Sir Hugh, all he could hear was laughter at his expense. The temptation to slit some gizzards was almost overwhelming. Not wishing to cap off his day by being declared an outlaw as well, he led his troop off at a gallop over the rolling hills towards Southampton. *This is indeed a bloody Egyptian bloody day - yesterday everything seemed so rosy, my prospects good. Now that blasted de Frage is roaming the countryside Scot-free, out for revenge, my reeve is dead, my mill burnt and I've still got to make good my tax bill.* By nature, Sir Roger was not overly superstitious, but was compelled to think the worst. Perhaps his enemy was working magic against him. This he feared as any man would. *Beelzebub has many acolytes.*

They had ridden hard but only made it to the Common before the curfew bell sounded. Justin reported that they'd shut the gates. 'They've got strict instructions not to open them to anyone - when I told them who you were, they said not even you.' *I bet that Eccles has something to do with it.* After what he'd done to the poor man, he wasn't surprised.

'In that case we shall go to St. Deny's Priory.' Sir Roger decided. 'It's only a couple of miles outside town. The Prior is a friend of mine.' If he were lucky he would get a monk's cell for the night, though his men would have to sleep in the stables with the horses. It took five minutes of banging on the door to be let in. An irritated monk was about to complain but, on seeing the nature and number of the party, thought better of it and scurried off to find Prior Framlington.

Wreathed in smiles and making his unannounced guests most welcome, the Prior led them through gloomy cloisters by guttering candle light. A kindly man with a twinkle in his eye, he was spiritual councillor and father confessor rolled into one.

'So how are you?' the aged Framlington enquired, his bon-homie engendered by the hope that one day soon Sir Roger would endow a chantry.

'Dreadful, I feel cursed. I think a sorcerer works magic against me,' opined Sir Roger, unburdening himself of his woes to Hugh the Prior over a supper of coarse brown bread and thin gruel. *Hugh's a good man,* he thought. *He eschews the trappings of wealth that most clerics now flaunt.* Money was corrupting the Church.

'Don't worry. We can fight the demon. You'll need an amulet,' the old man instructed. 'We'll start with a Paternoster charm, Christ the Alpha and Omega.' He took a scrap of parchment and wrote a magic formula:

$$
\begin{array}{l}
\text{S A T O R} \\
\text{A R E P O} \\
\text{T E N E T} \\
\text{O P E R A} \\
\text{R O T A S}
\end{array}
$$

'You must hide this under your right foot - it will silence your enemies. Follow the path of divine St. Augustine. Believe the doctrine of Original Sin and the necessity of Divine Grace - then you'll be saved.'

'I fear the fires of Hell. They seem perilously close.' Sir Roger could not be so sure about his faith. 'I suppose that's what keeps me from straying too far from the path of righteousness.' *And the amounts I pay for you monks to pray for me.* Together they explored the subject of sin a little further. *I have the blood of innocent souls staining my heart.* He was on the point of confessing his most perfidious deed. 'I suffer from the Sin of Lust. I cannot help myself,' he admitted half-heartedly, unable to bring himself to divulge his terrible crime.

'You must be careful or you'll spend eternity immersed up to your neck in ice. That will be your punishment in Hell,' the Prior told him. As they talked long into the night Hugh would not give him comfort; it was not his style.

'What's a man's life worth?' asked Sir Roger, still vexed by his recent dealings with his Sergeant.

'You cannot put a value on life, Jesus says…'

'Let me rephrase the question.' Sir Roger interrupted. 'If one man is indebted to another for his life, saved, say, in the heat of battle, what obligation does that engender?'

Prior Hugh thought for a moment. There was only one example that came to his mind. 'Remember the Great Alexander?'

Sir Roger nodded. *Of course I do.* He loved tales of Alexander. 'My favourite story is the one about the gems that were owned by demons and his barons have sticks and stones thrown at them, but then Alexander uses them to enchant his mechanical monster army so he can become invisible and fly over the enemy.'

Prior Hugh smiled indulgently at the childlike telling of the tale. *I prefer Aristotle's version of events* - but that was not his point. 'Alexander's life was saved by his friend. If I remember rightly, he chopped off the arm of a foe about to slay his master. Alexander couldn't bear being beholden to anyone - after all, he was king and his friend his subject. So he found fault with his friend, provoking an argument and, in a fit of rage, slew him.' He added, looking deep into the knight's eyes: 'Remember, my son, Alexander was a heathen and I am *sure* he roasts in the netherworld for his sin.'

Sir Roger found the similarity alarming. The message was clear: follow Alexander's example and hellfire awaits. *But then again, that fate probably waits for me anyway.*

Sitting on the edge of the stone shelf covered with a simple straw pallet, he had to fight hard to prevent himself from running into the cloister and shouting out his confession for all to hear. He lay down on the hard mattress, covering himself with a thin blanket, and shivered inwardly, imagining torments as the light from his candle flickered and cast phantasmagorical figures on the ceiling's rough plastering. He thought on Prior Framlington's story. *I can't kill my Sergeant in cold blood.* But the feeling of indebtedness was becoming more onerous.

'Can you do me a favour?' asked the Prior next morning, after Sir Roger had attended Mass and taken Communion. 'We've been instructed by the Pope to remit half our reserve funds to the Peruzzi Bank for collection and shipping to Avignon. It's a lot of money and you could deliver it safely.'

It had been a surprising request, quite unusual, but even on detailed examination the Papal seals were definitely real, identical to ones they had in their library. The Prior had been suspicious but concluded they were all in order. Cardinal Alberghini's letter spoke vaguely of a financial crisis, an earthquake that had destroyed one of Christendom's most sacred shrines, and that funds were needed for a new crusade to fight heathens. The need was great because all these problems had come up together.

'It must be bad if the letter comes directly from the Papal See. It says our bishops are fully aware of the position and urge our speedy compliance,' the Prior continued. 'It's not for me to question, but something is not quite right, I just can't put my finger on it.'

The Prior entrusted a sizeable chest of money for delivery to the Peruzzi Bank, which was substantial and fortress-like, with arrow slits in an otherwise blank wall flanking a door made mostly of iron. Unlike the other houses in the street, where the upper floors were timber-framed this building was solid stone - even the windows on the upper floors were covered with iron grills. Sir Roger noticed a wreath of fresh flowers tied with red ribbon nailed firmly in its centre. He rang the bell and waited as bolts and bars were withdrawn.

'Put it there,' said a suave Italian, pointing to an empty space in the underground vault that contained a strong room full of chests, deeds and other valuables. Like all those engaged in his profession, he was richly dressed, sweat staining his fur collar. 'I've been told to await instructions about shipment.' The Florentines owned the largest banking group in the world, with branches as far afield as the Levant, Cyprus and Alexandria.

Sir Roger also kept most of his money there. The banker went over to an iron-bound box with his name on it. Opening the lid, he could see that the various leather bags hardly covered the bottom. *Not much, easy come, easy go - my new fortune is all but spent.* But, looking on the bright side, he now had a castle and had invested in many thousands of sheep that would yield a handsome income. He examined his ledger and made a perfunctory count of bags, taking one for immediate expenses before closing the lid. *I need to buy a suitable gift for Lady Elizabeth if I'm to win her favours.* He also knew it would be wise to pay the rest of his tax.

'I'll arrange for Whytethorne to collect it soon,' he said, referring to his box. 'It's just as safe here as at Ipers.' The bank might not have a moat like his castle, but would take more than a log to batter through its stout doors.

'Built to withstand a hard knocking. The walls are a yard thick. Will you stay for some wine?' the Italian offered, but Sir Roger declined.

'I must find Master Eccles,' he said, keen to proceed with business. The merchant owed him an explanation. He dismissed his troop. The men were relieved; the thought of hanging around had little appeal in a town filled with alehouses. 'And see that you don't get into any trouble.' He knew his parting words would be in vain, for men-at-arms with time on their hands and money in their purses could only lead to trouble.

'Angel Inn, mid-afternoon,' he said. It was one of their favourite drinking holes. 'You two, with me,' he ordered, picking a couple of his men-at-arms at random. His status demanded at least two bodyguards and Sir Roger hated being pestered by beggars. Crossing the street to Eccles's emporium, which was opposite the bank, he established that the merchant would most likely be at the Weigh House.

Accepting the offer from Eccles's factotum to rub down and stable his horse he set off to climb the walls. He was mindful that the King had ordered him to make an assessment of Southampton's defences and see how well the docks were defended.

He was appalled.

The Barbican was a sink of corruption in a sorry state of repair– masonry crumbling, metalwork nearly rusted away, walls dripping with slime, corners stinking of piss and shit. Its primary occupants were rats and whores who propositioned sailors from the doorways of flimsy booths. Trade was brisk as drunken men copulated flagrantly against mildewed brickwork. A sergeant and five ill-equipped soldiers guarded God's Tower, which was the main gate from the waterfront. They snapped reluctantly to attention when Sir Roger announced him- self and his intentions, asking them what they would do if they were attacked.

'Run away,' answered a toothless soldier. The sergeant looked embarrassed, but it was true. But then, no one had *ever* attacked the town. Climbing to the top of the gatehouse, Sir Roger could see gaps in the walls.

'We put barricades across them at night,' said the Sergeant, but Sir Roger was no longer listening - he had heard enough. *Eccles is right - town's as vulnerable as a lamb before a wolf's jaws.* The docks were bustling with activity, their whole length crammed with merchantmen being unloaded. The sergeant knew each vessel.

'Spaniards, Gascons and that one,' he pointed at a brightly painted Mediterranean galley, 'is a Venetian spice runner - don't get many of them here.'

Intrigued, Sir Roger decided to take a closer look. He did not reach the vessel before Eccles spotted him as he passed the door of the Weigh House.

'De Bohun, is that you?' The merchant was still wary after their last meeting.

'Just the man I've come to see.' Delighted to have found him so soon, Sir Roger shook his hand vigorously. Remembering the token in his boot, he felt that it was fate that had led him to spend the night at the Priory. His soul felt cleansed, so he refrained from mentioning the incident at the gate the previous night.

'Looking at what passes for our walls?' asked Eccles.

'Is that *them*?" Sir Roger said sarcastically, pointing at a stack of wooden palisades.

'Yes, they get put in gaps at night and they're bunged there in the day. Useless, one push and they'll fall over.' It was obviously Eccles's pet subject. 'It's hopeless,' he added, 'I keep telling the Council but they say proper walls would mean we can't get goods straight off ships into warehouses. We'd have to go through *that* gate,' he pointed to God's Tower, complaining that it was always blocked up with riffraff, alluding to the drunken sailors who occupied the hospice. 'You must be thirsty, come up to my house.'

They threaded their way through the crowds on French Street, a wide thoroughfare with rows of multi-coloured, timber-framed houses.

'Everyone must be making a great deal of money,' observed Sir Roger, comparing it against the filthy, shabby warren of narrow streets in Northampton. Though Southampton had its poorer houses, here they had wide frontages with little alleyways running to long gardens behind. Upper floors protruded over pavements, giving shelter from rain and from night soil tossed out by slovenly maids too lazy to wait for rounds of the dung carts. Though there was little evidence of that on the main thoroughfare, the town fathers, he had heard, were strict on trying to enforce their ordinances. Sir Roger glanced up at the signs denoting the occupations of tradesmen that hung from the eaves of their houses: barrels for wine merchants, boots for cobblers.

'Looking for anything in particular?' asked Eccles.

'I want a gift for a lady,' he said, peering into shadowy side streets where a mass of small artisan's houses stood either side of alleys no wider than a handcart, upper storeys practically touching. Eccles saw a familiar movement out of the corner of his eye.

'Watch out!' He tried to dodge, but was too late. A squealing pig shot out from the alley, chased by a pack of unruly boys, knocking the merchant over into a pile of rotting cabbage leaves. 'Ruddy urchins!' He shook his fist in rage at the disappearing gang. 'There's just no regard for Ordinances any more. They're supposed to sweep all the streets.' Grumbling, he brushed the clinging garbage off his fur-trimmed coat, and he continued muttering under his breath all the way to his house.

'Strong stone footings,' he said, giving his stonework a proprietorial and cathartic kick. His house was detached, standing alone on a double-sized plot of land, with three floors. It was one of the grandest in the street and had an extensive orchard at the back. Eccles led Sir Roger down into a vaulted cellar, where rows of barrels contained olive oil and wine.

'Try this,' he said, offering his guest a Venetian glass beaker of wine before pouring one for himself. It had a rich, fruity bouquet. 'To making good business,' he proffered a toast.

'This is excellent wine. I'll take three barrels,' said Sir Roger, in ebullient mood, his troubles of yesterday forgotten.

Chapter 24

The Imp from Hell

The merchant was quite surprised by Sir Roger's request as they walked back towards the docks. Wine, *yes*, provender, spices, that sort of thing, *yes*, but perfume…

'Yes. Where can I buy perfume?' The knight had made up his mind. He wanted to woo Lady Elizabeth with a bottle of Attar of Roses. Eccles knew just the place, Johannes the Apothecary - a fellow of wholly unknown origins. To some he was Bohemian, to others Spanish, though Eccles suspected he was a Jew. They set off at a brisk pace through a maze of alleyways that soon had Sir Roger completely lost. Their destination was a tiny shop in an unnamed alley. It had a wall filled from floor to ceiling with rows of jars, flagons and flasks of every conceivable shape and size. It had a welcoming aroma quite unlike the street outside, whose stench was overwhelmingly of sewage tinged with rotten fish.

The apothecary was a wizened little scroat dressed in black who looked Sir Roger up and down. 'Sire requires a love potion; he wishes to seduce a lady of virtue,' he said, in an accent that could have been from anywhere but here.

Sir Roger nodded. *Indeed I want to seduce a lady, though I believe this one has little virtue.* He looked down on to the top of the apothecary's bald pate - it came up to the middle of Sir Roger's chest.

'And what would his lordship like to achieve with this perfume?' he asked as Sir Roger thought for a moment.

He wanted to say that he desired to create thoughts of willing wantonness. However, Prior Framlington's admonishments were still ringing in his ears. *For the sin of lust you will be immersed up to your neck in ice.*

The perfumer understood the silence implicitly. A tongue-tied client invariably had wicked intentions toward a member of the fair sex. Immediately, he started flitting around rows of containers like a caged bird as he filled a delicate glass bottle with a few drops of pink liquid, followed by a dash of this and a pinch of that, while all the while waving his arms, uttering strange words and singing tuneless incantations. *Definitely a Jew.*

'Have a sniff.' He proffered the unstoppered bottle to Sir Roger. 'This is guaranteed to make even the heart of an ice-maiden melt.'

It had a sweet, musky fragrance, reminiscent of the scent of fresh flowers combined with newly mown hay and morning dew. The apothecary stoppered the bottle with a cork, sealing it carefully with wax.

'That will be five shillings,' he said. *Another fool parted from his money,* he thought as he happily handed over five pence worth of rose water and lavender oil in a sixpenny bottle.

'I've got someone you ought to meet,' said Eccles as they walked into the sunshine. They passed the Angel Inn. It was filled with foreign sailors.

'Venetians,' ventured Eccles, 'rowers from the spice runner.' Sir Roger thought he spotted his green boar rampant motif on some of the men and waved. *Having a drinking contest with my men, if I am not mistaken.*

Entering the Weigh House, which was the port's commercial hub for administration of trade, it took a few moments for his eyes to adjust to the shadow. Eccles pointed to an immense beam, which was delicately pivoted with considerable precision and was being used to weigh goods. Puffing his chest out, he boasted that it was one of the marvels of his fair town. Sir Roger was impressed; it must have come from a massive tree. He could see lines of clerks on high stools writing up ledgers by the light of flickering oil lamps.

In the central hall customs officials were arguing with a heavy-set sea captain who was shouting in a variety of languages. 'Be careful with them, don't you fools appreciate how *delicate* glass is?' he shouted in mangled French.

Eccles inspected an opened crate full of elegant glassware. 'A new piss bottle?' he said, turning a green vessel with a long thin neck, a wide end and bulbous bottom between his fingers. 'I like the gilding on this one,' he observed, holding it up to a weak light that came through shaved horn windows. 'I bet it's expensive, though.' Some bottles were decorated with gold fig leaves. Others were plainer and cheaper.

'Need a bigger end to fit my sausage,' proclaimed Sir Roger, loudly enough to turn heads. Still tipsy from Eccles's wine, he made a mental note to purchase one. It was fashionable to use these at night so the servants could then collect the urine and sell it to tanners for curing leather. Eccles guided Sir Roger over to a Venetian captain with a fulsome brindled beard who was wearing rugged mariner's boots. He had an air of menace that served him well when dealing with difficult customs officials.

'Why can't I buy thirty sacks of wool?' He was gesticulating wildly. 'What do you mean, there's an embargo on selling wool?' He was mimicking the official's squeaky voice. 'Pah! I haven't come this far to be fobbed off with barrels of stale herring.' Nor was he about to let his real business become common knowledge, *especially when there is good money to be made out of the English*. 'You can keep your stinky fish.' He threw his hands up in disgust and turned away. 'Make them see sense.' He put his arm round Eccles's shoulder. 'Sorry, my friend, it is harder to earn a living these days. Your country only produces wool; there is, how you say, bugger all else to fill my holds for the return journey.' He shrugged as he continued his charade. 'At least herrings are cheap.'

The merchant had met Captain Bandolini at the Peruzzis on a previous evening and was keen to acquire as much of his cargo as he could, but like all canny merchants, he was looking for a better price.

'Would you like to see my ship?' The Venetian took a long look at Sir Roger, eyeing him up like a tailor measuring for a new suit. 'You look like a fighting man, *si*?'

Sir Roger smiled and nodded and left it at that. It became obvious that he was a martial man of considerable status when his bodyguards, who had been lounging in the sun, snapped to attention and closed in behind them.

'He's in charge of our coastal defence,' said Eccles helpfully.

'*Ah. Si. Commandatore.*' The captain bowed deferentially.

Sir Roger was fascinated by the long, sleek vessel that was built for speed above all else. He had never been on board a Venetian Galley, or any other galley. Whenever he'd crossed the Channel, it had always been on a cog, which always made him seasick.

'Her name is the *Il Rondone*,' announced Bandolini. He wanted to say that it was named after the bird and was 'the Swift' by name and by nature, skimming the waves at speed, but his command of languages, at which he was adept, did not stretch that far. She rode high in the water; her central hold was empty and ready to be filled with barrels of fish or whatever cargo could be negotiated. A row of beechwood oars were laid on each side with benches for two rowers on each oar, and a single central mast carried a rolled up triangular lateen sail. She had only a small defensive structure either side of her mast. The brightly painted stern had a superstructure housing captain's quarters and cookhouse. Canvas awnings stretched across benches, shading them from sun. Otherwise, Sir Roger could see no accommodation for crew.

'Where do they sleep?'

'In hammocks, like all sailors, see.' He pointed to a series of hooks above the benches. 'They go across here. These ships are all right for our home waters - it's warmer there. Here we get cold. I had to pay double for a Channel crew.'

In the cabin stood a rack of crossbows, other weaponry and half a dozen pavisses, big rectangular shields all painted with the Lion of St. Mark. 'In case we get attack by pirates,' explained Bandolini.

A few of the crew were lounging about, playing dice, but generally there was little activity. *Most*, thought Sir Roger, *are probably enjoying whores in the barbican.* In the comfort and secrecy of the aft cabin Sir Roger seized the opportunity to proffer a way he could make the Venetian's trip worthwhile.

'I've lots of wool I could sell,' ventured Sir Roger, giving Eccles a conspiratorial wink. 'Good grade too.'

Bandolini's eyes lit up.

'I can't bring it here - too many prying eyes. You'll have to take your ship up the coast. Round the headland there's a beach, you'll see some fishermen's huts. I'll bring my wool there, it's out of the way.' His tone was conspiratorial. He was conscious of edicts and Southampton's zealous customs men.

'How much wool can you sell me?' *My prayers are answered;* Bandolini made the sign of the Cross on his chest before clasping a surprised Sir Roger in a bear hug.

'I could get five... maybe six wagonloads by next week, all from Hampshire and Wiltshire sheep.' He made a quick calculation; three sacks of 250 fleeces per wagon and £8 per sack would make at least £120. Even though Handley had probably doctored the lot, it would go a long way towards replenishing depleted funds. He had to admit his Bailiff *might* have done him a favour. Bandolini offered four ducats per sack, with a Venetian Ducat worth roughly the same as an English Pound.

'Not enough for the risks involved.' Sir Roger looked for support from Eccles, wanting Nottingham prices. These were the most recently agreed in the trade.

Eccles nodded, happy to confirm that it was good grade wool. *After all, his castle is a major consumer of my provender, so I'll go along with him and play pass the parcel.*

'It has a nice firm fibre, not as good as Cotswold but much better than East Anglia.'

Bandolini understood. It was something to do with the length, softness and strength of the filaments.

They bargained back and forth, eventually settling on seven ducats. With a shortage of good English wool inexorably spreading across Europe from the embargo, Bandolini knew he'd make a handsome profit, whatever grade it was.

'I also have five tons of soda ash for making soap, but I don't know if you lot,' said Sir Roger, referring to Venetians, 'wash.'

'We do wash from time to time. Is it pure?' asked Bandolini, eyes lighting up.

Sir Roger nodded.

'I'll buy that too. We use it to make glass.'

They would make the final arrangements for the transaction later. Sir Roger indicated to Eccles that he had other things to discuss with him. 'Can I trust him?' he asked, once they were alone.

'No.' Eccles was curiously emphatic. 'There's something very odd going on.' He had wondered why the Venetian had come at all. 'He wasn't carrying much cargo. For one of these ships to make a profitable trip to England, they have to be full. His hold was almost empty other than the glass and that decent wine. The rest looked like someone else's rejects. He's taking too much interest in the castle, and has been seen walking the walls. He's thick with the Peruzzis, but I suppose he would be, being Italian. Let's walk a bit, I've something else to show you.'

As they ambled back through the streets Eccles pointed out the properties owned by foreign merchants. 'What do you notice about them?'

'Nothing much.'

'Look on the doors.' Each had a wreath of fresh flowers nailed in the centre of the door, similar to the one he had seen earlier on the Peruzzi Bank. 'He arrives and suddenly they've all put up garlands. I've never seen *that* before. It's probably nothing. They say they've had an instruction from a Cardinal, on the Pope's authority to celebrate some girl's martyrdom - hacked to death by heathen Saracens. She was supposedly a Florentine. They've been told to leave them there for a month. Apparently it will ward off evil spirits and bring them prosperity.' Eccles had a sinking feeling - *as if they're being marked out for life or death, like the Israelites at the time of Moses.*

Their walk took them up a wide boulevard that ran from the docks to an ancient stone gatehouse with a solid oak gate and iron portcullis. This was the entrance to the Castle, which was King Edward's principal storehouse and sited on a small hill at the northern end of town. It consisted of a twenty-foot-high curtain wall surrounding an old round bailey and dominated the mass of narrow, poorer streets that followed the curve of its walls - no gardens here. Passing through the gate, they entered the courtyard of a fortified warehouse guarded by twenty soldiers.

'Where's the Mayor?' Eccles asked the duty sergeant, who waved vaguely in the direction of the bailey. They found him in animated discussion with the town's chief tax inspector.

'I hope we're not interrupting?' ventured Eccles, who knew something on the subject about which they spoke. The two men turned, rapidly changing topic.

'The King's ship, *La Nicholas,* is due soon,' announced the Mayor. 'It's already two weeks late. I hope Hawthorne is all right.'

The men nodded. Like themselves Hawthorne was a leading merchant of the town. The Mayor knew Sir Roger and introduced him to the Tax Collector.

'Sir Roger has the place at Ipers. Do you know it?'

They all did. His tower was clearly visible on the other side of Southampton Water.

'A tax inspector. You must be *very* busy at the moment.'

The other man nodded. He had shifty eyes, always darting around, never fixing on anything for long.

'I've been instructed to review your defences,' Sir Roger informed them curtly. 'They *really* need attention, and I *suggest* you recruit at least fifty more soldiers as soon as possible.'

There was an awkward silence - soldiers were hard to come by at short notice. They also needed arming and training, all of which cost money.

'Until then, we're supposed to rely on *your* troops,' replied the Mayor lamely.

'My chief concern,' Sir Roger went on, 'is the barricades by the docks. I'm going to recommend that you apply for funds to build walls immediately.' He was about to comment on the Barbican when the King's Bailiff arrived, ordering porters to put sacks of cloves into the Spice Store. The harassed official touched the peak of his cap while shouting at a stream of porters lugging sacks of spices.

'Over there - how many times do I have to tell you? Put cloves next to ginger, not saffron, it taints it. Sorry about that.' The Bailiff came over and joined the conversation.

'We were talking about Captain Hawthorne. He should be back from Bordeaux already.' The Mayor crossed himself. 'He's a canny operator - I hope he's all right.' He returned to the business at hand. 'What should we do?' he asked obsequiously. *Ah, the knight with a fortune.*

'I've been reconnoitring your walls,' Sir Roger answered blandly, knowing it would take months or even years of negotiations to get any decision about revamping Southampton's defences. 'You fall into my bailiwick for coastal defence, but I'm short of men.' He had lost too many at Dunbar. Almost as an afterthought he added: 'What do you know about the Venetian?'

'Something to do with the Pope,' replied the Mayor. That answer surprised them all. 'I'm told that he delivered a bundle of documents bearing Papal seals to the Peruzzis and to the local abbeys and monasteries. His manifests confirm that he's come direct from Marseilles. I suppose he's on Papal business - but he's not flying his flag.'

Sir Roger digested this information. *Framlington's letters came from the Pope - the Venetian must have been the carrier.*

'I'm going to buy as much land as I can afford and build another row of houses,' said Eccles as they strolled back from the castle. 'I'm going to build a new street.'

They passed through an area alive with breweries, stables and smithies built against the town wall; blacksmiths were hammering out ploughshares, making nails and other useful items. Next they descended into a quiet square in which stood St. Michael's church.

'It's the oldest in town - built by the Normans,' said Eccles proprietorially. 'I worship here.'

'Charity, good sir knight.' A high-pitched, whiney female voice startled Sir Roger, who couldn't see anyone trying to attract his attention. The passers-by took no notice and seemed intent on going about their business. Again the pleading voice: 'Please, some charity and I'll pray for your soul.'

Eccles pointed to a wooden cell attached to the church's wall. 'It's our anchorite. She's quite mad. She's been living in that shack for over five years now.'

Sir Roger rummaged in his purse and handed a couple of worthless coins through a crack in the door.

'Bless you. Give me your hand.'

Religious hermits had to be obeyed. Sticking his hand in, he felt his palm being stroked. The stench was awful. The hidden voice, now quite surprising for its tunefulness, began uttering a mystical prediction. 'You will meet a devil, but be not afraid, this will protect you.' The anchorite placed a tatty token of indeterminate origin in his hand that looked remarkably similar to the one he kept in his helmet.

'I'm fated to meet devils,' he muttered as he turned it over, putting it into his purse.

Eccles's premises were a hive of activity; several girls were unpacking Venetian glass. The room smelt headily of wine and spice.

'Everything for gentlemen's larders, I hold the town monopoly for olive oil,' he was proud to announce. 'May I introduce my wife, Mistress Beatrice?' Eccles presented a plump, expensively dressed woman.

'A great honour.' She gave a little curtsy, as if Sir Roger were royalty.

Eccles's hall was richly decorated with tapestries and a couple of fine painted cupboards.

'So, have you worked out the de Bohun's account?' Eccles asked his clerk.

He nodded and handed an itemised list to his master. 'You owe me five pounds. Don't worry - your credit is good. Pay me when you get cash from the Venetian.'

In Eccles' bureau behind the hall there was a sizeable iron-bound chest that attested to his wealth. Sir Roger watched with interest as he opened it with a large key and ostentatiously placed a bag of money in it. It was full. On the table lay bundles of parchments and scrolls with red wax seals.

A horn inkwell stood next to a carved wooden tally board. A pewter mug held tally sticks bearing names that recorded debts and transactions. Eccles notched a new stick with five cuts and split it in two, giving half to the knight. He wrote Sir Roger's name on his half and put it in the pot. Appetising smells wafted in from the kitchen at the side of the house. Several crones sunned themselves in the yard, one of whom Eccles introduced as his mother.

'So *you* are the rich knight from up the road,' she observed. 'My son talks a lot about you.'

Eccles winced. 'I must apologise for my mother, age has robbed her of her mind and her manners.'

The family and servants assembled in the hall for lunch. Eccles fussed about the placement of his noble guest and proudly sat him next to his daughter Mary, a vivacious eighteen-year-old who spent the meal in uncontrollable giggles as Sir Roger told her outrageous stories. They admired a pair of gold candlesticks encrusted with semi-precious stones and intricate enamels.

'My father says they come from the Kingdom of Rus. Do you know where that is?'

'No. It's somewhere in the East, far away.' His friend, Eguerand had mentioned the place, said the inhabitants were horribly violent.

Eccles watched as they admired the sticks.

'Aren't they lovely, cost me a great deal. They're for sale if you want them.'

Mary was rubbing her fingers up and down one in a suggestive manner.

'Do you ... Sir Roger?' asked Mary coquettishly.

—⚭—

His men were still at the inn. Sir Roger ducked low to enter the noisy tavern. Dan was cavorting on a table with what looked like a short, very ugly, woman with long arms. Sir Roger was horrified. Dan was dancing with a devil's imp. At this point it emitted a loud shriek. Dan handed the creature a biscuit, which it ate greedily.

'*What* in the name of Heaven and all the Saints is that?'

'I bought it from the Venetians.'

'But what is it?' He'd never seen so repellent a creature. 'Is it a dog or a devil?' *The anchorite was right!*

'She's called Zuzu. She's an ape from the Barbary Coast.' Dan puckered his lips and the ape did likewise. 'She loves me.'

The other members of the troop were weeping with laughter. Dan sat down and Zuzu combed his hair with leathery fingers, looking for lice. She wore a tatty skirt around her middle and had a leather collar to which was attached a stout chain.

Sir Roger was revolted. 'How much did you pay for that thing?'

Dan looked around 'All my money, and theirs,' he waved at the troop. 'She's our new mascot.'

Sir Roger's heart fell, but he took it in good humour. If they wanted to squander their pay on this imp from Hell, so be it. At least they weren't drunk. Collecting their horses, they rode back down to the docks, the ape sitting behind Dan. When Bandolini saw them approach he crossed himself and spat.

'So you bought that *thing*.' Bandolini said vehemently.

Zuzu snarled displaying long yellow fangs. Bandolini told Sir Roger his crew had acquired it at a water stop at Cadiz after they had passed through the Pillars of Hercules. 'It bites.' This he knew from bitter experience.

Wary from what Eccles had told him, Sir Roger and the Venetian settled down to negotiate. It was interesting how the captain continually slipped in questions about the levy and beacons. Sir Roger probed as to where he was going next and when.

'Home.' Bandolini was unequivocal. 'Straight across the Bay of Biscay, and soon, before the stormy season.'

'I'll meet you on Thursday at the beach.' The small fishing hamlet of Lepe would be ideal. 'I want half the money up front, please.'

'Half? That's too much.' Bandolini was cautious. 'Anyway, how can I be certain you'll be there?'

Sir Roger assumed his honest face. 'You can trust me. Am I not a Christian knight? I'll be there. Eccles can vouch for me. I'm not hard to find.' He pointed at the tower of his new castle, clearly visible in the distance. 'And also I'm the district's military commander,' he said authoritatively.

A man with unlimited power is not someone to cross, Captain Bandolini decided.

'I'll give you a third now.'

This was acceptable.

'Wait here. I'll get your money.' Bandolini disappeared into the galley and returned with a leather bag full of gold ducats.

Sir Roger ruefully wished the coins had been silver, as there was an acute shortage of silver coinage in England. *But I shouldn't look a gift horse in the mouth.* The two men shook hands. He was whistling to himself. His luck had changed - he had had an excellent day. On the ride home, his mind turned to Lady Elizabeth. There was a ruined chapel near the beach that would make an ideal spot for an assignation.

The next couple of days passed quickly. A long hunt yielded a couple of fallow deer and a small boar. Hawking produced some spectacular kills, with Ariel, his other peregrine, taking a crane. The rest of the time was spent practising the arts of war, target jousting and swordplay. Despite an extensive search, Gwyn reported no trace of Sir Eustace. It was as if the earth had swallowed him up.

Sir Roger set himself a rigorous regime, vaulting on and off his steed wearing his *gambeson,* a heavy mail *hauberk* and a coat of plates. He'd seen Mauney do a somersault similarly attired, but that trick was beyond him. His new helmet, a *bascinet,* had a pig-faced visor and fitted the shape of his head and had more mail to protect his neck and shoulders. He'd got this from Spens's squire at Dunbar. *Poor old Spens.* He remembered Agnes's love arrow. *The ostrich feathers will have to wait.*

The weather was unusually hot for the end of September. Exhausted and sweaty, he drank copiously, ordering a page to sort out and prepare his bath. *I see Lady Elizabeth is admiring me from the battlements,* he noted with happy arrogance as he gave her a coy wave. *I think I'll make my move.* In the tub he imagined being inside her. *I'll have to separate her from her companions.*

This did not prove difficult. After a cursory inspection of his damaged mill, he had found her walking alone near the stream. Sidling silently up behind her he slipped his hand around her waist, making her start. She giggled flirtatiously. He found her violet coloured eyes irresistible. Drawing her close he kissed her deeply, she responding with equal fervour. They broke apart, fearing prying eyes.

'I'm making a delivery of wool to the beach tomorrow.' He told her of his plan. 'I'll meet you at the derelict chapel.' He gave her the directions, reached into his purse and took out the perfume. 'A gift for you.'

She pulled out the stopper, sniffed, and gently dabbed some on her wrist. 'Attar of roses with lavender, it's my favourite,' she cooed happily, before skipping back to the Manor.

Chapter 25

Captain Leon's Necklace.

The wharfs of Bordeaux were all but deserted. The main wine convoy had sailed and, with the threat of war looming ever larger as the French army advanced through the Santonge, even local vessels had departed to seek safer harbours. The cog *La Nicholas* stood alone. Her outward journey had been a nightmare. Sailing in the grain convoy, a fleet of galleys had attacked them, and during the fight the ship had sustained major damage necessitating this enforced stay in port. Captain John Hawthorne watched nervously as the dockhands struggled to roll the last barrels of best Bordeaux wine up on deck and into the hold. The Captain had seen too many barrels smashed on the dockside through clumsy stevedores.

'One hundred and fifty two barrels already loaded.' The first mate told his captain as he handed over the tally stick. 'Full to the gunnels.'

Hawthorne was a month overdue and getting edgy. He had been in port much longer than planned. He had considered his predicament and decided to gamble all. He had winkled out the best reserve stocks of wine from the merchants, arguing that it would be better they were drunk in England, albeit at half price, now, with a promise of more if Bordeaux survived the coming siege, rather than for nothing by the rampaging French if they succeeded in breaking in and sacking the city.

'If we don't get this lot home safely I'll be bankrupted by this war,' he told his first mate. 'If we do we're in clover. Good,' concluded

Hawthorne with a knowing sigh. His wife would be worrying as she waited for him at home in Southampton.

The Captain had leased the *La Nicholas* from the King for this voyage. She was of solid clinker construction and rounded at both ends, with a single mast with a crow's nest for three bowmen at its top, as well as high defensive wooden castles placed fore and aft, which he had added for the voyage – if they were attacked by pirates this would be their last refuge, otherwise he hoped that just the sight of them would deter would-be attackers. For additional armament, and placed in his castles, he had acquired, at significant expense, two springalds - large metal and laminate cross bows mounted on wheeled trolleys that fired heavy spears over hundreds of feet. These were very effective against rowers and boarders, and had saved his bacon on the way down. *Will they save me again?* He watched as raucous gulls wheeled over returning fishing boats, diving into muddy water for offal as the fishermen gutted their catch. On his own, it would be touch and go.

'Are you *really* sailing for England?' It was a tall archer dressed in brown.

'Who's asking?' Hawthorne looked languidly at the inquirer and saw that he led a sizeable contingent of soldiery.

'William of Northwich,' answered the archer, 'and forty of my companions, since you ask. Cheshire bowmen, fed up with not being paid and desiring to return to their families in England.'

Manna has fallen from heaven Hawthorne made some quick calculations.

'Get extra barrels of water,' he ordered his mate. 'Have you got food?'

'How much will we need?' asked William.

'If we have a fair wind, it should take three weeks. Get biscuits and hard tack. The chandlers should have enough.' *What joy, my very own archers.* 'I hope you have lots of arrows.'

They had plenty and, curiously, some spears for the springald. How they had come by them, he would ask later. With weather fair, he determined to go far out to sea to avoid enemy galleys that usually lurked off La Rochelle. The decks rapidly became cluttered with archers' paraphernalia. Five wagons full of kit and possessions appeared on the dock. 'You'll have to leave that here or we'll sink,' ordered Hawthorne.

'Then we won't come,' replied William truculently. And so began the long process of what would be taken on board. By the time each man had donned his fighting kit one wagon was empty; once they had taken up bedroll and mess kit, they emptied a second. Their weapons – bows, arrows and short swords - made up the third wagon, including a dismantled springald, answering Hawthorne's question. Tents were in a fourth, and bundles of clothing, accumulated booty and foodstuffs in a fifth. There was much grumbling as each archer was forced to carry all this on board. A large crowd gathered for an impromptu auction. If they couldn't take their wagons and horses, then they would sell them to the highest bidder. They didn't make much. There were no takers for the tents, which were unceremoniously abandoned in a heap on the quay. The ship looked a mess, with every nook and cranny filled with boxes, bedrolls and assorted barrels.

Hawthorne didn't care that his crew were unhappy and said so to his first mate.

'Tell them it's the price of security.' They had thought that safety in numbers would protect them on the way down and had been wrong. They had fought hard to get safely to Bordeaux, taking several large stones from enemy mangonels through the deck and sustaining damage to their rudder. This time, Hawthorne hoped the ocean's vastness would swallow them up. For such a large vessel, *La Nicholas* had settled low in the water, making her easy to board. It would be a slow trip home. Maybe they would make Southampton by the first week of October, but Hawthorne doubted it.

The tide was on the ebb and he could wait no longer, so he ordered that they should release the hawsers fore and aft. Sailors ran up and down cursing as they tripped over the clutter on the deck, raising the great square sail. On shore the crowd dispersed, taking their bargains. A company of the Seneschal's men-at-arms appeared, galloping along wharfs, shouting for the ship to return. The archers jeered, hurling abuse back at them.

'We hadn't told them we were going home, I think he's upset! But,' said William as he stood beside the captain and held up his fingers and rubbed them together on his thumb, 'no money, no fight. I've been watching your preparations and we left it to the last minute.'

'No money, only fight, my friend.' Hawthorne also rubbed his fingers together. '*That's* the deal if you want to get home safely.'

'It is *indeed* a deal.' William nodded in agreement. 'Let's hope St. Christopher will protect us.' He looked up at the purple sail with its golden figure bearing a young Christ on his shoulders and made the sign of the Cross.

It was hot. The archers stripped off their gambesons, rolling them up to use as pillows. There was hardly enough breeze to fill the canvas, so the Captain ordered out the sweeps. Four rowers manned each oar. Four oars on each side and the ebb tide took them ever faster out towards the sea.

—ɯ—

'I'm getting too old, I can't see properly, my joints ache and I want to die in my bed,' said Captain Leon Txillida as he rubbed a painful cut in his salt-cracked skin. He scanned the empty horizon with his son, Juan, who stood beside him on the quarterdeck of the *Izquierd de Dios* – 'the Left hand of God'. 'I'm going to finish this necklace then retire.'

The news delighted Juan, who for some time had wanted to be master of the sleek, black-painted whaler that was a hybrid between a galley and a galleass.

Leon cursed the Genoese. 'They've have left nothing for us.' With supplies of water running low, they would be forced to return home empty-handed. 'They've scared off the English or forced them into convoys. One more prize, that's all I want. Just one fat cog and I'm going to retire.' For the past twenty years Captain Leon had been chasing whales out of the small Basque port of Ribadesella, braving tempestuous seas to hunt the mighty leviathans of the deep that regularly congregated in the Bay of Biscay. In the wine convoy season he turned his hand to piracy, amassing a fortune plundering ships of all nations that had the misfortune to cross his path, not caring whose flag they flew as long as their holds were full. For the *Izquierd de Dios* and her sister ship *Sorginorratz* 'The Dragonfly', the season's pickings had been lean. The French and their *bastardo* Genoese allies had seen to that.

'They should stick to the Mediterranean - we don't poach their prizes,' opined Juan, still sore that the French authorities in Belle Île had refused to give them their usual payoff to prevent them from attacking fishing vessels. 'Maybe we should make friends with the English instead,' he said half-heartedly.

Captain Leon shook his head. 'Maybe we should have breakfast with the devil and be done with it.' Theirs was a family enterprise - his brother-in-law commanded the *Sorginorratz*; sons acted as officers, and crews came from surrounding hills and maritime villages. Ribadesella was at the end of a road from nowhere that went on to nowhere else. Cruising far to the north, criss-crossing shipping lanes, they hoped to pick off a straggler or brave loner.

Juan had climbed the stubby mast to the whale look-out platform.

A shout. Hope!

'Where?' Leon screwed up his eyes to see what his son was pointing at.

'There, can you see it?'

He had to admit he couldn't. His eyesight was failing him. Then, squinting hard, he could make out a fuzzy purple blob on the horizon.

'Man the oars,' Leon shouted as adrenalin took away the pains of arthritis. The rowers propelled the whalers forward with urgency; it was the sort of prize they wanted, an English cog wallowing hull down. No doubt her fat belly was full of wine. He respected the English. They always fought hard, but he had always prevailed, boarding quickly and butchering the crew and collecting their ears for his necklaces.

It had been the venerable Father Ignatius who had started him off. *Remember, my son,* he had told an impressionable young Leon Txillida, who was still debating what career to follow. *At the Day of Judgement you will be called to enumerate all your misdeeds before you can enter the Kingdom of Heaven.* As Txillida had chosen piracy, for which profession killing men was obligatory for success, he decided that the best way to keep track of each sin was to keep a memento. He did not bother to differentiate between Christian and Mussulmen ears, nor did it matter that the ears did not come from his actual victim – many had been thrown into the sea before his gruesome harvest. It was the *number* that was important – and one ear looked very much like another when dried.

This one, my sixth, will be my last, he decided. *Only ten more men will die at my hands before it is complete.* He had strict rules - fifty pairs of dried human ears on a platted leather string and he had to have killed the man himself in combat, or hung him, or, better still, had him flayed alive. He enjoyed the latter the most. He called it 'undressing' his victims, and then he used strips of their tanned skin to make his woven braids. When the time came, he would be able tell St. Peter with complete accuracy that he could account for two hundred and ninety souls consigned to the hereafter, courtesy of Leon Txillida.

'Shall we put up shields?' asked his son, knowing it was sometimes prudent to protect rowers from the odd arrow or crossbow bolt that might come their way.

'No, they only get in the way,' answered Leon, fiddling with the leathery garland that hung in anticipation around his neck. For rapid hit-and-board attacks, the key was to grapple and then get the whole crew, rowers and all, to overwhelm their opponents. Speed was essential and his experience of attacking in this manner had always been successful, so he saw no reason to alter his tactics. So the few shields they possessed would remain in the hold, as they always did. They might sustain extra casualties, but it was a merchantman they were attacking, not a warship. *Like blood on the claws of eagles.* He looked up at the red tips of white *lauburus* motif, a rounded cross of curved scythes, in the centre of his black triangular sail. The gap narrowed.

La Nicholas was making slow progress as Captain Hawthorne headed out into the Bay of Biscay, trying to avoid going too close to shore. *Not many captains are brave enough to lose sight of land,* he had a good nose for direction, using the sun and the stars, and he reasoned that it should be safer.

The wind freshened. White horses flicked across the tops of the waves, though the swell was not too great.

'From the wrong bloody quarter, too,' the Captain complained to his first mate. The strengthening north-westerly would only serve to drive them back towards France. 'At least this lot have only just started eating.'

For four days, William had cursed his ordeal and retched in misery. Now, finally, he had found his sea legs. Looking up at the sail, he wondered how much longer his living hell would last.

Captain Hawthorne was pleased to see that the leader of the archers no longer had the green pallor of seasickness. 'Get some food inside you.'

'Where do you think we are?'

The captain didn't answer when a shout came from the crow's nest lookout.

'Triangular sails to stern of us, on the horizon.'

'Not far enough, sounds like trouble.' It was near noon. *Sharks*, thought Hawthorne as he climbed the rigging to confirm the sighting. He could just make out two black triangles in the far distance. 'Basque bastards,' he muttered to his first mate. He knew who it was. Captain Leon favoured black. He also knew that not many mariners survived an encounter with the dreaded Leon. Hawthorne crossed himself and thanked the Lord for William. Assembling the crew, Hawthorne instructed his boatswain to break out their weapons. They had a fight on their hands.

The crew and archers assembled on the deck amidships. The weapons chests opened and the crew picked their weapons of choice. Some were armed with cudgels to crack heads, others axes to cut ropes, or spears to repel boarders. Hardened leather awnings were erected to protect the steersmen from crossbow bolts.

'Let us pray,' intoned Hawthorne, dropping to his knees, his men doing the same. Over the years, he had learnt a form of words that provided succour to their souls. 'By our Lord Jesus and St Christopher under whose sail we travel, grant us deliverance from the pirate Leon.' He knew how to fortify men's spirits.

'Bloody Basque bastards, they're real devil-spawn.' Hawthorne pointed to the streaming pennants. 'They're the worst. They'll definitely try to board. They're only interested in plunder.' He did not feel confident; usually the high sides of a cog made it much harder to board than sink, but his ship was riding low in the water. He had his steward pour him a beaker of strong wine. 'I always have a drink before any fight, settles butterflies in my stomach.' *This'll be my second fight this year. Last time we had other ships in convoy, this time we're on our own.* He shuddered involuntarily. 'Here, this will do you good.' He offered the refilled cup to William who drained it in one.

'What do you think?' asked William.

'It's going to be a fight to the death.' Hawthorne told William about their enemy adding, 'Leon collects ears from those he kills and makes them into necklaces. Time for action, William,' he observed. 'The men fight better if they know the Lord is with them.'

'We archers put faith in our weapons.' William started to sing tunelessly. The refrain was picked up by the archers unpacking staves from storage boxes, looping hemp on bone knocks before testing the sit and draw strength of their bows. Most wore padded jerkins and bascinets, favouring these to the pikemen's rimmed helmets. Few bothered with chain mail, as they were going to have to shoot fast. William ordered his men to don their surcoats. 'If we're to die we'll go down wearing the Cross of St. George.' Strapping on wrist guards and three-fingered gloves they were ready for action.

'What sort of arrow heads should we attach?' William held out a selection that came in many shapes and sizes, giving the Captain a run down on each. 'Same for shafts, heavier ones for short range - better penetration.'

'You decide,' said Hawthorne, not used to choice.

'We'll use flesh cutters for oarsmen and armour piercing for men-at-arms. Have you got anything for fire arrows?'

'I've got a couple of barrels of calking tar,' offered the Captain. 'We can mix it with lamp oil.'

Long arrows wrapped with cloth were dipped into the sticky black liquid. Enclosed lanterns were lit and placed in each of the castles.

William rummaged around and came up with serrated barbs that would snag canvas. 'Perfect. We'll set their sails alight.'

The enemy vessels were driven on by numerous oars - whale hunters were sturdy boats with high forward prows for cutting through the Atlantic chop in winter and a platform for harpooning their prey. Though smaller than the cog, each was well over half as long the *La Nicholas*.

'At least they don't have a ram to sink us,' the Captain told William, who was having regrets about leaving dry land. 'Whalers aren't built for ramming. These buggers are going to try and board. We have to stop them boarding at all costs. If they get on deck it's a fight to the death.' *It's our cargo they want. I've got to keep them at arm's length.* Hawthorne knew that if he did, he had an even chance of escape: the ocean swell favoured *La Nicholas*, and her fore and aft castles were high enough to give advantage over the sleeker balingers.

Hawthorne held his hand up and looked at the sun. *Just passed its zenith, it's going to be a long afternoon.* 'Split your men fore and aft, I'll have my boys in the crow's nest; they know what to do.'

Carrying crossbows and pulling up baskets of slinging stones and quarrels three men climbed aloft. It would be hard to be accurate while pitching back and forth.

'Grease the spears - make them harder to grab. And bring up soap.' Two small barrels of viscous liquid were brought on deck. One was mounted on a long pole and had a string attached to its bottom.

'Nothing like soap for making them slide about,' observed Hawthorne, helping William lace up his arm guards. 'Tip it on their boarding ramps.' He gave his final orders to the first mate. 'Clear the decks! We're in God's hands now.'

'Wind from the left, boys,' William shouted, his men ready for action.

With so many men crowded into the castles, the springaldeers had difficulty manoeuvring their weapons.

'Get some into the waist,' ordered Hawthorne as his seamen pulled the springalds around, winding them up with a pulley and winch and aiming them by moving the spear tray up and down. The pirates closed, oars sweeping rhythmically.

'It's all new to me. I've only ever fought on land.' William was in his thirties and had been fighting on and off since his teens. The enemy were now nearing four hundred yards from their stern. 'By the way, they're nearly in range.'

'You're kidding me.' Hawthorne expressed surprise, but then he'd never seen a longbow in action before. The enemy moved apart; coming from either side. 'Give them a taster of fire. The sooner we inflict casualties the better.' Hawthorne watched as ten archers mounted their bows and loosed off a volley. He could not see if any landed on the enemy, but an oar slewed awkwardly as the balingers surged ever closer, their harpoon platforms now crowded with eager boarders.

'Conserve your arrows. Don't fire too fast. Just maintain a steady rain and concentrate on the central sections.' William knew that discipline had to be maintained and over-eagerness curbed. This would be a lengthy duel.

The stern springald was wound up, manoeuvred into position and fired, its spear narrowly missing the crowded platform before lodging firmly in the coils of rope that had been readied with grappling hooks on the *Izquierd de Dios*'s prow as it came perilously close to the cog's stern. This unexpected missile caused much consternation and feverish activity amongst the Basques as they tried to dislodge it. A weapon such as this changed the level of danger they faced and sent the pirates scurrying back to find their cowhide shields.

'That gave them a fright.' The first mate had come to stand beside him. Both men watched as the archers picked off the stragglers. 'Impressive, I must say.'

The gap between the vessels had widened slightly and Hawthorne ducked involuntarily as the enemy loosed off a volley of crossbow bolts that whizzed overhead. The rear castle archers had the pirates at right angles to them - oarsmen pulling as hard as they could. They were fast, but now the rain of arrows was taking a greater toll of rowers who had little or no protection from the stream of missiles that fell on them. As wounded men dropped their oars so the rhythm broke, suddenly the whaler slewed.

Fire arrows, with fabric wrappings soaked in oily pitch ignited in the lanterns, were quickly fired at the Basque's sails, black smoking parabolic trails curving through the sky. The first fell short, but a second and third found their mark. Soon several arrows were firmly lodged in the enemy's sail, making it catch fire. The Basque captain yelled at his sailors to douse the flames with leather buckets of seawater. Concentrating on exposed men, the archers took a terrible toll. After much effort the Basques soaked their sail, trying to raise it again – but with several long, charred gashes in it, it was useless.

'Get ready to repel boarders!' Hawthorne shouted, watching as the sea wolves crowded the boarding ramp. The vessels were now only twenty feet apart. He felt a certain satisfaction as his forward springald sent its wicked shaft into the close packed bodies, skewering three men on one spear - once he'd seen them manage four.

'Aim at the tiller men. Them...' he instructed William, pointing to sailors manning rudders.

A steady stream of arrows arched into the enemy vessel's stern, making it sheer away. The springald, at maximum elevation, scored another hit, as the heavy wood fletched iron spear plunged into their enemy's bowels.

'Let's hope that makes them ship some water,' said Hawthorne with a grunt of satisfaction. The professionalism of the archers at work impressed the Captain, as did the power and accuracy of their war bows.

As the afternoon wore on, so the swell increased. Rolling waves made operating springalds increasingly difficult. A couple more attempts were rewarded with misses.

'Don't waste ammunition,' shouted the Captain, acutely aware that the balance of the struggle could easily tip towards the Basques. 'Make each spear count.'

The two whalers had slipped astern, positioning themselves out of range. It was not hard for them to keep pace with the wallowing cog.

'It's not over yet,' Hawthorne remarked to William, who had returned to his side during the lull. 'See. They're putting up awnings and shields to protect their oarsmen. They were over confident first time. Still, it will make boarding harder.' *They didn't expect bowmen.*

Both vessels now sported dirty canvas sheeting over their rowing benches and more cowhide shields were handed up from holds to protect the men on deck. 'They've become turtles. This is where it gets difficult,' he mused. 'Drop more fire on them.'

The flames took quickly on greasy canvas and men with buckets made easy targets. The pirates dropped back to reorganise.

Again their pace quickened; Captain Leon was not yet ready to quit. The English could see boarding parties readying themselves behind their clumsy defensive shields. This time they were going to bear the losses.

'They're going to try and board us again. Get your men to shoot at anyone trying to swing a grappling iron. They have to drop the shields before they jump, that's when they're vulnerable. I'm going to turn hard into the wind when they are about thirty yards away. They won't expect that, so be ready. Then we'll straighten up again and see what happens.'

The archers fitted their heaviest bodkin arrowheads, ones that could easily pierce armour and leather shields.

This time the enemy vessels closed with dramatic speed, each aiming for the amidships, trying to sandwich the cog's low midsection between their prows. The Captain gave the order and the huge tiller heaved over, turning straight toward the starboard galley, so that, instead of their prow dominating amidships, where it would be easiest for the Basques to swarm aboard, they found themselves overshadowed by towering castles, from where the archers loosed volley after volley into them at short range. The boarding parties took the brunt of a hail of arrows; the springalds both managed to get their heavy spears to rip through canvas into the rowers, causing them to break rhythm. Another stream of arrows hissed through the air. Captain Leon was running up and down, exhorting his rowers on before he went down, one arrow through his leg, another in his shoulder.

Hawthorne, aware of his predicament, ordered radical action, running out his sweeps. 'Back the oars!' he shouted, hoping he was not too late.

His helmsmen pushed the tiller with all their might, stopping the cargo vessel in its tracks. The manoeuvre had the desired effect. The first balinger, misjudging the angle, swerved in panic - too late to prevent loosing oars that splintered against the cog's stern. The respite was brief. The *Sorginorratz*, an iron-spiked boarding ramp swinging menacingly from the prow, got to within grappling distance before the archers could switch target.

Ropes with iron hooks arched across between the vessels, catching rigging and rails. Sailors with axes had to brave the missiles that came thick and fast as they hacked away at ropes while the archers dealt with the throwers. The springaldeers fired on the down roll; a broad-bladed spear sliced through the flesh of packed boarders, decapitating two before pinioning an unfortunate whale hunter by burying itself into woodwork, leaving him to wriggle like a harpooned fish.

'Steady, steady!' Hawthorne knew he had to keep a cool head as he grabbed the pole with the liquid soap. Judging the bucket to be over the ramp, he pulled the string, releasing its contents onto the plank. It made the boarders slide chaotically around, losing their footing. Several armoured men fell helplessly into the sea, the weight of metal taking them rapidly beneath the waves. More men on the ramp's end tried to jump the gap, only to be run through with spears. One by one the grappling irons were cut away.

'That's him, that's Leon.' Hawthorne pointed to a grey-haired fellow ranting with fury on the first whaler's poop deck.

William could see the garland of ears quite clearly as it closed again. 'He'll be my gift to you,' said the tall archer as he drew his bowstring to his chin, but the last restraining rope fell away, making the cog lurch forward. The arrow missed, shaving the side of Leon's head. A final brave Basque sailor tried swinging another grappling hook, only to fall like St. Sebastian, transfixed by arrows, before disappearing under foaming water. Again the whalers fell away out of range.

Hawthorne summoned William to take stock. 'How many arrows have you left?'

'One and a half barrels, that's twenty-five left for each man and ten springald bolts. If they try hard, we'll run out.'

Hawthorne looked at the sky. The duel had been going on for at least three hours. He realised as the sun burst through clouds that, at some time during their fight, the wind had changed direction. It was now pushing up from the southeast, which would help immeasurably as they ploughed on.

The balingers were going to try again.

'Bring all your men to the aft castle. Aim at their captains and men-at-arms.'

The sea was getting choppier. Again, like great water beetles, the Basques surged forward, and arrows struck home into crowded decks. This time they broke off before even getting to grapple range, and instead of slipping back they curved away for home.

'They've had enough,' whooped a relieved Hawthorne, wiping the sweat from his brow.

The English jeered and the archers waved their familiar two-fingered salute.

'I started out with ten barrels of arrows and I have only one left.' William made a quick calculation. 'My guess is we fired near on six thousand arrows!'

Two of Hawthorne's crew had been killed and three more badly wounded trying to free boarding lines. The archers were unscathed, though most men had cuts and bruises. Two larboard sweeps had been splintered fending off a whaler, but otherwise *La Nicholas* was unscathed.

Hawthorne gathered his men. 'Let us give thanks to the Lord and the war bow.' He dropped to his knees and others followed. Only the Grace of God, and William and his archers, had saved them all from a watery grave.

As evening fell so the wind rose. *I hope God has finished with us.* Captain Hawthorne raised his eyes to heaven. If it was not to be death from man's hand, he hoped that the Good Lord would spare them, for he did not know where he was. His sailors reefed the purple St. Christopher sail and settled down to a perilous night. As long as he could run east with the wind all would be well. Somewhere out there to the north was a wild and rocky coast where many ships had been wrecked. He prayed as hard as he could that they were not on a collision course.

—⚜—

Captain Leon felt warm blood trickle down the side of his neck. As a final irony, his ear had been clipped and cut in half by the Englishman's last arrow. He surveyed what was left of his crew and, for the first time in his life, wept. There were so many arrows sticking out of his vessel and crew that it looked like a porcupine that had rolled in apple blossom. The plunging metal spears had holed his hull and his carpenter had to work feverishly with squares of leather to plug leaks or he would sink before reaching home. Nearly three-quarters of his men had some sort of arrow wound; over half would not make it home. Already bodies were being tossed unceremoniously over the gunnels to feed the sharks. He winced with pain as his son pulled out the shaft piercing his leg, its wicked iron head poking out through his canvas trousers. Another had grazed his shoulder, leaving a deep gash that had rendered his sword-arm tendon useless. 'Don't.' He held up his other arm. He knew what his son wanted to say. *We should have deployed shields from the outset.* But the damage had been done by a deadly blizzard of iron and goose feather. Retirement was no longer optional. It was compulsory. He had fought his final battle.

—⚜—

Father Ignatius's successor was surprised when the Madonna's statue that looked down from on high above the altar received what he thought were garlands of dried flowers, but he was not tall enough, nor did he possess enough will to examine the necklaces closely - as far as he was concerned, it was an honour for the Blessed Virgin to be adorned in this way. If only he knew which of his parishioners to thank.

Chapter 26

A Matter of Trust

There was a chill in the air. The last gasps of summer were fading fast. Sir Roger picked himself a Warden pear from his wife's prized tree and bit into its dull, purpley skin. Its flesh was hard and tart and mouth-puckering, and he spat it out before throwing the fruit away. A neighbouring apple tree proved a better choice. Its sweetness was in goodly contrast as he mulled over the events of the last few minutes. It was rare that he was rendered speechless. But as he had entered Master John's room, he had instantly known that the monk was indulging in the Sin of Onan as he knelt on the floor. It was the hand hidden under his cassock and the tumescence protruding out of the front that was a sure giveaway.

'That's disgusting,' he had said eventually, quite shocked. He'd come looking for the chaplain to consult him about something, but could no longer remember what. 'Give me one good reason why you should not pack your bags and leave right away.'

Red-faced with humiliation, Master John's brain had gone into overdrive. He had been replaying the story of ravishing Sir Hog's virginal daughters that the minstrel had told him, in graphic detail, in his confession. It was a tale that always induced thoughts of lust beyond his control. John had grasped at straws and grabbed the wrong one.

'I know a secret,' he said, clutching at straws.

'And are you going to share it with me or will it remain your secret?' Sir Roger had asked as he pulled the terrified tutor to his feet by his throat.

'It concerns your wife and the minstrel.' *Oh Lord, I've done it now.* Master John could not control the words as they spilled out of his mouth before his brain had the ability to put on the brakes. 'They were alone together in the solar...'

Sir Roger stopped him saying anything more. The filthy pervert had said enough. He let him fall to his feet, where he clung on, begging not to be dismissed.

'I think that we should forget this ever happened,' said Sir Roger. *Thank you for that.* The thought had been nagging him ever since Whytethorne's comment. Head down, he crossed the courtyard with grim determination, mind churning, until a wicked smile crossed his face. *So she's been unfaithful has she?*

He looked up and almost walked into the Reeve, who was sporting a shiner of a black eye.

'So Walt, who gave you that?' Sir Roger asked pointedly.

'I walked into a tree, Sire,' Walt replied, unwilling to reveal the truth. Sir Roger knew it must be Handley's work, having given the Reeve two pounds, nearly a year's wages, when the villagers had confirmed his appointment. Handley had seen the transaction and, no doubt about it, wanted a share. Walt shifted uneasily from foot to foot while Sir Roger continued to stare. Walt's front teeth were reduced to stumps and a prominent nasal wart sported several course bristles. His weather-beaten face spoke of a lifetime's toil in the open air; hands calloused from years of cutting reeds for thatch.

'Well, I hope it was not too much.'

Walt had been forced to hand over five shillings.

'No, Sire, my wife got new linen. I have enough left for a fine trousseau for Lucy, and an ox to boot.'

Sir Roger waved Walt away and went and lay on the bank of his moat, watching as the colours of evening flushed the heavens. The sun was getting larger as it slid toward the horizon. A vole poked its head out from a bank opposite, its whiskers twitching. A snowy barn owl swooped silently, hunting rodents. It was one of those brief moments when God was in his heaven and all was right with the world, even if it wasn't. A solitary cloud reminded him of an angel. Sir Roger always hoped that the Almighty had assigned one to watch over him and his family. A mass of swallows was busy scooping up insects as they skimmed the surface of his moat. He closed his eyes and conjured up an image of Lady Caroline. He hadn't given her any thought since leaving Oxford, but she had certainly left a lasting impression... Those eyes, those pursed lips, that golden hair, those pert breasts... Would he meet her again?

He knew there would be trouble; the harvest had been unusually meagre. What corn there was had been gathered into stooks and needed to be threshed by the second week in September before the haystacks could be made. When they next met, Sir Roger told Handley to do a deal with the Tide Mill at Eling, and to make sure they had enough flour to see them through the winter, otherwise his granary would struggle to keep everyone fed. The Bailiff read his master's mood and decided the time was ripe to get back into his good books by revealing how much profit they had made by doctoring the wool.

Sir Roger's opinion of his Bailiff rose. *He's a sly old fox.*

It was with feelings of foreboding that Sir Roger returned to Winchester to pay over the remainder of his tax. After the debacle with the Under-Sheriff, and in need of spiritual sustenance before going straight to the castle he dropped into the Cathedral, pausing to pray to the reliquary of St. Swithun. The saint, in his view, had not been kind enough. There had been thunderstorms in July that had flattened crops, affecting Sir Roger and his tenants badly. Already there was grumbling across the country where it was the same story, with many promising fields wrecked prior to reaping.

In the Lady Chapel the floor tiles looked suspiciously familiar. Sir Roger recognised them as the same pattern as those in his new kitchen. The penny dropped when he noticed the pattern suddenly change for one of an inferior quality. *So that's where they came from...* He was about to leave when he noticed a novice monk polishing an ornate casket, one he had not seen before.

'It belongs to St. Iodocus,' the monk said, opening it reverentially so Sir Roger could look inside. It contained hair and nail-clippings, embedded in silver, placed on a velvet cushion. 'They continued to grow long after his death. They say that he protects against shipwreck.' The young man closed the lid again.

Up at the castle the Sheriff was in residence. 'The Banneret returns,' proclaimed Sir Hugh de Lacey laconically, with a suitable flourish, his greying hair cut in fashionable pudding bowl style. Sir Roger was greatly relieved when the Sheriff told him that his men had corroborated his story concerning the trouble with Sir Eustace. 'Indeed you were wronged. I've issued three court summons and will have him declared outlaw. That should flush him out.' He spoke in a series of clipped sentences as if he had rehearsed what to say. 'My man spoke out of turn. I realise that you acted out of self-defence.'

The knight noted a hint of deference. The Sheriff was offering his hand of co-operation and recognising his authority as local military commander. *Thank goodness, he wishes for harmonious relations.* He had let it be broadcast that he would pay a year's wages for information about de Frage's whereabouts. Rumours abounded. Other acts of brigandry were often linked to him and, having such a distinctive scar on his face, at least some of the sightings were verifiable.

Sir Eustace and his band of ne'er-do-wells had taken over where the four Folville brothers had left off. The Folvilles had led a notorious gang and had been declared outlaws for numerous acts of larceny.

'According to my sources, at least one appears to be going straight and has joined the King in Flanders. Let's hope Sir Eustace does the same. Frankly, I don't want *their* sort of trouble here,' said Sir Roger. The Folvilles most infamous act had been the kidnapping of the King's Justice, Sir Richard Wyloughby.

'That's the price for dealing dishonestly I suppose,' said the Sheriff, who prided himself on his fair dealings. 'Teach him to be too greedy.' Having already sentenced the four Folvilles for heinous crimes,

Wyloughby had reneged on his promise to release them after a hefty bribe had come his way. The remaining gang members had taken a dim view of this, joining forces with the Coterels, a group of similar ilk, and had taken Wyloughby on his way to market. 'They demanded over a thousand marks and got it too!' The Sheriff lowered his voice. 'Would your family pay if they received your fingers?'

Sir Roger shook his head, shocked. 'How many did they cut off?' he asked.

The Sheriff was counting thoughtfully on his fingers. 'Three murders, three robberies and at least one rape, and that were in only two years; then the eldest Folville gets pardoned. Helped put down the Lancaster rebellion, I believe. Then the bastard starts all over again and jumps a party of merchants near Leicester. Got away with two hundred pounds and then burnt that watermill - or was that his brothers? Anyway, it don't matter, all as bad as each other... I could do with that sort of money,' he continued dreamily. 'Somehow it doesn't seem right, every time they declare him an outlaw he manages to wangle a pardon. Comes from having a powerful patron, I suppose. What did you ask?'

'How many fingers?'

But the Sheriff wasn't listening. 'Get yourself a powerful patron,' he repeated himself. 'A magnate, a bishop or an abbot, and it gives *carte blanche* to go on a crime spree. There's always a man of substance behind these gangs. Everyone knows that the Folvilles split their ransom with the Tuchet family up at Markeaton. Do you know them?' Again the Sheriff didn't wait for an answer. 'I met Sir Richard last year. Never really got over having his fingers cut off one by one.' He flexed his hands, folding down three fingers on his left hand to answer the question. He pointed the index finger in Sir Roger's direction. Hardness returned to his voice. 'I won't tolerate any of that nonsense. I like law-abiding citizens in my county.' *Military commander you might be, but I'll be damned if you start upsetting the status quo.* 'Now you've got a castle, can you house two of my constables of the peace, and can they use your lock-up?' the Sheriff asked. 'You can run the Hundred Court, we had to do it from here, but it's a bit far to your neck of the woods. You can keep a quarter of the tax and fines. All manorial fines are yours anyway.'

Sir Roger smiled. This was a definite step up. *I must send him a book as a gift.* He felt the need to cultivate this new friendship. It was more than he expected.

'I know it means more mouths to feed,' the Sheriff continued. 'But it means more men to defend your castle should your friend Sir Eustace put in an unwelcome reappearance.' Sir Hugh wielded real authority in the county. There was a small moment of silence while both men sat back in their chairs.

Sir Hugh leaned forward and in a true inquisitor's fashion suddenly changed the subject. 'How many sheep do you have?' he asked blandly. Sir Roger had nearly four thousand five hundred at last count; keeping them with shepherds in small parcels spread throughout villages across the region.

'About a thousand.' Everybody lied when telling the taxman about numbers of sheep. Added to which, he didn't want word to get out that he was dealing in wool on the side, as that was supposedly illegal. *And duff stuff at that.* In retrospect, he'd profited from Handley's scam. *If I'd sold my wool through normal channels I'd be lucky to gross one or two pounds a bale after taxes - those bastard middlemen and hauliers take all the profit. And there's the Venetian who's going to take more...*

He steered the subject back to safer ground. 'I met with William de la Pole at Northampton and am thinking of joining his English Wool Company. What do you think?' The older man was always a good source of advice. There were nearly seven thousand sheep around Winchester and St. Swithun's, and he knew Sir Hugh was also thinking of joining the English Wool Company.

'Sharp as a razor.' Sir Roger detected a hint of sarcasm from the older man. 'He seems to have bankrolled this expedition to Flanders single-handed. I don't trust him, but he has the knack of making money. The Midas touch, they say - has his hands in many pies.'

And the upstart from Hull suckered me into buying the wrong type of sheep... But Sir Roger envied his commercial skills. *Somehow, though, I feel it's more honourable to earn money from chivalrous activity.* He thought of Walter

Mauney. Here's someone who earns his money the right way - capturing foes and collecting ransoms. Great knights are remembered through feats of arms in the ballads sung across the land. Sir Roger considered himself good at the art of fighting. *The other way relies on the trustworthiness of others - and whom can I trust?*

—∭—

At Ipers all available wagons were loaded with wool and ash. Handley had conjured up more scarce canvas woolsacks, from where nobody knew. Secrecy would be paramount for the operation's success. They had to get the goods to the beach without attracting attention. Nor was it an everyday occurrence that a Venetian galley pulled into the ferry beach at Lepe, and the last thing Sir Roger wanted were beacons being lit. Any strange vessel could trigger a full-scale alarm. For the next two nights, with a full moon, they would be able to move the wagons in darkness.

As he rode back from visiting Sir Hugh, the dilemma of his wife's alleged infidelity continued to trouble Sir Roger. He had wrestled all day and eventually decided not to broach the subject *just yet*. The temptation presented by Elizabeth beckoned strongly. He was not going to let her slip away unfucked. *If my wife finds out then...*

It would be useful ammunition.

~~*Talk of the devil.*~~ His wife was waiting for him in the courtyard with a look that spelt trouble.

'What are you going to do about your new mascot?' she said pointedly as he dismounted in the courtyard. 'She terrifies poor Horace and Eloise.'

These were her lap-dogs. It was whispered that she loved more than her children. She had decided not to inform her husband that she thought she was pregnant *just yet* as she was not sure who the father was. She would broach the subject of Zuzu instead, who was rapidly becoming a force to be reckoned with. Not only was the ape immensely strong, often tearing barrels apart in her searches for food, but awesomely noisy when provoked.

The ape resided, attached by a long chain, in an old kennel placed on the pigsty roof, near the kitchen. As dogs neared her she would hurl dung at them and would ride around on the pigs, grooming them for lice. Otherwise, when together, she and Dan were inseparable. She was particularly fond of beer, drinking herself into a stupor.

Sir Roger shrugged. He, too, had spent some time considering the ape. The near humanness of her hands bothered him, but he was impressed with her strength and agility. As a mascot, he was unsure. On balance he felt he disliked the creature, but had to admit he enjoyed her antics.

Chapter 27

The Gathering Storm

It sounded as if the Genoese in the Conference Hall were at each oth-er's throats, squabbling like dogs scrapping over a bone. So raucous were their raised voices that their goings on could be heard across the cloister, where, on the other side, Simon and the two French Admirals were making their way over with rising consternation at the thought that their new allies might just as easily declare war on each other than help them attack the English ports. Their threats and counter-threats could be heard echoing around the stone walls and beyond. Béhuchet likened them to unruly children as he held both men back; he wanted a word in private before entering the lion's den.

'Your principal target in Southampton is the Peruzzi Bank and it should be full of money,' Béhuchet informed his surprised fellow Admiral of his plotting with the forged documents as they strolled towards the Italian disharmony. 'Simon assures me that his magic pow-der will blow off the door.'

'What if these morons get there first?' Quiéret was sceptical.

But Nicolas Béhuchet's agile brain had mastered that possibil-ity. He outlined the details of his plan. 'My contact at the Holy See has done his job well. All you have to do is find the right building. The Genoese will have these instructions from the Pope.' He handed Hugh Quiéret a couple of sealed documents that bore genuine heavy Papal seals, though the contents had been drawn up with his full knowledge and connivance. 'They inform our new friends that they are, under threat of excommunication, not to touch buildings belonging to fellow countrymen. I advise you to create a diversion that will keep them occupied long enough at the other end of town. Simon here is a quick-thinking lad. I'm sure he'll think of something when the time comes.'

Simon nodded; he'd been to Southampton before, while on his spying trip, and it was his recollection of its poor defences that had swayed the decision that the town should be the target. He remembered seeing the bank and remarking that it looked well-nigh impregnable. That was before meeting the Magister and learning about the power of his wondrous powder.

A look-out rapped on the door with the butt of a spear and an uncanny silence replaced the cacophony.

The Admirals entered the hall. The Italian contingents were sitting opposite each other down a long table smiling as if butter would not melt in their mouths. The delegation of neutral Sicilians judiciously separated Guelphs and Ghibellines, and Béhuchet was pleased to note that the nightmare of Italian politics had not tainted the Kingdom of France. To their surprise Prince John of Sicily started holding forth on the subject of rebellious Flemings. His views were trenchant and uncompromising.

'I would chop them all into small pieces, and pull down the walls of Ghent,' he pronounced, waving effeminate hands in the air, as usual embarking into waters that were way out of his depth.

'Enough!' ordered Béhuchet brusquely, bringing the chatter to a close. 'First let me congratulate my colleague on capturing the *Cog Edward*. The prize money will be substantial.' This was an understatement. They'd captured what seemed to be the King of England's treasury. Hugh had also been amused by the fact that the weavers to whom he sold the wool complained that when they opened the sacks the stuff was duff - a thin veneer of quality surrounding coarse rubbish. *Typical of the English, always trying to cheat.*

'And none for you, Guelph arselicks,' sneered Ayton Doria, unable to resist a swipe at the Monegasques, having taken a hefty cut of the prize money. 'All you get are meagre takings from Guernsey.' He watched Carlo Grimaldi stiffen, his hand slipping to the hilt of his dagger. Béhuchet saw this too, signalling calm, but internecine warfare continued across the table.

'There's enough to fulfil my dream of constructing a gibbet at Monte Carlo only for Ghibellines,' Grimaldi riposted, 'and I will book a place on it for you.' He turned to Béhuchet. 'If it weren't for the money I'd sail my fleet into Genoa instead and boot all the pricks like him onto the benches of my slave galleys.'

Béhuchet rose angrily, smashing his fist onto the table and fixing both Genoese admirals with a withering gaze. 'Enough of this non-sense, *gentlemen*.' He emphasised the word harshly. 'No more politics at this table. We should be celebrating our mutual victories. Guernsey is ours thanks to Carlo. I am pleased to report that my campaign on Jersey yielded much booty. Half the buildings destroyed and all crops burnt. The English will starve this winter.' He paused theatrically, slowly drawing in his breath. 'I don't care a fig where the Papacy oper-ates from,' he said, this time fixing just Doria with a steely glare - *as long as it remains in my pocket*. He narrowed his eyes. 'You agreed to leave your petty squabbles behind. Concentrate on Southampton, and no doubt you'll live to enjoy the rewards of your labours.' His look was eloquent. No more quarrelling. 'Your leader for this expedition will be my colleague Hugh Quiéret. I have business elsewhere.'

He felt bitter that he had to hand over command of the forthcom-ing assault. *If my King commands I must obey - he'll get fewer truffles though...* Quiéret had been standing quietly behind his colleague and now taking a pace forward, he settled himself into the newly vacated chair. He thought about making a witty quip but decided not. He, too, wanted to make the right impression on their Italian allies. Already they knew he was a ruthless operator and that kindness was not a word in his vocab-ulary. Doria had seen his cruelty first hand when he had hanged the remainder of the English crew from the cross beam of their sail. He'd watched as the prisoners had been made to carefully fold the sail away by a smiling and seemingly benevolent Quiéret, hoping and thinking this was a sign of mercy, before they replaced it with their own bod-ies. The dangling bodies reminded him of bunches of grapes as they swung to and fro on different lengths of rope. If he had captured the Englishmen he would have spared them a quick death and chained them to his lower oar bank instead. *Never waste good man-power…*

'I want to hit Southampton on Sunday morning. Catch them in church.' He snorted like a rampant bull scenting cows in season as he contemplated the destruction to come. 'Make it known throughout the fleet that I will pay a prize of one hundred *livres* to the first man to breach the town's defences.' It was a generous incentive.

At least the French aren't fussed about breaking the sanctity of the Sabbath. Doria, like all Mediterranean sailors, knew that the time to hit their traditional foe, the Mussulmen, was when they were on their knees at prayer, so why should the English be different?

'And how much will we get, if it's not too delicate a question?' He knew the answer but felt it important for the sake of his captains to have their terms restated.

'Half is what you agreed. God willing half of Southampton is what you'll get.' It was a generous deal and satisfied his backers. They had put together a substantial fleet. Doria had assembled a private syndicate that included twenty large Mediterranean galleys, each carrying around a hundred men-at-arms. The Grimaldis had added a further fifteen. The King of Sicily sponsored three of Doria's galleys, putting his ineffectual son, Prince John, in command. Catalans from Barcelona, ever eager for larceny and the lure of plunder, provided another ten vessels of differing sorts and Quiéret, along with his flagship, had a handful of substantial war barges from the ports of Normandy and Picardy.

'We must be careful, in our assault, not to attack or damage property belonging to Spain or the Florentines. These are for you.' He handed out the letters and watched as Doria and Grimaldi examined them carefully before opening them. As expected, the deception was perfect. 'The Pope orders us, under pain of excommunication, not to attack or destroy any buildings with bunches of dried flowers on their doors. These will be easy to identify,' reiterated the French Admiral. 'Avoid the flowers. As my colleague Béhuchet pointed out so eloquently: we are out to wreck all that enables them to trade. Assemble squads to destroy the Customs

House, Weigh House and Town Hall. My Normans will take the Castle. We have a novel idea for getting inside. This young man, Simon de Pressi, is going to blow it open with his gun.'

Simon nodded his acknowledgement. His earlier demonstration had been far better than expected. The fact that the hatch, ostensibly three inches thick, had been an illusion didn't trouble him one jot. His carpenters had used two thin sheets of wood held apart with spacers to make the hatch *look* three inches thick.

When they returned to the Admiral's bureau at the Clos, Simon took out a heavy bag containing a hundred and fifty shiny, newly minted gold coins that he'd found hidden in a small box on the *Cog Edward*, and handed it to his wide-eyed master. Béhuchet had never seen these obviously newly struck coins before. They had a leopard on one side and the English king enthroned on the other. He held them up with his Master of Coin's appraising eye. They were small and quite thin. Were they worth it? He wasn't sure, they looked more like test samples than actual currency, but gold was gold.

'Will you keep them safe for me? Just in case. Buy me back quickly,' said Simon, hoping his master would have a shred of decency if he were to fall foul of the English. Having sampled the delights of England, with their cuisine and creature comforts he did not want to spend more time than necessary in the land of the Saxons. Quiéret, in a generous moment, let him keep the money as a reward after the vessel's capture as it had proved to be a veritable treasure trove.

'Have a safe voyage, young man. Remember, if you fall into the wrong hands, play dumb.' Admiral Béhuchet clasped Simon's hands. 'If there is, God forbid, trouble, use the pseudonym of Guillaume de Bapaume.'

Simon was also thrilled that his new Augsburg armour had been delivered. He was deeply grateful; he had never been on a raid, had never tasted the glory of victory and was keen to test his master's gift. When it first arrived he had worn it all night.

When he begged his mistress to let him have sex wearing it, she refused categorically. 'That's creepy. You can save that thrill for when you rape a poor little English girl. When you come back a real man of war....'

Chapter 28

The Miracle of St. Iodocus

Lady Alice bided her time, waiting for Handley to slip out of the kitchen. She had seen him slide in there and knew from his furtive glances that his purpose was probably nefarious. She needed to neutralise him before the secret of her pregnancy became hard to hide. The Bailiff had been happily going about his business - he and Max were indeed cooking up a scheme - when she caught him unawares. Drawing herself up to her full height, she became imperious, as only a lady of breeding could.

'If you ever disobey me, or if you ever mention the minstrel to my husband, I'm going to tell him that you made improper suggestions and tried to force yourself on me while he was away.' No one would doubt the word of a Lady of the Bedchamber to the Queen of England, and he would surely hang, however much he tried to plead his innocence.

Handley gulped. He had only just wormed his way back into his master's good books. The thought was too ghastly to contemplate, so he put on his most obsequious air and bowed low, knowing he was beaten.

The grass is starting to green up the moat, the water is nearly clear, and that man is firmly under my thumb. She felt triumphant as she went to inspect her collection of roses and fruit trees. Her pride and joy were her Warden pears, acquired from the Cistercian Abbey in Bedfordshire. They were late ripening, cooked well and could be stored throughout the winter. She counted them as she often did. It was the first year that the trees had borne fruit. Where there should be eight, now there only seven. She frowned and looked around. A crime had been committed. On the ground some distance away she saw the missing pear with a neat chunk bitten out. Someone had filched one, but who? She shrugged and dismissed the thought; she was in no mood to play detective. Her grapes were swelling nicely on vines clambering over trellising and a ripe purple plum took her fancy. As she savoured the tangy, sweet taste she noted that they were starting to attracted wasps. For some reason their wiggling yellow-and-black backsides brought to mind her cousin Elizabeth, who was starting to get on her nerves. *Why is she staying so long, didn't she say she was only staying for a couple of weeks?* Then the penny dropped, that was before her husband returned. *Ooh, the little minx...*

—⚊⚊—

Five ox wagons laden with wool left Ipers at dusk. They would have to make several trips. The night was clear, with a blowy, gusty wind. Silver-edged clouds, illuminated by the moon, scudded by, and owls were busy calling, hooting balefully in the woods as they made their way along the track. A nightjar whirred and an occasional fox yipped, in turn making a dog bark in one of the fishing hamlets that dotted Southampton Water's edge. The operation went smoothly and, by dawn after the first night, many bales of wool were secreted in woods close to the shore.

Sir Roger watched nervously as more cloud scudded in from the West, praying that the wind would drop. The lookout on his tower had seen the Venetian pulling down from the town. *He's on his way.* The part payment gave Sir Roger a warm glow of confidence, he would make good money. The wind, though, was not going to abate, and only grew stronger as he and the Ox stood on Lepe Beach watching the waves make white horses, with flicks of spume. He was not unduly worried; the Solent never produced dangerously large waves. The tide was at its lowest and they could just make out the old causeway with its leaping stones that gave the place its name. The builders on his castle had prised up many of these great dressed blocks for his foundations. Sir Roger climbed the headland. Way off in the distance he thought he could see the Venetian, moving slowly against the tide into the teeth of an ever-strengthening wind.

He told the Ox to keep watch. 'Send word to me when it nears the spit. I'll be at the ruined chapel.' He had an assignation to keep. *Will she be there?* He mounted his palfrey and galloped off through woods and small fields to the nearby hamlet of Eccesbury. He was not so confident of *this* rendezvous. *Meet me at the derelict chapel at Eccesbury. It's not far, it's opposite the tithe barn.* He'd given her vague directions. Eccesbury was a place of ghosts avoided by most. It had been a town where a thousand souls had lived before the arrival of the French. The storytellers told of a defeated army, led by Dauphin Louis, coming from the landward side. It was they who had wrecked the church, pulling it down, and slaughtering the inhabitants with considerable brutality that left bitter memories. What had provoked the French to this untoward violence no one knew. The roofless ruin had been deconsecrated and, while the Manor's owner had plans to rebuild, this had yet to happen.

His worries were unfounded. Lady Elizabeth's white mare was tied to a post. A few hovels surrounded a pond and a small stone convent, where a handful of poor nuns still prayed for the souls of the departed, stood nearby. He hitched his horse next to hers. The wind moaned through broken window slats and the door banged angrily behind him. She was kneeling at the broken altar. She looked around, a shaft of watery sunlight catching the flaxen colour of her hair through the broken beams in what was left of the roof. Within moments their tongues met in a passionate kiss. They had not even spoken.

Unbuckling his sword, he slid it through to bar what remained of the door. Feverishly she divested him of some of his clothing, getting to work on the laces supporting his stockings until his braes were down by his knees. The urgency of their passion precluded any foreplay as they made love on the dilapidated altar. *I'll have to pay a heavy penance for this pleasure.* It was a fleeting thought as he thrust deep into her, feeling her contract violently in orgasm many times. *This is the sin of lust at its worst*. But he didn't care. She was a squealer, not a moaner. They hardly spoke a word. As they rested, half clothed, reality started to filter back.

Someone was shouting.

'Sire. The Venetian has passed the headland.' It was Ralph, who he had instructed to fetch him when the galley got close.

He kissed Elizabeth again. 'Until next time.'

She helped him on with his clothes and held out his hat. 'You know,' she whispered in his ear as he readied to leave. 'You're the best lover I've ever had.'

He smiled; she had the shamelessness of a Southwark whore.

The arrival of Ralph, who had been foolish enough to go to the convent to ask for the whereabouts of the chapel, attracted the attention of a couple of nuns, who emerged from a wicket gate to wag their fingers at a dishevelled Elizabeth. The younger of them, her pockmarked face contorted with anger, started shouting about defiling a place of worship. Sir Roger rode over to the irate women. Baiting these holy harridans was too good an opportunity to miss.

'Good Lord no, she is a lady with properties in the town and we were discussing farming matters. She slipped on the stone floor and became undone.'

'Ploughing her furrow more like.' The eldest nun, bent double from years of toil, cackled through toothless gums. He took a ducat from his purse, placed it on his finger and thumb, and flicked it into the air.

'There. You saw no one. Go and buy new candles.' He tossed it to the younger nun, who gaped with dismay at the bounty. This would buy a year's worth of silence, and candles as well.

He galloped off towards Lepe and within ten minutes he was standing on the beach with his men. It was obvious the Venetian was in trouble. He was far too close to the shore.

'He's going to hit the bar.' A fisherman pointed to a choppy patch of sea that roiled by the spit. 'There. Go over that and she'll more as likely be a goner.'

'I bet she hasn't got a pilot.' Others were ready to proffer advice. 'I don't think he realises that that's a spit.' The fishermen raced to haul their fishing boats off the beach. The galley would need all the help it could get if it were to avoid being wrecked.

Standing at the stern rail, Bandolini, too, was having regrets that he didn't have a pilot to guide him. His rowers were nearing exhaustion from their struggle against wind and tide. His enquiries about the dangers of the Solent shore had revealed no dire warnings as to its treacherous nature. Mostly he'd been told to avoid getting stuck in the mud. The lead man's shout made him run to the prow. Suddenly he could see the steep drop and roil in the water that marked the bar's edge, and he had to hang on for dear life as the *Swift's* prow dipped alarmingly as it crashed into a wall of water that broke high over the bow, swamping the vessel. The galley reared up, slamming into a second trough before being flung about like a cork in chopping cross-waves. Bandolini had tackled the Siren's Whirlpool, but this was far worse. The first wave caught him by surprise, sweeping his feet from under him. It was only by pure grit that he hung on to the fore rail. Lurching horribly, the galley plunged again and started to slew around.

'Keep her bow to the wind,' he shouted vainly to his rudder men. It was a futile order as they, too, had been swept off their feet. Waves crashed into the *Swift's* exposed flank, sending another sheet of water high into the air and across the rowers' benches. The galley heeled over and, hard as the oarsmen worked, they could not turn her back into the wind. The swirling undertow caught them off-balance as the oarsmen struggled to stay on their benches. The leeside oars shattered and the current dragged the helpless vessel into the submerged bank. Meanwhile, the fishing boats had cleared the beach and were making for the far side of the stricken *Swift*.

Sir Roger looked on helplessly, feeling an overwhelming sense of guilt. 'It's all my fault,' he admitted to his sergeant. Then he remembered his visit to the Cathedral. *How curious, only two days ago a young monk told me that a prayer to Iodocus could prevent shipwreck. It must have been an omen!* 'Pray to St. Iodocus,' he shouted, making his men get to their knees, 'Pray as hard as you can, it will save the ship.'

From his knees, he could see Bandolini skittering across the deck galvanising his crew into action. Men hurried to the mast and started to raise the sail. Several were flung into the sea and dragged under by the current. There was a brief respite until a new squall sent a swirling gust of wind into the half-raised sail. A grinding noise told of the ship's bottom being dragged onto the shallow bar, and there she stuck. Her mast twisted, snapping like matchwood, a tangle of ropes and canvas falling over one side.

'Pray harder,' he shouted, as everyone prayed at the top of their lungs for St. Iodocus to intervene. He looked up. *Heaven be praised, the saint has answered our prayers.* Having worked their way round to the far side of the treacherous spit, the fishermen were cutting away trailing wreckage and attaching lines to the grounded galley. He could also see the crew were hard at work with leather buckets, emptying bilges. A relieved Sir Roger watched the rising tide calm turbulent waters, and as an hour passed, so more control returned to the stricken vessel.

News of the shipwreck spread like wildfire. Someone had lit the beacon on the headland. 'Get that put out at once' Sir Roger was furious, having given Sir Hog a dressing down about irresponsible beacon lighting. 'Go, and stop others being lit, *ride fast.*'

Lady Elizabeth had followed and arrived at his side sometime during the excitement, her white mare tossing its head in the wind. He should have sent her back to the castle; however he was too wrapped up in the drama to do so. Together they watched as the broken mast was disentangled and shrouds cut away and the galley eased off the sand bar. The flotilla of fishing vessels helped to pull the battered vessel to the beach. A gangplank was lowered and anchor lines run up to stunted oaks that lined the shore. Sir Roger strode over as the first quaking Venetians tentatively made their way down the ramp. Behind them, Bandolini was issuing a stream of instructions liberally laced with expletives. He crossed himself as he jumped onto the shingle, and then knelt in prayer for a couple of minutes.

'That was close,' he commented as Sir Roger helped him to his feet. 'I hope it will all be worth it.' He dusted the sand off his knees and started to take stock, examining his hull for damage. After a couple of hours he declared himself satisfied. He crossed himself again and gave thanks. They'd lost half their oars and mast, and the twisting motion had opened caulking in the hull. It would need to be re-pitched and sealed before she was seaworthy. It would take several days of work to make the necessary repairs.

'Perhaps it is a blessing,' Bandolini said. He could take the opportunity to clean off the barnacles and weed from his hull, and make their passage home much smoother.

The wind finally abated to a mere zephyr. The tide turned again and retreated, and by afternoon the sea was calm. An exhausted crew lounged in the bright sunshine while a crowd of locals eyed them with suspicion. Late in the afternoon about thirty heavily armed men came galloping along the beach on well-lathered horses. As Sir Roger had feared, the beacon had been seen. It was John de Bokland and the muster that controlled the adjoining twenty-mile stretch of coast from Christchurch to the edge of Southampton Water. Sir Roger waved to his neighbour.

De Bokland took off his helmet and pushed his mail coif back over his shoulders, giving a half-hearted salute. 'What have we here?' He could see that Sir Roger had everything under control.

'A bloody false alarm.' Sir Roger was pleased to see that de Bokland got there so quickly. *At least he's on the ball.* 'Call it a trial run,' he said, patting his armoured colleague on the shoulder and giving him praise for arriving so quickly.

Pure luck. De Bokland had been on patrol and tossed a coin as to whether he would take his men west or east on manoeuvres. They'd seen the rogue beacon and galloped over.

De Bokland's men milled around. This was no French raider and the sailors were not threatening. Some were sat in huddled groups on the shingle, while others were rigging pulleys onto trees to bring the galley further up the beach. The bodies of four drowned crewmen had been retrieved and were laid out on the sand. The priest from the nearby parish was kneeling beside them saying prayers.

Sir Roger managed to whisper something into Elizabeth's ear. Surreptitiously she moved her horse closer to de Bokland and contrived to distract his attention. While de Bokland was admiring Elizabeth, Sir Roger managed to catch Bandolini's eye. *'Go with me on this'* he signalled.

Drawing his sword, he held it to Bandolini's throat. 'I arrest you for spying for the French.' Bandolini's eyes widened and he spluttered. 'You are my prisoner,' Sir Roger continued. De Bokland's men-at arms dashed forward to surround the Venetians on the shore.

Those still on the stricken galley watched with horror. Some rushed to the aft and, before anyone could stop them, had armed themselves with their deadly crossbows and taken refuge in their central castle around the mast. A foolish soldier ran up the gangplank and was shot through the leg by a crossbow bolt.

Sir Roger then related Eccles' concerns about the Venetian to de Bokland, and explained how he'd lured him to this spot on false pretences. Enough of this could be corroborated if need be.

'I shall take this man back to Ipers and hold him there. Tell your men to surrender.' And, as if to emphasise the point, he pushed the point of his sword further under the captain's chin. Bandolini's hands were then tied behind his back.

'Are you sure of this?' De Bokland was suspicious by nature. A thought occurred to Sir Roger. Perhaps he could be bought. *De Bokland has to outfit thirty men, which must be costing him dear.* Times were hard, after all, and knights had expenses, especially those who had command of the muster.

A glorious sunset was developing over the salt marshes to the west. It would be dark within a couple of hours. Sir Roger still felt guilty and knew that he had to resolve the situation quickly. He strode back over to Elizabeth. 'Do you want to go back to the convent for the night?'

She shook her head. 'I want to stay here with you.'

Bandolini, who up until now had been silent, suddenly shouted something in Italian to his crew. 'Gentlemen,' he pleaded, turning again to the two knights, trying to work out the relationship between them. 'It seems we have something of a tricky situation here. Maybe I can offer a solution? Some of what you say is true. But I am not a spy. I was paid by the Pope to come to Southampton and deliver some letters to the Peruzzis. Apparently they have struck a deal with the Genoese and French that, if they were to attack, then property and buildings belonging to them would be spared. I swear on all that is holy that is all I know.' He spoke appalling French at double speed, which the knights had great difficulty in understanding. The gist, though, was clear enough. They let the Venetian continue blithering on. 'My country has been at war with the Genoese for many years. My only son, God rest his soul, was killed by them only two years ago. I hate those sons of bitches.' He crossed himself, spat and related the story of Cardinal Alberghini's visit.

'So, you mean to say that the French are going to attack us?'

'Yes, I think so. But where or when I cannot say,' answered Bandolini cagily. The Venetian cleared his throat again, desperately looking for signals. 'No, of course not, you're right, we are not here to trade. Why would we want your Lenten leftovers?' Sir Roger knew he was referring to the barrels of salted herrings. 'Though a full cargo will make up for a lot, as you can well appreciate.' He looked pointedly at Sir Roger, who raised his shoulders slightly and glanced quickly at de Bokland.

'The wolves are at the door, gentlemen, and Southampton is the fattest sheep in the flock. Look at the place, stuffed full of riches with only a handful of men and no walls to protect it,' said Bandolini, as the truth of the situation dawned on him.

The Commandatore wasn't expecting his lieutenant to turn up. This was not planned. He lowered his voice. 'I have money on the galley.'

Inwardly, Sir Roger sighed with relief. *I was correct about the Venetian having an ulterior motive. Now buy him off and we can all profit from this.*

De Bokland signalled to his men to release the captain and crew.

The blood red ball of the sun slipped over the horizon. The sea had become calm. Only an occasional cat's-paw ruffled the mirror surface as everyone stood to admire the beauty of the sunset. Fires were built and the small, heavy chest carried ashore. There was food enough for all, bread and herrings from the hold and ale offered up by the fisherwomen. The locals would happily supply the Venetian with whatever pitch and materials they could for his repairs; ducats were not something they saw every day.

Sir Roger led Bandolini a hundred yards up a gloomy track into the woods. Pulling aside some branches, he revealed the pile of woolsacks and ash. 'Here they are. They're all smugglers living here, so I'm sure, for a small consideration, they'll help load your boat. It's not too badly damaged I hope? I'm sorry about the arrival of my friend. Everyone is jumpy right now. You'll be pleased to know that I have honoured my part of the deal.'

'A couple of days and she'll be seaworthy again.'

'I prayed hard for you,' said Sir Roger and he told him of the omen as they strolled back to the beach.

'I saw, thank-you.' Bandolini reached into his purse and took out a gold ducat, giving it to the priest. 'Build a shrine to St. Iodocus and place it by their graves.' He pointed towards his drowned seamen. 'Perhaps it will save others too.'

'It's a miracle, that's what it is,' said the priest jubilantly, leading off into prayer. He'd been jealous of Fyscher's painted church. Now he would have his own shrine. *I'll make it a place of pilgrimage for seafarers.* He let grandiose ideas run riot. He would need more than a golden ducat to realise his dreams.

As they sat on the beach, Sir Roger realised that he had not formally introduced Lady Elizabeth to de Bokland. It was a small world and it could be tricky if he knew her husband. If he did, then he would have to swear de Bokland to secrecy and would be in his debt.

'John,' he leaned over casually. 'I do believe you have not been formally introduced to Lady Elizabeth Rochester - my wife's kinswoman.'

'I don't believe I have had the pleasure.' This was a relief. *But why should de Bokland suspect anything untoward?*

The seamen had made a couple of rudimentary screens of branches, as they were going to be camped there for several days. The evening was pleasantly warm. Sir Roger took off his robe and made a pillow. *It was probably a miracle, God works in mysterious ways. We should give thanks to St. Iodocus.* But as he stared into the flames it was not heaven, but hell, that dominated his mind. Miracle or not, he felt tainted by his sins. He had defiled a holy place and lied, he could not help himself. He had acted on impulse. *She makes me so horny. I'll buy an indulgence, just in case. I don't wish to spend my afterlife assailed by demons.* Poking the fire with a stick, he watched as sparks spiralled up to meet the stars. *The devil has many ways of tripping up the faithful.*

The fishermen had taken advantage of their launched boats and the calm sea to net a school of mackerel. They had brought over more food and drink, and so, instead of near rancid herring, fresh mackerel were cooked on sticks over red-hot coals, their sweet flesh all the more delicious for the circumstances of their impromptu feast. Lady Elizabeth listened enraptured as the Captain told her tales of the marvels of the Orient.

'They're not all bloodthirsty savages,' he was saying. 'In fact they are, in my view, better educated and more cultured than either the English or French. The ones to avoid' he told her earnestly, 'are Barbary Pirates. They only want slaves.' He described his race through the Pillars of Hercules with its great Rock, *Jibal Tariq*, corsairs on his tail. 'Thank the saints I've one of the fastest ships in the Mediterranean.' *And it was half-empty.*

'I've never been with so many real men before.' She fluttered her eyelids demurely, an act of virginal innocence. Sir Roger watched her flirting with the men around the campfire. He would tan her backside for this. His thoughts drifted back to the goings-on in the chapel. After a while, the day's exertions caught up and he drifted off to sleep. When he awoke the fire was getting low. Finding more wood, he stoked it up again. He could not see Lady Elizabeth or Bandolini in the circle of sleeping figures.

The moon was full and he gave an involuntary shiver. Nights were getting colder; autumn would be upon them, with winter not far behind. He went to relieve himself. As he did so he heard a familiar sound - the same squeal of delight that he had elicited only a few hours before. *She is a whore!* He was thinking about interrupting their tryst when another shadowy figure emerged from the gloom. De Bokland had sidled up to Sir Roger. He, too, heard the noises.

'Your wife's kinswoman is totally shameless,' he whispered. *I got a fistful of ducats for turning east not west, so I won't enquire as to what the 'Commandatore' was up to. That name suits the boss.* 'I'm glad I could be of assistance. Commandatore!' He held his purse and made it chink before rousing his men and riding off into the moonlight.

Sir Roger stalked off to find his horse. He was happy with his share of Bandolini's money, which was much more than he had been expecting, more than the value of his wool, so it had not been a bad day's work. Kicking his men awake he gathered up his complaining troop. *So today we've all succumbed to Venetian gold.*

Chapter 29

Under False Colours

Sir Eustace, meanwhile, decided that it would be safest if he and his gang travelled north to visit his sister, Honoria, at Markeaton where she resided, married to Sir John Tuchet. He'd only met her husband once, at her wedding nearly twenty-five years before, and he'd only seen her twice since. He hoped he would get a friendly reception. He also knew that her husband was patron to the Coterel gang, about whose beastliness minstrels had been telling tales in taverns the length of the land, invariably corrupting his name to Tutcher to rhyme with butcher.

Brother and sister looked at each other for some time. He noticed that her hair had gone white and she had crow's feet round her eyes. She was several years older than him and he could remember well the raven-haired beauty with whom he had committed an act of incest, at her instigation, shortly after he had attained puberty. She ran her manicured fingernail down his face in none too gentle a manner as they caught up on old times. *That scar's new, it's an improvement…*

That evening a sumptuous meal was produced in his honour. Sir Eustace told about the trouble with his neighbour. 'He's an insufferable, arrogant prig, and I want my revenge.' Lady Alice's slap had only served to increase his desire to humiliate her. It was a burning obsession that made him seek out only red-headed whores for his gratification.

The Bandit-Master, as Sir John was frequently called, was as Sir Eustace remembered: he had a jovial, round face with a bushy avuncular beard of salt-and-pepper, big, innocent brown eyes, and was slightly running to fat, though this belied brute strength. He always smiled and laughed as he killed; something he did frequently, with a sudden burst of unimaginable brutality that would come out of nowhere. One moment he would be all bonhomie to his victim, the next minute the poor wretch would be gutted like a fish or bleeding his last as his throat was slashed by a special razor-sharp knife he would conceal in the palm of his hand. This was a weapon he had acquired from his crusader father, who in turn had got it from a member of the Assassin Sect.

It did not take long for Sir Eustace to discover a soul mate in his host. They revelled in each other's dark personalities and found much common ground in their all-abiding loathing of clerics.

'They would love nothing more than to see me burn in hell,' Sir John spat out the word 'they' with virulence. 'But what do I care, they're pigmies. Odious little men who deserve what they get. I have my gangs harass them at every opportunity.' Eustace's brother-in-law warmed to his subject. 'Them and these new magistrates, I let them know *I'm* still the power around here.'

Next morning, the brothers-in-law headed to the stables, where the quantity and quality of horseflesh was enough to make any man drool with envy.

'This one belonged to Sir Richard Wyloughby; I want you to have it, a gift from me.'

Sir Eustace, for once, was too stunned to say anything. Wyloughby had been the victim of a recent successful extortion and the steed was a pure black stallion worth at least sixty gold marks or more. As they returned to the hall, arms over each other's shoulders, a plan was conceived.

'Why don't you pretend to be this de Bohun fellow? Honoria could have the women make up some surcoats and a banner with a green boar.' The two men laughed. 'I'll lend you some of Coterel's men.' *De Frage's marauders, has a nice ring to it*. Sir Eustace relished the thought.

—⋙—

'Safe journey! God speed!' *Thomas is such an old woman.* The Bishop of Nottingham bade farewell to the portly head of his household, and returned to his work. The Bishop, being still young and of a martial disposition, had aspirations to make a mark in the forthcoming campaign in Flanders. He had decided to send his non-essential baggage on ahead - papers, spare clothes and anything that might make his stay in the land of the weavers more comfortable. He would join with his contingent of knights and men-at-arms the following week, and, since he had only been able to hire one ship, it would have to make two journeys.

Thomas was nervous. 'There are bandits and robbers in the woods,' he had complained to his master. 'Why can't we have more men-at-arms to protect us?' But the Bishop had been adamant.

'You're not carrying enough money to warrant more than the three I've allocated to you,' he said dismissively. The truth was he wanted to make an entrance, a show of strength when he arrived in Antwerp.

Thomas reached Grantham without incident, leaving early the following morning. His worst fears were realised when they were ambushed within three miles of town. In a leafy glade, a knight wearing a green boar rampant motif and an old-fashioned cylindrical helm signalled them to stop. The three men-at-arms, seeing they were outnumbered as more men with green boar uniforms appeared, dropped their weapons and fled.

The knight was surly and unpleasant, ordering the clerks and servants to lie on the ground before his men ransacked the Bishop's boxes, strewing papers in the mud.

'Who's the leader?' he asked brusquely.

Timid Thomas raised his hand. 'Strip him and tie him to a tree,' the knight ordered while he, too, lifted his surcoat and dropped his braes. Keeping his helm on, he sodomised the terrified secretary while his men happily did likewise to the rest of the party.

'I'm Sir Roger de Bohun,' he whispered, repeating the name several times to make sure that the cleric would remember it after his ordeal was over. 'I'm going to spare your life so you can tell everyone how merciful I am.'

'Take their habits.' He ordered Falke to strip the monks. 'You never know when they might come in useful.'

Chapter 30

Safe and Sound

After endless days of ocean from horizon to horizon, the sight of land was at least cheering. It was only when Captain Hawthorne recognised familiar landmarks on the coast of England that he could finally relax. He was safe at last. After their brush with the Basque pirates they had been becalmed before encountering contrary winds. It had taken all his skill to navigate by the stars before catching the warm current of the Gulf Stream that swept them to safety. He knew it was home from the jagged white spikes of the Needles that guarded the western end of the Solent. Safety was less than a day away. He raised a toast to St. Christopher in fine wine. Their drinking water finished, the crew and passengers on the *La Nicholas* had been reduced to drinking their way through several casks of his wine, spending the last few days in a drunken haze. A shout from the lookout in the crow's nest alerted him to a vessel on the horizon; there was a galley coming towards them.

'Let's hope it's not hostile,' said the Captain, making a quick sign of the cross. As far as he knew there were no English galleys, so chances were it might be a pirate.

'Bollocks,' muttered William, ordering his men to string their bows again.

'So near, yet so far,' whispered Hawthorne under his breath. 'It would be a tragedy to succumb in sight of home,' he observed to his first mate as the two vessels closed.

'It's Venetian.' A relieved crewman pointed to the Lion of St. Mark streaming from the mast. The *Swift*, her repairs completed and hold filled with Sir Roger's ash and wool, was on her way home. The captains waved to each other.

Home also beckoned to Captain Hawthorne, who pointed to the distant steeples of Southampton, waving at passing fishermen whose boats chased the last mackerel shoals of the season. For all its adventure, it would be a most profitable trip, and clear a tidy profit. He would be back in the bosom of his family and lay his ship up for winter. The port was bustling as he spotted an empty berth near God's Gate and the archers, who had not enjoyed the voyage, suffering from seasickness and lack of provisions, tumbled down the gangplank in an unseemly rush. In homage to dry land, several knelt down and kissed the dock.

William was last to go. Still drunk, he thanked the captain effusively.

'No. It's *you* I must thank. We would be resting in a watery grave had it not been for your archers.' Hawthorne added: 'I'll arrange a feast for you.'

This sounded an admirable idea; however, William was conscious of the need for a cart to carry their equipment and headed off into the town. After a fruitless search he was about to give up. Still, he did not relish the thought of lugging all his kit back to Cheshire. Then, joy - outside the Wool Hall, three carts were standing empty and idle. On his way in, in the gloom, he bumped into a man whose breath smelt worse than anything he had ever encountered. The brute swore and called him a pea-brain, but went straightway to the carts.

Handley, business concluded, wanted to get drunk. Clutching his receipt from the Monopoly Consortium for their remaining fleeces, he searched his purse for coins. There were none. Then he remembered the prostitute he had been with earlier that day. *The bitch must have thieved my money.* A tap on his shoulder made him spin round. Involuntarily his fist flew toward William's face who, with the lightning reactions of a man used to violence, caught his fist mid-punch.

'A fine way to treat a fellow who wants to do a deal with you,' quipped William. 'I wonder if you would sell or rent one of these carts.'

'Where do you want to go?'

'Cheshire.'

Handley made a calculation. It would take weeks to get to Cheshire and back. Perhaps he might get four pence a day for a cart and three a day for his men. And if they could pick up a load of freight for the return journey... 'One pound, plus you sort out food and lodging for my men.' That would net a tidy sum and, if he were clever, his master might not notice a missing wagon or two.

William tried to haggle. 'That's too much.' They could only find eighteen shillings and six pence. It was all the money from the dockside auction of their goods. Lack of cash was the reason they had left France in the first place.

'Give me that, too.' Handley pointed at a fine tablecloth. 'And if it's a deal I'll be in the Three Bells.' He strode off, feeling happier.

'Do it, William,' spluttered an archer. 'I don't want to have to lug my entire kit all the bloody way home.' One of them was sent after the retreating figure. Deal concluded, William and his men set off for the feast.

The archer's feast was hastily arranged, with pork, capons, fresh bread and butter and good English ale aplenty. The Captain made a speech in praise of the longbow and the following morning, equipment stowed on Sir Roger's wagon, they set off home. Southampton's euphoric mood continued. With the delivery of the rest of Sir Roger's wool and safe arrival of *La Nicholas*, it had been a good week.

That Saturday night, the senior burgesses met at the Mayor's house to try Captain Hawthorne's wine. The Mayor commented on its excellence as he drained his fourth glass. 'You should get at least £6 a barrel.' He was a major purveyor of fine wines and knew quality when he tasted it. 'Is it all as good as this?' His mind was calculating fast. This was worth a minimum of eight pence a gallon.

'Be assured that some is *even better*.' Hawthorne was confident of clearing nine hundred pounds for his cargo. He would live handsomely on his profit, building a new ship to replace one he had lost.

'I'll take fifty barrels.'

Mayor Sampson stood up and raised his mug. 'I propose a toast to our continued good fortune.' The company got to its feet. 'To Southampton, long may we prosper!' The party wound down and the leading townsfolk made their way home. Tomorrow was Harvest Festival, the first Sunday in October.

Eccles looked at the setting sun as it set directly behind the tower of de Bohun's castle. Eccles had not met up with Sir Roger and had heard only vague reports from Lepe. *Aristocrats are all the same, they're your best friends when they need something - otherwise they're self-obsessed petty tyrants...*

Chapter 31

The Granddaddy of all Boars

'I thought he loved me,' Clothilde confided to Nunny, tears streaming down her cheeks. 'But now I see he is as fickle as the rest of them.'

'Who?' asked Nunny, as Norah Segrave was called. She was a well-born widow fallen on hard times and presently head of Lady Elizabeth's household. In her mid-thirties, she had a long, angular face with smallish eyes, a wide mouth and teeth like a horse. She wore her hair in a bun under a tight fitting wimple, giving her a severe visage; however, the French girls soon discovered this concealed a heart of gold. As far as Nunny was concerned, she had been forced to seek a position that she felt was definitely beneath her status.

'*Le Crevette.*'

'You mean Dan Digby.'

'*Oui.*' Clothilde had not yet mastered much English. A shrimp by name only, after his play with the hat they had had a couple of passionate sessions in the stable and she had found he was no shrimp in that department. Then she had caught him canoodling with her friend Beatrice and, instead of joining in, as Dan had asked, she had stalked off in a jealous rage. However, Clothilde and Beatrice both agreed that Dan was more fun alive than dead.

'I was going to make him a mushroom stew with some of these,' she said, giving Nunny some white Death Caps she had collected and telling her how deadly they were.

Nunny was intrigued. The French girls who had come with Lady Alice had much more knowledge about which fungi were edible and which were not. Instead of throwing them away Nunny put them into her purse. *They might be of use...*

—ɱ—

Having come back from her amorous adventures several golden ducats richer, Lady Elizabeth had behaved as if butter would not melt in her mouth. She enquired solicitously of Lady Alice if she wanted to come for a ride, though she could not really mask the insincerity in her voice.

Alas, in her condition, Lady Alice felt she should not. *The little bitch might be behaving as if she's decided to take up holy orders, but you can't fool me.* She watched Lady Elizabeth lead out her white horse. With an exaggerated sigh, and downcast eyes, Elizabeth said she was off to visit a local shrine to contemplate.

Even though Lady Alice felt that it was not seemly for a woman to ride alone she also felt a hint of jealousy. Deliberately barring her exit from the castle, she asked pointedly as to when her cousin was thinking about going home. Her patience with her kinswoman was wearing thin and, as far as she was concerned, the sooner the little trollop was gone the better.

'Oh, soon,' came the airy reply as Lady Elizabeth ducked under the outstretched arm with a 'fuck-you' expression on her face.

Lady Alice could not put her finger on the source of her unease, but suspected that her husband was paying too much attention to this slut. Little things: this newfound piety and desire to pray at local shrines didn't ring true. *What had Sister Elfreda said about some happening at the old Chapel? That had been on the same day as my husband had been to Lepe.* It might only be a rumour, but she would investigate further.

Sir Roger, meanwhile, found it hard to moderate his ways so as not to arouse suspicion, his ingenuity well-taxed to come up with safe meeting places for their trysts. Lady Elizabeth's sexual inventiveness never ceased to amaze him. *My little tricksy vixen,* he called her, on account of her owning and wearing a fox fur cape. *My big dog fox,* she called him and together they called themselves *Monsieur and Mademoiselle Reynard*. This time the shrine in question was not a shrine but a deserted woodcutter's shack. She bent over and presented her perfectly rounded pink buttocks to him and, as he took her from behind, she let out a little yelp of pleasure. He mounted her like a dog, something his wife would never let him do.

—⟋⟍⟍—

Early next morning, the castle courtyard was alive with men and dogs. The autumnal air was crisp and scented with the aroma of damp fallen leaves. Golds and browns sparkled as a mist percolated in wisps through beech trunks. The women of Ipers were out early, combing pastures and woods for edible fungi. Blackberries glistened and needed picking before the devil got to them, and Max was busy producing an endless stream of pies and tarts filled with all the delights of field and hedgerow.

Sweet-scented wood smoke drifted from the village houses as hams were prepared for the coming winter. Serfs and villeins alike prayed that God would keep them from starvation once this season of plenty was over. Sir Roger, mounted on Theseus, his favourite hunting horse, was filled with rising excitement as the party made its way to the yeoman's cottage where the boar had been last reported seen. Boar was his favourite quarry. *It might be Satan's own animal, bred in the pits of the netherworld but it is also a noble beast.*

'What weapon am I going to use for the kill?' he asked Alfred. Would he go for the kill on horseback or on foot? The ritual for the hunt had been laid down over many generations and Sir Roger needed to resolve many of these questions.

'Up to you, Sire.' Alfred, a stocky, wiry fellow skilled in tracking, had hunted with many gentlemen and was unafraid of expressing strong views. 'A worthy foe should be tackled on equal terms,' he opined. 'On horseback you risk losing a horse through bad luck. On foot you only have yourself to blame.' *Only the bravest men will go on foot, or the most foolish. Or is he just a brave fool?* Time would tell.

Sir Roger, too, was well aware of this and knew that his reputation in the district hinged on his decision. He had never hunted such a formidable quarry, if the tales about this beast were true. He couldn't show weakness now - not that he really needed to, seasoned warrior that he was. He had made up his mind. 'It shall be on foot with spear. What do you think?' They rode on together. 'Will it be as big as he says?'

Alfred knew the yeoman was not prone to exaggeration. 'If he says it's the Granddaddy of them all I believe him.'

In the distance beater's horns reverberated through mixed oak woodland, and huntsmen cried out their familiar halloos. Sir Roger's hounds, his prized alaunts, scented the air. They galloped across streams and through thickets before coming to a halt, a wall of tangled brambles covered with enticing blackberries barred the path. Sir Roger reached over, picking the juiciest, sweetest berries. A hound picked up some scent and started calling. Horns blared and men shouted.

The chase was on again.

A squealing sow with three stripy piglets burst from the undergrowth and headed at speed into a dense patch of gorse. Once inside her prickly fortress, she turned to face the dogs. Sir Roger took pity; she was not the object of the hunt. It was her mate that he sought. The dogs were called off.

Hunting was thirsty work, and Sir Roger called for a flask of wine, draining it in one go. The cool elixir refreshed him, its alcohol taking subtle effect. In the distance more horns spoke of a new sighting, galvanising him into action again. Digging his spurs into Theseus, he weaved through the trees at full tilt. He urged his mount on; maybe he would change his mind and tackle his adversary from horseback after all. He felt the weight of his boar spear, jabbing it down as if striking his prey; the weapon was wickedly sharp, with a crossbar to stop the animal riding up the shaft. *No, I will still make the kill on foot,* he decided, as blaring horns and yelping hounds signalled their quarry had been cornered.

The alaunts had cornered a massive razorback under a blackthorn bush where it grunted and squealed aggressively at anything that approached. Darting, snapping dogs tried to bite the enraged beast. One got too close and was ripped open by the wicked yellow scythes that slashed from side to side. The boar's piggy black eyes showed no fear, as he kept his tormentors at bay with brief charges. The huntsmen formed a ring, keeping a safe distance. As Sir Roger rode up, he eyed up the formidable tusks on his adversary and reckoned they were even larger than the ones embroidered in his banner.

He would go in alone, he declared, dismounting and tossing his spear from hand to hand. It might be foolhardy, but he was feeling invulnerable from the heady mixture of wine and adrenalin. His prize would not retreat. Alfred stayed close behind, weapon at the ready, just in case.

Sensing that its new adversaries were all on foot, the boar charged, scattering yelping hounds like chaff. Paying the price for overconfidence, Sir Roger had no time to react and was flung to the ground. He only just avoided being cut by Satan's hell-beast as it slashed sideways with its ivory knives. Rolling over, he pulled the spear point round catching the boar's shoulder. The wounded monster squealed as loud as the Devil's Trumpet and rounded with incredible speed. Up again, Sir Roger turned to face his adversary, but tripped on an anthill.

Ignoring dogs biting its backside, the beast determined to finish off its human tormentor. Spittle flecked its cheeks as it renewed its deadly onslaught. The moment was critical, the fraction between life and death. Sir Roger acted on reflex and instinct alone, plunging the base of his spear into the anthill and as best he could, aimed the blade towards the heart of his enraged adversary. He mouthed a quick prayer, a God-help-me-now-dispatch-this-servant-of-Beelzebub. Then it was all over. He felt the blade slide in up to the crossbar. The sturdy shaft snapped like a twig as it took the whole weight of the stricken animal, which must have died the instant it was pierced through the heart.

Huntsmen crowded round and Alfred congratulated him with deep respect. 'What a trophy! What a beast! It's the biggest I have ever seen.'

'Thank you, Lord,' Sir Roger whispered, crossing himself. It had been a close shave and, as he stood triumphant over his trophy's head, he was quite unprepared for Satan's final revenge, as he would later call it. The animal's heart might have stopped, but its brain still retained a spark of life. It slashed its razor-sharp ivories one last time. A white-hot lance of pain shot through Sir Roger's calf, but his euphoria was such that the pain evaporated. H only noticed it again when Alfred called for a bandage. The tusk had ripped through boot leather and then flesh down to the bone.

Alfred pulled off the damaged boot and flushed the wound out with vinegar that he always carried for just such an eventuality. He was pleased to report that no major blood vessels were broken, noting that otherwise blood would have been spurting everywhere.

'That's a nasty wound. We should take you home right now.' Alfred expressed his concern as he cut the torn top off the boot, replacing it carefully onto his master's foot.

'This is going to hurt some more,' said the huntsman, taking an iron he had been heating in the fire. He cauterised the gash before applying a spider web and herb poultice that he carried in his pouch, and then binding the wound.

Sir Roger was adamant that, though in considerable pain, he wanted to see the beast dismembered first. *Pain is personal, I must not let it spoil the moment.*

The carcass needed to be rendered manageable. They could have carried it back to the castle whole but, as Alfred explained, the meat tasted altogether better if it was dealt with while the body was still warm and before the blood congealed. Some cleft sticks and staves were cut from a nearby coppice while Alfred searched through his saddlebags for special knives and cutters. These he placed beside the carcass.

A wooden tripod groaned under the weight as the boar's blood was drained into a flask. Its belly was slit and innards removed. The lights, stomach and intestines were fed to eager dogs as reward for their bravery; the tongue was cut out and stored for the feast that would follow. Heart, liver and kidneys were wrapped in some fat and sizzled on twigs over a small fire the beaters had built. The delicious aroma of cooking made the hungry men salivate. They offered Sir Roger the heart. As he bit into it, fresh juices ran down his chin and a dreamlike expression passed over his face. He would later say that it was one of the best things he had ever eaten.

Alfred peeled off the bristly hide; the tough leather was perfect for making cuir-bouillé armour plates. Then, taking great care in jointing up the cadaver with his razor sharp implements, he deftly removed each leg and split up the rib rack. By the time he had finished, the body had been divided into many parts.

Sir Roger was helped back onto Theseus. His leg throbbed mercilessly, every movement bringing another stab of pain. But he had faced Death, in the form of Satan's Beast, and come through his ordeal. That was all that mattered. The boar's head was placed on a pole and, horns blaring triumphantly, trophy held high, the hunters returned to the Castle.

The procession reached the moat as the sun settled over the horizon, horns alerting the household to the hunter's return. Lady Alice came into the yard to greet her husband, who raised his hat and waved. In his joy, he forgot his wound. Dismounting, the pain overwhelmed him again. This time he fainted, sliding unceremoniously to the ground.

'Take him into the hall.' Alfred was quick to react.

Lady Alice looked on as her unconscious husband, face deathly white, was carried into the hall and laid out on the high table.

'Is he alright?' she asked, deeply concerned.

Master John listened to his chest. 'Still breathing and heart pumping, Ma'am.' He unwound the bandage. 'Get warm water and the juice of crushed garlic.' His father had been a successful barber-surgeon, so he had seen many such wounds and he knew that wounds treated with garlic rarely went septic. With a bowl of warmed water, he carefully re-cleaned the gash. 'I need needle and thread,' he demanded.

Sir Roger recovered consciousness, remembered the anchorite's token that lurked in the bottom of his purse, and placed the scrap between his teeth. Before applying a new poultice, Master John neatly sewed the wound shut with strong thread. It required many stitches. The agony was near unbearable as the needle was repeatedly driven though skin. *I will not utter a sound.* Sir Roger was determined not to show any weakness, silently reciting this mantra as he bit into his sacred token.

Handley had returned while Sir Roger was feverish and garbled something about something. But his mind had been so befuddled by Master John's concoctions that Sir Roger had sent him away.

—◊◊—

'Let's see how it's doing,' John said unctuously as he removed Sir Roger's bandage a couple of days later. He bent down and sniffed. 'Still garlicky, no pus and not gangrenous - wound's healing well.' This was a relief.

'It's itching a lot.' Sir Roger had to resist the temptation to scratch. He had received enough wounds to understand that this was a good sign. He could stand again and tottered downstairs using a crutch. *Tomorrow is Sunday and I want to show myself.*

Chapter 32

So Much for New-Fangled Weapons

All week provisions had been taken aboard the Franco-Genoese fleet and weapons honed in readiness for action. The excitement was palpable as it prepared to leave the safety of the Scheldt Estuary. From there it took a couple of days hard rowing to reach the lee of the Isle of Wight, where they anchored, undetected, in a deserted cove in the late afternoon. The Admiral looked nervously at the nearest headland, but still no beacons had been lit.

So far so good.

He could not believe his luck, the English were indeed a dozy lot.

The Master Mariner snuck ashore and placed several markers on the beach; he then spent several hours watching the shoreline from their anchorage, gauging the way the water receded from the cove. If his calculations were correct, it should be rising in the morning. This he told the Admirals with a fair degree of uncertainty, hoping the regularity of the tides on the English side of the Channel were similar to those of his home port in Picardy. If the tide was too low, it would mean wading ashore in mud; if it was high, they would be able to jump straight onto the beach.

Hugh Quiéret gathered the commanders on the French flagship for their final briefing. Wine was served, along with a light meal of bread and salamis. Ayton Doria took out some dice and pointedly inveigled Carlo Grimaldi into a game. Carlo won a hundred ducats in the first few rolls, but got distracted and missed Doria switch the loaded dice.

'Double or nothing,' offered Doria, hiding his smile.

Grimaldi agreed. He was up, and was in fulsome mood, having agreed a truce for the duration of the campaign. After three consecutive wins, Grimaldi suspected the dice were loaded and was about to accuse the Ghibelline bastard scum of cheating, but a don't-you-dare glance from Hugh made him stop and pay up.

'That man,' said Quiéret, watching as Prince John of Sicily preened himself in a corner of the cabin, 'is as useless as a eunuch in a whorehouse.'

Doria shook his head. The Prince spent endless hours in front of a Moorish glass mirror, preening. 'You're telling me. But I'm saddled with him.' His father's plea to Doria was to try and make a man out of him. 'I'm sure the nonce can't fight.'

No one was impressed with Prince John. His father, the King of Sicily, was of hard-fighting Norman stock, brought up on crusading and sieges. His son was the opposite and a grave disappointment to the old man. However, the King was a key Ghibelline supporter and had twisted Doria's arm with money. This was a make-or-break adventure for him.

Then it was down to business and tactics. 'I *insist* that my Normans take the castle.' Hugh was adamant in his argument, while Ayton shook his head disparagingly.

'Admiral, I beg to differ. My boys are battle hardened, yours are a mixed bunch of gutter-trash,' he said disdainfully. *I bet he'll come crawling back.*

The Admiral chose to ignore the last remark, and ploughed on with the briefing. 'We've got our secret weapon,' he said, pointing to Simon de Pressi, who smiled nervously. Simon gave a run-down on the defences of the town with a map he had prepared from memory.

Admiral Quiéret finally summed up the meeting. 'Remember the houses of our Italian and Spanish friends have bunches of dried flowers hanging on their doorways. Make sure your men leave these well alone. The soldiers and men-at-arms all have allotted targets - the rest, you may loot and burn at will.' He looked at the nascent moon. The plan was simple. Doria's men, and those of the Grimaldis, were to concentrate on the area of the town closest to the docks and empty the warehouses; the Normans, using Simon's untried *ribaud* and ladders, would break into the castle. The town was to be comprehensively and systematically ransacked, warehouses first, then street by street, house by house.

'Call me if you need me, which I think you will.' Doria then went over to where Simon stood. 'I bet your gun won't work, son. Believe me, you'll need something bigger than that,' and he climbed down the rope ladder into his waiting jolly boat.

—∿—

Next morning, Quiéret stood on the rear castle of his Norman barge. His excitement was infectious and men cheered as sails were raised and the great fleet got under way.

'Is it going to work?' he asked Simon, remembering Doria's last comment. Though he never admitted it publicly, the Admiral had little faith in this new weapon, but Simon was ever the optimist.

'Of course it will! You saw my demonstration.' He had to keep up the pretence. He was loath to admit that he'd had little success in real tests. The *ribaud* was inaccurate and had limited range. It most probably wouldn't even make a dent in a castle gate. The gun was just for show, as his master had cogently explained to him. His job was to find the Bank, blow off the door and purloin its contents.

The fleet looked magnificent. Norman barges with multi-coloured striped sails and rows of shields mounted along their sides and Genoese galleys, their upper works painted black and yellow. *My hornets*. Quiéret's thoughts were proprietorial as he watched as his oarsmen rhythmically stroked the calm waters of the Solent. In all there were over one thousand fighting men and nearly seven thousand or more oarsmen, sailors and non-combatants, clerks and personal servants, all hoping for a rich haul of booty and slaves.

'I dread what *they*'ll do when they come ashore.' Doria looked into the belly of his galley, where all manner of weapons were being sharpened and handed out. The journey up the Atlantic coast had been tough and his men were in the mood for mayhem. He knew exactly what they would do, but he didn't care. It would be a nightmare for any townsfolk who fell into their clutches.

Feverish activity gripped the fleet as each man prepared, making steam rise into the chill autumn air. It was St. Francis of Assisi's Day. Admiral Quiéret, kneeling to receive Communion from his personal chaplain, was not sure the saint, renowned for his kindliness, would have approved of the bloodshed that was to come. 'Still, I must make peace with God - just in case. 'On other vessels, a smattering of warrior clerics also conducted rudimentary church services.

Simon fussed over his precious *ribaud*. 'Be careful!' he ordered his four gunners as he ran his hand down the iron tube barrel that was bound with metal straps, before stroking the bulbous end. The bell makers had assured him that casting it in segments and binding the tube was just as strong as casting it in one piece. It would be mounted on its wooden framework when they got it ashore.

Quiéret, too, wondered if it would work. He also rubbed the strange contraption as he made his final tour of inspection, and, leaning forward, he admired his reflection in Simon's burnished breastplate, enquiring if it was really from Augsburg. He liked the look of it. After the capture of the *Cog Edward* he, too, was considering a new set, but was still undecided whether it should be German or Italian. Simon was pleased he had made his valet polish it to a mirror-like shine. His new helmet sported a plume of black and white ostrich feathers.

'I like those, too,' said the Admiral, with more than a hint of jealousy. His own helm had a battered mastiff on top that had once been gold plated. 'Once we've found the bank we'll organise a diversion. Have you got enough of your magic powder?'

Simon nodded, rechecking his supply of fuses and his tinderbox. He had been wearing his armour for an hour and was finding it cumbersome. He hoped he wouldn't have to do anything too strenuous.

Across the fleet other leaders were completing their preparations. Pacing up and down his galley's central walkway the Genoese Admiral addressed his oarsmen. 'You may go ashore once the town is secured.'

A great cheer went up from the rowers, all free men, who relished the idea of sacking a whole town. After four months at sea, many had yet to go ashore - wine, women, pillage and retirement had been the main topics of conversation.

'Heaven help anybody caught by that lot,' said Pietro Maruffo, one of the Genoese captains, as they assembled for their final briefing. Wearing canvas trousers, few rowers had shoes or proper weapons. Most were armed with eating knives, clubs and, occasionally, a hatchet.

'Concentrate on emptying the warehouses - load any wool or wine into the *navises,*' ordered Ayton Doria, making their priorities clear. He had thoughtfully brought along three capacious sailing ships that rode high and empty ready to be filled with bulkier booty, bales and barrels. 'Don't let the rabble loose until the town is secure and make sure everyone understands the signal for retreat.'

'What about those Satan-spawn Grimaldis? What are they going to get?' Maruffo hated Guelphs.

'Less than us! We'll just have to be quick,' added Giorgio Spinola, knowing all about Guelph trickery. 'If I catch one I'm going to slit his throat just for the pleasure of watching his blood spurt out.' They both laughed; but Admiral Doria was in no mood for bickering and told them to shut up.

'Slit a throat when it's dark if you have to. I gave my oath to the French that we've left our feuds behind.' He also reminded them not to attack any neutrals ships, as there was a strong likelihood of there being a Spaniard in the harbour.

Carlo Grimaldi relayed the same orders to his captains, only his invective was directed at Ghibellines.

Fog banks shrouded the shore, hugging the water. It was low enough for lookouts in the crows' nests of the taller ships to see over the top. The fleet edged cautiously forward into the mist, the water flat calm, and as hoped, the tide rising. Admiral Quiéret watched as porpoises broke the surface, chasing mackerel that had sought security under the shady hulls, their flashing blue bodies jumping clear of the water as they tried to escape the jaws of predators beneath.

'Do you think it is an omen of things to come?' He said to his Master Mariner, pointing to the fish so close to the boat. From across the water wafted the sound of church bells summoning the faithful to their devotions. *There'll be a lot of killing today* - he crossed himself - *and on a Sunday, too.* The Admiral had few qualms, and attacking unprepared and unarmed civilians on the Lord's Day of Rest was not one of them.

—⧞—

'That fog is as thick as a sheep's fleece,' the toothless soldier reported to his sergeant, before returning to play dice in the guardroom of God's House Tower. Because nothing ever happened on a Sunday, the wooden barricades along the dockside would remain in place until after church.

Dressed in their finery, Eccles and his wife made their way to church. His fur-edged robe was in keeping with his status as head of the Oil-Sellers Guild. 'Are you coming to Matins?' he asked Mary, his only child, who he adored above everything else.

'I'll come to Evensong, if that is alright with you.' She was nearly eighteen and ready for marriage. Opposite, on the Florentines' door, a garland of dried flowers still hung in its centre. The whole house was closed, windows shuttered; they had gone to Bristol on business. *The town seems to have emptied of foreigners.* Eccles realised that none of the usual international crowd had come to the celebration of Hawthorne's return. He passed his mother and servants who were in the kitchen; they had already made their devotions.

'Look, I got these yesterday.' His mother showed off her new shoes. 'A bargain at thruppence.'

Eccles smiled benignly. He had already paid the shoemaker five pence just so he would sell the shoes to his mother at a knock-down price. He had given her the money and it made him happy that she was happy. More often than not the old woman no longer knew who she was or where she lived.

He, too, looked at the fog that shrouded the harbour but was pre-occupied, distracted by the anchorite who was uttering dire warnings. *Stupid woman, I wish she'd shut up.* Then he stepped in fresh shit slopped out of an upper window and cursed under his breath. *Town ordinances about refuse collection needed revising.* He made a mental note to bring it up at Council's next meeting.

—⁓—

Slipping through the mist one by one, the raiders ran their bows onto the shingle at the town's edge. Ramps swung down and sailors ran out anchors. Men-at-arms and crossbowmen slipped silently along the base of the walls until they reached the wooden barricades. Anyone they encountered, mainly drunks and whores, were swiftly put to the sword. Bowmen shot down those who tried to raise the alarm. A makeshift battering ram made swift work of flimsy defences and within minutes the attackers were inside the walls. A flood of armoured warriors fanned out, killing everyone in their path.

—⁓—

'*Agnus Dei*, Lamb of God, bless our …' the vicar of St. Michael's stopped mid-chant as he was about to say 'harvest', when a flaming torch came crashing through the stained glass window behind the altar. Loud shouts came from outside, alarming the congregation. Someone opened the church door to see what was happening, only to reel back inside, clutching his throat. The square was full of panicking people being chased by men-at-arms flailing swords and axes. A hail of crossbow bolts cut down those that ran outside. Terrified survivors ran back into the church, shutting and barring the door. Above the din, Eccles heard the anchorite scream one last time before she was pulled from her booth and beheaded.

More torches crashed through windows, setting tapestries and drapes alight. Fire took hold of the decorative stooks of corn that were part of the Harvest Festival. Acrid fumes caught in Eccles's throat and, seized by panic, he ran blindly into the vestry looking for his wife, where he was almost knocked senseless as the door burst open, slamming him into the wall. The screams of the dying filled his ears and, wife or no wife, he knew he had to escape. Using the bodies of dead townsfolk as cover he worked his way on his belly to his garden where he hid by his cesspit getting glimpses of the horror that now engulfed his town.

Paralysed with fear, he watched as a group of soldiers grabbed his beloved Mary and bundled her away. Hot tears rolled down his cheeks as he prayed for her life. *At least she's still alive.* What future awaited her, he could not tell. He was powerless to stop heavily armed men hurling all his possessions onto the street and empty his cellars of stock. His strongbox was so heavy it took four sailors to carry it off. He wanted to shout out, to do something, but utter helplessness overwhelmed him as he struggled to maintain his precarious grip on the pit's edge and a new drama unfolded.

He watched as, for amusement, some soldiers hitched ropes to the beams of his house and pulled it down using draft horses, first front and then back, leaving a vast pile of rubble. Everything he had striven for in life collapsed, his family destroyed. *God has forsaken me.* Sliding into the foulness, he cursed himself for not having been stronger in demanding stouter walls. Cursing his own greed, he decided to die fighting and, thus resolved, hauled himself from his stinking hiding place. His fine robes ruined, his hat lost as he surveyed the flattened ruin of his house, he realised that he was alone. Opposite, the Peruzzi Bank remained untouched. Each time a band of raiders passed they looked, saw the dried flowers and went on. Now he understood their meaning, but too late.

—⚏—

From his vantage point on top of the King's warehouse, Richard Imberd the Bailiff could see enemy ships and watched in alarm as smoke arose from the first fires.

'No surrender. I'll go and summon help,' he shouted to his sergeant as he grabbed a horse, mounting bareback and joining the mass of fleeing townspeople. The Castle gate closed behind him and the portcullis came crashing down as two hundred Normans rushed toward it. His bowmen started to mark their targets.

—ᴍ—

'Keep up, men.' Simon, by now pumped up with adrenalin, had outrun his gunners. 'Put the *ribaud* up here.' He selected a spot just out of bowshot where his men set up the elaborate wooden frame and fitted the barrel; his six-foot long gun looked painfully inadequate. *Elevation, distance, charge… merde,* he swore inwardly. He hadn't a clue, so he carefully ladled in some more black powder before loading a weighty iron bolt. *It'll be a miracle if it hits the gate.* It wasn't the distance that worried him. He knew from his trials that these bolts would go at least twice the present distance. It was just that they didn't always fly straight.

'This ain't going to do nothing to that,' commented his gunner with a disparaging look as he surveyed the massive portcullis and iron-studded door more than two hundred yards away.

This is the moment of truth. Simon was acutely aware of the enormity of his task. *I hope no one important is watching.* A feeling of hopeless inadequacy came over him as he touched the fuse. The *ribaud* bucked fiercely as the missile hurtled at the gate. *Bull's-eye!* It went through the portcullis and into the door. Hearing the bang, Quiéret strode to his side. Reloading, they fired again. This time the heavy bolt struck the stonework spinning high into the air.

'Just as I thought,' observed Quiéret, 'useless.'

'No, I'm sure it'll work. Double the charge,' Simon ordered. It proved the *ribaud*'s undoing. The explosion blew the muzzle off, bursting its seams. Two gunners standing closest took the full brunt of the blast. One, writhing in agony, was holding his guts in; the other lost both hands. Simon felt something slam into his chest, knocking him off his feet. Quiéret looked down, offered his hand and hauled him back up.

He shrugged. 'So much for new-fangled weapons,' the Admiral said quietly, shaking his head. Summoning his leading knights, he issued a stream of new commands. 'Get scaling ladders. One hundred *livres* for the first man over the wall.'

The Normans rushed forward, each man eager for the prize. Desperate defenders tried pushing the ladders away with long pikes, slashing with swords at those who clung to the battlements. A pile of broken bodies was growing at the base of the wall.

'Make yourself useful,' Quiéret ordered Simon. 'Get Doria and crossbowmen. Hurry!' Prickling with shame, Simon slunk off to find the Genoese Admiral.

Though he said nothing, his I-told-you-so expression said everything. Genoese crossbowmen started picking off the defenders, giving covering fire as more ladders were put up against the walls. Still the castle guards managed to dislodge them.

Doria brought up his reinforcements. 'We'll attack in three places. Your boys need practice at this sort of thing. You need my monkeys.'

The Genoese sailors could climb far quicker than bulkily-clad Normans. A steady stream of arrows and stones continued to rain down. The twenty men of the garrison and the remaining warehousemen were whittled down to ten and, unable to repel agile mariners, were overwhelmed, with their bodies joining the growing pile of corpses at the base of the wall. Everyone found inside was summarily executed.

Simon examined his handiwork without satisfaction. The *ribaud's* bolt had pierced the door, its point protruding through four inches of wood, but that was all. *Not the right tool for the job. Round shot would be better...*

—◊—

The streets were filled with fleeing people carrying whatever they could. Roving gangs of freebooters slew whoever they caught. Oarsmen, now set ashore, hunted down women, taking turns to rape and murder. More disciplined groups of men-at-arms systematically looted houses, torching wrecked shells.

Through this mayhem, Captain Hawthorne slipped unnoticed, arriving at the dockside in time to see *La Nicholas* being crewed up and taken out to sea by drunken Norman sailors. He felt the irony of the moment - to have escaped Basque pirates on the high seas only to lose it all in his own home port. He watched distraught. His great fight had been for naught. No longer caring for his own safety, he didn't notice the soldiers. He died quickly, his throat cut, his body skewered by a sword.

—ɷ—

From his mansion at the town's north end, the tax collector watched a pan-icking stream of humanity. Gathering up his family and servants, he grabbed a sword. Taking as many bags of money they could carry, they joined the fleeing masses. They did not stop running until safely outside the walls. Looking back, he could see smudges of smoke rising into the still morning air. The bells of the nearby Priory started tolling in alarm. Groups of villag-ers gathered on the road, where, instead of offering assistance, they started robbing the refugees of their possessions. A gang advanced menacingly on the tax collector, but, seeing his weapon, thought better of it.

Now two streams of people moved in opposite directions, towns-folk running from carnage; country folk armed with clubs and pitch-forks, attracted by the commotion, entering the maelstrom intent on adding to the town's woes.

—ɷ—

Admiral Quiéret was increasingly satisfied. Other than the losses at the Castle, his force was unscathed. Leaving Doria to empty the King's warehouse, he sought out the Monegasque leader.

'It's miraculous,' he remarked to Prince Grimaldi as they stood in the Weigh House, 'that no-one has put up any resistance.'

Grimaldi agreed. Many men sweated profusely as they worked to remove the beam of weighing scales. Over a century old, it had been a marvel of its age. With much grunting, the Monegasques finally hoisted it off its pivot.

'Well done.' The Prince was delighted as he admired his handiwork and congratulated his crew. 'It will make a perfect ceiling joist for my new palace.'

'These'll make good additions to my collection,' Doria said, show-ing the admiral Custom's Seals. 'I picked some up on the Guernsey raid. Every town I sack, I try and get the seals. If there's one thing guaranteed to annoy a King, that's his townsfolk losing their seals.' He laughed. 'They don't seem to be able to operate without them.' *This is going to be a most profitable bit of piracy.* He poked through a pile of broken Venetian glass piss bottles that were now strewn across the floor.

An out of breath man-at-arms signalled the Admiral. 'We've found the Bank,' he whispered discreetly, giving him directions.

'Get de Pressi,' he ordered, before turning back to Carlo. 'You stay down here in the docks and finish emptying the warehouses.'

From his hiding place at the edge of the pit, Eccles watched with interest as a knight in shining armour and an ostrich plumed helmet arrived at the door of the Peruzzi Bank, where several other senior-looking individuals joined him. They were soon deep in discussion.

'Here's the bank. Open that and retrieve some glory,' said the Admiral.

Simon looked at the impressive door set in a high stone wall and went off to collect all his kegs of gunpowder.

'We need to put some weights on them,' he said, instructing his remaining gunners to pile wood and stone on the barrels while he carefully laid a trail of black powder from the pile. This done, everyone disappeared from view.

'Here goes,' said Simon as he struck the tinderbox. He lit the fuse and ran. The resulting explosion took the front right off the building. The blast knocked Eccles back into his pit, deafening him. The French swarmed through the rubble, slew any guards who remained alive. It did not take long to find the keys to the vault. With joy in his heart, Admiral Quiéret saw that, as his colleague had promised, it was full of chests of treasure.

—ɯ—

Itching in his leg had kept Sir Roger awake for most of the night and now his mood was foul. Pacing painfully up and down the solar, he was in the process of haranguing his obdurate Bailiff, who had been particularly evasive about certain items in the manor's accounts, when a distinctive noise, a clear explosion, came from the direction of Southampton. He recognised it immediately. *That's the same noise as that made by Magister Frakenham's magic powder. Someone is using gunpowder!* He limped up the tower and in the distance he could see columns of smoke, more than usual, rising from the town. Church bells started ringing with an insistence that told of something untoward.

'We'll finish this discussion later. Let's find out what's happening,' Sir Roger said, heading for the courtyard. A dishevelled figure, riding bareback, clattered over the drawbridge. It was Southampton's Bailiff, Richard Imberd. Sliding off the horse and pointing, a jumble of incoherent words tumbled out.

'The French have come, raise the alarm, light the beacons, summon the muster,' was what he meant to say.

'Calm down.' Sir Roger had dealt with panicked men before. 'Breathe deeply.'

'It's happened.' This time he was coherent. 'Thousands of pirates have captured our town. It's a nightmare.'

Sir Roger felt the blood drain from his face; he had just sent the remainder of his wool to Southampton. Adrenalin surged through his body as he issued a flurry of orders. Suddenly his leg didn't hurt any more. He ordered his groom to get Samson, his war-horse, ready for battle. An iron triangle alarm was rung vigorously, galvanising the garrison into action. Everywhere men scurried around, putting on armour and gathering weapons. Soon the yard was filled with horsemen. Reinforcements arrived as hobelars answered the call to arms. A stable boy led out Sir Roger's warhorse and his palfrey. His armourer filled a cart with his armour, lances and all the accoutrements for his steed, throwing the thickly padded green caparison and saddle on the top.

'Be careful,' Sir Roger barked, wincing with pain as his armourer laced up shin protectors. *I'll get the light stuff on now.* He'd put the rest of his kit on when he arrived at the battlefield and took stock of the situation. *Always eat before a fight, that's what cousin William says.* He stuffed his mouth full of bread, washing it down with wine and taking some dried sausages from a plate Max had prepared. Half an hour later he kissed goodbye to his tearful wife and prepared to lead his troop to Southampton.

'Raise the drawbridge,' he shouted to Lady Alice. 'Let no-one in without finding out who they are.' If this was an invasion rather than a raid, he was glad his loved ones were behind stout walls. With Gwyn in front carrying the Green Boar Banner and Dan, Zuzu perched precariously behind, leading about fifty men, he galloped round his moat before heading off.

It took an hour to reach the bridge over the Test Estuary, pushing their way none too gently through refugee clogged roads. The afternoon was as windless as the morning had been. At the crossroads they met the first men from Winchester. Recognising Sir Hugh de Lacey, Sir Roger immediately went over to confer.

Sir Hugh was close to tears.

'So it has finally happened. We must drive them off. Stop them coming inland.' So far there had been no reports of mounted enemy knights and all action was confined to town, so it was probably not an invasion. Sir Roger asked what other fighting men had answered his beacon on Farley Hill. It had been alight for some time, blazing out the warning and summoning the muster. As if to answer the question another column of soldiery raced into view. Sir Roger knew from their banner they were Sir William de Palton's men. Their numbers had swelled to over two hundred fighting men.

'So,' de Palton inquired, taking off his helm and shaking out his white hair, 'who's in command?'

Sir Roger, though theoretically outranking de Palton, remembered his wife's jibe at his feast and decided it would be diplomatic to defer command to the older man as he knew the layout of the town better. The Sheriff and his Commander nodded their heads in agreement. *Let him have his moment of glory.*

'Gentlemen, I have no plan, we must drive them off and save what's left.'

The knights and soldiers readied their armour. Sir Roger, now encased in padding, mail and plates, had difficulty in mounting his destrier. Sir William expressed his concern.

'Hunting accident,' replied Sir Roger through gritted teeth, the pain making him nauseous. 'Fucking boar ripped my leg.'

Without further ado their forces advanced through extensive market gardens where fruit and vegetables were grown outside Southampton's walls.

―⁂―

Eccles pulled himself out of his cesspit and sat in his garden. His house was in ruins, his wife was still missing - almost certainly dead - his possessions purloined. He wept until he had no more tears. Then, gathering himself together, he went in search of a weapon. *If I'm going to die then I want to kill as many of the bastards as I can.* He crept into the street, but his part of town had gone quiet. The Peruzzi Bank was a shell, emptied of its contents. Smoke from fires made hiding easy. Occasionally roving bands hurried by, easily recognisable: the enemy either wore armour or were near naked muscle-bound savages. Bodies were strewn everywhere; men, women and children, all equal in death; hacked limbs lay casually in the road, as if waiting for a new owner. A dog ran down the street carrying an arm. A group of dancing oarsmen paraded a baby impaled on a spear. Eccles vomited. Corpses dangled from charred beams. Another group came into view. These were not enemy but local villagers. They, too, had worked out that the houses with the garlands were untouched and broke into them instead, looting the premises, not caring who owned it. Whooping with delight, they scurried off into the smoke.

'Master Eccles, is that *really* you?' It was a loud whisper. 'I thought you must be dead.' Startled he looked round. There, hidden behind a wall, were several men. He recognised his chief porter.

'We must do something.' Eccles found an iron tipped club. 'Come with me.' The weapon gave him confidence. As they dodged up alleyways, being careful not to be seen, the numbers swelled until at least fifteen followed along in a crocodile. It was time for revenge.

―⁂―

From his temporary headquarters in the Town Hall, Admiral Quiéret took stock. Money from the bank had already been successfully spirited into the cabin of his ship *without the Italians getting a whiff.*

'Far more than expected,' he crowed to Simon as they surveyed the rest of the rich pickings, which exceeded their wildest dreams. They had taken wine, gold, wool, cloth, and spices in abundance. The Genoese had also captured many young women, who stood wailing and weeping, fearful of their final fate. Mary, Eccles's daughter, was among them, clothing torn.

'Take them to my galley,' ordered Doria as they were roped together. Their origins would conveniently be forgotten when they were sold as slaves. *When I return to Genoa I'll be rich enough to sway the elections.* He rubbed his hands together with glee at the thought.

Hugh had never seen the Italian so pleased with himself and asked what he was going to do with his share. Doria had made his mind up. He was going to be a power broker. He would become a political puppet master and he puffed out his chest, imagining himself in the Palazzo Pubblico giving Simone Boccanegra what for.

His dreams, and those of all the raiders, were brought back to earth with a jolt. An out-of-breath skirmisher brought the news they had dreaded: enemy knights and soldiers had been spotted approaching from the north.

'We'll hold them tonight with crossbows.' The Admiral issued a stream of orders. 'Assemble men; we must defend our ships at all cost.' He was acutely aware that his fleet was presently stranded high on the shingle, having missed the evening tide. It would be a long night.

Raiders' bloodlust satisfied, the killing had now stopped and drinking began. Most were eating butchered pigs and chickens, cooking them on makeshift spits over the smouldering ruins of houses. Sergeants combed streets for stragglers. Units of crossbowmen and *pavissiers* headed for the enemy, each pair operating as a team - one to fire his crossbow, the other carrying a shield and short pike to combat enemy men-at-arms.

—◊—

Prince John of Sicily had steered clear of the main action, preferring to avoid any real fighting. With his squires he was searching a fine mansion near the West Gate for valuables. A well-stocked pantry yielded wine and food. In an out-house they found a cripple.

'There, I've bloodied my blade,' he said, running his sword through the unfortunate's neck, he shrugged his shoulders as his victim drummed his feet on the floor as his spirit departed. The Prince wanted to show that he, too, had dealt out death, not that he enjoyed killing defenceless civilians. *I'll be a hero after this.* The Prince wiped off the excess blood from his blade with a rag. *My overbearing tyrant of a father will not be able to complain any more. Now I'll be able to relax in my scented lemon groves, compose poetry, play my lute and dally with boys.* All criticism extirpated. They were about to leave when they heard whimpering from a closet. Inside a girl, no older than twelve, cowered, scared out of her wits.

'Take her as a slave. She'll fetch 20 marks in Genoa market,' estimated one of his acolytes. But the Prince had other ideas.

'No. I want to ravish her first,' he informed his squires, who were of a similar bent to himself. 'She'll do. This young flesh is perfect.' He had watched as oarsmen rounded up and raped women with a mixture of disgust and excitement. The urge to do the same was overwhelming. He grabbed the front of her dress, ripping it off, while his men pinioned her face down on the table. He sodomised her so she would still be a virgin when she went on the auctioneer's block. Sated, he felt like a real soldier and allowed his squires to follow suit. When they had finished, they bound her hands and pushed her into the street. 'Take her to my ship,' he ordered happily.

He did not expect the group of vengeful townsfolk that rounded the corner, led by a bareheaded madman, his face burnt red down one side and brandishing a club. Eccles's men grabbed the Prince while driving his squires back into the house and forcing them to make their escape through the garden. The first blow took him by surprise as he tried to draw his sword. Out of instinct, he put his hands up to protect his head, but the club smashed into his knees.

Eccles landed a body blow as his old porter tripped him up with a stave, flooring the Prince.

'*Arrêt. Je suis un prince*,' he pleaded in French, but to no avail. He tried a different tack, 'I'm worth a fortune in ransom money.' The crowd of sullen Englishmen led by the wild-eyed fanatic, covered in excrement, looked at him in amazement.

Again the Prince begged for his life. 'Look, money.' Clumsily he found his purse and shook out some gold coins. 'I'm worth much money.' The realisation dawned on him that the crowd did not speak his language. 'Ransom, ransom,' he whimpered pathetically, hoping that there was a universality in that word, as he tried to scrabble back towards the door. He thought there was a glimmer of understanding in the madman's eyes.

'Ransom, I'll give you ransom you Frankish bastard. Now you'll die.' The reply came in perfect French as Eccles smashed his iron-tipped club into the cowering prince's head. The first blow broke Prince John's hand. A second whack smashed his teeth, the third knocked his bascinet clean off, and a fourth splashed his brains across the ground. The crowd took his weapons and stripped the corpse before hacking him limb from limb. The old porter quietly went down on his hands and knees and scooped up the money.

Chapter 33

Zuzu's Prisoner

The sun was setting when John Bokland and his muster arrived from the west. His forty additional men was a cheering sight. On any other day everyone would have stopped to marvel at the sky, clouds suffused with yellows, oranges and reds, but there was no time. The light was fading fast.

'Good to see you, *Commandatore*. Any orders?'

'No plan. William's in command. Let's throw these bastards out of town and save what we can.' *Commandatore* - the Venetian had called him that and he liked that title. *It has a certain ring to it.*

Sir William had noticed that the gates were still open and realised that their enemy had made a mistake as he watched groups of Genoese crossbowmen take up positions at the end of a field of cabbages. *If we're quick...* 'We must secure the Bar Gate. You keep them busy, while I sneak some hobelars round the side.'

Sir Roger closed his visor, the dying sun glinting off his lance point. With Bokland, and flanked by uniformed men-at-arms on foot, the knights looked magnificent and felt invincible. They might not be much of an army, but they were fired up and eager for action. The cabbages, all in neat rows, were between the chevaliers and Genoese. The *pavissiers* had set up lines of shields between houses lining the gardens. Each window had a crossbowman, often two, loosing quarrels at advancing men-at-arms, who zigzagged forward seeking any shelter they could. It didn't take long for the charging horsemen to reach the shield wall. A few crossbowmen ineffectually loosed off their weapons in their direction before running for cover. Sir Roger aimed his lance point at the back of a fleeing Genoese, running him through. Pulling it out, he steadied Samson, who pawed at the ground and whinnied with excitement at the smell of blood. His warhorse seemed to relish battle. Sir Roger skewered another, but this time the point stuck firmly in his victim.

'Blast!' he mouthed several oaths and, though Samson pulled back as taught, no amount of shaking could remove lance from body. No time to waste, he drew his trusty morgenstern and started flailing out at the remaining shields, which were soon outflanked and overwhelmed as groups of soldiers entered each house, flushing the enemy out. The Normans in charge of the gate tried to put up a fight, but were too drunk as the hobelars rushed them and summarily slaughtered them on the spot.

William de Palton encouraged them on in the last glimmer of dusk as their little army of deliverance entered the devastation. The liberators were confronted with corpses dangling from collar purlins alongside shop signs, on streets illuminated by brightly burning houses. They faced an enemy that flitted through the shadows, occasionally loosing off a crossbow in their direction.

Bar Gate secured, Sir Roger signalled Justin to help him off Samson before putting him somewhere safe. He winced with pain as he dismounted and he limped into their new headquarters. Charitable as ever, Sir William put his colleague in control of the gate.

'I'll establish where our enemies lurk.' The old warrior was in his element, shouting orders, sword in hand, men-at-arms at his side, spring in his step, and he entered the game of cat and mouse that ensued, fighting scrappy actions amongst smouldering ruins. The English soon learnt to avoid blazing buildings. These, they found, illuminated them as targets for the Italians, who kept to the shadows. It would be a gruelling night.

—⚒—

Prince John's squires found Admiral Quiéret at the Town Hall and reported the fate of their master.

'Died like a man, cock in his hand,' he observed dismissively. He'd have to write to John's father, the king. He'd concoct a glowing report on the heroic death of his son. *All lies, but good riddance.* The French Admiral had other worries now the muster had arrived in force. Above him, beams carried their quota of English bodies. They were lowly clerks who had tried to defend their place of work, throwing inkwells at his men. They swung slowly to and fro as a slight breeze sprung up.

On a table in front of him were the Town Charter and Common Seal. *These will make fine gifts for my master, the* Rightful *King of France.* He swept them into a large leather sack.

The Hall was emptied of all its plate and treasure, candlesticks and crucifixes from ransacked churches safely stowed aboard their ships. In a final triumphant act he emptied his full bladder on the threshold before ordering his men to burn the building down.

The ever increasing breeze fanned smouldering timbers so that many houses burst back into flame. The charred ruins were burning fiercely again, flames illuminating surrounding streets and alleys. Posting sentries, Sir Roger sent a team to reconnoitre the walls towards the Castle.

Ordering the portcullis be lowered, he settled back into a chair in the officer's room to await events. *Now no one can enter or leave the town without my knowledge.* Some tallow candles had been found and guttered in the rising wind. Zuzu sat in a corner wearing a red jacket and was concentrating on grooming herself. Every time Sir Roger caught the ape's eye, she raised her lip and hissed.

'Hell spawn,' he hissed back.

The Sheriff came in and sat down at the guardroom table. He was close to tears with exasperation. 'What next? The King will have to be told. He'll be as mad as a cut snake.' He didn't relish being the one who had to tell him about this disaster. *We'll cross that bridge when we get to it.*

The thought was distressing enough. 'We must drive these pirates off first.'

Sir Roger, too, had been struck by an unwelcome thought. 'I hope I haven't lost my bloody wool. I delivered five wagonloads last week. All I bloody well had,' he moaned bitterly, conveniently forgetting what he had sold to the Venetian.

De Lacey was sorry to hear that. 'What in heaven's name is that?' Nor had the Sheriff noticed the ape in the gloom of the corner until now. He jumped up in startled amazement when he saw her.

'Meet Zuzu, she's our troop mascot.' Sir Roger motioned with his hand disconsolately. 'I hate the beast, gives me the creeps.'

Sir Hugh sat down, taking off his bascinet. Much to his consternation, Zuzu casually got up, sauntered across and climbed up the back of his chair. Perching beside him she proceeded to search his hair for lice.

'Can you get this thing off me?'

'Sadly no. If you put your helmet back on she might stop.'

Sir Hugh replaced his headgear with alacrity. Zuzu looked around for more amusement and, seeing none, went back to her corner.

The success of blowing open the bank's door had cheered up Simon. *Vindicated!* he thought triumphantly. He'd returned to his ship and taken off his armour, which had been starting to get uncomfortable.

'Look at this,' his valet pointed to a deep dent where the piece of exploding gun had struck him. Simon examined the damaged breastplate with the realisation that it had probably saved his life. *Thank you, oh gracious Toad.* His thoughts then turned to what his mistress had said - *you can fuck a little English girl in that suit.* A string of women were being shoved on board, so he picked one at random – young, pretty but catatonic - then led her to the captain's cabin and enjoyed himself before letting his valet have a turn.

All the success aside, the Admiral was still smarting from the debacle at the Castle. Along with other Normans, he had endured a barrage of snide comments from their Italian counterparts about their storming abilities. So when word came that the English occupied the Bar Gate, he galvanised them into action.

'I'll lead them,' Simon volunteered, now rested and eager to show willing. *Hero of the hour can become hero of the day.* The chance for more glory was too tempting, he told his valet as they strapped his armour back on.

A fighting retreat did not appeal to the Admiral; he really didn't want the English controlling the walls while he tried to re-embark.

'Split your force in two.' The Admiral gave his instructions, but Simon was only half listening. 'One group should attack along the wall and get the others to come through the streets. Have them in a pincer movement. I saw that the Castle has a good supply of pitch torches. Use them.'

—⟶⟵—

Sir Roger made a spur-of-the-moment decision and promoted Dan to sergeant. The men respected Dan and Sir Roger had noticed that they often deferred decisions to him.

'Does that mean I'll get more money, Boss?'

'Don't push it!' Sir Roger was in no mood for lip. He put Dan in charge of a group of hobelars. Dan armed himself with a pike and called Zuzu, who climbed onto his shoulders.

This was his first action. Sergeant he might be; experienced in warfare he was not, although he considered himself a skilled stave fighter, having been a pilgrim to the Holy Land where often he had only a stout stave to fight off rogues and bandits. A thrill of excitement coursed through his body as he tried out several manoeuvres with the weapon, getting a feel for the blade. However, having never killed a man before he felt his stomach churn with nervous anticipation. Cautiously, they made their way along the wall to the neighbouring tower.

One of his hobelars pointed at the line of torches coming in their direction. From their vantage point they could see the column split into two.

'You'd better go back and tell H.Q.,' he instructed the archer.

Patrolling south of the gate, the Ox also took one look at the approaching column and returned to the gatehouse. 'Torches coming from the Castle,' he announced, out of breath. 'What shall we do? He feared they were heavily outnumbered.

'We fight. There's been enough cowardice to last a century,' said the Sheriff gruffly. *There can be no retreat.*

Sir Roger stood with difficulty. His leg throbbed horribly and he had trouble putting weight on his foot. He ordered Justin to ready his destrier.

'Let's see if Samson can do what he's trained to do.' Sir Roger said a silent prayer hoping that the many hours they had been spent working with this horse in all manner of combat would now pay off. The streets were dark, scary and hellish as the wind whipped up showers of sparks from the still-flickering flames. Sir Roger could feel the animal quiver as he was helped up. He leant over whispering calming words in Samson's ear, before putting on his bascinet, not bothering to lower his visor as he wanted to see as much as possible. On either side of the warhorse Sir Roger's men were on foot, led by his faithful Ox.

Normans emerged from narrow side streets, rounding a corner, carrying torches aloft. The puddle of light illuminated only a few feet in front as they peered nervously ahead. Their destination was concealed in gloom. The soldiers in front slowed, as apprehensive men will do. Suddenly, snorting and rearing, a mounted knight came at them out of the darkness, their worst nightmare becoming reality.

Samson's training was impeccable, advancing slowly at an angle, kicking out with his hooves. Some Normans tried poking flaming brands towards his horse but Sir Roger flailed with his morgenstern, whirling it round, striking heads and crushing helmets with ease. 'Don't-poke-that-at-me,' he yelled, cracking another skull between words. The line of pikes, spears, swords and shields on either flank of the prancing horse slammed into their disorientated foe, stabbing and slashing like a well-oiled machine. The Normans bunched, those behind pushing forward, those in front falling back. They could not stem the relentless onslaught of knight and men. Those trying to defend their heads from the spiked ball were speared through undefended ribs or sliced up by Gwyn's falchion, his oversized curved meat cleaver severing arms and necks with equal facility. Sir Roger crushed any head he saw. In panic the Normans fell back in disarray and fled for their lives.

'No pursuit,' ordered Sir Roger, withdrawing back into shadow again, curbing his instincts to chase the fleeing men. 'We don't know what's around the corner. We'll make them fear the dark,' he growled to Gwyn. 'Norman men-at-arms are one thing, Genoese crossbowmen are another - I'm not going to risk an eighty guinea warhorse….' He could see *pavissiers* advancing past a burning building. They would have to employ a different tactic to deal with them.

Finally reaching the walls, Simon ordered his men forward with trepidation, now bitterly regretting his decision to lead a counter-attack. It was much further from the safety of the ships than he had anticipated and he was rapidly becoming exhausted. The weight of his new armour was more like a millstone, but he clung onto the thought that he was in command. In a momentary lapse of concentration he let his mind drift away from matters at hand: he'd become a Roman emperor riding his chariot in a triumphal procession.

Reality returned abruptly with the sound of twanging bows as the first arrows came hissing out of the darkness. With only two men able to walk abreast, they cautiously approached the tower. One man fell, another tripping over his body before it was pushed into the void. Fizzing out of the gloom, a shaft glanced off his Augsburg plate, a second went through his shield, striking his mail coif as he struggled to maintain his balance.

'Sons of bitches,' he cursed and pulled the arrow out before breaking it into bits. The tower which was their objective loomed out of a fiery backdrop. More arrows and Simon realised their firebrands were acting as beacons. He shouted to his men to throw away their torches. Quickly these were flung onto roofs as yet untouched by destruction. Crouching down, he edged slowly forward towards the tower's door. He was no more than a couple of yards away when, through the limited field of vision his visor afforded, the door swung open to reveal a screaming banshee.

Inside the tower, Dan remembered his father's words of advice: *if in doubt, yell as loudly as you can, it will startle and demoralise your enemy.* Thus, with Zuzu screeching, aping his shouts with a shriek of her own, Dan burst out onto the battlements with the ape hanging onto his head. To Simon it was a seven-foot tall, twin-headed, ululating monster. Rooted to the spot, fear made his bladder and bowels release involuntarily. All around his colleagues fled but he was unable to move. Then one of the heads spoke to him in broken French.

'Yield, you are my prisoner,' said Dan, thrusting his pike tip under Simon's chin and hauling him unceremoniously back into the tower, where he was stripped of his weapons and hogtied.

Employing different tactics, a few men showed themselves fleetingly in front of the Genoese. Sir Roger slipped quietly with the remainder of his men through alleys, circling round behind, and suddenly charging out at full gallop, flailing his morgenstern from side to side as he crashed through their line. Before they had time to react his men-at-arms were again butchering with swords and axes.

Between bouts of fighting, Sir Roger had time to inspect the carnage wrought upon the town and its inhabitants. Corpses littered the streets; male corpses stood out like white fish stuck in mud, stripped of clothing by rampaging oarsmen, women's clothes were of no use to them. The English ventured as far as the Town Hall, which was now blazing furiously. Sir Roger watched the clerks fall one after another as fire severed the ropes. He was appalled at the massacre. Suddenly a blackened figure emerged from the smoke. Sir Roger raised his morgenstern, ready to crush another skull, when a voice he recognised spoke to him.

'Is that you, de Bohun? It is I, Alfred of Eccles.' The merchant burst into tears of relief and clung, shaking violently, to Sir Roger's armoured boot. Together they returned to the Bar Gate.

—m—

The chastened Normans fled back to their barges and steadfastly refused to return to the fray. If their boats had not been stranded so far up the beach, they would have put to sea.

'No more forays,' ordered Quiéret as he listened to reports of English counter-attacks. He went with Doria and Grimaldi back to their beachhead. 'I don't want more losses. Get as many ships afloat as you can. We leave at dawn. We'll meet in Dieppe to divvy up the booty.'

'I concur; I want to live to enjoy my prizes.' Carlo Grimaldi nodded in agreement; his Monegasques occupied the South Gate and God's Tower, having been driven to the town's edge by de Palton. With caution as the watchword, an uneasy standoff reigned, with neither side capable of taking advantage in the dark.

Chapter 34

A Slip of the Tongue

The horror of his experience had left Eccles a gibbering wreck as he tried desperately to unburden himself to the Sheriff, often choking between words. All he could do was repeat the word 'terrible' over and over. Sir Roger stepped in and offered succour and charity.

'Come to Ipers, stay until you have found your feet again,' he said, as the merchant slumped to the floor and made himself into a ball of pity in the corner of the guardhouse.

The knights listened to descriptions of the rapine unleashed by oarsmen that were shocking beyond belief. The fact that other Christians should do this on a Sunday was unthinkable and barbarous. The Sheriff was most galled by reports of looting by local villagers as he listened to the tales from survivors, and was furious that Englishmen had probably stolen as much as the pirates.

'Something I would expect of Mussulmen,' ventured de Palton, for those who fought them attested to their cruelty towards Christian womenfolk and their disregard for the sanctity of the Sabbath. Their deliberations were interrupted by the return of Dan, who pushed a simpering, hogtied Simon de Pressi through the door.

'I've captured one of them,' he boasted. 'I hope he's worth ransoming.'

The word 'ransom' suddenly made Eccles start up from his corner and, with surprising clarity, he recounted the slaying of Prince John.

'The only reward I wanted was to see him die. All the money in the world will never make up for today,' he said, bursting into tears once more. Inconsolable, he slumped back, alone with his grief.

'What have we here, then?' They crowded round and, in the candlelight, examined their captive and admired his shiny new armour.

'I'll have those.' Sir Roger pointed to the plume on Simon's helm - these were a dream realised. Simon was untied. Rubbing his wrists, he tried to restore circulation to his numb hands.

Bokland took out his dagger threateningly. 'Talk, or I'll cut your tongue out.'

Remembering his master's advice, Simon tried to play dumb, but under the pressure of the knife details started to spill out.

'I have never been on an expedition like this.' Simon sweated profusely, his mind racing. 'I've never witnessed sacking a town. I'm a man of peace.' This drew a wry laugh from the Sheriff, who took over the interrogation.

'Who is in charge?' He was a practised inquisitor, forcing questions out in rapid, staccato succession, never giving his victim time to organise his thoughts as he flicked his iron-studded gloves none too gently across Simon's cheeks.

'Admiral Quiéret led us - he gave the Italians free rein.' Simon added quickly that he had been shocked by their brutality.

'What's your name?'

'Simon de Pressi,' he said quietly. He stopped and took a deep breath, hoping they had not paid too much attention. '*Mon nom*,' he now said as clearly as he could, 'is Guillaume de Bapaume.'

'What did you say before that?'

'Nothing.' His mind was in overdrive. 'I said *s'il vous plaît*, please, I didn't hear the question. Guillaume Bapaume, my name is Guillaume Bapaume.' He knew he had made a mistake. The alias he had agreed with Béhuchet was Bapaume. Trying to back pedal-served to compound his errors. 'To think' he continued, thoroughly confused, grasping at straws, 'that someone once said Italians were civilised. I came as an observer,' then it slipped out, 'with the *ribaud*.'

'What? What happened?' Sir Roger was all attention. 'Repeat what you just said?'

'My name is Guillaume de Bapaume, I'm just a poor knight, I came along with the cannon but it didn't work.' Simon tried to make his role insignificant, telling them that the *ribaud* had been left in the Castle ditch.

'Find it,' Sir Roger ordered Gwyn. 'First thing in the morning.'

'If you're so humble and a poor knight, how come you've a five hundred *livre* suit of armour?' The Sheriff was accurate with his valuation and Simon knew it. He would have to concoct another lie that was believable - but was spared the effort. The interrogation ended as Bokland clattered in to report on the situation at the south end of town.

'Got 'em bottled up in God's Tower and the Barbican,' he recounted breathlessly. 'I'm not going to winkle them out tonight.'

Taking Simon's helmet with its ostrich feather plume, Sir Roger tried it on for size. *Not a bad fit,* he thought as he lifted the visor.

Again something jogged Eccles out of his misery. 'He's the bloke who made the front of the Peruzzi Bank disappear,' he said quietly to the Sheriff. 'I saw his men pile up barrels; he lit something and ran away. After that there was like a thunderclap...' he waved his arms wildly, trying to emulate the effect of an explosion, '...blew me into my frigging sewage pit, made the whole front of the building turn into smoke. Strong magic, whatever it was.'

'I thought I heard an explosion.' Sir Roger told the Sheriff what he knew about gunpowder. 'Put it in your report.'

Monday's dawn was cold, freshened by a brisk north-westerly breeze. The tide had risen and the raider's ships pulled clear of the shingle and joined their fleet offshore. One by one the last galleys and barges slid off the shingle until only those of the rear-guard remained. Admiral Quiéret was becoming more and more agitated, he was ready to leave, but there was no sign of Simon. His questioning was met with shaking heads. 'Didn't he lead the expedition to try and capture the gate?'

A man nodded. 'I thought he came back with you.' Everyone shook their heads again.

'*Merde!*' The Admiral swore many blasphemous expletives as the truth dawned. Simon was dead or, worse still, in enemy hands. 'That *is* a veritable disaster.' *Mon Dieu, what shall I tell the Toad?*

The Genoese hornets had already raised white sails with red crosses that flapped noisily, waiting for sheets to be tightened. They were riding low in the water, holds and decks crammed with booty, waves lapping at their gunnels. *Simon is lost – that's bad*, thought Quiéret, so he gave the order to depart.

Gaps in walls and along wharfs were being fought over as the English knights pressed forward with their men, trying to prevent any last remnants of their enemies from leaving. The final rear-guard of *pavissiers* and crossbowmen held their ground, retreating volley by volley. A few remaining men-at-arms ran along the beach, torching fishing boats and nets. On the rest of the fleet, halyards and sheets were pulled tight, wind filling sails; whooping with joy and shouting obscenities the oarsmen put their backs into their task and, like overweight water beetles, the fleet sped towards the Solent and home. The last Italians broke and ran for their ship. It was too late. The English charged down the fleeing men, cutting them to pieces before rushing up the gangplank of the last galley. There would be no mercy, no quarter given. Those who surrendered were made prisoners.

'Strip them and hang them from the masts.' And, as an afterthought, de Bokland added: 'Cut off their privates, give them something to chew on as they strangle.'

Ayton Doria ordered that the captured women be paraded. With his armour removed and a beaker of what was proving to be a rare and fine vintage wine, he ached from his exertions of the previous twenty-four hours, but he was not so tired that he didn't want some amusement.

His boat had twenty women captives. These were bundled into his cabin. Most had torn clothing, their eyes reddened from weeping, their worlds ripped apart and bodies violated most brutally. *All these will make good price.* With a practiced eye he evaluated each one as they were pushed roughly forward. Mary, Eccles's daughter, tried to show dignity in adversity, jutting out her chin and managing to spit onto the Admiral's blood-stained shirt. He liked the spunk of the girl. The rest were ushered back down to the hold. Mary wanted to struggle, tried to struggle, but with men pinning her arms it was hopeless. The Admiral enjoyed his prize before settling down for his well-earned sleep. *I know exactly who I'll sell this one to.*

—ııı—

Prior Framlington was in tears as he surveyed the ruins of the Peruzzi Bank and directed his monks and labourers to find and bury the dead. Though he hoped it would be otherwise, it came as no surprise to find that the bank's vault was empty. He thought back to the letters from the Papal See and only now started to have doubts as to their authenticity.

Thoughts of how such a tragedy could occur, and how unprepared the town had been, were major topics of conversation as the knights rode back through the scene of destruction. Charred corpses still swung from burnt beams. An eerie silence descended on normally bustling surrounds. Few returned to survey the wreckage of homes and workplaces. The vexing question was who should tell the King, and, more pertinently, *what* would they tell him. From his temporary headquarters in the Bar Gate, the Sheriff had summoned a bevy of clerks from Winchester to make an inventory of damage and try to assess losses. Bokland rounded up some peasants who had obviously been looting empty houses. In normal circumstances he would have hanged them, but he'd seen enough death for one day. He made them dig grave pits instead.

Hobelars were sent to get carts, as those inside town were found to be smashed and useless. It would take many days to assess the extent of the damage and so the painful process of clearing up began.

Sir Roger, relieved of his armour, which had been packed back onto his cart with his weapons, found it difficult staying on his horse. The pain in his leg was savage, but he bit his lip. *Duty first*, he told himself. He didn't notice de Lacey approach.

The Sheriff was concerned, watching Sir Roger swaying and mouthing silent words. 'I'm going to send Bokland and Palton to the King. I'll write personally.'

Startled, Sir Roger straightened up.

'William tells me you're hurt. Leave some men to garrison the castle and go home.'

Sir Roger readily agreed. Like all the others he hadn't slept for a long time.

The Sheriff continued. 'I'm issuing warrants for the arrest of the Mayor, the Bailiff and the Tax Collector for gross dereliction of duty. Part of this mess is down to them.'

'Imberd should be at Ipers.' Sir Roger remembered the Bailiff's arrival at his castle. 'It was he who raised the alarm.'

'And he should have defended the castle and King's possessions. Take him too. It was your monkey-man who captured him.' He pointed to Simon. Rain was falling steadily. Drops hissed on smouldering ruins, extinguishing the last fires. Pools of congealed blood liquefied, running red as rainwater started to clean the streets.

'Gwyn, Digby,' Sir Roger issued instructions to his sergeants. Dan was to bring his detachment to Ipers, the rest were to remain in town. And so, weary to his bones, he and his small entourage made their way home. Zuzu sat behind Dan, watching their captive. Whenever she saw Simon looking at her, she peeled her lips back, revealing yellow fangs, and hissed quietly. Simon wanted to cross himself, but his hands were tied behind his back. Any feelings in his arms were long gone and he feared they might drop off. He knew, too, that his captors were determined to make him suffer as punishment for sacking their town. In an attempt to hang on to his dignity and sanity he contented himself with sticking his tongue out at the ape, a fatuous gesture that afterwards made him feel foolish as it drew a stream of abuse from his fellow travellers. With the mangled remains of his *ribaud* slung between two ponies, the procession trudged along a road still clogged with refugees. Halfway home, the rain increased to driving sheets. Lightning and crashing thunder increased as the storm unleashed its full fury. A trickle of water found the gap between Simon's hauberk and padded jacket, coursing down his back, adding to his misery.

They reached Ipers Castle by mid-afternoon. Sir Roger was soaked to the skin and completely numb with cold. He slid unceremoniously into the arms of his servants and was carried inside. There was, at least, a roaring fire in his new fireplace.

'Your wound looks nasty.' Master John pointed at the angry red gash. 'Keep it clean,' he said, wiping it gently before Sir Roger settled into his wooden bathtub.

Sir Roger thanked the Lord that Dan had had the foresight to send a messenger to alert Max to heat up the cauldrons for this purpose. A procession of servants kept it filled with hot water. As the reviving liquid reached his neck, so the tingling heat penetrated his aching body. This was aided by a piping jug of mulled wine that worked from inside out.

The Pantler was fussing about like an old hen. Max, on cue, came flustering out of the kitchen, and with characteristic flourish, produced a steaming bowl of pottage and slab of finest white bread, which Sir Roger devoured with relish. He had not eaten anything other than a bit of dried sausage for over twenty-four hours. *My cousin was right; always fight on a full stomach.* Somewhat revived and wound bound, he limped back to the log fire, absorbed in his own thoughts. It was only slowly that he noticed that every corner of the room was full of sullen, disconsolate people.

'I'm sorry I disobeyed you. I had to let them in,' Lady Alice admitted, 'I couldn't leave them in the rain. They've been arriving since yesterday. There are more outside, all the buildings and stables are full.'

Somewhat refreshed and by now in a forgiving mood, Sir Roger recounted to her the events that had befallen Southampton. Not that he needed to say much, as the refugees had no doubt unburdened themselves of their ghastly tales. He could tell, though, about fighting through the night and driving off the pirates.

'The bastards have gone, leaving three hundred dead.' This raised a weak cheer. His nature was not to brag. *It is better if descriptions of my exploits came from others.* Remembering the Sheriff's instructions about arresting Imberd, he sent for Whytethorne, who summoned the guards.

The Southampton Bailiff, who had been seated on the other side of the hall, huffed and puffed about the indignity of his arrest, but Sir Roger paid him no heed. 'You're a disgrace. I should have you put in chains.' Sir Roger was glaring. 'But I won't.' Using his booming voice so all could hear, he vented his spleen on the hapless custodian. Those high up in the town's hierarchy, and there were a fair sprinkling who had sought this refuge, listened to his tirade with trepidation. Their greed and indolence had been an open invitation to the raiders, and they had reaped the whirlwind. Their cowardice would be called to account.

'I had to raise the alarm,' Imberd stuttered pathetically.

'No. *Your* duty was to defend your master's property, to the death if need be.' Sir Roger was implacable. But he left it at that. It was true. *How could a man be expected to fight armoured men in his Sunday best?* But it was not for him to say. The King would decide what justice should be done. They had been caught with their undergarments down and had to accept the consequences.

A whimpering Simon de Pressi was pushed through the door, dripping wet and still tied. In all the fuss he had been forgotten, left outside for another hour while his captors had got dry clothing. On hearing that he was their prisoner, recumbent figures rose out of gloomy corners and from around the walls. Someone tripped him up and then, in turn, they started to spit on him. A few kicked him as well. Sir Roger waited until the crowd had done enough then signalled for him to be taken to the cells.

'Feed him. I'll have his armour. I'll question him about the *ribaud* and the bank in the morning.'

Chapter 35

I've Lost your Dog

F lushed with success, the French fleet made swift progress across the Channel. A following wind, wine and elation with victory meant that the first galleys reached Dieppe next morning. Ayton Doria was full of admiration for the stamina of motivated men. The slower Norman war barges took longer to return. Once on dry land, Doria and Quiéret took stock, exhorting rain-soaked crews to unload sacks of wool and other booty into dockside warehouses as quickly as they could.

'We lost two hundred and twelve men, excluding oarsmen, and one ship,' the Admiral told him after a roll call was completed. The Normans had taken the brunt of the casualties at the castle and during the night. Ayton Doria had lost many good men in the rear-guard action and it hurt. Both men had been surprised by the ferocity of the counter attack and, though it pained them, agreed that the English, who they believed were supposedly craven cowards, had fought back with uncharacteristic vigour. It was the loss of Prince John that was Doria's uppermost concern during his return journey, and he wondered how to tell the King of Sicily about his son's ignominious end, hacked to pieces by a mob. He shrugged; the prince had been useless from the start. He started composing a letter. *'Your Majesty, he died nobly,'* would suffice. He would dress it up so it sounded as if he had died bravely, but there were too many witnesses for the truth not to emerge.

'Thinking what to say about Prince John?' Quiéret echoed his sentiment. 'Not much we can say. I'm far more worried about de Pressi.'

'You lost Toad's lapdog. What will he say?' Doria shook his head in a disparaging fashion. 'I hope he won't force us to mount another expedition to retrieve him.' His campaign season was over and he was looking forward to spending his winter sampling the joys of the French court and its fair maidens. With the weather turning worse, his galleys could not tolerate rough seas. The Genoese would beach their ships, divide up their spoils and enjoy the fruits of their labours. 'He was right, though,' continued Doria. 'The English were ill prepared. Southampton *was* poorly defended. I won't have problems in recruiting.'

They watched the pile of treasure grow as clerks worked hard recording all the valuables taken. *What am I going to give my wife? What prize ornament shall I send her?* He removed a pair of gold candlesticks set with enamels and jewels that caught his eye.

'These will do nicely.' He turned them around, admiring the delicate tracery of the enamel work, idly wondering where they had been made.

'Leave it where it is,' Carlo Grimaldi ordered his captain when asked what to do about the weigh beam. 'Our fleet returns to Monte Carlo as soon as we've divided up the prizes.'

'No,' Ayton Doria was forcefully insistent, pulling rank. 'It's booty and comes off your boat.' *Anything to irritate this conceited Guelph.*

'I'm not leaving my fleet to the mercy of an Atlantic winter.' *Anything to escape this arrogant Ghibelline.* 'I intend to spend Christmas at home in my castle overlooking the sea. *Any* more time spent with you will sorely try my patience.' He was considering trying his hand at town building and some piracy closer to home next year. *A stab at Genoa would not come amiss.*

Quiéret had other ideas. He wanted to revictual quickly and hit England again, or so he expounded enthusiastically to the Italians, thumping his fist into the palm of his hand. A bold thrust up the Thames before Christmas - but he was unable to garner any support from his allies. The plan was put on hold until the weather improved.

Carlo Grimaldi agreed to remain on the condition that he kept the beam, and he refused, point blank, to be in the same fleet as Ayton Doria. He would extend his contract with the French, which, to date, had proved *most* lucrative.

The Admiral sat down, quill in hand and wrote a brief report to his colleague in Rouen. *The only bad news in an otherwise glorious triumph was the sad loss of your dog. He ran away and did not come back when called. Q.* He did not know who might read this letter as there were spies everywhere. *He'll know who I mean.* Summoning a messenger, he gave him the note and urged him to make haste.

Chapter 36

Walt Repays His Debt

In retrospect, it had seemed strange to Prior Framlington that only the religious houses nearest to Southampton had been instructed to remit their reserve funds to the Peruzzis. The Prior had visited a number of abbeys and churches and pieced together a rather worrying picture. Once he had compared the documents he'd been sent with others he knew to be genuine, he had come to the inescapable conclusion that something was fishy. At first he was reluctant to call the documents forged; he just couldn't put his finger on what was wrong. He decided to make his way to Ipers to consult with Sir Roger, who welcomed him into his hall. Sir Roger, for whom creating forgeries and disseminating half-truths was part of his stock-in-trade, listened with interest. He sent for his prisoner to be hauled out of his cell.

Simon had been left locked up more for his own protection from the refugees than as a punishment. It gave him time to ponder on his dilemma. Scratching idly at mildew on the stonework, he had never felt more miserable in his life. This was made worse by Zuzu, who would climb onto his cell's window and defecate through the opening.

The first time this had happened, he had been lying on the straw mattress provided by his captors. He had been contemplating his fate and counting little black flies as they danced back and forth in the centre of his cell when he saw a pink ape anus point though the bars. This proceeded to spray him with semi-liquid and totally odorous faeces that made him vomit. His sense of misery increased and he dreaded his tormentor's visits, for she would sneak up without warning and, even though he tried to move his mattress to get it out of the way, that foul beast was unerringly accurate, always seeming to sense where he was. He had been in there for what seemed to him an eternity. Each day a trencher of food and a pitcher of water were provided. A single thin blanket was all that protected him from cold and damp. Often days passed without human contact, and it was only a small consolation that the food was passably good.

He was scratching his eighth line on the wall when he heard voices outside. The door was opened and the Ox hauled him out of his cell and marched him off to Sir Roger, who was appalled at his prisoner's condition and berated his Sergeant accordingly. Simon was supposed to be a man of breeding. The smell was overwhelming, so Sir Roger ordered that he be thrown into the moat to be cleaned off. Simon was led out and stripped before being flung unceremoniously into the cold water. He was then given some old clothes that were ill-fitting and made him look a scarecrow.

Sir Roger handed him a beaker of decent wine. 'Drink that, old chap,' he said, full of false bonhomie.

Simon drank, and had his beaker refilled a couple of times before he realised he was getting tipsy.

It was obvious that Simon was not a fighting man, so what or who was he? Once they had made him comfortable, they set about finding out more about the purpose of the raid and specifically the details about the pillage of the bank. It did not take long to coax answers. Back and forth, lie, half-truth, lie, truth - Simon found it harder and harder to keep up as some food and more wine was produced. His inquisitor was more skilled than any he had encountered with the Toad, but then the Admiral liked to rely on pain to get his answers.

'So, let's start at the beginning again. You say your name is Guillaume de Bapaume.'

He nodded. 'My father is a modest knight and we hold lands near Bapaume. He's old now.'

Sir Roger worked back over the old ground, this time speeding up his questions so they came at Simon, bam-bam-bam, before finally hitting on the subject of a ransom.

'So, what are you worth?' he said pertinently. *What is any man worth?* This subject had been vexing Sir Roger for some time, and his problem about what to do with his Sergeant still weighed heavily on his mind. Ransom demands had to be drawn up correctly. 'Two thousand Marks? Three thousand?' It would be split between Sir Roger and Dan, with Sir Roger due the lion's share.

'We're poor now my father has lost all his money,' said Simon. 'I don't think you'll get more than two thousand.'

They settled on one hundred gold Florins, which was close to the same value in Marks. Simon knew that his master had the money because he'd given it to him himself just in case of this very eventuality.

Still, Sir Roger was intrigued about the fine suit of armour. 'It's mine now, by the way,' he added. What had the Sheriff said, worth at least five hundred *livre... There are many lies that need to be exposed with this Frenchman.* Something did not add up. *A poor knight who does not appear to be a fighting man, yet he wears a suit of armour that I would wager more than my life for.* That could wait for another day.

He deemed Simon had suffered enough, so he offered him parole. 'You must swear an oath that you will abide by the terms of your parole and await delivery of your ransom.' Once this was paid 'Guillaume' would be allowed to return to France.

'There, now you are free to enjoy my Castle and its surroundings. Don't venture too far,' warned Sir Roger. 'It would be unwise for you to wander or say too much. There are many who might wish you ill after the goings on in Southampton.' He examined the man who stood before him. *So he knows about gunpowder - Eccles identified him as the chap who blew the Bank. I wonder if he's the Frenchman who met the Magister.* He'd work on that, trap Simon into an admission, but not today; he could see his prisoner was fully on the defensive. 'Finally, you're not to hurt the monkey!'

With that he was dismissed and Edgar the Pantler was told to find Simon suitable accommodation. The part about the ape galled, for

Simon had spent his days plotting what he would do when he got hold of that filthy, vile creature…

Prior Framlington had been quietly snoozing in a leather seat by the open fireplace while the interrogation had been taking place, sadly, he did not speak adequate French to keep up with what was being said. He awoke with a start. Sir Roger filled him in: there were two Admirals in France, one aristocratic and one a jumped-up-Johnny, as far as he could work out. The jumped-up one had the ear of the French King and was the chief architect of the raid, but had not come along. He got their names, Hugh Quiéret and Nicolas Béhuchet, but had not heard these names before. He made a careful note to report them to Mauney so that his spy network could start to keep tabs on them. The most alarming feature of their policy was the hiring of the mercenary fleet from Genoa. This was war on a larger scale than he or King Edward had anticipated. Simon had been vague about the letters; he certainly knew about them and his obtuseness was a give-away. If they had really come from the Pope, he would have said so.

'We must get word to his Holiness about the forged letters.' The old Prior had trouble getting his words out, wheezing badly. The hard work of dealing with the clean-up was taking a toll on his health. But he was now absolutely convinced that the instructions they had received from Cardinal Alberghini did not have Papal blessing.

The only seaworthy boat that the raiders hadn't taken or sunk was an old coastal trader owned by nearby Bewley Abbey. They would need all of his considerable powers of persuasion to get the Abbot to agree to provide it for a perilous voyage across the Channel to Brittany, home of one of England's allies.

—m—

As predicted the Abbot came up with a whole string of excuses in a reedy, squeaky voice. 'What about pirates? Who'll pay for it?'

Sir Roger couldn't believe his ears. Didn't the Abbot realise this voyage was of national importance? *But then he is as wet as a fish's wet bits.*

'For God's sake, they stole the Church's money,' he said, his voice rising out of anger and frustration.

'Well, *we* were lucky. *We* had our money ready to take to Southampton but the French arrived first. So it wasn't *our* money.'

This was the final straw. Sir Roger seized the Abbot by the wrist, making him yelp with pain and complain.

'And I'll hurt you a great deal more,' growled Sir Roger as the Prior looked on. His patience was wearing thin.

'We can't let them get away with stealing our money' said the Prior. On that all the men were agreed. 'I would help pay, but they took all our cash.'

'Who'll pay if our boat is lost?' the Abbot squeaked. It was one of the Abbey's most valuable possessions.

'The King will pay. As District Commander I have the power to requisition your boat in emergencies anyway, and *I* say *this is an emergency*,' Sir Roger said forcefully, fixing the Abbot with a steely stare before finally letting go of his hand.

'Who'll go?' It would be an arduous and dangerous journey that could take at least a month or two. Sir Roger and the Prior looked at each other and then the Abbot, who luckily had a suggestion.

'I'll send Brother Anselm. He's worldly wise and should be able to slip unnoticed through France. We'll have to take the risk and hope that God looks kindly on us.'

On the way back, the Prior asked if Sir Roger really had the power to requisition his boat.

'I don't know. You don't know. And he certainly doesn't know- but he believed me. That's what counts.'

Both men laughed.

The church bell tolled noon as Sir Roger climbed to the top of his tower. From his eyrie he could see for miles in the clear, still air. In the distance to the east he could make out a smudge of wood smoke from Portsmouth. In the west were the jagged white teeth of the Needles that guarded the passage through the Solent. He watched as a sorry procession of dispossessed humanity plodded back out over his draw-bridge, ejected and dejected. The Steward had complained that the castle's supplies were emptying at an alarming rate, so his hospitality had worn thin. *My family and castle must come first.* His scar was healing well and itched madly. *I must not scratch my scab.* He resisted temptation.

He was so engrossed in his thoughts he did not notice that he had been followed. A hand crept round his thigh. His Little Vixen wanted to play. 'Not here, someone might see us,' he said, startled.

'But it's been *so* long.' Lady Elizabeth's eyes sparkled, and he could feel his erection growing. It had been a fortnight. The day before Michaelmas they had met in a woodcutter's shack in the forest. His wife, too, had been cold and elusive since their night of passion after the feast. *Something's up there...*

'Soon. *Very* soon.' His mind was racing. *Where would be safe for a little tryst?* 'We'll meet at Abbot's Well.' This was half an hour's ride across the heath.

Sir Roger was correct to be worried about prying eyes.

Handley was keeping tabs on his master, surreptitiously orbiting him like a fly near a dung pile.

Does my master know about the minstrel? The Bailiff still wanted to get back even with *that bitch* his mistress. Seeing Lady Elizabeth go up the tower and come down moments later, followed shortly by Sir Roger, he knew something was afoot. In matters of *la chasse des femmes* he had his master's measure. The smirk was a giveaway. Should he follow him or her?

'I'm going for a ride, anyone care to join me?' announced Lady Elizabeth, while complaining in a slightly too loud voice about being tired of being cooped up. 'I need some fresh air,' she said pointedly. The other women were quick with excuses. They had an embroidery project to work on, or a complicated game to finish. Elizabeth was pleased that her unpopularity allowed her freedom to come and go as she pleased.

'I won't go far,' she assured Lady Alice, who was worried for her safety with so many people on the roads. 'I'll take good care.'

As soon as she was out of sight, Lady Alice called Nunny. 'I think minxie is up to her tricksies,' she confided. Nunny agreed.

The Bailiff had busied himself pretending to mend a water butt when the lady made her appearance in riding attire. Wrapped in her fox fur cape, Lady Elizabeth casually trotted off on her white palfrey. She was followed shortly by Nunny, who saddled a nag and asked the surprised Handley if he had seen which way her quarry had gone. Then, as he had predicted, Sir Roger emerged shortly afterwards and summoned his ostler and falconer.

'I want Uriel,' he ordered. 'And come with me.' Uriel was his favourite goshawk, used for hunting small game, and named after the archangel who stood with his flaming sword by the gates of the Garden of Eden.

So he's going hawking is he? Handley slipped quietly into the stables before following at a discreet distance.

Walt the Reeve had gone to the Steward to talk about the serious matter of his nephew Edwin, who was his sister's boy, fathered by Fyscher the Priest. He'd been apprehended with a barrel of wine and was unable to explain how it had come into his possession.

'The lad's not altogether there,' said Walt, tapping his head. That didn't surprise the Steward, for everyone knew Edwin was simple.

From the corner of his eye the Reeve watched the procession of riders leaving the castle. When Handley emerged on his own, his suspicions were aroused. Something untoward was going on. *This should be interesting.*

'Got to go,' Walt said abruptly, bidding the Steward a swift goodbye, and he followed after the Bailiff.

It had only been the previous week that the Bailiff had thrown Walt into a manure heap, so thoughts of revenge on his foul-breathed antagonist put a smile on his weather-beaten face. The afternoon was glorious; autumnal tints of russet and gold glowed in the trees. Old Man's Beard covered hedgerows with fluffy tufts and, high above, the air was filled with migrating birds. Walt wondered where the swallows went as he pulled the peak of his felt hat down to shade his eyes from the bright sunshine. Looking at the sun always made him sneeze. Taking a bite from an apple, he followed the furtive Bailiff who, in turn, was shadowing his lord. Walt liked his master, he was Reeve thanks to him and his gift of two pounds had been *exceedingly* generous.

Sir Roger took his goshawk to a nearby warren and made a show of releasing it at rabbits. The low-flying bird made an unexceptional kill, quickly executed. Using this as an excuse, he sent bird and minder home, then spurred his palfrey on for his assignation.

His chosen trysting spot, Abbot's Well, was a low stone shrine hidden in the woods. Lady Elizabeth's palfrey stamped and snorted a welcome. The bulk of the building was beneath ground level, with a flight of stone steps leading down to a wellhead. After circling around and checking they were alone, Sir Roger ducked under the lintel. Lady Elizabeth was standing demurely wrapped in her fur and was dimly illuminated by the sun through a shaved horn window. He always marvelled that it had never been stolen. However, according to popular superstition, it was cursed, so heaven forbid that anyone should think of removing it. Closing the door carefully, Sir Roger started to undo his clothes.

The Little Vixen revealed that she was already naked inside her fox fur. Soon they were locked in a passionate kiss.

'I have bad news,' she whispered, pushing him away with manicured fingers, getting words out between kisses. 'My husband has returned from Flanders and needs me. I have to leave tomorrow.'

Their lips locked again while this statement sunk into his lust filled mind. It made his desire for her even more urgent; foregoing any foreplay, he lifted her up and prepared to enter her.

Nunny had maintained a discreet distance and had secreted herself a short way away behind a screen of hazel coppice. From there she watched as Sir Roger scouted round the shrine. When she was sure that she wouldn't be noticed, she crept carefully up to the window. A horn strip had slipped, leaving a chink through which, when she got down on her knees, she could see the lovers entwined. She watched for a while with thoughts of excitement fighting with revulsion. It was as she had suspected, and she wondered whether it was her place to tell Lady Alice, who would not be pleased. All that mattered was the humiliation of her mistress. She would have to think on that. She carefully crept away again.

Handley dismounted close by and he, too, crept forward. He wondered if he should catch them *in flagrante* or if he should just watch. *If I burst in, I risk being run through with his scimitar.* He was too engrossed in his voyeuristic instincts to notice Nunny, who was similarly preoccupied until they bumped into each other.

She let out a stifled yelp as a clammy hand closed over her mouth. Together they took a step back, treading on a twig, which snapped loudly.

Everyone held their breath in the silence that followed.

Sir Roger's penis deflated with alarming speed.

All the protagonists tried desperately to maintain the utmost silence.

A deep voice boomed out, loud and melodramatic, in an eerie, ghostly fashion. 'Leave it alone. Don't you know that window's cursed? You should be ashamed of yourselves. Be gone, you thieves and vagabonds.' Walt moved silently from his hiding place.

Having watched Handley pulling Nunny back Walt launched his attack. *I can always claim that I'd just been passing when I saw a damsel in distress and had gone to her rescue.* It was payback time and, armed with an iron-tipped quarterstaff, face wrapped in a woollen scarf so as not to be recognised, the Reeve pulled his hood over his hat. Letting out a muffled cry he rushed at the pair and, tripping them up with his pole, they fell in a heap. He swung a glancing blow onto the side of Handley's mouth, sending a rotten tooth flying. The second strike was altogether more satisfying, catching his erstwhile tormentor smack in his testicles, making him double up in pain.

Helping Nunny to her feet, Walt admonished her for being a Peeping Tom. 'If you tell *anyone* what you saw I will kill you, Mistress Norah,' he whispered in her ear, hissing her name threateningly to emphasise his point.

Handley was doubled up, holding his privates. A hard shove sent him to the ground, face forward, bottom up, and Walt could not resist another swinging blow onto such a juicy target before melting away.

Still in pain, the Bailiff and a flustered Nunny ran to where their ponies had been tethered, only to find that their mystery assailant had undone the traces. They had to chase after their mounts through the woods. On his ride back to the castle, Handley spat out a second then a third tooth.

Sir Roger, his ardour cooled, drew his trusty scimitar and edged nervously out of the building, looking and listening as he scouted gingerly around for the source of the commotion. There was no one. A few ruffled leaves, a scrape in the mud and the imprint of a hand, now filling with water, were all that remained of their potential discoverers. A flash of white caught his eye and with his sword point he turned over a human molar. *Who could our mystery saviour be? And who had been the Peeping Toms?* In the mud he saw three sets of footprints leading away from the love nest.

The Little Vixen's news had come as a surprise, though it was not unwelcome. Their continued affair was doomed and the close shave bore testament to that.

'Gone,' he said with relief. Lady Elizabeth pulled him back. If anything, the interruption had heightened her passion. This time there would be no going back.

—◊—

Rosy-cheeked after her exertions of the afternoon, Elizabeth found her entourage of maids. 'Get packing, we leave tomorrow,' she informed them brusquely. 'Where did you get that?' she asked Nunny, who sported a mud stain on her dress. Blushing, Nunny spluttered something about slipping on moss in the courtyard before hurrying off. She knew she had been rumbled and sought out Lady Alice.

Mindful of Walt's threat, she erred on the side of caution, reporting her mission had not been fruitful. 'I can't bear to stay with that whore any longer, Milady, and I wondered if there might be a place for me in your household?'

Lady Alice was delighted and offered to tell her cousin when she saw her next. 'It's so boring here. I need the companionship of someone intelligent.'

At this Nunny's expression of perpetual disapproval cracked into a beaming grin.

'You should smile more often,' Lady Alice complimented. It was the first time she had ever seen Nunny smile.

'I think I'll be able to.' Norah gave a short laugh, whinnying like a horse.

Lady Alice liked Norah, who was able to read and write, in itself a rarity, and was surprisingly well-informed on manners, sewing and other feminine arts. With her impending confinement, Lady Alice would be grateful for a skilled pair of hands. *She'll be good company too, when my husband will no doubt be his usual monosyllabic self and won't provide any worthwhile conversation.*

—m—

Sir Roger made a detour, stopping at his mill.

'At least another month before we can start milling again.' Handley was there, making a show of inspecting progress.

'Lost a tooth?' Sir Roger asked casually. When Handley instinctively put his hand up to his mouth, his suspicions were confirmed.

'It was knocked out in a fight I had with some monks.' Handley opted for a half-truth. He said there had been a tussle - that much was true. He embellished the story about having been caught netting carp in the stew ponds. 'I was only trying to fulfil my promise to get fish for the moat.'

In truth the monks had caught him and made him put the fish back, but the Bailiff had sneaked back later, this time cleaning out the pond. *I should've waited till the buggers were in prayers the first time.*

The Bailiff watched his master depart and resolved to stir the pot. *Fyscher the Priest is always good for a juicy bit of scandal.*

'I wouldn't have had him down for an adulterer,' said Handley conspiratorially, knowing he was talking to the village foghorn. The priest was *fairly* good at keeping the confessional's secrets, but other confidences would usually ebb out sooner or later. And a titbit as salacious as this…

Sow the seeds. We'll see what happens.

Chapter 37

The King is Not Amused

De Bokland and de Palton waited impatiently for over an hour as the Sheriff fussed around, obviously reluctant to hand over the set of vellum rolls that contained the catalogue of disaster listed in a dry accountant's hand. He had struggled to sum up the suffering, and in the end he had not found adequate words to convey the human misery. 'Your best bet will be to go to London. Have a safe journey.'

The two knights found a city in chaos. The threat of invasion was on everyone's lips. Teams of Londoners were frantically driving lines of stakes into the Thames to try and stop raiders coming upriver. All shipping had ground to a halt and no amount of coercion could secure them a passage for Flanders.

'Try the Tower,' one Captain said helpfully.

By contrast, the Tower was an oasis of calm, which was explained away by a newly appointed King's Councillor to whom they explained their plight. 'Thick walls,' he said almost casually. 'Frenchie won't get over these in a hurry. The Royal dispatch galley leaves tomorrow. I'll get you passage on that.'

'Thank goodness someone understands,' said a relieved and grateful de Palton.

It had finally stopped raining when they boarded the galley. The rowers all bore the King's livery and the Captain ordered cast off from the wharves below the Tower. A great chain that barred the river was lowered and, after weaving carefully round many obstacles, they were soon making good speed. Crossing the North Sea was easy, a following wind helping considerably, and the two knights, with a pair of faithful servants in tow, made landfall in Antwerp. Finding the King, however, proved far harder.

'He's gone, the army's gone and he didn't bother to tell anyone of his plans,' said the first English official they managed to collar.

'Too many spies, Frenchies have eyes and ears everywhere,' added a helpful merchant, whose duty was to sell the infrequent wool deliveries. 'From what I hear he's gone to meet the Emperor.'

Eventually they tracked down a royal Marshal, who told them that, from what he'd heard, the King was supposed to be at a place called Herk, eighty miles away.

'In which direction?'

To which the reply was a vague and airy wave of the arms. With weary hearts and on borrowed horses, they set out on their quest.

'And will we ever find the Holy Grail?' quipped de Palton to his companion after trying to elicit directions from yet another sullen Fleming. In the end it was easy.

Follow the mud.

'Herk?' they asked.

Follow the mud.

At least it had dried to leave a fairly decent road; peasants would point at the brown swathe trampled across the countryside. Having arrived at Herk full of hope, they found the city was all but shut up. The army with all its hangers on and camp followers, had left, and so had their money. Herk had played; a friendly army is a bonanza for all those with something to sell. Now dressmakers were hard at work as the more willing ladies of the town spent their earnings.

Again their hearts sank. The English had moved on.

'Where to?' they again asked. Another nameless weaver pointed to the churned road.

'Mechelen.' It sounded more like an insult than a place.

'How far?'

But the man just shook his head. Mechelen, they discovered finally from a group of disgruntled soldiers, was the first town of any size south of Antwerp, fifty miles back in the direction they had come.

They located the camp by the smell: a mixture of wood smoke and ordure, of cooking and crap. Spreading for miles across the fields and orchards, and located just outside the town's walls, rows of smaller tents were interspersed with grand marquees belonging to the magnates and senior clergy who accompanied the army. As far as the eye could see, thousands of banners and flags belonging to all the noble houses of England and her allies - Hainault, Juliers and Bavaria - were like flowers poking through dirty snow. Carts and horses clogged up every road and thousands of men seemed to be milling around aimlessly, busying themselves with nothing. Several fields had been turned into a massive wagon park filled with rows of every conceivable form of wheeled transport. Some were filled with barrels of arrows and other ordnance; others were gaily-painted coaches of noble ladies who travelled with their husbands.

The two knights, veterans of campaigns against the Scots, had never seen such an array of men and might before. The King's tent was the grandest, with the royal banner proudly streaming from its pinnacles. It was, in fact, a series of brightly coloured tents joined together, with decorated dormer windows around the uppers of the poles. Outside, the King's household troops in red, green and gold livery were standing on guard.

'I hate being the bearer of bad tidings,' said de Bokland, taking a deep breath. The journey's end would be the start of their tribulations and they had endlessly rehearsed what they would say: a major seaport despoiled, sacked and up in flames, royal warehouses emptied and booty carried off by the enemy. 'I've never met the King before.' De Bokland ran his fingers through his hair and tried in vain to brush the dust off his clothing, but it was too ingrained to respond. He bemoaned the fact that Sir Roger wasn't with them as they tried to summon up some shred of dignity and courage.

'I think it would be wise to talk to one of his advisers first,' ventured de Palton. 'I know Chancellor Stratford.' This eminent churchman, who had once been Bishop of Winchester, was now Chancellor of the Exchequer. Finally, too, here were people who could speak the same language.

A helpful archer pointed out the Chancellor's magnificent tent. 'I know he's there,' the man added helpfully, 'saw him go in just a moment ago.'

The ostentation of their surroundings after weeks of dreariness made their task much harder. The Court was a chaotic affair. A further magnificent royal marquee had been set up for the meeting between the King and the Bishop of Cambrai, so they were told by one of the many soberly clad clerks who sorted through mountains of documents in the outer part of the tent. Money seemed to be no object. The small talk continued for some time while they waited patiently for an audience.

'The Chancellor is a very busy man,' observed an avuncular bishop who seemed to be in charge. 'Can I be of assistance instead?'

'We need to see him in person, please.' Then, apropos nothing, de Palton added: 'This lot must cost a pretty packet.'

The knights were surprised when the bishop remarked that the King was short of cash. They could make no sense of it. Soldiers deserting due to lack of pay, yet here it seemed money was no object.

'Wait here,' the bishop ordered and disappeared into the main body of the tent before ushering them into Stratford's presence. The Chancellor, they could see, was a worried and much harassed man. With little time for formalities, they were made to stand while he signed a stack of parchments and had a clerk affix great weighty seals on each. At the end of this task he looked up and wiped a bead of sweat from a receding hairline.

'I hope,' he said wishfully, before offering them a couple of chairs to sit on, 'that you have good news.'

'I'm afraid, Your Eminence, that it is not so.' They explained the nature of their business; Stratford was deeply shocked.

'Does anyone else here know?'

They shook their heads side to side in unison. Stratford left right away to seek an audience with his Majesty. Scurrying out through a side flap, the Chancellor soon returned red-faced and out of breath. 'I have only told him that it is of great importance,' he declared. 'I haven't dared tell him what it is about. I'll leave that to you,' he said ominously.

They waited for what seemed another eternity in an ante-chamber before a uniformed flunky came out and indicated that the King would receive them now, ushering them into the Royal Presence.

He had been jousting and was wearing a full suit of plate armour, burnished and gleaming, with a gold crown mounted on his bascinet. His knee and elbow protectors were embossed with gold and he had an embroidered surcoat with gold lions on red, quartered with blue *Fleur de Lys*. On his shoulders he had the square signifiers of a banneret emblazoned with the three lions of England. The two knights waited on bended knee while the King was divested of the weighty metal. They handed over the Sheriff's letter and watched while the King sat at a bureau and examined the seal, expertly checking the edges of the wax for signs of tampering.

He frowned intermittently while reading the letter in silence, before getting up and pacing round his tent. Arranged on perches around its walls was a selection of his favourite hawks. He flung the letter down and took a morsel of meat from a silver platter, which he fed to a peregrine. It gulped the titbit down before letting out a strangulated squawk. He'd brought thirty falconers with him on this campaign.

The ominous silence was only broken by the tinkling of silver bells gracing the hoods and jesses of his birds. After what seemed an eternity, he spoke to the travellers. 'And you've come straight from there?'

'We have, your Majesty.'

'Why has it taken so long for this news to reach me?'

The knights explained that they had come by way of Herk. The King's face reddened and he started shouting at a couple of heralds who were doing something of which he disapproved. 'This is a catastrophe, gentlemen,' he acknowledged, lowering his voice again. 'You will go back and bring all those mentioned in the report to the Tower. I'll instigate a Commission to question and punish guilty parties. You are dismissed.' He then strode out of the room.

De Bokland and de Palton looked at each other as if to say 'thank God'. That was it - no tirade, not even a 'how sorry he was for the suffering of his subjects' - just 'punish the guilty parties.' Wearily they got up and shrugged, unsure as to what to do next, for the King had not been forthcoming with instructions. They were heading back out when a herald accosted them.

'The King says he will see you tomorrow. I'll arrange suitable accommodation,' he said. 'You are also commanded – invited - to attend the banquet.' He told them the King would be exercising his new role as 'Imperial Vicar'. This was the honour and title bestowed on him by Emperor Ludwig. All pomp and no substance. 'But then His Majesty has been all promises and no money,' he added, rather candidly.

—✖—

The King strode majestically into the banqueting tent in his scarlet velvet robes, richly embroidered with religious and heraldic devises though the Great Crown of England was missing from his head. All around nobles were dressed in such finery that the two knights felt ashamed at the dowdiness of their travel clothes. From the side-lines they watched the unfolding spectacle while a garrulous courtier kept up a running commentary to a small group of his neighbours. Bokland and Palton had never been this close to the hub of power and were fascinated by the sights and sounds as great men came and went, some prostrating themselves before the enthroned King as if their very lives depended on it, while others merely nodded as if to an equal.

This display of royal power was meant to impress allies and coerce waverers into the fold. The Bishop of Cambrai fell into the latter camp and was undecided as to his loyalty and whether to support this King's 'rightful' claim to the French throne. However, so their mine of information told them, the Duke of Brabant still refused to come in person and had sent a couple of lawyers to represent him instead.

'Grovellers - keeping their noses in the mud.' Their commentator turned out to be a knight in the service of the Margrave of Juliers. 'Even though the Duke is supposed to be one of your King's principal allies, he's presently playing hard to get! He needs to secure allegiance from these northern Lords if his spring campaign is going to bring results. To date he's failed to draw the French army into battle and they've only fought some vicious skirmishes. The Bishop's bluff has been called,' continued the knight, 'because, as Imperial Vicar, the King has the power to strip the Bishop of his rights on pain of Deprivation.' This, they knew, was a harsh punishment for any cleric of standing - but hard to enforce, as it was also politically motivated. The whole exercise served to deliver a blunt message about the King's authority and encourage waverers, such as the Duke of Brabant, to join his gallant endeavour.

The Bishop was seated on a deliberately uncomfortable backless stool watching as the stream of supplicants and allies continued to parade past until suddenly the procession stopped.

'It's decision time for the Bishop,' revealed their commentator in whispered tones as a hush descended over the proceedings. But the Bishop was not going to give in easily, needing more time to consult. He phrased his response carefully - the worm wriggled and was deftly off the hook. The King frowned. A herald read out another summons to the Bishop of Liège and the Count of Flanders, also notable absentees and firmly entrenched allies of the enemy, to attend the King at the end of the month.

'I think Hell will freeze over first!'

It was all to do with money. The King's allies were calculatingly venal and had accepted promises of large amounts of cash to support Edward's claim to the French throne. An English army would also give them the necessary military strength to take castles and towns away from France. De Bokland and de Palton were startled at the sums on offer. The German Emperor had been promised four hundred thousand florins.

'He's received a tenth.' The secretary was obviously privy to much confidential information and, as the day wore on, so the knights elicited more juicy gossip.

'The surrounding towns have been stripped of cash and still he behaves as if nothing's wrong,' he continued, but the knights were no longer listening to this catalogue of fiscal woe; the royal trumpeters sounded a fanfare and the King ascended to his throne. He stood there in his ermine-lined scarlet cloak and raised his arms; in one hand he held his orb and in the other his sceptre. 'Both got out of hock for the occasion!' elaborated their guide.

'My friends.' The King had a strong, clear voice. 'Today you will be pleased to hear that we have concluded a pact with our cousin the Count of Hainault. In May next year we meet in the Cambrésis, and from there we will drive forward and depose the Valois Viper, that treacherous usurper to my French crown.'

The whole tent erupted into cheering.

He held his arms aloft again. 'I am the rightful and lawful King of France, my claim is just and, with God's Will, we shall be triumphant.'

The sides of the marquee were raised and trestles groaning with food and wine were carried in. The knights found a space at the bottom corner of the tent and enjoyed a feast the like of which they had never tasted before. The King watched the feasting, drinking wine from a gold- and jewel-covered goblet, but not eating. After a while there was another great fanfare and the King rose from his throne and left.

Shortly afterwards, a herald came over to the knights. 'The King will see you now. Follow me.'

They were led out behind the throne into a bright blue tent with silk hangings that depicted hunting scenes. Thick oriental rugs covered the floor. The King had changed, having taken off his Vicar's heavy cloak. He was wearing a scarlet brocaded tunic embroidered with gold stars; his shirt had puffed melon sleeves, his cloak was scarlet with a blue petal scallop edge, his stockings were of finest woven red wool and he had a jewelled girdle around his hips. Four pages attended him. Several magnates, ministers and bishops, ten in all, were seated on chairs while the King stood in the centre of the tent. The two knights got down on their knees and prostrated themselves before the King, noses to the floor, which, thankfully, was not muddy. He signalled for them to get up.

'These gentlemen have just come from England and they bear terrible news.' An audible drawing-in of breath came from the seated councillors. 'Our fair and noble town of Southampton has been brutally attacked and sacked by Admiral Quiéret and his Genoese allies.'

He paused, watching as the full import of what he told them sunk in. 'The crown has suffered grievous losses. I will let these men tell you what happened.'

De Bokland went first and described the events of the sacking. When he got to the part about the relief of the town, the King interrupted him. 'And how is my good friend Sir Roger, and how does his castle fare?'

De Bokland gave a brief description and informed him that his friend was suffering from a hunting wound.

'Remind him about the report on the guns.'

'He is aware of that, your Majesty. In fact we managed to capture a French *ribaud*, and a knight called Guillaume de Bapaume.'

'The Sheriff says that he also blurted out the name 'Simon de Bress', does this mean anything to you?'

'I thought I heard the man say 'de Pressi' but I can't be sure,' interjected de Palton. 'Sir Roger is holding him for ransom.' de Palton had noticed this slip of the tongue but had not paid it any heed- until now.

'Ah. Tell him to take the gun to the Tower when he delivers the prisoners. I want copies made of it.'

De Palton interrupted again, fearful of a regal rebuke, and informed him that the *ribaud* had exploded and been abandoned. 'Well, tell him I want better copies,' retorted the King. 'I have a letter here for the Sheriff. You and de Bokland are to be in charge of garrisoning the town; the Wardrobe will pay for two hundred soldiers. Get walls built. I will consider the matter of the Seals later.' He was abrupt in his manner and made it clear that their audience was over, turning on his heel. The knights were then ushered out of the tent and, bearing a bundle of letters of instruction, they set out, with some trepidation, on their journey back to England. It had started raining again.

'How bad was it?' asked Mauney, when they had gone.

'Read for yourself,' said the King brusquely, handing over the Sheriff's letter. In suitable terms, it catalogued losses of life and property, noting the brutality of rapine carried out on a Sunday. It outlined the cowardice of the King's servants and their dereliction of duty and listed items of the King's possessions that had been stolen- 270 surplars of fine woven cloth, 50 sacks of cloves and 136 sacks of wool. It reported the theft of 194 tuns of red wine intended for the King's use and that a further 40 tuns of wine had been drunk by the raiders. It had been particularly galling to relate that the King's Agent had only purchased *La Nicholas's* cargo on his behalf the day before the pirates had taken her away.

It reported how the King's Tax Collector had fled, and had suspiciously sold ships to the Spaniards only a short while before the raid. It bemoaned the weigh-beam's removal and the stealing of the seals, adding details of a mysterious explosion that removed the front of the Peruzzi Bank, and the emptying of its contents. Craving his Majesty's indulgence, it gave an account for work that had already begun to repair Winchester's walls should the French return and strike inland, asking that further funds be allocated for this purpose.

Only one French prisoner, it continued, had been captured, Guillaume de Bapaume, and as a postscript the eagle-eyed de Lacey mentioned that he had uttered a name something like 'Simon de Bress' that he had rapidly retracted - it might not be important except the knight had been wearing *very* expensive armour and that he had been instrumental in blowing up the Bank. The missive ran to several pages.

'De Pressi. Simon de Pressi,' said Mauney. 'I've heard that name before, but where?' He scratched his head.

—◊—

'Got it!' exclaimed a triumphant Mauney after a couple of day's diligent work. 'It's been nagging at me and now I remember.'

Several times he had been close, this time he was certain. He went back into the King's tent.

'You showed me some papers about six or eight months ago. Something to do with testing armour in Rouen.'

The King shook his head. His spies were meticulous and tried to copy every document they could.

'We can have a look,' said the King. 'I think they are in my library.' He travelled with an extensive bureau of files that he called 'his library'.

It had no real books, but all these documents were bound, whenever the bundles became thick enough. Fifteen fat volumes were brought in. Three hours later, one of the perusing clerks called out to Sir Walter.

'I think this is it, Sire.'

'Show me.' And sure enough, there it was, 'From Simon de Pressi to Admiral Béhuchet'. Often these letters from spies were just digests, but this one was copied in full.

He went off to find the King. 'We've got our man. Look, here, our Fat Little Pig gave him a five hundred *livre* suit of armour as a gift.' To the English Béhuchet was not 'The Toad' but 'The Fat Little Pig'. The following page contained a report from the spy referring to his diligent work 'his most trusted right hand man Simon de Pressi…'

'My God! Do you think Sir Roger is aware of who his prisoner is?' asked the King.

'I doubt it,' replied Mauney, shaking his head.

'That man possesses all the secrets of the French navy. I want him brought here as soon as possible.' The King summoned a secretary and started to compose a letter to Sir Roger. 'Put it into Code C.' It was his most complex cipher. 'I don't want word of this getting out.'

Chapter 38

Take Him Somewhere Quiet.

It took Brother Anselm more than a month of arduous riding to reach Avignon from Brittany. It took two whole days of sitting resolutely in the antechamber at the Papal Palace before he was allowed in to see the Pope. He had progressed from archbishops to lowlier cardinals, but each time he had repeated what he had been told to say by Framlington, who had also issued a dire warning: *He who blocks your entrance to see His Holiness is probably implicated in the plot, so be extra vigilant.*

The latest cardinal was of a different calibre; the cut of his robes had been carefully conceived and was of expensive cloth. Unfortunately he, too, never returned.

'Alone,' Brother Anselm said again, trying not to let desperation creep into his voice. 'My instructions are specific. I must see the Holy Father alone.'

Finally, the ever-courteous Cardinal Alberghini put his head round the door.

'You still here?' he said and Brother Anselm detected a hint of exasperation in his tone, 'I'll tell His Holiness.'

I must get a note through without this man finding out, Anselm thought. His opportunity came the following day. Anselm had seen his adversary leave, so he took his chance.

A servant arrived balancing several plates of fruit and sweetmeats.

'Let me help you take that in,' Anselm said with a smile, grabbing a bowl of apples and slipping his note of introduction carefully between them. The Pope looked at him with curiosity and thunder but Anselm was quick to grovel while he read the note.

'So what is this bad news from England, I already know about Southampton.'

'I have a letter...' and he reached inside his robes for the hidden pouch that contained the offending documents. The Pope read and reread them, examining the forgery.

'You say six houses sent funds?'

Anselm nodded. 'Do you know how much?'

'Church funds were in excess of thirty-five thousand marks. The raiders emptied the whole vault.'

The Pope drew in his breath sharply.

'Did you know I have been waiting in the antechamber for two days to see you?' The Pope shook his head and Anselm decided to be bold. 'My Abbot said to tell you that he who prevents me seeing you is probably one of the guilty parties, and your secretary has known of my presence for the past three days.'

'In that case, please sit outside for another day, then I'll have you sent away.' Then the Pope offered Anselm his ring to kiss. The audience was over. Anselm had played his part and, being worldly-wise, he decided he would see and sample the cardinals' play places for himself, for the abbot had given him ample travel expenses that he had squirrelled away for an opportunity such as this.

'I shall have that man excommunicated.' The Pope shouted angrily. 'He attacked a Christian city on a Sunday, that's sacrilege. Draw up a Bull immediately.'

'Who for?' his Secretary enquired.

'Admiral Hugh Quiéret, of course, he was the leader.' He held up the Abbot's letter. 'Four churches burnt with their congregations still inside. It's disgraceful. He can burn in Hell for what he did.'

'What can you tell me about this?' He placed the forgery on the table and watched Alberghini, waiting for a reaction. The Cardinal's face went white.

'Nothing. What should I make of it?' He was going to brazen it out.

'I'm disappointed with you,' said the Pope quietly, summoning the Captain of the Guard. 'Take him away, somewhere quiet and remote, and wall him up. No one must know.' He turned back to his Secretary, who had collapsed onto the floor. 'That should give you enough time to repent on Earth before you account to St. Peter.'

'That bastard Béhuchet made me do it,' he cried, hoping that a confession might change the Pontiff's mind, but it didn't.

'He can be excommunicated as well.'

Before they took the Cardinal to a derelict watch tower overlooking the Mediterranean and immured him, they subjected him to the rack, ensuring that both arms were ripped from their sockets. Instead of heavenly choirs of castrati, he had the raucous cries of gulls and croaking caws of ravens to ease his passage to Purgatory. The Captain of the Guard reported back that it had taken a week for his soul to be harvested by the Grim Reaper.

Chapter 39

Here's Hoping

Admiral Béhuchet gave a shudder as if someone had walked over his grave. 'You think Simon might have been captured?' he said quietly to Quiéret when they finally met, 'not killed.'

The other man nodded. He had been vague with his co-Admiral, none of his returning Normans had been very coherent about what happened to Simon. One man had seen a two headed demon, another thought it was a banshee; a third had seen him fall. Whatever it was that had come at them out of the tower that Sunday night certainly seemed to have been endowed by the supernatural, of that they were all sure.

The Toad felt enormous relief when a ransom demand arrived addressed to 'The Lord of Bapaume' for his son Guillaume. His man had waited at Bapaume Castle to redirect any messenger. The demand had arrived a couple of days before, but the carrier who brought it could give no clues - 'A monk gave it to me on the road,' he said blandly. 'Paid me with Venetian ducats.'

'So his real identity might still be a secret?' Béhuchet missed his right-hand man more than he cared to admit. Small things that were normally done remained undone; the details that Simon would usually provide were missing. His empire was already starting to fall apart at the seams, imperceptibly perhaps, but he noticed.

'I hope so.' Quiéret, too, had noticed a change in his colleague. *He loved that boy too much.* Not that he minded, he would use this weakness to advantage. In the games that would follow he would need to gain the upper hand. *After all, I'm the sacker of Southampton!* It was time for him to press his suit with his King for the return of more of his lands.

Béhuchet searched through his coffers for the leather bag of money given to him by Simon. 'Here they are,' he said, spilling the coins out on his table. They were gold, but unlike any he had seen before. Fresh from a mint, they bore pictures of leopards and looked similar to florins. He counted out one hundred, keeping the rest, *for my expenses,* before using a strand of wire and a lead seal with a bee on it. This he entrusted to his henchman de Coudebeq. *There - here's hoping…*He would need to find a brave smuggler willing to undertake the crossing.

Chapter 40

The Court is in Session

In the month that had passed since its destruction, Southampton remained more or less deserted. With fear of the pirates' return uppermost in most people's minds, few could bring themselves to try and salvage the remnants of their possessions. A few stray dogs wandered the streets, and burnt-out shells of houses rotted away under torrential rain as storm followed storm out of the west. Survivors huddled together in the few undamaged houses and tried, in vain, to make sense of their predicament. Those leading citizens who had not fled or been massacred, were languishing in Winchester Castle awaiting trial.

Eccles had escaped this fate. He, at least, had been brave and fought back. Now, as he scrabbled through the ruins of his house for the umpteenth time, he felt angry, fulminating on the latest iniquity. *That bastard Sir Roger has reneged on his debt - no tally stick, no pay he said.* All his pretence to being a God-fearing nobleman who honoured his obligations had evaporated. The merchant had hoped that Sir Roger was different. *No. He's just the same as all those other blood-suckers who by dint of birth rule over us.* Sir Roger had flatly refused to pay his debts, so the merchant had, like many other homeless refugees, taken up residence at the Priory.

Prior Framlington had worked tirelessly to comfort the sick and heal the wounded, but his resources were running low.

'I'll try and put moral pressure on Sir Roger next time we meet, but,' he had explained to Eccles, 'without witnesses or tally sticks how can the debt be verified?'

The ceaseless rain had not improved matters either. It was turning into a winter of discontent.

'I'm going to write to the King and ask for an abatement of our taxes and a remission from the new levies,' the Prior continued. The Priory had been speculating on wool and had borrowed heavily against next year's fleeces. 'The money-lenders might have gone for now, however I feel sure those leaches will be back to collect their dues sooner or later.'

Eccles was in two minds about what to do as he discussed the future. 'Should I now forsake the worldly life and take up holy orders?'

'The people look to you for leadership.' The old Prior had wise words for him. 'Someone has to provide an example, and you fought back. You did yourself a great service killing that nobleman, even though we are commanded so not to do by the Scriptures.'

Eccles was not so sure. In retrospect, he felt that killing Prince John of Sicily had been a mistake. *I could have done with the ransom.* The thought continued to rankle as he returned to the ruins of his house, where he pushed hard on a fallen beam that had once supported the floor above his office. Rain had loosened the rubble and he got the splintered wood to move. He could see an object buried underneath that he thought he recognised: it was a dull grey metal semi-circle. He scrabbled harder, finding a sharp stick that aided his excavations, and soon he had unearthed the pewter pot that had once held his tally sticks. *The contents must be here somewhere.* If so his money worries would be over for the time being. *I'll enjoy shoving my half stick up his nostril!* But the little pot was empty and a ton of wood, tiles, plaster and rubble covered the rest of the floor. He sat and wept with frustration. He would have to find some workers to help move all of this before he could claim his prize.

—∾—

Sir Roger sat back in the privacy of his solar and had a pang of conscience that he had dealt so harshly with Eccles, but he dismissed these thoughts from his mind. *My coffers are damn nigh empty and the longer I can keep my creditors at bay the better.* Any excuse, however flimsy, would suffice, and the lack of the other half of the tally stick had come to him on the spur of the moment. *I like the merchant for all his urban pretentiousness.* He would try and make it up to him when he saw him next. It was time for his court. Whytethorne had given him a foretaste of the day's proceedings. A dispute had arisen between Gregory the Cooper and Cecilia, the widow of the Reeve murdered by Sir Eustace's men, over field boundaries, and there was also the case of Edwin the Idiot and the barrel of wine.

'I'm convinced it is to do with the fact that the widow has rejected Gregory's advances,' Whytethorne had affirmed to Sir Roger as they sat reviewing the case. 'After all she is most eligible. She used your money to hire Gregory's plough to turn her fields, which, by the way, run parallel to his. I think our Gregory has assumed this to be an invitation to plough that other furrow.' Then the trouble had started.

In these dreary early November days, there was little to amuse the populace, so a big crowd was expected. A stream of wet peasantry, villeins, franklins and assorted yeomen and women were presently making their way to the hall. Gwyn made sure the crowd gave way to the Steward and saluted with appropriate smartness, crashing the iron butt of his fighting stave onto flagstones so sparks flashed.

The hall had been decked out for the occasion; the dais, where the head table normally stood, had been cleared. A row of benches flanked two seats. Sir Roger's chair was raised above the Steward's and that was higher than the jury benches, this was as expected. When discussions had taken place in Winchester about his appointment, it was made clear that the Sheriff had final say, but Sir Roger would be the primary dispenser and arbiter of the law. His men-at-arms stood forming an aisle in front of the rows of benches provided for the upper echelons of village society and local community. The rest stood against the walls. A fire roared up the chimney and those standing nearest to it steamed. The smell of damp clothing, mould and packed humanity made the household's ladies sniff at their lavender-filled nosegays. Seated in the minstrel's gallery, they could survey proceedings at their leisure or retreat to the private quarters as they pleased.

Nunny accompanied Lady Alice and together they joked about the weather. She had grown to like this woman and her acerbic wit. For the last week they had workmen clambering all over the roof in the rain fixing drips - the new roof leaked like a sieve and little streams of water that percolated through the ceiling had to be traced and slates realigned accordingly. *Build in haste, and you get shoddy workmanship….*

Servants handed out goblets of warmed spiced wine to arriving dignitaries; Whytethorne shook off his cape, took a proffered goblet and, in one gulp, drained its contents. 'By golly, that's good,' he commented as he held it out for another. The irony was not lost on him when he was told that the wine in question came from the disputed stolen barrel. The Pantler banged three times on the table.

My cue. Sir Roger adjusted his newly acquired Italian felt hat. It had been dropped by one of his fleeing foes at Southampton. Someone had picked it up off the beach and given it to him. *If the cap fits…* It had a peaked brim, a fine pearl pin and some elaborate feathers that he suspected were from a rooster. His Hall was packed and silent, punctuated by a few coughs; he noticed with amusement the steam near the fireplace.

The land dispute was first. Cecilia was a big, meaty, red-faced woman in her early thirties. Her husband's untimely death at the hands of Sir Eustace's ruffians had left her with three children, the last of whom was still a babe in arms. It was hard to pinpoint where the mewling noises emanated from through the layers of clothing, but it was there somewhere.

The other protagonist, Gregory the Cooper, was skinny, pug ugly and a patent opportunist. Most of the village thought the haste at which he had tried to press his suit on the widow unseemly, but agreed that when God had the perversity to grant poor Gregory a lopsided visage, finding eligible partners for marriage was always going to be difficult. For all his physical faults, he was a popular man with the ability to make even the sourest of individuals smile and laugh. He and

Cecilia glowered at each other across the tables at which black-robed legal clerks from Winchester sat, facing the bench.

The Jury was made up of most of the district's freemen - the miller, the franklins, the sergeants of the levy, a couple of local grain merchants, Alfred the Huntsman, the Steward, the new Reeve and other worthies from the neighbourhood. They sat on the benches provided and tried hard to look serious. Handley the Bailiff was responsible for the smooth running of proceedings; he was a changed man since his mysterious assailant had rearranged his smile. All those who had the misfortune to be collared by him could not fail to notice that his breath no longer had the foul rotting smell of before. While no one could say it was pleasant, it was certainly an improvement. In fact, one or two serving girls at the alehouse were even prepared to accept his advances, which further improved his humour.

'The Court will come to order!' He relished saying those words; it was his dream come true. The Estate Clerk started out reading the statements of claim and counter claim. The crux of the matter concerned the boundary posts that seemed to have mysteriously moved by several yards shortly after the Reeve's death.

Immediately Gregory jumped up and started shouting. 'It's a lie, I never moved that post.' Several pairs of hands pulled him down and told him to shut up.

It had been the jury's job to look at the whole question and their self-appointed spokesman, Alfred the Huntsman, got to his feet. 'My Lord, it is true. The posts certainly do appear to have been moved, we found some old holes. But we cannot be sure - you see we also understand that the Reeve,' Alfred crossed himself as he mentioned the recently deceased, 'had moved some of the posts himself last year.'

This time it was Cecilia's turn to splutter. The truth was the Reeve and his neighbour had not been on good terms, ever since the affair of the geese. Villagers remembered fondly the to-ings and fro-ings in his gaggling flock that would regularly reduce in number. A fox was blamed, but the location and nature of the pile of feathers showed that the fox had two legs not four. Half the jury had had the pleasure of sampling Gregory's quite delicious roast goose and were not inclined to the Reeve's widow, who made sour ale. The other, more compelling, truth was that the widow's children were not old enough to help her farm her holding and she had gone to Gregory to ask if her hired man could borrow his plough and team. Gregory had been *most* forward and not only offered his oxen, but also asked for her hand in marriage.

'If not wedlock, then how about a little carnality,' he had suggested smuttily, for Cecilia was known to be a feisty woman. It had been when she was on her way home, in a fury that only women get into, that she had noticed the boundary posts had shifted significantly.

Gregory's explanation of the events elicited gales of laughter. The man had a real talent to amuse and Sir Roger, who was feeling a bit like Solomon as he sat on his throne, saw the humour too. 'That's enough,' he boomed. He leant forward and whispered into Whytethorne's ear. The Steward rose to his feet and addressed the Jury. What had they found?

'We've been unable to decide. The boundary posts have definitely been moved, but we cannot establish by whom,' concluded the Jury's Foreman. 'We do have a solution; we feel that indeed the widow and Cooper should get married. That would solve all the problems!'

Ribald laughter broke out around the hall as Gregory jumped up onto the table and with a flourish got down onto one knee.

'I may not be the most pleasing of men to look at, but as God is my witness I will be a good and faithful husband.' He looked around at his audience and gave a broad wink. 'And I can roast a mean goose…'

The Hall erupted and a unified cry of 'Marry him, marry him,' rose out of a hundred throats. Cecilia rose with all the dignity she could muster; the baby hidden in her garments awoke at the sudden movement, felt hungry and started to cry. She turned and walked towards the exit. The noise was terrific and even dogs joined in with baleful howls. When she got to the door she turned and faced Sir Roger and the jury of twelve men. The Hall went quiet.

'I will,' she said in a quavering voice and fled out into the lashing rain as cheering erupted all round.

A hush settled over the dimly lit Hall. The two pointed mullioned glass windows let in little light and lamps set beside the fireplace cast a puddle of light in their immediate vicinity and no more. The wind howled and the roof moaned as the bedraggled figure of Edwin, in chains, was half dragged into the room's centre and deposited on a stool in front of the dais.

'How do you plead?' asked the Steward.

It took him several attempts to find any words before he managed to blurt out 'I'm innocent.'

'But you confessed to your crime.'

'I d-d-d-d-didn't. P-p-p-pain hurt Edwin. I w-w-w-wanted to make him stop.' He raised a manacled hand and pointed to Handley. The ends of his fingers were still bloody and torn where a thumbscrew had been applied.

Whytethorne leaned over to the clerks. 'Read the man's confession.'

The clerk stood and read the whole confession, which had been transcribed during torture. 'I stole the wine.'

'There, you admitted you did steal the wine.'

'But I wasn't under oath.' Poor Edwin remembered this clearly and repeated again as loudly as he could. 'I w-w-w-wasn't sweared to God. D-D-D-Devil took my tongue.'

Sir Roger was amazed that an idiot such as Edwin could conjure up this defence until he remembered that he was the verger. In fact, he was rumoured to be Fyscher's illegitimate son - his mother had looked after the priest for many years. He looked at the round face topped off with a brown thatch and then at the priest - *there's a distinct similarity.*

'What do you mean?' asked Sir Roger.

'He hurt me so much I just 'fessed to make him stop.'

Handley had to admit to himself that he'd let his sadistic streak get the better of him that day, but now he denied the use of excessive torture.

Whytethorne turned to Fyscher, who sat next door to him. 'I thought you were supposed to have been at the interrogation to administer the oath.'

'I'm sorry, but I had to go to Winchester to see the Bishop, I've only just got back.' He'd deliberately absented himself on a flimsy pretext. *I can't condemn the boy - he's all I've got...*

'What does legal precedence say about confessions not under oath?' Sir Roger leaned over as Whytethorne conferred with the priest and a couple of jurors who had sat in courts before.

'We think that his testimony is not sound, my Lord. If there is no oath then the Devil can indeed take a man's tongue and make him condemn himself so that he can claim his soul for the hereafter.' Sir Roger remembered the story of the lettuce leaf.

'The accused will stand. Tell the bench how you came upon the wine.'

Edwin rose from his stool drooling, eyes rolling around like a blind man. 'I was bringing it to his lordship here, like I'm supposed to do.' He mumbled his words into his thick matted beard. In truth he'd been taking it to the priest, everyone knew that, and if Godless Gwyn hadn't caught him no one would have been the wiser. But the Ox had been on the prowl looking for an excuse and a victim and he hated the new Reeve.

'We believe that you found the barrel as you say you did,' pronounced the Foreman of the Jury, having conferred with his fellows, 'but there is no evidence that you were going to give it to his Lordship. So we still consider this to be a matter of honour that will have to be proved by combat.' The leading juror turned to Sir Roger. 'Will you nominate the court's champion?'

Gwyn licked his lips in anticipation; he would enjoy beating up Edwin.

But it was not to be him. 'It will be...' and there was a pause as Sir Roger eyed up his men-at-arms. 'You.' He pointed at Peter, who had no last name. 'You need to redeem your honour.' He had been seen holding back in a cowardly manner during the fighting at Southampton and had not really been brought to account for his actions at the time. Fyscher breathed a sigh of relief - *the lad's strong enough to beat Peter.*

'You will fight with rammeshorne staves until one side is bloodied and bowed.'

This seemed to please the villagers, who now had a contest to look forward to. Edwin had the unpleasant habit of defecating on their doorsteps and needed a good beating, and rammeshornes, three-foot long ashwood poles and iron devices shaped like ram's horns, pointed and sharpened with no real use other than for fighting judicial duels, were a good weapon for delivering pain.

'The duel will be fought ten days hence on the Green. That should allow enough time for your torture wounds to heal.'

Chapter 41

Punished for a Crime they did not Commit

'It's a joke, it has to be.' Sir Roger took the sweat- and rain-stained sheet of parchment and examined it carefully. The ink had run making it barely legible. The message, though, was clear enough. He was wanted for robbery, larceny, rape, sodomy and murder. Sir Roger de Bohun, declared outlaw in three counties, reward offered. The size of the reward could only be guessed at, as the amount was smudged into illegibility, but from the extent of the smudge it must be substantial.

'I think not,' said Handley. He had been relishing this moment from when he had been given the 'wanted' notice, acquired by the carter who had taken the archers to Cheshire. 'It's definitely for you. It was posted by the court in Stoke-on-Trent. John the Carter thought you might want to see it and stole it from the notice board. 'Your' exploits are the talk of the Midlands.'

The carter corroborated the story; he had been passing when he had heard the proclamation being read out. 'So I pinched it when no one was looking,' he said.

'It's outrageous,' Sir Roger spluttered in fury. 'Who is responsible?' *And who might be looking to collect that reward?* He didn't know. Later that evening, unable to sleep, he took his candle and came down into the empty hall. All court seating had been cleared away, with the exception of the accused's stool, standing alone in the hall's centre. Moving it to the fireplace, he idly used a long poker to stir the ashes, watching as spirals of sparks wafted up the chimney. *I bet it is Sir Eustace's doing- it has to be him.* He felt a hand rest gently on his shoulder. It was his wife. He had been so deep in thought that he had not heard her approach. As he turned, and in the dim light, he could see she'd been crying.

'I'm pregnant,' she said softly. The bump in her tummy was just starting to show and she knew she couldn't hide it any more. Her anxiety was terrible and she had become unable to eat.

A welter of emotion ran though his head. *He who is without guilt should cast the first stone.* They'd both broken their marriage vows. He'd strayed with Elizabeth and others knew it too. *They were at the window.*

'Whose is it? Is it mine?' Sir Roger spoke softly, dropping the words so that they were barely audible. 'Or is it the Minstrel's.'

He watched his wife gasp. *How's he found out? Who's told him?*

'What are you going to do?' she asked.

He let his mind revert to his other problem and changed the subject. 'To start with, I think I should see the Sheriff and swear an oath of innocence before the Bishop. I am convinced that this is Sir Eustace's doing.'

'Come to bed, *mon amour.* There is nothing more you can do, and I'm cold in bed without you.' She led him back upstairs by the hand, hoping to repair the damage to their relationship. They lay side-by-side without speaking, neither daring to start the conversation. Eventually he turned his back on her and tried to sleep.

He was glad Elizabeth had gone, though it had been his most exciting sexual liaison to date. He saw the peril in upsetting his marriage. Before the acquisition of his fortune, he thought he would be reliant on his wife's inheritance - she was her father's only child - *and the way things are going I might need to rely on her good offices again.* For the moment he was too angry. He hoped the child would be his, but he doubted that he would ever try for another. *All this misfortune started when that turd Eustace floated across my moat...*

Next morning he prayed much longer and harder than usual. *Here I am, normally the giver of life or death, wanted as a common criminal alive or dead with an unreadable price on my head.* It was this that galled him most. *I want to know how much I'm worth!*

There was further bad news. 'Cook says that the flour is no good,' said Edgar the Pantler as he served his master his breakfast wine. 'He wants to know when our mill will be mended.'

Sir Roger nodded and promised to find out.

'I want the garrison on full alert. All strangers are to be stopped and searched and questioned as to where they were coming from or going to,' Sir Roger instructed Whytethorne. Being declared an outlaw meant that any citizen could arrest you and the State could confiscate your property. *At least I have been forewarned.* He gathered his troop and set out for Winchester.

For the first time in he didn't know how long, the rain had ceased and a watery sun shone in the heavens. The storm had stripped most of the leaves from the trees and flocks of rooks argued noisily as they tumbled through a mackerel sky. He watched a skein of geese flying like an arrow high above, out of the reach of even his best falcon. *A sure sign of winter* - though hawking was far from his mind. *I feel more like the hunted.* He had an unaccountable feeling of dread that the hounds must be close at hand.

Not much work had been done on the mill, as most people were reluctant to venture out in rain, preferring to drink ale around the hearth and tell stories or play dice. Today, with a gap in the clouds, workers swarmed all over the building. Carpenters had finished a new wheel and the Reeve was supervising it being hauled up into place. They stopped as their master approached.

'When do you expect to have it finished?'

The Reeve was optimistic. 'Once the wheel is up it won't take long for the gears to be fitted and grinding stone to turn once more,' said Walt.

Sir Roger decided it would be no bad thing to ensure that his Reeve knew about the warrants. An indefinable bond was developing between the two men; Sir Roger could not put his finger on it, but the Reeve was always keen to do his master's bidding, and not in the simpering, grovelling manner that often characterised the relationship between lord and subject.

'I want to thank you for picking a puny opponent for Edwin.' Walt was effusive. 'I will keep my eyes and ears open for any traitorous words.'

'A cask of good ale if you get the mill working before it rains again.' Sir Roger decided to add incentive to the labourers. 'And not from widow Cecilia.'

This prompted a laugh, and straining and heaving began with renewed vigour.

—⚒—

'That's him,' a voice shouted as Sir Roger and his troop arrived in the city. 'The great outlaw with his Green Boar banner!'

'What luck,' whispered Sir Eustace to Falke - they, too, had come south with mayhem in mind. 'Let's stir this up into a hornet's nest.'

Their plan had been to sow dissent and spread rumour, publicising the dreadful deeds of 'Sir Roger' and his band of thugs closer to home, but, glory be, their quarry had materialised before their eyes. A rush of people came from the marketplace and surrounding streets. They couldn't believe their eyes. Here was the outlaw, as brazen as could be. Bystanders stared and pointed and murmured to one another. A lump of dung was thrown in his direction.

'Get to the castle quickly,' ordered Sir Roger spurring his horse forward to escape the mob. Some of his troop drew their swords, not taking kindly to threatening behaviour. The commotion alerted the Sheriff, who emerged into the courtyard. He waved his hands in a calming motion and ordered his men back to their posts.

'Not what I expected,' commented Sir Roger, non-plussed, as he dismounted and handed the bridle of his palfrey to the nearest man-at-arms. His welcome should be one of deference- salutes and touching of forelocks. This time it was pointed pikes and knocked arrows.

'The most famous bandit in the land has come to call, and none too soon, my friend.' Sir Hugh was beaming. 'Come inside.'

They went through the hall to the private chambers. There Sir Roger took out the crumpled warrant.

'Did you realise that a month ago, when you and I were together, you were accused of stealing all the valuables and possessions of the Bishop of Nottingham? The hue-and-cry is, by all accounts, almost countywide. I think that you are a great magician to be in two places at once!' Sir Hugh roared with laughter. He was well known for encouraging alchemists to try their hands at turning base metal into gold, and when they failed he would have them burnt.

'I think de Frage is behind all this.' Sir Roger advanced his theory that his arch enemy was stirring up trouble and was about to float the idea of taking an oath when one of Sir Hugh's constables interrupted them.

'It's getting ugly out there, what should I do?'

A massive crowd, jostling and shouting, had gathered outside the gate, held back by a thin line of pikemen. It was only a matter of time before they flooded into the courtyard. Sir Roger's men struggled to keep their mounts under control. Zuzu had climbed onto Dan's shoulders and was bouncing up and down, shrieking at the mob. The pikemen were pushed back as the first of the mob broke through their line.

'Clear the yard of riffraff and drop the portcullis,' ordered Sir Hugh, dispatching a man to the gatehouse. With a rumble of chains it came crashing down, the heavy wooden grill with serried metal spikes pinning a poor unfortunate through the foot. There he remained, howling with pain.

Sir Hugh shook his head in disgust and continued. 'As I understand it,' he related, 'the Bishop of Nottingham's baggage train had just left Grantham when your impostors suddenly attacked them. They were stripped naked, tied to trees and sodomised. 'You' kept your helm on throughout and 'you' buggered the Bishop's Private Secretary before stealing all his valuables and setting fire to the rest.' The Sheriff spoke in short, clipped sentences. 'The gossip started in the marketplace a couple of days ago. I was going to send you a note, but it seems you have found out yourself. So there you have it. I should keep you here for your own protection.'

Sir Roger was appalled. His eyes widened. *My good name has been severely sullied and I am threatened with incarceration 'for my own protection'.*

'I must clear my name forthwith. We'll go to the Cathedral and I will swear an oath of my innocence.' He paused, feeling the need to get out of the castle. 'I'll swear on the bones of St. Swithun.'

'Good idea,' said the Sheriff, summoning the guard to ready their horses and clear the street. At least two people had died, crushed to death by the weight of those pushing to get into the courtyard when the grill had dropped. The mood was still ugly and a cry arose as the crowd saw Sir Roger and the Sheriff mount up. Surrounded by men-at-arms, they forced a pathway with their pikes down the hill to the Cathedral Precinct, followed by what seemed to be the whole population of Winchester.

Pleased with his handiwork, Sir Eustace took the opportunity to steal a pie. 'Keep them stirred up,' he told Falke. 'Let's have a few more martyrs. If we work at it we should have a full scale riot baying for blood.'

His band of thugs dispersed again into the crowd, egging them on, pushing and jostling. The Sheriff ordered his mounted escort to force the masses back and alarm set in at the front of the crowd as they tried to evade the horsemen. Men-at-arms were deployed, pikes menacing the bellies of the leading townsfolk. Sir Eustace shoved hard at one, making him yell as the blade slid into his stomach.

A service was in progress in the Cathedral, plainsong chant echoing through cloisters. Singing stopped as the level of noise outside became audible. The Bishop of Winchester, who was leading Mass, sent the Dean to find out the cause of the interruption. He was confronted with a chaotic sea of humanity pushing Sir Hugh's and Sir Roger's men backwards - towards him. A horseman was pulled from his saddle and assaulted by the mob. He had to be rescued by men-at-arms, who dealt brutally with the assailants, slashing them with pike blades. Several injured men and women lay on the ground by the door.

'Get through the door,' shouted Sir Hugh in a state of near panic. The Dean only just got out of the way as horsemen made a dash for safety.

'What is the meaning of this?' The Bishop's stentorian voice echoed around the cathedral's magnificent interior, as did the clatter of hooves on the flagstone floor. 'This is sacrilege!' His face was puce with anger. 'How dare you violate the House of God?'

He strode towards Sir Hugh, Sir Roger and the rest of their men, who were quickly on their knees, their heads bowed with what they hoped was suitable humility. Sir Roger remembered the times he had to take punishment on behalf of his prince, not many times, he had to admit. Not because they were that good, but because they were rarely caught.

'As well you may pray that the Lord forgive this intrusion into his holy house.' The bishop recognised the pair. 'Tell me, what is the meaning of this civil disorder? Are we attacked by the French?'

'No, may the Lord forgive this trespass,' the two men answered in unison. Still kneeling, Sir Hugh led off with an explanation. The Bishop held up his hand to stop him.

'Come with me,' he ordered. It would be more appropriate to hear this sorry tale in his private chamber. The Dean asked what he should do.

'Keep the door barred till I return.' And with the pair in tow he marched up the nave, past the relics of the Saxon Kings of England, and went into the robing chamber. 'This is a very serious matter. I heard this story about you yesterday.' He looked directly into Sir Roger's eyes. 'Is it true?'

'No, upon my oath and upon all that is sacred, it is not.'

'I can provide his alibi,' testified the Sheriff. The Bishop nodded as if to acknowledge the fact, and signalled that he, alone, should go.

'You have nothing to answer for. This man has.' The Bishop was in his fifties, and was tonsured in the manner of the Augustinians; his eyebrows were remarkably bushy, his face angular and his lips thin. He had fought the devil at every turn and could see into men's hearts.

'If you are blameless,' he said flintily, fixing Sir Roger with steel grey eyes that froze even the warmest of hearts. 'First you must make confession.' *Which should be interesting*, thought the Bishop.

The Ipers village priest, Fyscher, had been to see him, an event so unusual that he had found it most curious. *Is this pre-planned?*

The priest had relished the opportunity to drop his lord in the shit, nor could he bear the thought that he would be forced to condemn his son. He had told him about the slaughter of the monks and that he suspected his Lord of being an adulterer. The Bishop had been delighted to hear of these sins. Now he, too would be able to gain a portion of Sir Roger's fortune. Many hours of prayer would need to be said if forgiveness was to be granted, *and a man like this will not have the time so he'll have to pay me for someone to pray on his behalf...*

'I will do so willingly.' Sir Roger wondered what he should confess; he had not made confession for several days, not since his escapades at the well with Lady Elizabeth. Was lust his only sin? He was not too sure.

'But first you must fast. You must remain here and pray all night at the tombs of the saints.'

Sir Roger was shocked. He was already tired, hungry and thirsty, having not eaten or drunk anything since leaving his castle early that morning. He had to prove his innocence before God and the Bishop or be torn apart by the mob, so he steeled himself for the ordeal ahead. *I will lead my men by example*, he swore inwardly to himself. *If our paths ever cross again, I will make Sir Eustace suffer for this.*

Leaving Sir Roger on his knees in front of St. Swithun's relics, the Bishop returned to the Cathedral door and ordered it opened. He emerged, crosier in his hand and mitre on his head, and addressed the angry multitude. It took some time for the tumult to die down as passions were still running high.

'Tomorrow Sir Roger de Bohun will swear an oath that he is innocent of the crimes he has been accused of.' He had to raise his voice. 'This will be after Matins. Tonight he will fast and pray, as will his men, who have also been accused with him of heinous acts of outlawry and defilement.' He waved the crowd away. 'Now go home.'

Reinforcements had, by then, arrived, and in an orderly fashion the crowd was dispersed. As the horses were led to stabling, Dan regretted having brought Zuzu along. She sat disconsolately on her master's saddle. He secured her chain to his pommel and whispered comforting words in her ear. *I hope she doesn't get up to any mischief…*

A young priest was charged with leading the men through their ordeal through the night. 'You will kneel in front of the Saintly relics until sun up tomorrow,' he ordered. 'This is in penance for defiling God's holy place and disrupting our worship.'

To ensure that the penance was done properly, six burly monks armed with birch whips made the men strip to their shirts. 'If anyone speaks out of turn or complains, they are to be flogged at the altar.'

The pain of kneeling became excruciating after only a short while. The agony extended through their thighs and up their backs. They prayed. The louder they prayed the easier it was to bear the agony, and so the night wore on in a babble of prayer. Sir Roger resorted to sucking on the anchorite's token, which he wore around his neck, this allowed a little saliva to flow and wet his parched mouth. In his mind, he relived the episode of decapitating the monks and tried hard to fathom the depths of his iniquity.

Zuzu, meantime, found being alone very frightening, so some time after dark she tugged away at her collar, eventually loosening it enough to get it over her head, breaking free. She climbed out of the stables and headed for the Cathedral. The night was cold and starry, so she climbed up the great building's west face to seek what warmth she could from the stones. She found a roosting pigeon, which she grabbed and ate with relish, sucking warm blood from its breast. Far below, she thought she could hear her master bellowing his prayers. By morning it was cloudy again. There was a brief sunrise, full of promise, but scudding clouds soon filled in from the west. There was a bustle of activity below. Soldiers arrived early and had taken up their positions. A steady stream of citizens were making their way to the cathedral - those who arrived first would get the best places. Zuzu shifted round to watch. A small boy saw her and tugged excitedly at his father's robe, pointing.

'Look Dad, one of the gargoyles moved.' The father, obviously a baker from his dress, looked up but saw nothing. Zuzu moved again. The boy pointed again. This time his father gave him a sharp clip round the ear and shoved him along. There was an impressive array of city dignitaries and this time all was decorum. Each wore their best suit of clothing. Women, too, had on their finery, many with fur collars and cuffs. The guild's musicians played trumpets and beat drums and a procession was formed of the mayor and his aldermen.

The last twenty-four hours had seen five people crushed, spiked or trampled to death in the near riot and dozens had minor injuries, but the mood of the crowd had changed, order had been restored.

The penitents had been allowed to wash and generally make themselves presentable. It had taken some time to restore circulation to their legs. On his first attempt to stand, Sir Roger had crashed to the floor as his legs gave way. He was very thirsty indeed and he could not resist thrusting his head in the washing bucket and taking a draft of water, and he thanked God that his rank gave him the privilege of being first at the bucket. Somewhat refreshed, he addressed his men. They knew nothing of the attack or the buggery of the monks and were appalled at the crimes of which they were accused. Only as he told them did they realise the gravity of the accusations and the fearful trouble they were in. They were lined up in front of the congregation and forced once again to their knees.

The Bishop made a dramatic entrance in robes of scarlet and gold. He started the service and handed over to an archdeacon while he summoned Sir Roger to come forward.

'It is time, my son, for your confession.' He drew the knight aside to a confessional. 'I know you and he didn't concoct this as an alibi - how could you?' The Bishop's voice was dripping with malice as he hissed in his ear. 'You were breaking the Seventh Commandment at the time. I've heard all about your adultery - but for that you would have spent the night in a comfy bed. You're supposed to set an example...' He continued with his lecture on moral obligations while Sir Roger squirmed - never in his life had he been given a dressing down of this magnitude. It made him want to open his heart, and he was on the point of cracking and admitting to murder. His breath was drawn in, words forming on the tip of his tongue. And then the thunderbolt struck.

'And I know you have the blood of innocents on your hands. Getting your church painted is not proper penance.' The Bishop paused for his words to sink in. 'For the murder of ten monks, you must get ten monks to say prayers for their souls twice a day for a year.'

That's a tidy sum, thought the Bishop.

You bastard, thought Sir Roger.

'As for your sins, your night-long penance has absolved you,' said the Bishop, changing from despot to benevolent father. 'Now you must make your oath on the bones of the saint in front of the congregation.'

'All my sins?' asked Sir Roger timidly.

'All that you have declared to the Saint,' answered the Bishop, now keen to get on with the Service of Absolution. He went down the line of kneeling men and touched each on the forehead with the crook of his crosier. 'You are absolved of all your sins,' he intoned solemnly in Latin as he passed down the line. As the crozier touched the Ox, he felt a weight lift off his shoulders. He, too, had never confessed to the atrocity, which he had committed and now it was gone. All gone. He might get to heaven after all - though he doubted it.

The whole of the religious fraternity started chanting a plainsong anthem as the reliquary with the Saint's bones was removed from its alcove beneath the altar and brought forward. Four black robed priests carried the holy box aloft and, in procession, led the knight and the other penitents around the twelve Stations of the Cross; at each they knelt and crossed themselves. On completing the circuit of the Cathedral, which was almost finished - only the east end was still under construction - they returned to the high altar where Sir Roger swore his innocence before God and multitude. There was an almost audible sigh of relief as the proceedings came to an end.

Outside, those who had been unable to get into the packed Cathedral watched in fascination as Zuzu climbed to the very pinnacle of the square tower and sat there, picking at her fleas. Someone tried to sling a stone at her; this narrowly missed a stained glass window. A man-at-arms made threatening gestures so it would not happen again.

Dusk was well advanced when the men arrived back home. It had taken Dan a very long time to coax Zuzu back down from the tower, a situation made worse by the Bishop forbidding 'Satan's Imp' as he called her, from setting foot inside, so Dan had had to make a perilous climb up and down, watched by a large crowd, to retrieve his pet.

Sir Eustace, disguised in the stolen robes, watched as events unfolded with a certain satisfaction, revelling in the chaos he'd caused. It was he, after all, who had provided the intimate detail of the degradation, and it was he who had encouraged the sense of outrage felt by the good citizens of Winchester.

'I'm slightly disappointed,' he confided to his gangling henchman Falke. 'I had hoped we could make that prick suffer more.' The thought of his nemesis on his knees being flagellated through the night, put a spring into his step as he went to the yard where he'd stabled their horses.

It had been easy to rouse the rabble. The crippling taxes and lack of money was already driving prices down, craftsmen could no longer afford to keep apprentices, and trade was drying up. Combining this with the foul weather and fear of the French had made many a malcontent. He would travel the highways and byways a bit longer, putting together his army of the displaced, dispossessed and displeased. *We'll start our campaign for justice* - and put an end to the hegemony of money-grubbing barons - *by burning down their castles.* And he knew just which one, belonging to the King's Friend, would be the first on his list. He would be King Arthur's heir. *Better still, I'll be his reincarnation!*

Chapter 42

No Good will come of It

The only ship de Bokland and de Palton could find on their return to Antwerp was one going to Great Yarmouth. It was a ropey old cog, carrying a cargo of cloth, and was tossed about like a demented cork on the storm-lashed North Sea. Both men suffered most dreadfully from seasickness. Even on dry land, their troubles were far from over.

'Take'em or leave'em. They're all I've got,' said the Ostler, rubbing his hands with undisguised glee at the thought of selling broken down old nags destined for the knacker's yard at twice their worth. The two knights, exhausted from puking their guts out, knew that he had them over a barrel.

'We'll take them,' said de Bokland through gritted teeth as his long-suffering manservant hefted their heavy saddles onto sagging backs. They had no option- their horses were at the Tower in London where they had been forced to leave them. No amount of brow beating or flourishing of official warrants worked to produce better - the barrel had already been scraped clean.

'I've got two florins, one mark and twenty pennies left,' moaned de Palton, resigning himself to a slow ride and sub-standard accommodation. Incessant gales had all but stripped the trees of leaves; driving rain came in cold, stinging waves. Days later the two knights were nearing the limits of their endurance as they drove on on their decrepit mounts.

'I don't want to do that again,' declared de Bokland, relieved at finally seeing Winchester Castle in the distance. It was therefore by a lucky happenstance their arrival coincided with the end of Sir Roger's enforced penance.

'Here, these are from the King.' De Palton handed over the letters of instruction. 'And can we have some money, please.'

Hugh de Lacey took a long look at the indents for money and, with an exasperated shrug, turned his eyes heavenward. 'The coffers here are empty.' He cast his eyes dolefully towards the floor. 'I have enough cash to last us here another week.' He had just sent another strongbox of coin to London, wrung out of a reluctant population by his tax collectors' strong-arm tactics, and he told them so. He was equally disparaging about men for a garrison. 'I have barely enough men to hold this castle.' He was shaking his head unhappily as he took the royal warrants and placed them on a large, untidy pile of papers that occupied the majority of his bureau. 'I think these can wait till spring.'

'Money. I haven't spent the last month being eaten by bedbugs and fleas to be fobbed off with some more bits of bloody paper,' pleaded de Palton, who was close to breaking point. 'Come on Hugh, at least pay half, be a gent.'

The Sheriff gave way, handing over two paltry leather purses. 'There just isn't any more,' he said with a shrug. 'We've had some fun and games here.' He related the story of Sir Roger's penance. 'Speak of the devil! Here he is.'

Sir Roger, still sore at the knees and smarting from his ordeal, entered the Hall to say his farewells to the Sheriff. His eyes lit up when he saw the weary travellers.

'Well, well. Who have we here?' He hugged his friends as if they were long lost brothers. 'I'm headed home - care to join me? I'll send a galloper ahead and make sure we have a feast when we get home.'

The two men shook their heads.

'I'm going straight home - but thanks for the thought,' said de Palton. 'My old bones need a proper feather bed.'

'I hear you've spent the night being beaten.' De Bokland had to suppress a laugh as Sir Roger told him of the warrants.

'It was a most uncomfortable experience. When I get my hands on Sir Eustace, I'm going to make him kneel on broken glass before I pluck his eyes out and cut out his tongue. No, I'll do that first - then he can kneel.' Sir Roger had been plotting an imaginary fate for his persecutor. The Bishop had given a stern sermon, admonishing the crowds for being beguiled by the devil into making false accusations. Sir Eustace and his men had slipped away, happy with the trouble they had caused.

'The campaign is not going well.' Bokland related the news from Flanders. 'In fact it seems to be a complete failure. The French are fucking cowards and won't fight. Poncy bastards, afraid of getting their armour rusty.'

The French had steadfastly refused to be drawn into battle; their mobilisation had been an empty vessel - a lot of noise but no action.

'The King has decided to stay put and hold court in Flanders. Magnates are grumbling that they need to be in England to keep their affairs in order and this cannot be done from some sodden tent pitched to protect an ungrateful bunch of rebellious weavers.' He painted a picture of bitter recrimination and petty jealousies against the Earls, who had been omitted from this foreign adventure. 'They might be organising the defence of the realm and its governance; instead everyone thinks they are lining their pockets and enjoying the womenfolk.' The two men laughed.

'As long as next year brings a change in my fortunes, I won't care.' Sir Roger moaned. 'I lost everything in Southampton.' He wished for a swift victory, with much booty and ransoms galore to be collected - but all that was in the future. Today there were more mundane duties - of having to take prisoners and *ribaud* to London for examination.

'They say the King has scoured most of the Low Countries and quite a few German cities to boot, borrowing from all and sundry, including the Jews, at rates of interest, it was said, of up to fifty per cent.' De Bokland told of their meeting with the Chancellor. 'Just what he does with this money no one knows - except that it isn't used to pay soldiers!'

'Can we trade in those nags we got in Yarmouth?' De Bokland was still saddle sore.

Fortunately the Sheriff had a better-stocked stable and provided new mounts for the knights.

'There's something very wrong going on. No one has any money.' De Bokland was a stickler in financial matters. 'We submitted for expenses at two shillings per day, that's our normal rate, had the sum doubled by our grateful Monarch then get fobbed off with a piece of paper 'payable by the Wardrobe at the Tower' - you couldn't take it with you when you go?'

'And can you collect our horses? Take the stabling charges out of what I'm owed,' added de Palton - he hated to think what costs might accrue if their horses remained in London. 'The King might pay us double but it don't make no odds if we can't get the cash.' To them, four shillings a day was a decent wage. 'There isn't any money anywhere.'

Whatever mints there were, and these were few and far between, were hammering out coins as fast as they could, but it was a slow business as most were lacking supplies of any precious metal.

'Delighted to help,' offered Sir Roger, all-obliging. *I'm looking forward to visiting the Tower, if the Queen's in residence it should be full of women.* And he wondered whether Lady Caroline would be there- *she of the silky skin.* 'As a precaution. I think we should travel back with banners furled and surcoats reversed,' he ordered Dan. 'We don't want a repeat of yesterday.'

'Looking forward to Martinmas?' asked de Bokland as he waved farewell.

Sir Roger nodded. He always enjoyed the Feast of St. Martin - the roast beef festival, when surplus cattle were slaughtered and salted.

'A sure sign that winter is on the way.' He pointed at babbling skeins of Brent Geese streaming overhead. The sight of the birds somehow made his pains increase. 'Get Edgar to prepare a hot mustard bath,' he ordered a rider to gallop ahead. 'I need to ease my aching joints.'

Sir Roger was quite unprepared for the chaotic scene that confronted them as they approached the castle. When they had left, peace and quiet had reigned at Ipers. Now it looked like a demonic livestock market, with many temporary pens filled with frightened animals.

Sir Roger spotted Whytethorne and asked what was going on. He was standing with Handley watching proceedings from a safe distance. A near riot was in progress as angry farmers pelted a line of men-at-arms with clods of earth. They, in return, made forays into the crowd, grabbing ringleaders and beating them up with pike staves.

Whytethorne expressed surprise when his master made his appearance at his side. 'You gave me a fright, Sir. I saw you coming but didn't recognise you without your banners.'

'Well, you're not going to believe what happened to us.' Sir Roger gave him a brief description of their ordeal, making sure that he disseminated the line that the severity of punishment had been because of the barbarity of the attack *and not because that bastard Bishop wanted to punish me. That*, he considered, *would not endear me to my men.*

'This lot arrived this morning,' said the Steward dejectedly, pointing at a crowd of irate serfs, villeins and other assorted farmers who were attempting to get payment for what they considered to be outright theft.

On the far side of the crowd, a large knight appeared to be in command. He strode over and removed his bascinet, wiping sweat off his pock-marked forehead with an iron-studded gauntlet. 'You must be de Bohun I presume.' There was a no-nonsense sort of approach to this man, who was juggling commands, shouting across to appropriately placed henchmen and drovers. 'I'm Sir Robert de Mansfield, I'm the King's Agent.' He flourished his warrant. 'I am tasked with collecting as much livestock as possible, especially draft horses and wagons, as well as foodstuffs for the army.'

Sir Roger gave the warrant a perfunctory glance. It gave Mansfield absolute power to use whatever necessary force he needed to fulfil his duties.

A pair of over-worked clerks battled to keep whatever scraps of paper and parchment they had dry and under control from wind and drizzle while laboriously attempting to write out receipts. Some peasants were trying to erect a temporary shelter out of wattle hurdles but without much success. It seemed that ineptitude was the order of the day.

'This is my last port of call,' declared a relieved Mansfield, having swept Kent, Sussex and Hampshire clean of useful animals.

'Aren't you going to pay these people?' asked Sir Roger, somewhat aghast.

'Payment is, sadly, out of the question. We ran out of money long ago.' Each animal owner was being asked to identify his beast and would then be given a receipt that would be cashable as soon as the Exchequer made funds available. However, since all the animals had been assembled into one great herd, it was nigh impossible for erstwhile owners and forfeited property to be reunited.

'How much of this livestock is ours?' murmured Sir Roger quietly into Handley's ear.

'None, Sire. I took the precaution of hiding our beasts in the woods. I told *your* Reeve to take them there.' Handley could not bring himself to call him 'the' Reeve. 'I took the liberty of going over to Sir Eustace's place and liberating all his livestock- seeing as he's not around. We sold those instead.'

Sir Roger smiled as he looked at the bill of sale. 'In that case, tell all these good folk to submit their claims to the Sheriff; he can sort this mess out.'

Mounted troopers were assembled in a line and, using the flats of their swords, they beat the aggrieved masses back from the pens and dispersed them grumbling and cursing. Disgruntled and disconsolate, they went back to their hovels and shacks, fulminating on the evils of war and the depredations of their rulers. Their Martinmas had been ruined.

'Care to join me in the Castle? I have a hot mustard bath being prepared.' Sir Roger extended an invitation to Mansfield and the knight was happy to accept.

'Impressive, eh,' Sir Roger said, noting that his walls had finally been furnished with wooden palisades and a sloping roof of wood shingles covering the walkways had been finished. 'Wet soldiers rarely make good watchmen.' He could not help boasting as he crossed his drawbridge.

Sir Robert was impressed, thinking how his lowly manor could be improved. When they came into the hall, he was bowled over by the fireplace.

Lady Alice joined them, welcoming her husband back. 'I was worried,' she said. 'I thought you would be back yesterday.'

Handley appeared, having silently slunk in. It was the knack he had of suddenly appearing unannounced by his master's side that gave Sir Roger the shivers. 'There'll be trouble in store for that,' he said in the whiney voice that annoyed Lady Alice so much.

'What?' She liked to keep abreast of the goings on.

'The animals, Milady. That is wrong, what is going on out there. No good will come of it.' For Handley to express an opinion was rare, but Mansfield was unrepentant - his only regret was that he had not brought enough clerks with him to make the operation run quicker. Sir Roger availed himself of his tub. The mustard stung his back, but the pain flowed out of his joints. Mansfield followed.

'Your Bailiff's right, no good will come of it,' he said, almost apologetically as he sank completely under the hot water. 'Thank goodness, once I've got this lot shipped I can spend winter hunting - I've had it up to here with abuse.' He tapped the top of his head. 'Must get on, can't stay for dinner.'

Max watched disconsolately as the knight took his leave. 'More food, a feast, hot water, no feast, no water, can't these people ever make up their minds?' he grumbled to Edgar. 'Now I've made too many wafers. Come,' he said solicitously, putting a huge greasy hand on the old man's bony shoulders. 'Come and enjoy the food of angels.'

Left alone with Alice, Sir Roger could not resist giving her a bear hug. He was not often overcome with emotion, but now tears welled up into his eyes. 'I don't think I have *ever* experienced anything as uncomfortable as spending the night on my knees being whipped.' He told her all about Winchester. *I've paid for my sins - all of them, my slate has been wiped clean.* The Bishop had been emphatic. *As long as you declared all your sins to the bones of the saint you'll be absolved and I did, so I am!* His heart sang with joy. *I'm not going to pay him for sins that have already been absolved...*

'I'm going to miss the trial by combat. What are the odds on Edwin?' he shouted out to Handley, who was lurking discreetly. There were always side bets and wagers.

The Bailiff thought for a moment. 'It was even money on Edwin and two to one against Peter. But there's a complication. Peter has done a runner- gone, vanished, disappeared.'

'Then I want to see Edwin right away.' The accused had been paroled, but was not allowed out of the castle precinct. He'd been put to work on roofing around the walls, and it only took a few minutes for him to come. 'It appears that the court's champion has gone,' Sir Roger informed him. 'If he doesn't come back in time for the bout you'll be freed unconditionally. Show me your hands.' He examined them - they were nearly healed. Somehow the message got through. The grateful verger gibbered and spluttered as he backed out of the Hall, bowing and scraping for all he was worth.

'No sooner here than gone again,' he told his wife. 'I have to go to London with the prisoners.' It would take at least a week, if not longer, to get there as the roads were in a shocking state of repair worsened, no doubt, by Mansfield's massive herd of animals.

'Have I got any cash?' he asked Handley.

'Not much, Sire.' The reply was as Sir Roger feared - he still had the Venetian's gold ducats, and it was apparent that these were all he had. They were no good to him until he sought out the services of a moneychanger who could exchange them for silver coin of the realm. It would be an uncomfortable journey with prisoners and *ribaud*. In the distance, he could hear lowing and mooing as the requisitioned animals were driven away.

Already there was a queue as his own serfs lined up for his clerk, who had set up a desk and inkwell near the door. Widow Cecilia was in floods of tears - her team of plough oxen had been taken. She saw Sir Roger and came running over, prostrating herself at his feet, a quaking heap of rags. 'How can I marry if I can't even plough my own fields?'

Sir Roger had no answer; he could not even give her a half-farthing, as his purse was empty. Nunny helped Cecilia to her feet.

We'll have to tighten our belts if we're going to make it through the winter. I'll take the saltcellars to London and try and sell them. Sir Roger felt sure he would get a good price for them in the capital. From the carefree spending days of summer, he was amazed how quickly his money had evaporated, and he fervently hoped Eccles would not find his half tally stick. *At least I've got some stout walls and a moat - at least I've had something of use from it. And I hope I still have my sheep.*

'After that trouble with Sir Eustace I'll have to change my emblems,' he said to Lady Alice, worried that the sight of his green boar rampant might spark off another hue and cry.

'I'll search my cloth store,' she said. The only suitable material they found was a bolt of red silk. Sir Roger remembered how expensive it had been. He had haggled with Bandolini for over an hour, but still it had cost him dear.

'I want a red sash for each man,' he instructed the women- it would have to do. It was also time to subject Guillaume to a more detailed interrogation. *And I know just the man to help...*

Bailiff Imberd and Simon had spent the last month at Ipers locked in endless games of chess. The Bailiff had lost all his pomposity, dreading the thought of being incarcerated in the Tower and facing a panel of inquiry. Simon, on the other hand, had regained some of his.

'Guillaume, you're coming to London too.' Sir Roger told him casually. Simon's heart leapt *This is the offer of a lifetime.* Here, on a plate, was a chance to see the heart of his enemies' power base for himself. *It just gets better and better,* thought Simon. He'd joined Béhuchet with the specific intention of seeing the world. He hoped his pretence of being William de Bapaume would hold.

'So how is my angel today?' Simon sneaked up behind Clothilde, grabbing her round the waist. *At least there is some pleasure to be had in this gilded prison of mine.* Once on parole, it had not taken him long to settle his affections onto Clothilde. She was far and away prettiest of Lady Alice's ladies-in-waiting, with her long brown hair and hazel eyes, she was a happy-go-lucky girl who bemoaned her fate, stuck near the windswept heath of the Forest - imprisoned, she said, amongst troglodytes.

'But then, *mon amour*, you came here.' She turned and gave her poor knight a kiss. 'Will you rescue me from the dragon and take me back to France with you?' There was something unfathomable about this man. She was usually a good judge of character - men were basically simple souls who could be reached by feminine wiles, but this time her instincts failed her and it annoyed her that she could not put her finger on what was different.

Women are mysterious beasts - but gullible. Simon assiduously continued to create his masquerade of being poor Guillaume. He was sure that the confidences of the bedroom would be relayed to her mistress and then to her husband. He knew this to be true when Sir Roger had picked up on the story of his one-armed friend and the suit of Augsburg armour - for he had only told her and no one else....

'So you've decided to travel incognito,' observed the Sheriff, looking at the red silk stripes sported by Sir Roger's men and handing over the rest of the prisoners. 'Take good care, my friend, these are lawless times. There are many angry men on the roads these days.'

Chapter 43

The Sons of King Arthur

A triumphant, crowing Sir Eustace rode out of Winchester, where his gang had taken advantage of the chaos and engaged in wide-scale theft, pillaging vulnerable shops and market stalls for foodstuffs. He was thrilled that his curse was obviously working. 'That'll teach him. Back to Caxton for Martinmas?'

'I think,' said Falke, taking off his monk's habit to reveal his phoney Green Boar surcoat. 'We should give it another go. Closer to home, more trouble for your chum.'

So again the band of bandits sought out suitable prey, which was not long in coming. A party of tax collectors were ambushed, netting a goodly haul of cash, and Sir Roger's name was bandied about so all could hear.

'Shall we kill the rest of them?' Already one had died, pierced through the brain with a blow from a *poignard,* its heavy stiletto blade ideal for stabbing through mail, or unprotected heads for that matter.

Sir Eustace shook his head and ordered they be let go. It would serve his purposes much better to let them run off to the Sheriff and tell him that his friend had been telling lies.

The Sons of King Arthur were in a buoyant mood when they rode back to Caxton Deverell Manor, where their bubble of happiness burst. The place had been abandoned. Even the factotum and servants had absconded, leaving an all-pervading air of decay. Falke ordered the gang to empty sacks and saddlebags onto the table.

'Beef is off the menu,' said Sir Eustace, barely capable of holding back his anger as he surveyed the dereliction. Their herd of fat cattle, so successfully rustled by his Normans in the summer, had also gone - and, from the tell-tale signs, not so long ago.

'Two, three weeks at the most,' said Falke, kicking a dried crust of dung in the courtyard and setting the men to work collecting wood and making makeshift repairs.

'We'll use this as our base,' Sir Eustace told the forty men who now made up the Sons. 'If we're going to be King Arthur's Sons I want you to pick names. You,' he chose a man at random, 'can be the new Sir Lancelot, and you can be Sir Bedevere.' He gave each a name, making them up when he had exhausted his knowledge of the real ones. *A sorrier bunch of renegades I have rarely seen...*

'You remember the Mummers,' said Falke to his obviously depressed boss.

Sir Eustace nodded.

'I saw them again. You might care to remind that fat oaf Mercurius of his obligation to you.'

A smile flickered across the scarred face as Sir Eustace remembered the gaily painted wagons and their pompous leader who had claimed to be the world's greatest actor.

It was Mercurius who had introduced Sir Eustace to the Arthurian Legend, ending with the words 'and in England's darkest hour, King Arthur will rise from his slumbers and rescue these devastated lands.' Sir Eustace liked to gain the confidence of his quarry, pretending to be a lone traveller, lulling his intended victims into a sense of false security before leading them into his ambush. This time the knight, again masquerading as Sir Roger, had joined the actors' caravan a mile or so away from where his men were hiding. It was during this interim that a second group of robbers, poorly armed ones, had launched their attack, and the 'noble' knight had been forced to butcher them to a man in a display of astonishing swordsmanship. The florid-faced actor, Mercurius, had been eternally grateful and would do anything to return the favour. Then their rescuer turned from being mister nice-guy, becoming demanding, wanting money. He'd then told them, quite forcefully, to go north.

'That's great news. Where?'

'In Salisbury.' That was less than a day's ride away. 'So he must have remembered your threat.' This thought cheered him; in his febrile mind he had a plan. *I can breach the castle wall….*

—⚇—

The Mummers had just finished a rendition of 'The Tribulations of St. Titus' outside the cathedral door and Mercurius the Magnificent, face flushed with wine and the adulation of the crowd, made his rounds with his money bag receiving a paltry handful of coppers. The next hand released a stream of coins.

'Remember me?' His hood was pulled far forward covering the face, but the voice had menace. 'You have a pact to keep.'

Mercurius jumped back as if stung by a wasp. *Oh shit, the devil has found me.* He realised he was surrounded.

They led him back to his gaily painted wagons. Mercurius had dreaded this moment. Saviour he might have been, but the man with the scar and lopsided grin had troubled his dreams.

'What do you want of me?' he asked querulously. His peevish manner came naturally. He, too, had seen the warrants, and realised how close his escape had been. Fear of obeying the scarred knight, believing that more danger lay northward, had made him do the opposite and come south instead. Once south, he could not believe that the brave and noble knight, the leader of 'the Band of Brothers' who was the saviour of Southampton, who's praises minstrels were singing in taverns for miles around, could be the same Sir Roger de Bohun as the one who had threatened him? As Sir Eustace had put it so delicately, Mercurius the Most Famous believed his own publicity. Believed that his fame was such that any hound could sniff him out.

You can never *hide from me. You're as easy to follow as a slug leaving a shiny silver trail and I'll squash you with similar ease.* 'You thought I was Sir Roger,' Sir Eustace laughed. 'I was joking - he's my commanding Banneret. I want you go to his castle and become his Christmas surprise gift from me.' Sir Eustace told the Mummers' leader what he wanted them to do. 'You'll be well paid.' He put a pile of cash, recently acquired from the tax collectors, on the table. 'Call this an advance. There's only one condition. You mustn't tell him who gave you to him.'

Mercurius looked at the money. It was more than they'd earned in the last two years and his mind was made up. 'I'd prefer it if you didn't mention this to my colleagues,' he said nervously. He'd never been involved in a caper of this sort.

Later that evening, when his entire troupe was gathered back at the wagons, Mercurius stood up and made his announcement. 'I have good news, I've got us a Christmas engagement, we're to perform for a great lord,' he lied. He still had to bluff his way into the castle...

Chapter 44

Witchcraft

Lady Alice was becoming desperate. The pains in her abdomen were getting worse. She had suffered a series of cramps during the night and was at her wits end. Fearing the loss of her unborn child, she sought out Nunny. 'A devil has found its way into my innards,' she said, as another wave of cramps sent her to the floor in convulsions.

'There's nothing for it,' declared Nunny, who had become insepa-rable from her new mistress. 'We must find a way to cast it out.' She rummaged around in her trunk of possessions, taking out a small, old and battered leather-bound book. 'This was given to me by my mother, she taught me a lot about herbs and magic,' she said.

'You mean resort to witchcraft?' gasped Lady Alice. There was a fine line of distinction between what the church considered medicine and witchcraft. This was generally determined by whether a man or a woman administered the remedy. However, in her present condition, Lady Alice was prepared to try anything.

'Not yet, my mother was a very successful healer and I have seen this done before to stop miscarriage and cure cramps.' Nunny remem-bered her childhood, growing up surrounded by bunches of drying herbs, and trips around woods and hedgerows with her mother, col-lecting different plants. 'I'll need help, I'll get Master John.'

After his embarrassment at the hands of Sir Roger, Master John had contemplated leaving. He, too, had noticed the sharp deterioration in standards. The raid on Southampton and a trip to the Priory had changed his mind. *I need stout walls and a well-stocked larder to keep me safe this coming winter,* he thought as he answered the women's call for help.

'Milady, you are sickening?'

Another wave of cramps swept through Alice's body as she flushed with sweat. Turning to Nunny, John mentioned quietly, 'I do not know much about the maladies of women. But I have performed several exorcisms before.' He fancied himself as a bit of a healer, practicing the laying on of hands and making potions. 'It's usually an elf,' he asserted with a good deal of authority in his voice. Nunny agreed; elves were the commonest cause of such maladies. They compared a list of ingredients they might need.

'That boar they killed the other week, what happened to the useful bits?' asked Nunny. She had noticed that Master John was forever collecting dead frogs and assorted berries and had a growing collection of dried animal and vegetable matter in his garret. From their first meeting, she had felt there was something unsavoury about this character and had often examined the contents of his room while he was otherwise engaged.

'I have testicles and pizzle, eyelashes, gall bladder and hooves.'

It was as she suspected: a respectable haul.

'Grind up a hoof, mix it with fresh chicken blood and boil until it becomes sticky. Make sure none of it burns.' She was emphatic. 'It mustn't burn. Then repeat *'abraxas ablates'* three times and add some of this.' She handed over a sachet of powdered mandrake. 'Add this at the very end.' She showed him her book, watching his eyebrows rise, fall and rise again. He could see pages covered in a mixture of tiny diagrams, charts and spidery writings.

'May I borrow this some time and make a copy? I've never seen some of these remedies,' he said, casually, as Nunny tried to retrieve the book as quickly as she could without arousing suspicion. She fervently hoped he had not seen too much, as she remembered her mother's words when she had given her the volume years ago on her deathbed. *Show it to no one she had said,* but now, in an unthinking moment, Nunny had broken her mother's edict. Instantly she became acutely aware that its revelation had placed her in danger. Not all of the spells and potions were for good. Hidden in amongst healing remedies were details on all manner of poisons and curses, and she did not relish being tried for heresy, the usual punishment for those in possession of knowledge not sanctioned by the Church.

'Start with this, Milady, we must try and expel the elf. It's a purgative. You'll vomit and pass turds.' She carefully measured out a few drops of dark green liquid from a tiny glass bottle onto a spoon made from rosemary wood. It was well known that spoons made from this wood had the power against poisons. She stirred the drops into a quarter-full tumbler of milk while making a series of incantations: three 'Hail Marys' followed by five *Pater Nosters*'. She gave her mistress the green milk.

An hour later, during which time Lady Alice had voided the contents of her stomach and bowels, Master John returned with a copper dish filled with thick brown paste. Smearing it into a square of red silk about a foot across, the same silk from which they had made the emblems, they rolled it up and tied it round Lady Alice's stomach.

'I've got a hazel switch. What do you want me to do with it?' he asked.

'Cut it in half.' He slit the twig with a small penknife and, taking Lady Alice's left hand, deftly pricked her finger. Dipping a quill in her blood, he wrote '*Christus + Exeunt + Christus + Salvate*' on the flat part of the twig, and started flicking her exposed belly so that red welts formed in a circle around her swollen tummy. Lady Alice wimpered with pain, but refused to cry out loudly. He made the welts into crosses with further flicks of the switch, and they continued smearing on brown goo until it was all used up.

All the while they chanted, beseeching God to deliver their mistress and save the child. Together they solemnly recited and Lady Alice repeated. 'This as my help against the evil late birth, this as my help against the grievous dismal birth, this as my help against the evil lame birth.' Over and over, for hours they prayed.

Nunny, realising that the afternoon was drawing on, said that they should take her to the graveyard. 'I've found out where a still-born infant has been buried.'

She had spent a long time - starting as soon as she learnt of her new mistress's pregnancy - looking for that grave. Such local knowledge was not easy to find as these resting places rarely had any sort of marker. The information had cost her dear. She had been shown it by a local midwife upon whom she had unloaded a great deal of her meagre savings. *Worth every penny, if I can save my mistress's unborn child then she and her husband will owe me a lot more.* In these uncertain times she, too, felt a strong need for protection.

Lady Alice bore the rituals with remarkable fortitude. Nunny noted highborn women fell into two categories: they were either screamers or stoics, rarely was anyone in the middle. Lady Elizabeth, she remembered coldly, was a screamer whereas Lady Alice was most definitely a stoic. The poor woman was sweating profusely as her ordeal progressed, reciting prayers for the unborn babe over and over again.

'It's time for the final part. Her Ladyship must step over the baby's grave three times,' said Nunny, summoning able-bodied servants.

'What are her chances?' asked Beatrice, deeply concerned that if her mistress died she'd be stranded in a foreign land.

'We must get there soon, before it gets dark. We don't want the stillborn's spirit entering her ladyship. The child was dead when it was baptised, the midwife told me. We want this imp out, not a new one in. Can you stand, Milady?' Nunny asked, as together they clothed a weakened Lady Alice in a warm coat and, with the aid of the servants, carried her out into the stormy afternoon. The graveyard was close by the church, only half a mile from the castle.

'So where's this grave?' asked John, puffing hard. He was not used to physical labour. Nunny pointed to a patch of nettles in the brambly corner farthest away from the church. A cross of white pebbles could just be seen through the weeds.

'Collect those, we'll make a potion to give her later,' she indicated to Beatrice, who had to use her shawl against the stingers. They manoeuvred Lady Alice to the grave's edge, stones clearly visible, and left her wobbling on her own - she swooned and collapsed back into John's arms. Nunny pinched her hard, making her stiffen.

I must take control. Lady Alice braced herself as pain brought her back to full consciousness. *I can do this. I must do this.* She forced every fibre of her body to obey; she had to make the three steps unaided otherwise the whole process would be for nought. 'Mother Mary, full of grace, bless this sinner and protect her unborn child,' shouted the onlookers, mentally willing their mistress on.

One step. Lady Alice could feel a rising wave of nausea; *the elf is making a determined stand.* She fought back sickness. 'Holy Jesus save this sinner and instil life in her womb.' *Two steps.* Again she suffered a body-wracking spasm and she knew it was time to fight the evil monster that had taken possession of her innards. She howled in rage and steeled herself for the final step, her mind drifting back into blankness. 'Blessed Spirit, expel the demon, make our sister whole again.' *Three steps.* She felt her waters break as, with the last reserves of her strength, she stepped over the crucifix a third time before collapsing into Master John's arms. Together they carried the unconscious woman back up the hill. The light was failing fast by the time they crossed the drawbridge. The Steward saw to it that the guards took over carrying Lady Alice's limp body up to her bedchamber. They laid her back on her bed and tried giving her a broth made from nettles collected by Beatrice.

During the night she gave birth to a girl. It lived long enough for Master John to perform a rapid baptism. He noted that the child had dark curly hair and long, elegant hands that reminded him of the minstrel. *I want that book, and then I'll have enough evidence to accuse that pot-faced cow of witchcraft.* His mind was made up; he always enjoyed a good burning.

Chapter 45

Two Can Play at That Game

Harold and Wulfstan Goedericson were identical twins in all physical respects. They were big, intimidating men who, through their malevolent presence, made life in Guildford follow the beat of their drum. They had never been seen together in public, using their secret to maximum effect in terrorising the inhabitants of the town. Barring an occasional wart, the brothers ensured that, scar for scar, they remained indistinguishable. Only their women folk, who they shared as well, could tell them apart. A dog had bitten the tip off Wulfstan's penis and this, as far as Harold was concerned, was a scar too far. While one engaged in highway robbery the other would be found in full view of respectable witnesses who could swear that Goderic Goedericson, the personality they shared, was seen, as large as life, strutting around the market square at the time of any alleged offence.

They had grown up in Somerset, so in Guildford no one who knew of the tearaway twins from Wells, and anyone who did fathom their secret risked having their tongues cut out. Three mutes could no longer attest to this double act, however hard they tried. Every couple of years the twins and their gang of acolytes would move to another town, beginning their cycle of violence again on an unsuspecting populace. To do this, they would buy an inn with a deep cellar, from where they would dig a network of tunnels that would come out in hidden corners around the town. They used their similarities to full effect, often creating elaborate alibis to fool the Seneschal of Guildford Castle, who was a weak and vacillating individual, and making him powerless to intercede. This was through choice; his share of proceeds from their larceny ensured that he kept his eyes tight shut. Still, the Master of the Royal Castle was unaware that Goderic, landlord of the Swan Inn, had a twin brother.

'I'm going to work the hole,' said Harold as the brothers planned their day. 'I'll be back after dark.'

—◊—

Roads were clogged with wagons laden with barrels, sacks of corn and wool, herds of draft and beef animals and the endless paraphernalia of war heading for London and the Medway ports. Occasionally there were disgruntled soldiers making their way back home, grumbling about lack of pay.

'What have we done to deserve this?' The Ox looked heavenward as if hoping to see the Divine One. All were agreed that mud and rain were God's punishment. But for what? There were a thousand sins that could have been responsible for this continuing deluge. Many felt that war had something do with it, but no one was sure.

The night had been an uncomfortable one.

'Ouch, shit, damn, blast.' Sir Roger stubbed his toe and hopped around in agony. This was not an auspicious start to the day.

'I bet it's going to be another Egyptian day,' Dan remarked, as he took a mouthful of food. 'My old master, God bless his soul, reckoned that there are thirty-two evil days every year, he said they usually fall on those days furthest away from feast days.'

'Too many for my liking.' Gwyn, who had been the only one listening, touched the hare's foot he had bought at Northampton. 'I'm a great believer in hare's feet.' He had several, adding one more for each narrow escape he had from death, attaching them to his left forearm. Many were convinced as to their efficacy in keeping the wearer out of danger. *I owe my narrow escape at Dunbar to these charms.* 'All the survivors from the sow wore them,' he said proudly, ignoring the fact that a few of those who were killed had worn them too.

'They must have used up their power. One foot, one save, three pence each!' proffered Dan, who had noted this superstition amongst several of the troop. He had acquired several of these feet and was making a brisk trade.

'I wonder if ape feet have the same effect?' Simon wondered out loud. Zuzu, sensing hostility, showed Simon her fangs in her usual manner.

The hatred Gwyn felt towards Dan had only increased with his promotion and the capture of Simon. *Not only is Shrimp-Turd-Digby - unjustly in my view - of similar rank to me, he's also about to become considerably richer with his share of ransom money. Opportunity, all I need is opportunity.*

'I want to reach Guildford Castle by tonight. We must be vigilant and push hard today.' Sir Roger hoped that they would be offered some hospitality. 'Robert Hardridge is the keeper, but he's a grumpy old curmudgeon.' It was a lesser-used royal residence, though there was particularly good hunting to be had in the rich Surrey woods. With those thoughts in mind, his troop and the Southampton prisoners - Sir Roger did not treat them as criminals - no one thought of these unfortunate men in those terms. Most had lost all their worldly possessions and some their families, all slaughtered by those heathen pirates on the Lord's Day. Sir Roger felt sure, and reassured them, that a panel of enquiry would exonerate them.

The road led into hilly Downs country, where they would have to negotiate a particularly tricky climb up a section of road known to all as the Hog's Back. In front, a wool train of fifty heavily laden mules was striving to make headway up the slippery slope. The road was narrow, without enough room for the horsemen to pass by. Far up the slope, an animal suddenly slipped and was stuck fast up to its belly in a deep pool of mud, causing everyone to stop as the pack animals involuntarily bunched up. A flicker of movement caught Sir Roger's eye. In the trees above the road he thought he saw a man running, then another.

'I think we have trouble.' His words were cut short as an arrow flickered out of the undergrowth, piercing a drover's leg. The mule train was caught in a confined space. *Like rats in a trap*. This is what Sir Roger feared most. He had decided to ride his destrier, Samson, as his warhorse needed exercise, and for such a valuable beast to fall to a brigand's arrow would be bad news indeed. He crossed himself and prayed rapidly for deliverance.

'Back, back,' he ordered, getting down the hill as quickly as he could. Dismounting, he handed the reins to Justin. The rest of the troop followed suit.

'Fan out,' Sir Roger instructed his men. With Dan and Gwyn, his hobelars started to climb up through the brambles and bracken and over the rocks; he wanted to gain height and come down on the robbers from above.

Dan handed Zuzu's leash to the nearest hand, which just happened to be Simon's. 'Guillaume…' He made a look at Simon that said *'don't you harm a hair on her body'*.

The outlaws were after woolsacks. More arrows found targets. Muleteers tried to get the tail of the train to reverse, but their attackers felled an animal towards the rear, blocking their escape route. Drovers sought protection amongst huddled, panicking beasts or fled into the woods. The troop climbed rapidly. The exertion of going uphill in his aketon and mail was something Sir Roger was not used to. *I wish I hadn't neglected my exercises since being wounded by that boar.* Soon he found himself lagging behind. He had to sit down on a rock to catch his breath. It was indeed another Egyptian day.

Dan, being nimblest of foot, had soon gained the high ground above the brigands. It had been a well-laid trap. He could see a rope concealed in mud so that when it was tightened a mule would be trapped in a hole, a couple of bandits lurking near its end. Signalling to the hobelars, he began to slide quietly down. Well-placed arrows took out the men on the rope; their bodies were quickly dragged back into the bushes and hidden. The ambushers had been ambushed.

From his vantage point, Sir Roger could instantly appreciate the nature of the trap and looked around for his men. They had disappeared into the hillside. He felt like a kestrel hovering over its prey as below him he saw a small party of outlaws running along a track that ran parallel to the clogged road; they had obviously made this path so that they could run up and down with ease and attack the convoy at whatever point they pleased. Stopping directly below, he could see they were a normal bunch of cut-throats and dispossessed peasantry. A couple had swords, and others were armed with clubs, crude spears and hunting bows. Their leader, a large, vicious-looking thug with a bascinet and iron-plated padded jacket, was intent on directing his men, who were concentrating on getting at the remaining drovers as they ducked and dived amongst the sack-laden mules.

Dan reappeared at his master's side and Sir Roger suggested they try and capture the leader. They'd have to be quick, for already the outlaws were getting the upper hand. Sir Roger plunged down the slope and the sight of a knight, gleaming sword in hand, had the desired effect. A couple of swift strokes disarmed the nearest peasant, quite literally. The next thrust took another through his throat and that peasant, too, went down in a fountain of blood, his carotid artery severed. Remaining gang members turned to flee, only to find Gwyn and more men-at-arms blocking their path. Their leader turned to face Sir Roger and, sword raised above his head, charged. Sir Roger parried the blow easily, smashing his buckler into the bandit's face, breaking his nose and front teeth. Dan appeared and, before the robber had time to do anything, had hogtied him face down in the mud. They caught six others. Cutting up the ambush cable into suitable lengths, they used the rope to hang the robbers from the lower branches of a large nearby oak, to cheers from rescued drovers. The victims danced and twitched some time and then were still, their urine spreading down their legs as bladders emptied in death. Their erstwhile leader was prodded to his feet, glowering with hatred. Three muleteers had been badly wounded, one was dead, and it took a long time to disentangle the wool train and get to the top of the pass. As Sir Roger had feared, an arrow had struck Samson; fortunately it was only a superficial wound.

Simon clutched Zuzu's chain, loathe to do anything that might upset her. He had spent the last few hours scheming and dreaming and plotting various ways for ridding the world of this travesty of a creature.

Dusk fell rapidly and it was night when they reached the castle gates. They were firmly closed. Shouts and exhortations came to naught and the bedraggled troop, with their captive dragged cursing along behind, made their way to Fish Cross market with its covered stalls.

'Food, drink and bed in that order,' said Sir Roger hungrily, having not eaten all day.

'Leave it to me.' No one was going to gainsay John Gwyn, the armoured giant, as he started hammering on doors. All along the narrow street candles flickered to life as citizens preparing for bed came to find out the source of the commotion.

A tavern, the Swan Inn, was located nearby, but the surly landlord claimed all his beds were full. This was not going to dissuade the Ox, who pushed their captive in front of them into the dimly lit parlour. A flicker of surprise crossed the landlord's face, and this was not lost on Sir Roger who whispered to Dan. He, in turn, slipped back into the street to keep watch. Even in the gloom one could see that the landlord was a man of similar size and build to the prisoner, though he quickly turned away.

'How can we please your Lordship?' Suddenly the tone changed to obsequiousness.

The room was half full of drinkers and attendant wenches who stared at the intruders. Sir Roger demanded more light and extra candles were brought. Some of those nearest the room's rear tried to slip out, but Gwyn blocked their exit menacingly.

'Disarm them all.' Sir Roger used his booming voice, and at once his hobelars and men-at-arms went from table to table, taking knives, daggers and couple of cudgels. One man, unwisely, tried to stab at a hobelar.

'Now, get food.'

The landlord made to leave.

'Not you - her.' Sir Roger pointed randomly at a girl.

The prisoner was kneeling, curled up, and was hiding his face on the floor. Sir Roger pulled him to his feet by the hair. His face was still bloody, his teeth broken, and his nose was crushed across his face, but these disfigurements aside, the candlelight revealed remarkable similarities with the landlord.

'Twins!' Sir Roger exclaimed. 'They even dress the same.'

They had, he quickly realised, arrived at the gang's headquarters. Bowls of steaming pottage and bread were brought out and passed to the Southampton prisoners, who still sheltered under the Fish Cross.

'We'll eat first and then deal with this rat's nest on a full stomach.' There would be no sleep in Guildford that night. 'Old gristly guts up there must be in on the racket.' Sir Roger pointed up towards the castle. For such a gang to operate so close to authority meant only one thing: collusion between chatelaine and robbers. He felt it was imperative to stop help being summoned. For the moment, he had the upper hand, but this might not last long. *Justice will have to be swift and thorough.*

'Get the women out,' he ordered, and they were herded, remonstrating loudly, into the street. One by one, the rooms were cleared and only those who could prove that they were innocent travellers were pushed out into the gutter, clutching whatever clothing they could. The remainder of Sir Roger's troop blocked off the exits to the marketplace.

A crowd gathered as inhabitants of the surrounding houses came out to watch as a rope was slung over the extended purlin that had the tavern sign. Sir Roger could see by the light of a newly lit torch that it was painted with an elegant swan. The landlord and his twin would hang together. The rest of the guilty, who Sir Roger judged thus solely on their presence in the inn after curfew, at least seven, would burn within. Even before life had left the twins' bodies, torches were thrown through the windows and doors. All those who attempted to escape were cut down.

As he mounted Samson and prepared to make his getaway, a thought came to Sir Roger and he stood up in his saddle. 'I am Sir Eustace de Frage; forget me at your peril.' *Two can play at that game,* he thought, as he led his men away down the dark narrow cobbled street. 'There's a barn over the river, we'll spend the night there.'

He had been to Guildford before and knew of a tithe barn belonging to the nearby Friary. He quietly sat on Samson, watching the bridge. No one followed. He could hear cries and shouts of 'fire' and thought that everyone was too preoccupied with the blazing building to give chase. It was possible they would raise the hue-and-cry tomorrow, but he doubted it. Looking back over his shoulder, he could see a glow as flames licked up to the roof. To be on the safe side, he set a rota of watchmen and had a couple of his men chop down some trees to block the road.

The townsfolk watched as the Swan Inn burnt to the ground. The fire even rousing Robert Hardridge from his bed. 'Who did this?' asked the Seneschal.

'He called himself Sir Eustace de Frage,' said another who had heard.

'Saint Eustace more like,' said a third, surveying the charred corpses. 'Twins, who would've believed it. We can live in peace again, thanks to him.'

Chapter 46

Foreigners

Christina, who did not have a second name, started her working day at cockcrow, sweeping around drunks who had collapsed, cleaning up their vomit, laying new sawdust and rushes and yearning for the pine forests of her far distant homeland. Many times she had thought of running away, even moving to the brothel two doors down the street, but she was unwilling to compromise and sell her body *I have to maintain my pride somehow.* She was sure that one day a prince, and if not a prince then a lordling, would come and sweep her off her feet, she felt sure he would not wish for soiled goods. At least the Tabard's landlord was pleasant enough. He had taken pity on her after her owner, a Baltic fur trader, had come to London to make his fortune with many thousands of squirrel pelts, those of the type that made up the Vair capes so sought after by the ladies of the Court. But he had been killed in a quarrel after a drinking bout, leaving the poor girl alone and unable to speak any known tongue. The landlord's wife, though, hated the lewd way her husband looked at Christina and she knew that he would fondle her when he thought no-one was looking, and so she treated Christina like dirt.

Every night, Christina curled up into a little ball and cried herself to sleep, trying to make herself comfortable in the corner of the cellar at the Tabard Inn she called her own. With few clothes and no possessions, she was only now, after two years, starting to understand the languages of the English. She had not been born into servitude.

In fact, quite the opposite; her father was a wealthy timber merchant. Her loneliness was compounded by the jealousy of other girls. She had ash blonde hair and azure blue eyes that marked her apart from the other serving wenches, who would be unnecessarily spiteful towards her, often stealing her tips.

—⁓—

The prisoners were cold, damp and miserable, and not used to sleeping rough. The Mayor complained bitterly as they were roused well before dawn.

'Count yourselves lucky you're not in chains,' growled Sir Roger, wanting to get on and put space between themselves and the irate townsfolk of Guildford. By the time dawn broke, they had climbed to the top of the last rolling hill from where, way in the distance, a grey smudge of smoke was still rising from the town centre.

The Mayor, looking nervously at leaden skies that threatened them with yet another soaking, pleaded for somewhere dry to stay.

'I know just the place,' said Sir Roger confidently. 'There's the Royal Stud Farm no more than ten miles away. We'll get a better reception there and they can treat Samson's wound.'

It was also the residence of the 'Keeper of the King's Horses South of the Trent', who was a drunkard of note. Secretly Sir Roger agreed with the Mayor; sleeping rough was no fun, though he did have the advantage of having brought his campaign cot along.

The Stud farm was truly a horse palace; King Edward kept a herd of twenty breeding mares, a mixture of war horses and smaller coursers, his prize racing horses. Each mare had its own stable and groom with its name proudly emblazoned above every stall.

'I've never seen such a place,' observed a new recruit in awe as the troop and prisoners were allocated some empty stalls so that they could bed down for the night.

As expected, when Sir Roger finally found the Keeper, he was deep in his cups, drowning his sorrows.

'How does the King expect me to breed horses if he takes *all* the fucking stallions with him to Flanders,' he moaned, offering Sir Roger a swig from his flagon. When he saw Samson, he perked up and, with a practiced eye, saw the answer to his prayers.

'You realise,' he confided to Sir Roger, 'you're like a gift from heaven.'

They went down the stalls looking at beasts. There were three black, one white, two white spotted and three iron greys. The black mares all had white blazons on their heads and white shins with long hair above their polished hooves.

'Can I borrow him?' he asked, pointing at Samson. He was not too drunk to spot the opportunity. 'I can give you a fine palfrey in exchange.'

'You mean lend.'

The drunken man nodded in affirmation. *Thank you God, this horse is exactly the quality of stud we need.* 'I'll get the grooms to treat his wound.'

Sir Roger had been having serious misgivings about this journey with Samson, as destriers were not good horses for long distance travel, so the suggestion was most welcome. An impressive barn full of oats made up his mind. He knew each horse would consume half a bushel a day, along with three loaves of horse bread, baked from beans and peas mixed with oatmeal. *The food alone must cost nearly tuppence a day.*

'The same as what I pay them lot,' he said to the swaying Keeper, indicating his hobelars.

'We don't spare any expenses here,' boasted the Keeper pointing at the oil lamps that illuminated each stall. 'I think that any cost of your horse's upkeep will adequately be covered by stud fees...' He paused, waiting to see whether there would be any dissent. There was none.

Having changed horses for the final leg of the journey, Sir Roger no longer felt it necessary to wear any armour, and had it stowed carefully on a pack animal. Dressed in a green travel outfit with a beaver fur collar, his Italian hat perched at a rakish angle, he looked forward to indulging in the pleasures that the city had to offer. A few heads turned as they reached Southwark, from where they could see the White Tower, newly whitewashed, across the Thames. It was an impressive sight. The prisoners looked with apprehension, wondering how long it would be before the commissioners got round to hearing their pleas.

Something though had been troubling him for some time. Whilst he found Simon a diverting companion; he knew from his body language that he was hiding something.

But what?

The man definitely was not telling the whole truth about anything, things just didn't add up.

'Are you really loyal and true to France?' Sir Roger asked, as they approached London Bridge. A solid stone gatehouse guarded the entrance with a few heads rotting on spikes. An occasional crow fluttered down to peck at scraps of flesh. 'Traitors and vagabonds,' he continued. 'Every man has his price, so I am told.'

'Why do you say that?' enquired Simon carefully, worried that this question might be loaded. His captor had the disarming habit of talking about something inconsequential, like the weather, before rounding onto a hard topic. He had a beguiling way of eliciting information, a snippet here and there.

'I'm interested. Take you, for example, a poor knight from Picardy. What would it take for you to change sides?'

'I hadn't really thought about it.' This was truthful. *What am I, Simon de Pressi, really worth, and to whom? Much more than my alter ego, the poor knight from Picardy.* Simon thought back to his conversation with Béhuchet on the road to Paris. In retrospect, he wasn't sure what made him tell Sir Roger about his uncle. To date he hadn't asked him anything about the gun, which was curious, since they had lugged it all the way to London between two mules. *Perhaps he doesn't know that it was mine.* This thought came as a relief.

'Look, that's new.' Sir Roger pointed to a curtain wall that had been added since he had last visited the Tower.

'It's all new to me.' Simon could see a large, forbidding fortress, no doubt replete with dungeons and torture chambers, but he supposed his captor meant the wharf that was under construction; the eastern end of the curtain wall was a mass of scaffolding topped off with a couple of cranes. St. Paul's Cathedral, with its square tower, dominated the city from on its hill, pale limestone gleaming in weak sunshine. All across the city, they could see many steeples. The rain had stopped and the capital of England looked newly washed. A mass of shipping of all sizes clogged the Thames as far as the eye could see, penned in by lines of stakes and a great chain. Simon was in his element, memorizing everything he could see. He was brought back to reality by the next statement.

'Look how many churches there are, like Oxford with its spires.'

'Yes,' said Simon, remembering his clandestine visit to steal the formula for gunpowder.

That affirmative confirmed it - Simon must have been there. *Caught you.* It had taken Sir Roger days of probing, gently laying the groundwork and gaining Simon's confidence, making him believe that the workings of his gun were of no consequence. Inwardly, he was thrilled. He held a bargaining chip of enormous value. *What did Mauney sell Guy the Bastard to Edward for? Yes, a thousand pounds.* It would be many months yet before Guillaume's ransom might arrive - he'd have this Frenchman telling him everything.

'Find a tavern,' Sir Roger instructed Dan. 'The Tabard is usually pretty good. Should be empty, it's not pilgrimage season.' He sent the troop and prisoners off to get some refreshment. 'You,' he indicated to the Ox. 'Come with me.'

They rode through narrow streets up to Cheapside, then towards the Cathedral. Everywhere was crowded with hawkers, gawpers, carters and dung carriers; some had errands to run, while others ambled aimlessly.

Gwyn was amazed at how his master navigated the narrow alleyways to where the goldsmiths did their trade.

'Guard the horses,' he told his Sergeant, before slipping down an alley behind the church. There was a row of cramped workshops, from which sounds of tapping and hammering could just be heard; he ducked into one of these.

'Is your master in?' Sir Roger inquired of a young man who was studiously working a piece of yellow metal. He did not look up, but pointed to the back of the shop where Sir Roger found the master goldsmith. 'Hello, Master Bernard.' The man looked quizzically at Sir Roger. 'Do I know you?' He spoke with a broad Norfolk twang.

'The King's Friend.' His master, he had noticed, always made a point of introducing him in those distant days, when they would sneak off together, as his 'Friend', it was an honour he clung onto, observing that no one else since was accorded the same epithet. It had been many years since he and the King had frequented London's streets in their teenage years, often in disguise, seeking ornaments and trinkets, golden gifts with which to impress the ladies.

'You made those silver chains for the Great Oriental Tourney.' Bernard scratched his head, a glimmer of recognition crossing his face.

'Tarts and Tartars. Yes, I remember it well.' It had been an unforgettable event - a jousting spectacular in Cheapside. The King and his companions had ridden out from the Tower dressed in oriental fashion, each leading a lady robed in ruby velvet on a silver chain. Heralds had gone before with trumpets, challenging all comers, and so many had wanted to join in that the party had gone on for three days. *I did well*. Sir Roger remembered getting to the last four, winning a half a gold salt cellar, and one of the best fucks ever from Lady Whatever-her-name-was, who, he discovered later, had taken his prize.

The Goldsmith thought hard - he loved a good yarn, vicariously living the life of a knight in his imagination. 'I remember you now. You helped abduct Mortimer. Sounded quite an adventure.'

'Did I tell you how we crawled through the drains?'

'No, can't say as you did.' Bernard thrived on hearing stories about the nobles of the Court.

'It must be eight years ago,' Sir Roger told him. 'I was much thinner then. We wormed our way through the drains. Full of rats, they were. I don't think I'd be able to do that now.' He patted his waist, which, he had noticed, had grown considerably since the arrival of Max. On October 19th, 1330 - the date was seared into his memory. *It was my first real adventure,* he recalled. They had crawled through the foul watercourses of Nottingham Castle and kidnapped the King's mother's lover. They had achieved complete surprise. 'He was in his nightshirt. We pulled him out the same way, then spirited the hapless man back to London, where we had him summarily tried and executed for treason - hung, drawn and quartered.'

'That's how I know; I had a front row seat,' added Bernard, remembering how he had paid a small fortune for the privilege. 'Some deaths are quick, but that one was horribly slow.' He shook his head disapprovingly. *Everyone enjoys a good execution and this one was memorable.* 'The poor soul was still very much alive when they drew out his guts and roasted them on a brazier; that made him scream. It's a ghastly way to die, having one's own innards cooked and served to you. Mind you, he deserved to suffer for what he did, I didn't feel any pity for him,' he rambled on, as if talking to himself.

Sir Roger had been there too, and agreed it was one of the most gruesome he'd ever attended. 'We had trouble enough with his daughter-in-law, Lady Agnes, at Dunbar only a few months ago!' said Sir Roger ruefully.

They talked some more. The Goldsmiths had only had their Royal Charter for a few years, in fact it had been favours to the young King and his friends that had secured them that privilege, it had been his first Charter.

'Queen Isabella's face was something to behold,' recounted Sir Roger, for whom the image of the shrieking harridan was as real as yesterday, seared into his memory. *You traitor*, she had screamed, *I gave you succour as if I fed you milk from my own breast and this is how you repay me.* 'When the King told her that this was his wish, she was in such a fury that he had to give her that exquisite gold incense burner you had made just to shut her up. He had intended to keep it for himself.'

'Where's the Queen now?'

'He bundled her off to Castle Rising. Good riddance. Anyway,' Sir Roger always said 'anyway' before he changed subject. Slowly he got round to the purpose of his visit, taking out his gold salt boats. 'How much will you give me for these?' Bernard took them and turned them over, making sure the leopard head stamps were genuine, and weighed them. *Eighteen florins worth of gold.*

'I'll give you twelve florins.'

They had cost Sir Roger over twice as much only six months before. He was shocked, he'd been hoping, at least, to get his money back.

'Money is in short supply at the moment; our King has taken it all to pay for his useless war.'

They bickered on for a while and settled on sixteen. *I've come too far to go away empty-handed.* He knew he was beaten as he reluctantly accepted the offer. Sir Roger followed the goldsmith into his back workshop, where he created his finer works. On the table was a crown, looking suspiciously like the Great Crown of England. But it was made of lead. Sir Roger picked it up and weighed it. It was heavy enough to fool all but the King. One side had already been covered with a veneer of gold leaf and the jewels looked real enough. Bernard smiled enigmatically and said that your boss wanted an exact replica, so that's what he'd get.

Cash, it seemed, would continue to attract a premium, and Sir Roger divided several of his more valuable gold coins into smaller change at a moneychangers as he rode back over London Bridge to retrieve his men. They were taking a leisurely meal at the Tabard Inn, a place frequented in the summer by pilgrims before they set out for Canterbury to pay their respects at the tomb of St. Thomas the Martyr. Now most of its tables were empty.

It was Zuzu that first attracted Christina to the large and, in her view, curious crowd of travellers. Some were attired in surcoats with a red silk stripe, while others had clothing that had been expensive but now was sorely in need of laundering. The ape was wearing a red frock.

'What's that?' she asked in a thick accent and singsong voice, her curiosity piqued. She'd never seen a creature like it. She'd seen plenty of bears, and this wasn't a small bear, nor was it a dog.

'It's a Spaniard,' joked Dan, unable to take his eyes off this vision of loveliness that had just entered his world.

The tavern attracted a polyglot of different nationalities, which was probably what prompted the argument between Simon and Justin.

Their subject was foreigners.

'*Les Anglais*,' declared Simon after some thought, 'are all mongrels. In France we are proud of our families. Do you know who your grandparents were?'

'My ancestor came to this country with Duke William from Normandy,' answered Justin proudly as he went for the jugular. 'All you Frenchmen are effeminate and far too proud for your own good.'

'No we are not.' Simon rose to the insult like a trout to a mayfly. 'You Normans are boastful and deceitful, not to be trusted.'

They sat back, pleased with their abusiveness. 'And what about the English,' they both turned on Dan. 'They're cowards and are drunk most of the time.'

'Useless whoresons,' he spluttered with indignation.

'What about the Flemings?'

'Bloodthirsty vagabonds, arsonists to a man, burn your house down as soon as cross your threshold.'

'So that makes the boss a bit of a Fleming after the other night,' said Gwyn, who rarely offered an opinion, picking up the conversation's gist. 'We met some German sappers in Gascony.' He weighed into them with relish. 'Dirty gluttons and ill-tempered to boot.' He recalled the fistfight that had ensued in the street. 'A bit like Burgundians, stupid and brutal.' The conversation petered out again; they'd gone through all the nationalities they knew and a few more beside.

'Where are you from, my lovely?' asked Dan, who had encouraged the lissom blonde, with hair so pale in colour that it was remarkable, to sit on his knee. She squirmed and giggled as he worked his hand steadily up her thigh. She let it get just so far before giving it a firm slap.

'Where do you think?' She had a singsong lilt to her voice. No one could guess: some suggested the more distant parts of England, while others ventured Saxony. 'I was born in Viborg,' she announced proudly 'I am Karelian.'

The party looked at each other; no one knew anything about Karelians. She then related the tragic tale of her life, of how she had been happily harvesting nuts in the forest with her mother when they had been grabbed by a marauding band of Finns. Her mother, she told them, had died from maltreatment at the hands of these ruffians.

'I was sold as a slave to a fur-trader and now here I am. I have been in London for two years.' She tweaked Dan's cheek. 'And I don't think you are drunk or a coward.'

'What is your name?'

'Christina.' She had hands of an elegance rarely seen and a grace that was as captivating as her impish smile. Though small, she was perfectly proportioned. Dan was hopelessly smitten. *I've never seen a more exquisite creature in my whole life.* His reveries came back to earth with a bump as Sir Roger reappeared.

'Duty calls, I'll be back for you this evening.' Dan said, hopefully, to his newfound love.

As they clattered over the bridge Dan broached the subject. 'Master, can I get married?'

'What, to her? But you've only just met.'

'Yes, but she is so lovely and so alone.'

In the short time they had been acquainted, Sir Roger had not thought of Dan as a man to put down roots and have a family. He didn't even have a house or a room to call his own.

'And what are you going to do for money?' enquired Sir Roger.

'Him.' Dan pointed at Simon. 'He's my money.' Simon smiled; after a couple of months, he was starting to understand English.

Christina watched the men depart. Her prince had come and gone and her loneliness returned. For a brief moment she had felt her shackles fall off, she had smiled and laughed with Dan and his monkey. *How many men had said they would return for me?* It was more than she dared count. A broom, thrust none too subtly into her hands by the publican's wife, ended her dreams.

Chapter 47

Traitor's Gate

The hurly-burly of the city gave way to a wide green and, beyond, the moat around the Tower reflected its enormity. To Simon it was even more imposing. On his previous trip to England he had seen quite a few castles; his master was keen on such details. This castle was almost as grand as that belonging to the King of France in Paris. He was about to say so when a brusque order was barked out by a sergeant in royal livery, asking them to state their business.

Sir Roger took out his crumpled travel warrants and handed them over for scrutiny. 'This is the Lion Gate,' he pointed out a pair of crudely carved felines to Simon while the sergeant disappeared into a courtyard. 'Ever seen a lion close-up?' Simon shook his head. 'Well, now's your chance.' He gestured to a semi-circular building in the moat.

'Sorry, no horses allowed inside, there's no room. Take them over there' A guard indicated a nearby stable block. Four men lugged the *ribaud's* broken barrel off its sling; it had proved to be a nightmare to transport. As they went through a series of gates, a pungent odour wafted into the tunnel.

'Berenger, you old scroat, where are you hiding?' shouted Sir Roger as he came into a small amphitheatre where the royal menagerie was housed. 'Berenger's the smelliest Dago I know, always got a nose full of snot, which, considering the stink is no bad thing!' he told the Tax Collector. 'Just don't stand too close to the cages.'

The Collector was overawed by the whole process of entering the Tower and failed to heed the warning. Still blinking from the tunnel's darkness, he stepped back without looking. A male lion, a mangy brute with a black mane, let out a fearsome barking roar, making the Collector wet himself involuntarily.

'Ajax has that effect on people.' Their keeper, a Spaniard called Berenger Darragoun, emerged from a corner booth to see what had upset his charges. He was wearing a leather butcher's apron, on which he continually wiped his hands. 'Come here, puss, puss, puss.' The big cat allowed Berenger to scratch it behind its ear. 'He's a big softie really.' His eyes lit up as he saw Sir Roger. 'Is that really you?' he said. 'I haven't seen you for years - my, you're a proper big man now.'

'Same smell. How are you?'

'Can't complain, he pays me twelve pence now,' boasted the Spaniard proudly, his accent so strong that he was virtually incomprehensible. 'Still not as much as them, though.' Berenger had come with the lions, which had been a coronation gift from the King of Aragon, and had proved indispensable. No one else would take the job as Keeper of the Royal Beasts, which numbered three lions and a leopard, in residence in cramped cages.

On seeing the leopard, Zuzu panicked, letting out an ear splitting scream. Shaking with near uncontrollable fear, the terrified ape clung onto Dan's head. The shriek aroused the rest of the beasts from their slumber and they started pacing back and forth, their yellow eyes glaring. The nearest lion, a female, snarled and swiped out with her paw.

'What do they eat?' ventured Dan, desperately trying to calm Zuzu down. She was reduced to a quivering mass, clinging tightly to his chest.

'I give them a quarter of a mutton a day - they eat well, they do.' The Keeper was keen to expound on the generosity of his master. 'The King allows two shillings and one penny for each animal.' He looked at Zuzu. 'Well, my pretty, you're a long way from home,' he said, cutting off a slice of the apple he had been eating and offering it to her.

Simon found the stench overpowering, making his way to the causeway across the moat.

'I spent hours fishing for pike down there.' Sir Roger pointed to some reeds growing precariously on a bank. A heron took to the air from where it had been searching the water's edge for creatures to eat, a crab here, a small fish there, speared, tossed up and swallowed. 'We'd take them to the kitchen, where we'd get the cooks to make us mousseline. Pike have green bones. Did you know that nothing else has green bones?'

Simon shook his head, only half listening to Sir Roger's prattle. Fish bones were fish bones - something to be thrown away with no further thought. 'You know the King well, then?' Simon, mistakenly, thought his captor easy to manipulate, having rapidly gained his confidence after being released from the lock-up.

'We grew up together, I was his companion,' Sir Roger answered blandly. 'The Queen is in residence, and Prince Edward.' He pointed to the royal standards. 'I had better go and pay my respects. First we need to find Brecke - he's the Constable of the Tower.'

'Looks more like a warehouse than a palace,' commented Simon, looking at a great untidy mass of clutter that filled every conceivable corner. 'Not that I've been to many.' He lied. *Of course I've been to lots of palaces with my master, he likes neatness and order.* He wondered how Marie was fairing without him. *Does she miss me?*

'That's new.' Sir Roger continued his guided tour, pointing to rickety wooden scaffolding. 'But then, this is all new to you.'

Their attention was taken by a loud clunk above their heads, and they watched as a stone ball sailed out across the river, splashing beside a floating target in the middle of the clutter of shipping anchored in the Thames.

'Just practising,' muttered the guard who had been seconded to take them to the Constable's quarters. 'It scares the hell out of the sailors. They've got a new siege catapult in case those Frenchies have a go. The young princes think it is the greatest thing. They've been limited to two shots a day. They get close, but still haven't sunk this one.' He pointed at the target made out of empty barrels. 'Hit it about once a week.'

Sir Roger remembered spending many hours climbing all over the walls with Edward, rescuing maidens in distress from dragons and wicked knights. 'That's the Traitor's Gate, and those are the traitors.' Three long dead skulls on spikes leered in the gloom. Simon was starting to feel uneasy. *Twice now he's shown me these heads.* The thought of his own head on a spike sent a shiver down his spine.

The Constable was waiting. Like most of the incumbents of such roles, he was well past his prime. 'Sir Roger de Bohun,' acknowledged Constable Brecke, who had been in deep conversation with a richly dressed courtier, 'you know Count Robert.'

Indeed he did know His Highness, the Count of Artois and his heart fell. Rarely was there a more pompous, odious, irritating man to be found in all of Christendom.

'Count Robert.' Sir Roger bowed low in deference to royalty, sweeping his hat off in an extravagant motion. *He's aged.* Sir Roger noted how the Count's hair had turned grey. It had been a couple of years since he'd seen him. *Not since the incident with the heron.* 'What shall I do with these?' he indicated to his charges.

'House them over there,' Brecke ordered, pointing to the Beauchamp Tower. 'How long are they going to be here?'

'I've no idea. I'm just the delivery boy,' replied Sir Roger. 'And who should I see to cash these?' He produced a Promissory Note. The Constable looked at it and pointed to the offices of the Wardrobe.

'Ask for Robert Woodhouse, he's the Treasurer. He's out until tomorrow,' he added helpfully.

The prisoners were led away with what paltry baggage they had with them, which was carried by the couple of servants who had come too. The troop were duly given some expenses money and sent off to find billeting in the crowded barracks.

'There's a strict curfew,' the Constable informed them. 'Gates are locked at sunset and opened again at dawn. My officers and men are not allowed out at night, but I suppose that doesn't apply to your men.' He looked at Sir Roger.

'It will apply to mine too.'

'I thought your men wore a green boar?' The Constable was usually a stickler for matters heraldic. 'Not very distinguishable, this red stripe.'

'It's only temporary.' Sir Roger told him of the episode at Winchester. The Constable nodded with understanding. They wouldn't bother the heralds with this technicality. Changes in armorial devices were their department, and working out who was who from their coats of arms was becoming an increasingly complex business. From a narrow window they could see the mangonel being readied for its second shot.

'Those blasted stones are the very devil to get hold of, they'd throw all the building stone given half a chance,' he sighed with remorse, 'but boys will be boys. You must go and see the Queen, she's in the Audience Chamber.'

This was an order. The evening sun streamed through the coloured glass windows where a pregnant Queen Philippa sat, surrounded by her retinue of ladies-in-waiting, including Caroline de Burgh. Queen Philippa beamed radiantly as she bid him welcome; she had an appealing, honest visage with widely spaced eyes set on a broad face, though he thought her lips were a bit thin. 'How's Lady Alice?' she asked.

Sir Roger wasn't sure how to answer this question. *I can't tell her she's suffering from an imbalance of her humours.* He remembered how gaunt and withdrawn she'd looked when he'd left. 'Well, I think,' he said, blandly.

'Give her our regards,' said the Queen, smiling sweetly. 'I hope you'll dine with us.'

'It would be a pleasure, Milady.' *Especially if I could sit next to Lady Caroline again.* He smiled in her direction. She fluttered her eyelids demurely.

'We look forward to hearing all your news over dinner.' And with that, his audience with the Queen was over.

With a couple of hours to spare, Sir Roger sought out Walter Milimete, the King's Chaplain, moral mentor and pet alchemist.

'You've shrunk,' he told the wizened fellow, who had a restless energy and very few teeth. He found him in his workshop, where like the Magister, who was a friend of Walter's, he experimented with anything he could lay his hands on.

Walter looked Sir Roger up and down. 'And you've grown. My, how you've grown.'

Sir Roger patted his stomach. He had been worried by his expanding girth, as all his clothes were becoming tight. *It's all Max's doing.*

'I've brought you a present.'

The old man clapped his hands with childlike glee.

'It's a French *ribaud*.'

Walter could not contain his excitement and wanted to see it as soon as possible. The broken tube had been dumped on the sward; Sir Roger kicked it as he passed. 'That's it. I've got the gunner who came with it. Do you want to meet him?'

'Of course.'

'I'll go and get him.' Then Sir Roger got serious and told Walter of his suspicions. 'I know he's been to Oxford and met the Magister - I'm sure that's where the Frenchies got the formula for gunpowder. He doesn't know I know that. Grill him well.'

But Walter was far more interested in how his good friend the Magister was. 'I had a letter from him just the other day, wanted a new pair of glasses. We often write to each other.'

'Did he tell you he broke them showing me how the stuff worked?' said Sir Roger, leaving Walter to prod and probe the gun. 'I'll go and get Guillaume.'

He'd left Simon with the prisoners from Southampton. A weird and ghastly din could be heard coming up from the dungeons beneath, rattling and shouting.

'It goes on all night too,' moaned a guard, who sat at a small table by the entrance.

'What, or should I say who, is that?'

'It's Moray. He's been here since that to-do at Dunbar. Weighted down with iron. No one's allowed to speak to him, they's the King's instructions. It's a penny to see him close-up,' Sir Roger handed over the coin. He couldn't resist the urge to torment Agnes's brother again.

'No talking mind. He's a demented son of a bitch. We feeds him well and make him comfy but, with all those chains and shackles…' He let the motion of his arms flopping to his side, and a slump of his shoulders, tell the rest of the story.

A flicker of recognition crossed the unkempt face; Moray was obviously not allowed a razor. Silently Sir Roger took out his cock and pissed into Moray's drinking jug, before howling like a dog. He flicked the last drops at the prisoner, who had turned his face to the wall, away from his tormentor.

'That weren't very nice,' said the guard. 'Know the gentleman of old?'

Sir Roger nodded. 'Don't give him anything to drink until he's drained his jug,' he said, giving the guard an extra penny. 'And make sure he does - I don't want him pouring my precious water down the drain.'

Collecting Simon from the Beauchamp Tower, the pair then returned to the remains of the *ribaud*. Walter was making a drawing, using callipers to make measurements. He pointed at the ruptures around the breach.

'This was his gun.' Sir Roger introduced Simon. 'Oh and this is Walter, he's a friend of Magister Frakenham in Oxford.' He paused, watching Simon's face drain of blood. 'Who I believe you know.'

Simon nodded weakly. The bubble of his confidence burst and his knees gave way.

'Bugger me,' Walter said. 'He's fainted.'

Sir Roger hauled Simon to his feet. 'I know it was you who stole the formula for gunpowder, I just needed confirmation - and you gave it to me this morning. The spires of Oxford, *oui*.' He kept his face close to the Frenchman's. 'I'll honour your parole if you promise to cooperate. Otherwise I'm sure the Constable will find you *suitable* accommodation.'

A vision of traitors' heads floated through Simon's mind. *I was a fool to underestimate my captor.* His life took a lurch in the abyss.

'You see, they haven't made it strong enough.' Walter's voice brought him back to reality. 'How much powder did you put in?' he asked Simon.

'Too much obviously, about double than usual.' He thought that was about a pint of powder. 'I wanted the missile to break the gate.'

'There, you see we've got a lot to learn about these things. I'm trying to make one myself. I'll show you tomorrow. I think they should be made like bells - all in one piece - you see, the mistake is that if you try to do it this way,' and he showed Sir Roger and Simon where the iron bands around the barrel of the *ribaud* had burst at the rivets, 'weakness, the forces inside the tube are enormous.'

Simon was reluctant at first to impart any information but was soon swept up by the old man's enthusiasm, and he told of how the French were experimenting with a breach system. 'There's little interest in these new weapons amongst our nobility,' he said dismissively. 'They see nothing chivalrous about what they call 'peasant weapons'.'

Wait until they see an arrow storm, thought Sir Roger.

'Was that really Count Robert?' Simon asked Sir Roger as they walked back to the Beauchamp Tower.

'Yes. Loathsome creature.' Count Robert was still an enigma. He had been banished from France for attempting to acquire his aunt's lands by scheming, murder and forgery. He had felt aggrieved that the lands that should have been rightfully his had been granted to his aunt 'by a lawyer's mistake'. He suspected the slippery hand of the Valois Viper in this complicated and often distasteful story. He'd gone from being his foremost advisor and friend to becoming his most hated foe. The mayhem the case produced resulted in him suffering perpetual banishment and the loss of all his remaining property. As a Capetan royal prince, he, too, now hated the Viper with a vengeance that burned and consumed every fibre of his being. His cousin Edward had offered sanctuary and paid for his upkeep, sometimes in seclusion and obscurity and sometimes, as now, back in favour.

'I met his confessor, a monk called Sagebran.' It had been early on in Simon's career. 'He told us that the Count used to make little wax models of his enemies and stick pins in them while chanting a 'Death Spell'.' He told Sir Roger how Robert of Artois had used poor Sagebran to tell the King about it, or rather he let it be known that he had confessed all to the monk and then let the Valois Viper drag it out of Sagebran by torture. 'I think it's wrong to subvert the sanctity of the confessional.' Simon did not often venture an opinion.

But on this matter he's got surprisingly strong views, Sir Roger thought.

'My enemy's enemy is my friend,' continued Simon, after a moment's thought, before adding, 'though whether the friendship of *that* man is a boon I cannot say. Trouble follows him as surely as night follows day.'

Chapter 48

Sir Hog Sends his Compliments

Justin always enjoyed wandering around the Tower: the whole building oozed royal power from every stone. He'd been several times with Sir Roger. He, too, was just mooching around with time to kill when their paths crossed. From across the courtyard, down an alley, the regular clank of hammer on metal caught their attention as every few seconds yet another coin was struck. Sir Roger had always had a fascination for watching men work, so over they went and popped their heads round the door. The Mint Master aggressively enquired their business.

'Just showing my squire where money comes from. He thought it grew on trees!' Sir Roger smiled and held out his hand assuring him that his motives were honourable. 'I was also looking for the Treasurer.'

'He's not here.'

Sir Roger could see that they were stamping gold coins. 'Can I have a look?' The Mint Master handed him one. It shone in the evening light.

'It's a new type of florin - we call it the 'Double Leopard'.' He pointed to the motif. 'King wants to use them in Flanders. We sent him a test bag to see if the merchants accepted them but they were taken by the pirates when they captured his cog.' From being monosyllabic the Mint Master suddenly couldn't stop talking but the noise was becoming intolerable. 'Goes on day and night,' they were informed, and they thanked their lucky stars that when they arrived at their rooms they were far enough away so as they could not hear its irksome noise.

'I shall wear my best suit of clothes,' Sir Roger said to his personal servant, who was fussing over his poulaines, polishing the scuffmarks. The prospect of proper food rather than the peasant fare he'd had to endure during his journey greatly heartened Sir Roger. *Enough of beans and watery pottage, I want cinnamon and ginger, pepper and saffron, almond cream and whortleberries and, maybe, even, my favourite, mousseline of pike.*

The Dining Hall, on the first floor of the White Tower, was full of elderly nobles. These would probably become the commissioners whose job it would be to interview his prisoners. Sir Roger thought he spotted Lady Caroline's husband. Etiquette demanded that he be announced and he stood patiently waiting his turn while the herald shouted each new arrival. He heard Count Robert's name and watched as heads turned to look at the prince.

'Sir Roger de Bohun,' boomed the herald again.

'Good to see you Roger,' the Count was all bonhomie and hail-fellow-well-met. Sir Roger remembered Simon's words - *trouble follows this man as surely as night follows day.*

It had amused Count Robert to use his confessor in such an underhand way, subverting the vows of secrecy that the confessional were supposed to hold, and he wished he had been a fly on the wall. It was he who had persuaded his young cousin Edward that he was the *Rightful* King of France, and it was he, through secret letters to his confederates in Flanders, that persuaded the Flemings to come out in favour of this claim.

'I saw you visiting Walter.' The Count had recovered much of his spirit since the King had taken him back into his favour and he looked well fed. 'I wonder if we'll have heron for dinner...'

The Queen and her retinue arrived to a great fanfare. There, to Sir Roger's joy, was Lady Caroline. He greeted her most effusively.

Indeed his heart's desires were served up in an endless stream of delicacies to appeal to every nuance of his palate. One ravishing dish followed another: pike as good as ever, served with fillets of smoked eel and a hot horseradish sauce; raisin stuffed quail were followed by pink venison chops with a rich dark gravy. There was *definitely* no heron.

The Queen afforded Sir Roger the singular honour of placing him on her right hand side. 'I'm fed up with only having these old men to talk to. They tell me nothing of importance or interest. You were at Dunbar were you not?'

Sir Roger nodded.

'Did you see Black Agnes? Was she really as brave as everyone says?' The Queen paused for a moment and then added, 'for a Scot. She did well to hold her own. Tell us of the siege.'

'She has my banner hanging over her fireplace, she told me herself,' Sir Roger had to pick his words carefully.

'I hear she got out her dusters.' Even the Queen had a sneaking admiration for Lady Agnes.

'They were dressed up, too.' And a hush settled amongst the diners while Sir Roger told them some of the gory details. How Agnes had dressed all her maids in their Sunday best, and with feather dusters and dainty handkerchiefs, they had gone around the battlements, wiping off dust and fragments of stones. He also told how she had alluded to the sexuality of the besiegers in less than glowing terms. The Queen giggled. Every so often Sir Roger would shoot a furtive glance at Lady Caroline, he caught her eye and blew her a secret kiss.

'We all ran out and those heathen Scots were shrieking and oinking at us. It was humiliating. And then they caught all of us napping. Salisbury made up a little ditty that we all sang.'

The Queen summoned the lute player down from the minstrels' gallery to give accompaniment. 'Your wife sent him to me - he's got the most wonderful voice,' said the Queen. 'I think he's called Michael. He's my favourite.'

Sir Roger eyed him up - *so this is the stealer of my wife's virtue*. He smiled. *Now is not the time or place, but, my fine voiced friend, we shall meet again.*

The Minstrel sang with the voice of an angel.

> *'She makes a stir in tower and trench*
> *That brawling, boisterous Scottish wench,*

Came I early, came I late,
I always found Agnes at the gate!'

The Queen and the other ladies clapped, not for the humiliation of the English, but for the bravery of a woman defending her castle.

'What about old rattle chains we've got locked up over there?' The Queen lent over and waved her napkin towards the Beauchamp Tower. 'I never quite found out what his sin was. My husband treats him abominably.'

Sir Roger smiled. *As did I - adding a bit of saltiness to his drinking water...*

He told them how Moray had been captured in the autumn. 'Well, we reckoned that we might bargain his life for the castle, Agnes being his only kin and all that. So we took him along the causeway, threatened to kill him if she wouldn't surrender. Go ahead she said, and good riddance. I think your husband took exception to this and decided to make him suffer, especially as I hear his family have absolutely no intention of paying his ransom.' *It is one of the problems with collecting ransoms, getting paid.* He thought about Simon. *How long will he be a burden to my pocket?*

'We shall be spending Christmas with my father and husband,' announced the Queen as her party prepared to leave the dining hall. 'We're to go over to Flanders in the morning, weather permitting, to join them. Your friend,' she said, referring to her husband pointedly, 'has decided, in his wisdom, to winter in Antwerp. Please give my kindest regards to your wife and thank her again for her gift.'

As he bowed down, he noticed Lady Caroline drop a small billet from her sleeve. Making sure no one saw, he carefully placed his foot over it. It was an invitation of his favourite sort; she must have found out that he was to be at dinner as it held instructions for a tryst, neatly written in tiny script. A walk along the walls, a stolen kiss, his heart raced in anticipation.

At the appointed hour, when they met, this would be courtly love, chaste and chivalrous; there would be no carnality, no lust, no sin - not this time anyway. Sir Roger had only set his cap at the lady a few months ago. He had wanted to joust under her colours, tie her ribbon to his helmet crest, but had left before they had really become acquainted. *She treated me with such disdain, so why the change of heart?* A clear gibbous moon, almost full, cast a silvery light across the Thames. A few dim lights could be seen in windows over on the south bank, the occasional sound of carousing drifted over the water. It was cold and the stones were slippery from the first rime of hoar frost. His eyes adjusted to the night and he could see emerging from a nearby tower, a hooded figure, his paramour.

'I hoped we'd meet again,' she said sweetly. 'I saw you arrive with that metal thing.' In the moonlight he could see her exquisite features. There was no colour in her lips but they were glossy with moisture, slightly parted so her breath was like little puffs of smoke. He wanted to take her and kiss her. He felt her hand find his as they strolled along the empty walls.

They made small talk. All the while Sir Roger's mind was racing, he felt it wise to err on the side of caution and play the part of the knight, chaste and noble. This time he would talk of love but practise chastity. He remembered a poem Justin had made up on their journey. It was entirely suitable for a moonlit stroll such as this - a fair damsel had fallen in with thieves and her guardian had tried with all his might to rescue her but he had failed. He enlisted the help of a black cat who was in fact a bewitched prince. Sir Roger had just reached the part about the rescue, when the maiden was to kiss the cat and restore the prince to mortal form, when Lady Caroline drew him to her and their lips met. He felt her tongue flick playfully over his.

'I must go now, good Sir Roger. I hope we will meet again soon, for I would like to hear whether the prince rescued the fair maiden.' And with that she was gone.

Numbly, his head reeling, his lips still tingling, Sir Roger followed and went toward his appointed lodgings. *But first I think I'll pay the Minstrel a visit.* A helpful guard pointed him to the servants' quarters. Michael was eating when Sir Roger came in.

'The Queen loves your voice, and I came to pay you my compliments.' Sir Roger continued praising.

'And,' said Michael, irritated by the intrusion that seemed to have no purpose. 'And who might you be?' He lacked deference.

'And, me? Oh, I'm a good friend of Sir Hog.'

Michael stopped mid-mouthful and looked around nervously - he was alone.

'I'm also the husband of a lady of Hampshire that took your fancy.' Like a cat he sprang forward, grabbing the minstrel's wrist. 'I'm Sir Roger de Bohun,' he said, putting his face within an inch of Michael's. 'And you are going to pay for what you did.'

'Please don't kill me, my lord.' The Minstrel made a pathetic struggle to get free of Sir Roger's grip, but couldn't.

'Kill you? I wouldn't dare kill the Queen's favourite songster. No, you come with me.' He led him out into the night. 'I want to show you where money is made.'

Keeping Michael's arm firmly locked behind his back, they went towards the mint. Michael begged and whined, then wheedled and flattered, but to no avail - Sir Roger's vice-like grip held firm. In the mint, two men rhythmically swung their hammers, each blow producing a coin. Between each action a new blank disc was inserted - their actions second nature.

'I fail to see what this has to do with me,' said Michael, getting bolder as they watched the coins falling into a bucket beside the die stamp anvil. Sir Roger, though, was counting the time between strikes and, judging his revenge to perfection, pushed Michael's hands, one after the other, into the coin mould as the hammer came down. A gratifying organic crunch came each time as the minstrel's knuckles were turned to pulp.

'You can sing all you wish,' Sir Roger said to the whimpering Minstrel, 'but you won't play your lute, or diddle with ladies, for a bit.' He turned and apologised to the startled minters. 'Put his dick where he ought not to have.' He kicked Michael back out into the alleyway, leaving him to nurse his wounds, and went off to find his bed. Sleep eluded him for some time - to be kissed so sweetly made his heart near burst with excitement.

He was up early the following morning. Dawn was only starting to colour the sky to the east. It was still and clear, and the trees and ground were covered in thick swathes of white crystal. The sun's first rays made spirals of steam rise up and join wisps of fog that drifted over the moat. Already there was a great stirring in the Tower as the royal galley, which had been berthed along the jetty, made ready. A stream of porters carried all manner of gaily painted wooden boxes, leather travel trunks and the rest of the paraphernalia of a household on the move. Rowers, all dressed in royal red garb, silently found their benches and mounted their oars. A bell sounded divine service in the chapel; Sir Roger crossed himself and went to prayers.

The women of the royal party were dressed in their furs; mostly finest Vair capes similar to the one he had bought for his wife. Lady Caroline gave him a furtive glance but otherwise he was ignored. He could expect no more, a secret kiss, a stolen moment. His heart would ache till they met again. *She's gone without her husband*, he noted. *If I make it to Flanders...* He watched as they boarded the galley, which nosed out into the Thames. A hundred backs put all their strength into pulling their oars in perfect unison; the royal standard streamed proudly from its gaily painted stern. *I hope they have a smooth crossing.*

Chapter 49

Dan Gets Married

'Both hands and feet - blood and guts everywhere,' said the Wardrobe clerk in a conspiratorial voice. 'Four ruffians held the minstrel, directed by a great lord. I'm told it was only through the Mint Master's quick thinking that the poor minstrel didn't lose his life. Minty apparently pulled his head out before the fatal blow... Can I help you?'

Sir Roger smiled to himself as he handed the clerk a fistful of indents for payment. 'Nobody seems to know who the lord was - he's certainly not a Tower regular,' the clerk said to his colleague before turning back to Sir Roger. 'We don't have enough coin.' The desperate official tried to fob him off with one excuse after another - the war had made gold and silver a rare commodity and much in demand. There had been a patent failure to collect any of the wool promised to the Staple. He ended with 'the Mint can't produce money fast enough.' At this, Sir Roger lost his temper.

'I don't care,' he shouted, his voice rising into a crescendo. 'That is the most fatuous excuse I've ever heard - do you hear that?' In the silence, the steady clank of the money hammer was clearly audible. 'That's money being made, go over there and bloody get some or I'll put your bloody head under the hammer.'

A royal messenger emerged out of a back room of the Wardrobe, which was filled with earnest clerks and elderly household officials who shuffled mountains of paper. It was obvious at first glance that chaos ruled this house and the royal councillors were not the most competent of individuals.

'How can I be of assistance?' It was the Treasurer who emerged from the back room. 'I couldn't help but overhear your tirade. Get his money, be quick.' There was easily enough - in fact, there was lots.

'Put it all in a proper moneybox. There.' He handed Sir Roger a small casket full of different bags of money with little labels all carefully written, each one in payment of one of the promissory notes over which he wrote 'Paid In Full' and signed his name. Then, handing over the key, he continued sadly, 'that's my good deed for the day.'

'Finally, thank you. Someone who can get things done.'

'Now you're sure you have been paid up in full, all your expenses, allowances, everything?' Sir Roger nodded his head; his tantrum had obviously worked.

'Sometimes it pays to get angry,' he replied.

'No, you are quite wrong.' The Treasurer laughed and he seemed pleased to hand over the money. He waited until Sir Roger had put the money away and then he whispered. 'No, you could have begged on bended knee, you could have kissed my bare arse, I would have given you the money just the same. This, believe it or not, you lucky man, was my final act as Treasurer, I've just been dismissed! Gentlemen,' he turned and addressed the assembled company. 'I have some bad news; I've just been sacked! That messenger handed me this.' He flourished a parchment with the royal seal. 'May God be pleased that I shall never again serve a master that has so little interest in my efforts,' he lamented bitterly. 'I've tried my hardest, and what do I get as thanks. This! It will end in tears - mark my words. That man just does not understand the burden he places on us, expecting us to conjure money out of thin air.'

The heron's revenge, thought Sir Roger, feeling, at last, a good deal richer. 'No Dan. Where is he?'

'He went back to the inn. I didn't give him permission,' said Gwyn pointedly.

Passing an armourer's smithy, Sir Roger bought his son a fine dagger. *A boy of his age should start to learn about weaponry - and I'll buy Alice some fancy fabric.* This would be his first Christmas as a Lord in his own castle. The prospect excited him, and he wanted to make it a celebration to remember.

'That one.' *Joy.* Sir Roger pointed to a coat made from camlet, which was a pale, thick, hardwearing fabric made from camel hair imported from Cyprus. He eyed up the garment; it had a sable collar and trimmings. He lined up all the women in the shop and on the street until he found one whose head came up to the bridge of his nose and was roughly the same build as his wife. 'Got to get the right size,' he said, squeezing a few bottoms for good measure, smirking happily. 'Try it on, please...' A pair of fur-lined kid gloves for an extra couple of shillings complimented the ensemble. He noticed that they made dolls with fabric off-cuts and bought one for his daughter. The shopkeeper wrapped his purchases carefully in a canvas bag.

When he finally arrived at the Tabard Inn he found Dan in a corner canoodling with Christina. 'Who gave you permission to sneak off?' he asked, annoyed at his disobedience.

'He did,' replied Dan. He looked at the Sergeant for confirmation, but received a stony stare instead.

If I can get you into trouble, Shrimpy, then I will, thought Gwyn,

'You were busy so I asked John and he said he'd tell you,'

Well I didn't and I'll deny it again. This Gwyn did.

'Honest, Master, I did ask him. I'm sorry,' Dan sounded contrite. 'Can I still get married?'

I wouldn't put it past the Ox to be lying; knowing how he feels about Dan, so I guess I'll give him benefit of the doubt. Sir Roger mellowed; his visit to the Tower had been stressful in so many ways and so satisfactory in others. 'Yes,' he agreed reluctantly. It was a toss-up, saying no would be to disbelieve him, and Sir Roger didn't want Dan to bear a grudge.

'Can I borrow some money? I need a ring and the marriage fine.'

Sir Roger coughed up five shillings. Dan raced off, acquired a silver band from a cheap jewellery store on London Bridge, and returned quite out of breath.

'Well, aren't you going to introduce the bride-to-be?'

'This,' said Dan, his heart near bursting with pride, 'is Christina.'

She had changed out of her work clothes into a blue velvet frock with gold embroidery on the bodice. She had kept this dress wrapped up in the bundle she used as her pillow and this was the first time she had worn it - in fact, she had not taken it out since the death of her owner. Brushing out the creases she looked demurely at the floor, hardly daring to raise her eyes to such a great lord. When she did, the blue of her eyes intensified. Here was the triumph of true love. Sir Roger was impressed while Gwyn seethed with jealousy and hatred.

Sir Roger acted as best man and the landlord gave Christina away. A drunken monk blessed their union. The landlord stumped up a dowry, giving Christina a couple of old pewter mugs, some wooden plates and a wine jug all wrapped up in a damask tablecloth. His wife stood shaking her head, irritated that she'd have to find a new cleaner. Dan came over and thanked Sir Roger most profusely as the impromptu wedding feast, his 'bride ale' was getting under way. More beer - good beer - bread, meat and fish were laid on the table and feasting began in earnest.

'I think we should leave them, our presence won't be missed.' Sir Roger signalled to Simon. It was true, he required loyalty and obedience from his men at all times and had a firm rule about never socialising - even at occasions such as this. Giving the wedding his blessing was enough. 'Let's go and visit the Winchester geese,' he said, pointing to the many houses of ill-repute that were close-by.

'Geese?' asked Simon.

'Yes, the Bishop of Winchester owns all the brothels and we call the prostitutes his 'geese'!' An array of quality horseflesh told of the nature of the pleasures on offer within as Sir Roger and Simon eyed up the different establishments.

'This is the best,' a satisfied young blade assured them, and on that recommendation they stepped inside. Indeed, a range of finely dressed young ladies presented themselves, all beauties in gossamer. A line of wooden tubs were filled by an elaborate system of lead pipes; raised benches lined the walls with more maids a-plenty to satisfy every whim.

'I fancy something dusky,' announced Sir Roger, as he admired the choices that the brothel keeper presented. Whilst Lady Caroline, with her pure white skin, had aroused his chivalrous desires, he felt more like satisfying his lusts on the likes of 'Black' Agnes. A half-caste girl caught his eye; he had seen a Negro once and had marvelled at the man's finely oiled muscular torso. 'That one.' He signalled for her to come over. Athène was her name. Her breasts were firm and pert with small perfectly round nipples - no baby had ever suckled on them - and two marks her price. *A fair one.* Sir Roger contemplated the pleasures that would ensue upstairs.

'Here.' He flipped Simon a groat, 'see what you can get for that.'

'Can I bring my friend?' Athène asked. Her friend, a petite brunette, flashed a perfect set of teeth. Sir Roger was in heaven.

'It's not often we have such a well-endowed knight of such status,' they said, admiring the size of his penis while giggling in unison. Time slipped by and it was near dusk when a clean and sated pair returned to the Tabard Inn. It was quite obvious that their travel arrangements would have to be put on hold. The wedding party was still in full swing, with most of the troop well and truly drunk. Gwyn had disappeared, leaving Sir Roger's banner rolled up in the corner.

'Sour bastard,' said the landlord. 'Told me to tell you he's gone home and he'll see you at your Castle, wherever that might be.'

What goes through an ape's brain is difficult to say, but Zuzu tried all her usual tricks to get her master's attention. Where before he would have scratched her gently behind her ears and given her a morsel of bread offered between his puckered lips, now she was fobbed off with a dish of ale. As the feast progressed, so Dan continued to lavish his affections on Christina. Zuzu felt like yesterday's toy, once played with, and now discarded. In a funk of jealousy she sat under his chair picking at lice. There she remained obstinately refusing to move, until Simon reappeared. Then, instead of her normal fang-baring, she went over and laid her head on his knee, and, very slowly, climbed into his lap and curled up. He was horrified - suddenly his hellish tormentor wanted to be his friend.

'We'll wear the Green Boar and be proud of it,' Sir Roger announced at breakfast, deciding he had had enough of skulking like a coward behind false colours. Clouds were rolling in again from the west, ominous portents of more rain. 'And we'll go back to Guildford, after all,' he said with a laugh 'It wasn't us who burnt the town, but that villain Sir Eustace and his red-striped men.'

The Seneschal was delighted to welcome the Banneret - the fame of his exploits were passing into legend. 'Mind you,' he said conspiratorially. 'The townsfolk have a new hero - Sir Eustace de Frage.' In the silence that followed, Sir Roger looked in astonishment at his host. 'What?'

'They call him St. Eustace and want to name a street after him for what he did.'

It was too much for Sir Roger and he shook his head, snorting with outrage. *If only he knew.*

'So Guillaume, your first Christmas in England; do you have any family?' the Sheriff asked. They had reached Winchester again, and were sitting by a roaring fire in the Great Hall. The conversation turned to the coming festivities.

'My Yuletide feast would not be complete without a roast boar.' Sir Roger thought of the hunt. His leg had healed well; only the long, livid scar remained as a testament to the encounter.

'I'm very tired, I think I will go to bed.' Simon rose and was shown to his sleeping quarters. He was getting bored and hoped his ransom had been paid. After the episode at the Tower he knew many of his secrets had been revealed. What was also clear was that his captor was treating him more like an equal. How he would get to France he did not know, but he would cross that bridge.

'Have you learnt any more about our mysterious Frenchie?' asked the Sheriff.

'Lots. We grilled him at the Tower. He's a pleasant enough fellow, but I still can't make his story add up. The armour bothers me. Says that a friend who lost an arm lent it to him. I'm sure that's a lie. It fits him too well. I mean, would you lend me fancy armour? No, you'd sell it.' The two men nodded and shrugged.

'Oh, by the way, a King's Messenger had an urgent letter for you. I sent him to Ipers. It was obviously important, he said he had galloped all the way from Flanders. How was London?' The Sheriff had a habit of delivering a lot of information followed by a usually unrelated question.

'Well, believe it or not, we all got paid!' And he told him about the Treasurer. He did not, however, admit to torching Guildford - *that seems to have backfired rather spectacularly!*

'I should warn you,' said the Sheriff, adopting a serious tone, 'that a party of my tax collectors was robbed. That gang that's pretending to be you did it. I'm told their leader has a scar running down his cheek.'

So Sir Eustace is back, thought Sir Roger. *We'll have to be vigilant...*

Chapter 50

The Ransom is Paid

At last Lady Alice felt well enough to get up. She thanked the Lord for sending her Nunny, who had been a tower of strength throughout the ordeal. Now, having been bedridden for a week after the loss of the baby, she was ravenous and told her so.

Nunny was more sanguine. 'At least you've got some colour back, Milady. I'll order up a meaty broth.'

Lady Alice had seen the infant's hands and felt slightly relieved it hadn't survived. *I'll tell my husband it was his, but only if he asks.*

'I'd never have got through it without you,' said Lady Alice, surveying the Hall, admiring its newness. She loved the carved mantelpiece with *her* eagle riding so proudly on *his* boar's back. Handley slunk in and coughed to attract her attention.

'What is it this time?' she asked, irritated that the Bailiff was constantly coming with queries. In her weakened condition, she found him tiring and tiresome.

'I know I have lots to ask, Ma'am. I've never put on a proper Christmas for the Master. He told me if I had any questions I was to ask you.' His breath smelt sweeter and his grin had fewer teeth. 'I've got the ash log.' The Yuletide log was a Norman tradition inherited from their Viking forefathers, but for Lady Alice, being from Brittany, it was meaningless. In olden days, it would have been carved with runes to the Norse gods, but the Church had outlawed such a pagan practice.

Suddenly Lady Alice became agitated and started pointing. 'There.'

'Where? What?'

'There's a spider's web. There.' She pointed to grey shadows just visible behind the eagle's wing and shivered involuntarily. 'I hate spiders.'

Nunny took the corner of her sleeve and was dusting away the web when she noticed the little phial of Godfrey's semen that Sir Eustace had concealed before being ejected from the castle. 'Look at this,' she said, removing it and holding it up to the light. 'What do you think it is?'

Master John, who had been helping the children prepare a nativity crib and half listening, came over. He recognised what it was immediately and started reciting prayers as fast as he could. 'Put it down,' he ordered, trying to be authoritative. 'Don't touch it. It's bad, bad magic. It's a curse. I must work to neutralise it…'

—ʍ—

'Is the Ox back?' Sir Roger collared Whytethorne as soon as he returned. 'And did a Royal Messenger leave me a packet?' The Constable nodded.

'Both came two days ago. I've never seen a man so foul tempered - I sent him home.' He paused. 'Is there trouble between you and him? He normally follows you like a devoted dog. Somehow, he's changed.'

'I know. I don't think I can trust him anymore. He saved my life once and now feels I owe him more.' *Not good, not good.* 'Let him cool off, I can't face seeing him yet.'

'This lot arrived while you were away,' said Whytethorne, pointing to a pair of gaily painted wagons parked near the entrance. 'Said they were here to entertain you for Christmas.'

'Well, I didn't ask them.' *It is extraordinary how this castle attracts all manner of strangers.* 'Who's their leader?'

A large, florid faced man with exaggerated features presented himself. 'Let me introduce myself, I'm Mercurius,' he said, in a rich baritone, pausing for effect. 'Mercurius the Magnificent. I'm the leader of Mercurius's Magical Entertainments, mummers of distinction, performers of diverse plays and entertainments who crave your protection over the festive season. In return, we promise to keep your household amused and diverted. We ask little else save some scraps from your table, stabling for our horses and a dry place to sleep.'

Good entertainment is a must. Sir Roger hired them on the spot.

'I thought you'd go for them. Why they should have come so far out of their way, I don't know.' The Steward was suspicious of strangers. 'The good news is someone has paid Frenchie's ransom!' He informed his master quietly. 'How they got it here, I don't know. Day before yesterday, this foreign bloke arrived and gave this to the porter and without so much as a by-your-leave vanished again.' He handed over a goodly sized leather bag full of coins secured with a wire and lead seal and a letter. Sir Roger read it; it was in French. Roughly translated it said 'Payment ransom, William de Bapaume.'

'One more thing,' said the Steward hesitantly. 'Your wife miscarried. She lost the baby. It was a girl. I'm sorry.'

Sir Roger took this news in silence, burying the pain and sadness. *Was it the Minstrel's or mine?* He didn't dare ask his wife, so would never know.

The Hall was still in uproar. Master John had gone into overdrive, surrounding the vial with numerous charms in an attempt to draw away the evil spirits. Sir Roger feigned interest before heading up to the solar. He kept eyeing up the King's letter in its leather pouch. The seal was not the usual one. It was the one that spelt trouble with a capital T. On its back was scratched a little 'c'; he searched through his strongbox until he found a tatty old hymnal that was the key to the code. He opened it. The letter, on a single strip of paper, was a jumble of meaningless letters and numbers. Slowly he worked his way through, his disbelief rising.

'Your prisoner not de Bapaume' it said. 'He's Simon de Pressi'. *Now that answers that question.* 'He's Béhuchet's *chef de cabinet.* Turn if possible. Bring to Antwerp soonest. Signed EIIIR'. *Will buy,* thought Sir Roger exultantly. *This can stay secret till after Christmas.* Then he remembered the conversation at London Bridge; he had not meant it in the way that it was meant, but now it was in earnest. He was about to count the ransom money when he heard a knock at the door. It was Handley.

Sir Roger sat back and listened to his Bailiff's catalogue of woe.

'Parlous, Sire, couldn't really be much worse.' Handley recounted the ploughing and sowing of the winter wheat and oats had been severely curtailed by wet and lack of plough teams. His flocks of sheep were proving equally difficult to muster. Murrain, that most dreaded of diseases, now affected two of his flocks and losses were mounting. Only a quarter had been put into winter pens and there was no sign of the rest. The mill had suffered a set-back, the river was so swollen that it had not been possible to mount the new wheel. *It's definitely the curse.*

'Enough. Go and tell Alfred we hunt boar tomorrow.' He ushered Handley out. *I hope Master John can lift the curse.*

'Let me look at that,' Sir Roger was now keen to see the source of the misfortune that had dogged him over the last few months. Master John showed him the vial.

'I don't think you should touch it,' he said, 'use these.' He handed Sir Roger a pair of tongs. He lifted it as if were red hot.

'What do you think it is?'

Master John shook his head. 'Necromancers use many powerful potions to cast spells. Could be anything - mandrake juice, bat blood, snake bile, hanged man's semen... Whatever it is, it's very strong if your bad luck is anything to go by.'

Too right. The last ingredient reminded Sir Roger of Godfrey with his underclothes cut away. *I bet this is Sir Eustace's doing.*

'First I thought I'd make a lead coffin, then bury it in consecrated ground. We have to trap the evil inside and surround it by souls of the shriven.'

Holding the offending article in front of him, like a man holding a toxic turd, he led Sir Roger to the castle's smithy. Using some scraps of lead from the roof they cast a container, dropped the vial into it and poured more molten metal to seal it in while Master John recited his catechism.

'There,' he said, as they poured cold water onto the hot lead, listening to the satisfying hiss. 'I defy any devil to get out of that prison.'

Taking a stylus Master John scored the surface with crosses and wrote 'Lord Jesus protect us from evil' into the soft shiny metal.

'Let's bury it.'

Sir Roger felt much happier after the lead lozenge, which was about the size of a hen's egg, was safely interred in the Churchyard. Fyscher caught the spirit of the event and made doubly sure by saying a full mass over the hole and sprinkling it with holy water.

—ɯ—

Unnoticed amongst the many coming and going from the castle, three robed mendicant friars watched and waited. They walked around the moat and eyed up the gatehouse. Some time in the next few days, when all were quiet and asleep, the Sons of King Arthur would strike a blow for liberty against the oppression of the King and his tax collectors. From a distance, they watched the procession go to the graveyard, but did not fully understand its significance.

'I'm going to make them suffer like I have suffered. I'm going to take that arrogant prick, Sir fucking pompous Roger,' Sir Eustace pronounced the words with venom, 'and humiliate him.' He was not in a forgiving mood, licking his lips at the thought of the pain he would visit upon the de Bohuns. 'I'm going to do to him what I did to that bishop's bum boy. And his wife too,' he snarled happily to Falke. His obsession with Lady Alice continued unabated and was beginning to affect his ability to reason. 'Then I'll kill him.'

Sir Eustace's force had swelled, becoming a magnet to all ruffians and outlaws. They were billeted in the abandoned buildings at Caxton, where, after his servants had fled, weeds had grown rapidly, giving an air of dereliction to the casual observer and easily concealing that, in fact, it was, to all intents and purposes, an armed camp. They were well armed, too, from their forays through the Midlands, and well-motivated by the sweeps of the taxman.

'Once we have the castle I'm going instigate a reign of terror.' He had been plotting and planning for this day. 'And when winter is done, we will evaporate like morning mists burnt off by the rising sun.' *Quite poetic*, he thought in his happily twisted way.

Increasing numbers of lesser knights would be happy to hire his mercenary band to plunder the fat riches of monasteries and abbeys and pillage supplies wending their way to the army in distant Flanders. A split of the profits would make the difference between penury and luxury for a lot of hard-pressed landowners. In return, all they needed to give was protection, and immunity from the law. *Ipers is suitably remote, Southampton's still in ruins. It'll make an ideal base for the winter. All we need is surprise.*

'What were they doing, Father?' asked Falke, feigning innocence. He waited for Fyscher to finish his mass before approaching.

'Nothing much,' replied the Priest as dismissively as he could. 'Burying something that needed to be buried.' *Already someone is interested, it must be a powerful charm.* He noticed that the monk who had asked the question had too much hair poking out from under his hood. He waited until the strangers had gone before digging it up again and hiding it in a fresh location. Now he controlled it, whatever it was.

Chapter 51

The Sacred Grove

Try as they might, there were no boar to be had on Sir Roger's estates and, as each hunt drew a blank, so Sir Roger's dudgeon grew.
For two days they had quartered every acre of his lands; plenty of fallow deer but no trace of boar anywhere. The temptation to stray into
the nearby Royal Forest was great, but it was strictly off-limits, even for
the King's Friend. No one could hunt there without express written
Royal permission and it was too late to ask. At the end of the second
day, Sir Roger stomped back into his Hall, ready to kill. The Bailiff was
there with a grin that could have swallowed a porpoise whole.

'I've got you a boar,' he announced with a great deal of relief in his
voice. *'What's Christmas without roast boar?'* Sir Roger had ranted on for
so long that the Bailiff thought he might have an apoplectic fit. When
questioned, Handley was reluctant to give details of the transaction
or how he had come by the carcass. But there it was, not the biggest
animal, but a wild boar none the less.

'Suffice it to say there were those who wish you well, Master, and
they hope to make your Christmas Feast complete.'

The sense of relief was tangible. With two days to go before the
feast, preparations in the kitchens were well under way. Max was mas-
terminding his finest hour.

'Humbly pie, humbly pie. The poor will eat their humble pies,' he
sang happily to himself as he laid out the livers, hearts, brains, tongues
and other edible entrails of deer, which, baked into pies, would be given

to the poor. There would also be mincemeat pies and haunch of venison for all.

A scullery boy was fussing about assembling the ingredients for frumenty, that indispensable pudding of preserved fruit, molasses and wheat that was always served at Christmas. The main task of cooking was still some time off but, as Max said, *preparation is everything*. And now, finally, better late than never, a fine young boar had been delivered. He would roast it whole on a spit. It hung in the larder next to geese, duck, pheasant, partridge, heron, hare, rabbit, chicken, deer and a steer that would all be consumed over the next fortnight.

'We need the head,' said Handley, popping his head round the door.

'Can't have it.' Max exploded. 'It will spoil the whole look of the dish, for what is a whole roast boar without its head, complete with an apple in its mouth!'

'We still need the head and be damned about the apple.' Handley was adamant. 'It's the price, I'm afraid. I bought it headless.'

Eventually Max was persuaded and, using the great butcher's knife that hung from his belt, swiftly removed the head.

He watched disconsolately, but with some considerable interest as Handley, Whytethorne, Sir Roger and the said head made their way over the drawbridge.

'Where are we going?' It intrigued Sir Roger, who followed in procession. The route was circuitous. Suddenly Handley departed from the track, going down into a hidden gully. *This is part of my land I have never visited.* Sir Roger slid down the bramble covered slope, *and with good reason*, he added to himself as he pulled a thorn out of his thumb. He had neither hunted nor ridden through this place. An almost invisible, sunken wooden causeway crossed over the bog that he had always considered impassable, to a rising of dry ground where a copse of ancient oaks stood. His eyes widened as he took in the sacred grove. *This is a place of heresy.* He felt cold and clammy. *This is where adherents to the old religion make offerings to the goddesses of fertility and farming and pray for a good harvest and I am party to this.* He was heartened to see a wooden crucifix. He had bullied Whytethorne and Handley into allowing him to come. They had made him swear on all he held holy never to reveal what he had seen to Fyscher or anyone else. *Especially not Fyscher. He can't be trusted* - his night on his knees in front of St. Swithun's relics had taught him that.

The trees were eerily ancient and gnarled, some so old that they were more like hollow stumps than mighty oaks. Here and there animal skulls had been placed high up on boughs. A circle of standing stones formed the copse's heart. To his horror, he saw that these were topped with dark red - *old blood smeared onto each point.*

About a dozen villagers, some whose faces he vaguely recognised, others new to him, materialised out of the trees and took the boar's head. He did not understand the language they spoke. It was not the English of his villeins and cottars, and it certainly was not the Latin of Mother Church. He watched as the worshippers revered the cross - *so Christ will not be offended.* Mead, he assumed it was mead from the honey smell, was poured into the beast's mouth and the head was placed high up on a trunk. More mead was poured over each stone, and, as soon as that was done, everyone disappeared as silently as they had come, just melting away.

As they threaded their way back along the hidden causeway, Sir Roger's mind was in turmoil. He had never expected to witness a pagan rite in this Christian land. He should report it to the Bishop and root out this heresy, but thought better of it. *I've given my oath, after all.* He also felt curiously privileged to participate in a ritual, albeit as observer, which was older than a thousand years, so Whytethorne had said. Perhaps, with all the terrible weather and the failure to plant their winter crops, another hand was needed to protect the future of his village.

The morning's frost had not melted. Ice crystals covered reeds; a bittern boomed in the distance. The cold had intensified, puddles of rainwater had solidified and Sir Roger found himself running and skating on their black shiny surfaces as if he were a boy again. The clear blue sky had given way to iron-grey clouds that gathered out of the north.

'If this cold continues,' said the Steward, looking at the moat, 'we'll be able to skate on it.'

As dusk fell, an eerie silence came down like a cloak. Even the wind was quiet. Sir Roger sat with Lady Alice and the children; they had been showing him their crib and he had been telling them stories of London and the Queen's banquet. He omitted any mention of Michael; he thought he would save that juicy morsel for an appropriate moment. Sir Hog would no doubt be interested to know that revenge had been served up. He had to laugh at the irony of St. Eustace at Guildford.

'Well I never,' he said in astonishment, as he peered through the crown glass panes of the solar window. 'Come, children.' He opened the door that led onto the battlements; a flurry of snow-flakes swirled inside and vanished. Outside, the dim light of the candles and lamps illuminated at least six inches of snow that had settled on the machicolations and crennelations. In fact, everything they could see was white.

Daylight revealed a world of virgin snow, already punctuated here and there with the paths of passing animals. Familiar routes were being trod, one set of prints at a time. The Watch noticed that an ominous set of three heavy boot prints had circled the moat and then disappeared north. Whytethorne sent a few men to follow them and report back.

'They led to horses that were tethered in the woods about a mile or so away. They've headed towards Caxton,' Gwyn informed him. He had returned to duty and, as the Steward reported, seemed in a much better mood.

'The curse amulet, Sons of King Arthur, and now scouts...' Sir Roger shook his head as he watched his hall being decked out with swags of holly and ivy. Mistletoe, too, was placed in bunches where kisses could be stolen. Master John thought this very unchristian, but held his tongue.

'Most villagers face destitution, Sire,' Walt reported. 'We've managed to plough two virgates since harvest. No one has managed anything near their allotted tasks. We know you can raise fines, but there's no money,' he continued. 'The purveyors were the final straw. John atte Wood has gone. Some say to join 'the Sons of King Arthur.'

Sir Roger's ears pricked up. This was the second time now he had heard mention of this shadowy bunch of villains.

'Tell me more,' he said. John had been a cottar, one of the lowest of the low.

'There's not much to tell, though in the ale house the other day a stranger to these parts was talking about them. Almost recruiting, I would say. They promise an end to taxes, freedom to the serfs and a virgate to each man of the finest land in any village they liberate.'

'Liberate from who?' *To usurp land from the crown is treason indeed. I must stop this nonsense at once, nip it in the bud.* Sir Roger made a mental note that once the Twelve Days of Christmas were over, he would root out this treasonous bunch- a thought soon put out of his mind when Mercurius appeared.

'What would you like us to perform,' he asked, 'and when?'

Sir Roger delegated the task to Handley, who, as the Bailiff, was de facto master of ceremonies. Handley noticed a girl dressed in particularly bright clothing who was part of the group.

'She's a Rom, comes from Egypt,' said Mercurius, who had paid a hefty price for her and was determined to recoup on his investment. 'From what I can establish, she was captured in Cyprus. I bought her last year. She's supposed to be a fortune teller, but her English isn't very good.'

The language the Bailiff had in mind had few words. 'She can also be my bed warmer.' He liked a challenge, and for three good silver pennies a deal was struck.

—∭—

'I think you should introduce your wife to mine,' said Sir Roger, leading Dan and Christina to where Lady Alice was sitting with Nunny. 'She's in charge of all the women in the castle.'

'I would like you to meet Christina, Milady. She's Karelian,' said Dan formally.

Lady Alice put out her hand graciously, expecting Christina to step forward and curtsey. Instead she burst into tears. Taken aback, Lady Alice tried her hardest to comfort the girl, wondering what had brought on such grief.

'Your cape,' Christina informed her, wiping her eyes, 'I made that.' Lady Alice was wearing her Vair cape, which, in this cold weather, she rarely took off. Christina could recognise her handiwork anywhere. These were the same squirrel pelts her owner had come to England to trade and Christina had spent many weeks sewing each tiny scrap of fur together, her fingers becoming toughened and strong from endlessly pushing needles through the soft leather.

Lady Alice looked at Dan and Christina and saw a couple truly in love. She looked at her husband. *You are a better lover than that minstrel.* Now she had tried another man, she could make the comparisons that her friends had talked about.

Zuzu, however, was still in what could only be described as an apely huff. She most certainly did not approve of Dan's new marital status and had sulked ever since Christina's arrival. She had even tried to bite her. In her own way, she now transferred all her affections to Simon, meticulously grooming his lank locks whilst baring her teeth at her erstwhile owner. *At least*, thought Simon, *it is better than being shat upon!*

Christina proved a big hit with all and sundry, being quick to volunteer for all manner of tasks. She rapidly became most in demand for her sewing skills as she repaired rips in the troops' clothing, sewing with deft dexterity and lightning speed. Her flaxen hair and the way she had of floating over the ground like an angel entranced everyone, with the exception of the Ox. He looked at her and only thought dark thoughts.

Dan had a grin that spoke of a man well satisfied, but he was concerned about Zuzu. She had not eaten for a couple of days, refusing even the choicest morsels he offered. Of course, he was not to know that Simon now fed her bread and carrots when no one was looking. Simon was not going to give Dan any comfort in that department. The humiliation of his capture still rankled and now, with his change in circumstances, he thought it best to keep quiet.

The meagre hours of daylight soon passed. A makeshift stage had been erected at the far end of the hall, lit with extra candles and concealed by a painted curtain.

A peal of phoney thunder and a clashing of cymbals heralded the start of the show.

'Ho ho harrrr.' A deep voice boomed out from behind a star-studded screen. Again, deeper, even more alarmingly, the devil was calling. An imp scampered across the stage. Then he appeared, all in red with wicked horns, a mask of incarnate evil and a long swishing tail. Mercurius looked magnificent, removing his mask to reveal a face painted blue, with gold stars on his cheeks.

The mummers danced and entranced their audience, who in turn clapped, cheered, jeered and groaned at a moral tale replete with knights and maidens, quacks and villains.

'Tomorrow,' Mercurius promised, 'the escape from Herod and the Blessed Nativity. And more,' he roared to the audience, as steaming jugs of mulled wine were brought around.

'Look what Daddy gave me!' said Harry in delight, holding his new dagger up so it glinted in the early morning sun. He practiced endlessly, drawing it out of its leather and wood scabbard, shouting '*En garde!*'

'Stop that at once.' Lady Alice reprimanded him; worried he'd stab someone. Her husband had told her how sorry he was to hear that she'd lost the baby. *Thank God he didn't ask whether I thought it was his. He seems preoccupied, somehow distant.* As if from nowhere, he conjured the canvas bag with her new coat.

'How did you know my size?' She was so delighted - it was quite unexpected and, as he had hoped, fitted perfectly. He smiled, keeping other gifts back, well hidden, to be given, as appropriate, during the next few days.

A steady stream of villagers climbed the slope to the castle, each giving their dues if they were able and receiving their allocation of new clothing from the stores.

'Can I have a word, Sire,' asked Fyscher, sidling up to Sir Roger. 'In private.'

They slipped away where they couldn't be overheard.

'After we buried the talisman I was approached by one of those mendicants that have been hanging around for the last few days. They started asking questions and I noticed that he couldn't have been a proper monk - his hair, for one thing, wasn't tonsured *and* he was wearing riding boots.' He paused to wipe a bead of sweat off his forehead. 'Well, I took the precaution of digging up that little lead box and putting it somewhere safe. Then I hid and watched. Sure enough they came back with a spade and dug up the hole. One of them got very angry indeed. I thought you should know.'

This news made Sir Roger feel edgy. *The curse might have been lifted but it hasn't gone away.*

When he returned to the hall, the party was in full swing. The village's poorest elements each came to the feast carrying their own cloth, cup, trencher and stool. At the feast's end, they could take away all that was left on the cloth.

From his seat on the dais, Sir Roger surveyed the throng. The experience in the marsh had affected him, subtly altering his perception. The site's sheer age and the place's power had brought home his own mortality and now he was worried. *I might be king in my own castle, but how safe is my castle?*

Below him all sat in eager expectation. A drum roll and cymbal crash, courtesy of the mummers, heralded the arrival of the roast wild boar. Four men had to manoeuvre it carefully from the kitchen on a great wooden board specially constructed by the carpenters.

'One cooked pig's head looks much like another,' said Max to Handley, who had complimented the chef on restoring the beast, replete with apple in its mouth and wooden tusks; Max had worked a small miracle in joining it almost seamlessly to the body. The boar was surrounded on all sides with roast geese, venison haunches and venison pies. A further tray was piled with capons and hams, after which a stream of scullery boys emerged carrying cakes, pastries, mince pies, white breads, brown breads, frumenty pudding and, finally, a cauldron of soup. All this would be washed down with ale, lots of ale. The food parade was accompanied by loud and prolonged cheering.

'That's it!' said a relieved Max Grossteste as he finally sent the last scullery boy through with the last loaf of bread. 'Now the game of 'find of the bean' can begin in earnest.' For somewhere, in one of the loaves, there lurked a solitary hard bean. He, or she, who found the bean, would become 'King of the Feast, Lord of Misrule'. As beans go, it remained hidden for a long time.

'The bean is mine!' Suddenly a roar arose from the far end of the hall - the bean had been found, and by none other than Mercurius.

Who better could be elected Lord of Misrule! Sir Roger surveyed the revellers. The Yule log crackled and hissed in the fireplace, spreading warmth throughout the hall. He raised his mug of mulled wine and called for silence. It took quite some time before all hundred and fifty banqueters were quiet. Loud belches followed in quick succession, as a contest to see who could be longest and loudest.

'I hear the sounds of satisfied eaters.' Sir Roger held up his mug again. 'Let us drink a toast to Max the Cook.' A hearty roar of approval reverberated around the beams, almost lifting the roof. More toasts were proposed from the floor.

'Better weather!' cried the ploughman.

'A reduction in taxes!' A carter drew a cheer. Everyone who wanted a say could have one, some more eloquent than others. Many deplored the war and the theft of their livestock by purveyors.

'Let us stand in prayer for all those who suffered and died in Southampton.' Fyscher called for a moment of silence.

Children were running about and dogs were going from place to place, begging for scraps. As dusk fell, so the party split into groups of men or women talking or playing dice or backgammon. Sir Roger and Master John retired to the solar for a game of chess; there the senior members of the household could escape the increasingly raucous fun and games led by Mercurius.

Not wishing to be outshone or outdone, Dan put on a performance of juggling and sleight of hand that was truly impressive.

'That, son,' said Mercurius patting him on the back, 'is some of the best juggling I've ever seen - and I should know, I've seen them all. Who taught you?'

'My father.' Dan told him his name.

Mercurius's eyes widened. 'I knew him well.' He reeled off a list of fairs. 'I wasn't called Mercurius then, though. So he was your father - well I never, I must have seen you as a nipper.' From that moment on, a bond formed between the two men.

'That thing,' Sir Roger said, as he forked the Chaplain's queen with a triumphant flourish, 'has attracted the attention of others. I hope you've done enough to neutralise it. Fyscher's got it and hidden it, now he controls it.'

It must be more powerful than I imagined. This made Master John more determined than ever to get hold of it again. He had intended to do just that, once the furore had died down and the snow had melted. Two moves later, it was checkmate.

It was well after midnight when the last revellers had either braved the cold and dark or fallen drunkenly asleep. The hall reverberated to the sounds of snoring. Outside it was snowing gently, great white flakes filling footprints.

Sir Roger lay awake, and in a flash of inspiration he knew what he would do with Simon.

Chapter 52

A Web of Deceit

The Sons of King Arthur were close to mutiny by the time they reached Sir Eustace's home. The cold ride back through snow drifts sometimes as high as their horses had been strength-sapping. The one who was Sir Bedevere was most vociferous.

'I hope you've brought us some food, we're starving,' he grizzled, echoing the gang's sentiments. They had eaten their way through the food stolen from Winchester and, without serfs or servants, there were no winter provisions stored at his manor house. At Sir Eustace's suggestion, they tried to mount a raid on a nearby village, but none knew the district well enough. Confused by the featureless whiteness, they had spent several fruitless hours floundering in drifts only to return empty handed.

'If we can walk across the duck pond,' said Falke to the men, 'then the castle moat will be firm enough to cross as well.' It no longer mattered whether their man on the inside opened the gates or not. All they needed were ladders and they could climb over the walls.

Sir Eustace wrapped his wolf fur cloak tighter and headed for the pond. None of his men were brave enough to venture onto the ice. They needed convincing. He watched as they continued to dither

'Cowards. It's firm, the ice will hold.' He walked slowly and deliberately to the middle of the pond, where he pushed away the snow with his sword and started to hack a hole in the ice. 'Thick. Thick enough for an army to cross.' He knew the moat would hold - he'd tried it already

'The castle's full of food and women,' he told them when they returned to the relative warmth of his Hall. 'All we have to do is take it. We need scaling ladders to climb over the walls and then Camelot will be all yours.' He made it sound so easy.

—⚏—

Having heard that the amulet was no longer in its grave, the Chaplain was on a quest. He had seen the power of the curse in action and was mightily impressed. From the moment the vial had been placed behind the eagle's wing, it had worked its malevolence with dreadful effective-ness. *Truly there is a devil in that bottle!*

'How much do you want for it?' Master John sat opposite Fyscher at his table.

'For what?'

'For the little lead box, silly. What did you think I wanted? One of your indulgences? They're not worth a farthing.' His tone was conde-scending, his manner arrogant.

Fyscher looked hard at the weasel opposite. He'd met the Chaplain's sort before, instinctively hating the smart-arse. He was one of those who were forever telling all those who would listen that he could recite the catechism in Latin by the age of five, and that the kindly monk in charge of the foundling home where he had been deposited as a babe found that within a year he'd learnt to read and write. From then on his rise had been meteoric, and had he not been caught in an unguarded moment, one that he now wholeheartedly regretted, he would have doubtless been a bishop or even a cardinal.

'What's it worth?' The bumbling Priest wasn't going to be trapped so easily by the Chaplain. *If he wants it that badly, he'll pay a good price.*

Master John thought about how much money he had.

'I'll give you five shillings.'

The Priest shook his head. He had other ideas. He remembered how heavy the talisman was. 'I think it's worth its weight in gold.'

—ᴡᴡ—

Harry had honed his new dagger to razor sharpness and it didn't take long for him to want to try it out, as all young boys are wont to do. Nor did it take long for his mother to discover his crime and notify the authorities.

'You know what that beastly son of yours has done,' said Lady Alice, holding up her favourite lapdog, Horace, under her husband's nose for inspection.

To his untrained eye, the dog appeared more moth-eaten than usual. 'Look. It's all your fault, giving him that dagger.' She pushed the squirming hound into his face. 'Look, damn you.'

He looked again and saw that chunks of hair, like a checkerboard, had been shaved off its back. He tried hard not to laugh.

'You men are all the same,' she said in disgust, comforting her pooch. *Now the brat deserves to be beaten on Holy Innocents Day.*

His wife gone, the chastisement of her son the next thing on her list, Sir Roger summoned Dan to the solar.

'Close the door, we don't want to be overheard.' He signalled for Dan to sit. 'Guillaume's ransom money has arrived. There's a problem, though. You mustn't tell him.'

Dan raised an eyebrow. Surely the etiquette of chivalry demanded the instant release of the parolee. He aired his concern.

'It doesn't apply in this case.' Sir Roger took out his dagger and placed it on the table pointing at Dan. 'You must swear a most sacred oath of secrecy, by all that is holy, and all the saints. Otherwise this dagger will surely cut out your tongue.'

'I swear by Almighty God, the Blessed Virgin and the Holy Trinity.' Dan swore holding the old hymnal. 'What?'

'Guillaume has been lying. He's been weaving a web of deceit.' Sir Roger groped around for suitable words. 'The King thinks he's called Simon de Pressi and he's only one of the most powerful men in the French navy. He's only the bloody French bloody Admiral's bloody Aide de Camp and we've got to get him to fucking Antwerp.' Sir Roger looked up at Dan, who stood open-mouthed at the stream of swear words. 'After fucking New Year. He's a clever bugger, I'll give him that - he nearly had me fooled.'

He took the dagger, gently opening the lead seal with its bee, and emptying the bag's contents onto his desk. There were exactly one hundred gold double leopard coins. They were the same as the Mint Master had shown him. *They must have been stolen from the* Cog Edward. *So that's where he got them.* He held one up so it caught the light and admired its pristine shine. *That bee confirms everything. Béhuchet must have paid the ransom.* It all fell neatly into place. He divided the pile. 'Two for me, one for you. Fair?' It was a rhetorical question, and Dan knew it. He nodded - *never look a gift horse in the mouth.*

'This one is for the lepers,' Sir Roger said, holding the hundredth coin. 'Not a word now.'

It was more than Dan had hoped for and he recounted his thirty-three gold coins with great deliberation; it was more money than he had seen in his whole life. He could build Christina the house he had promised her.

Another couple of inches of snow had been deposited during the night. Again, mysterious footprints stood out from the rest, being more recent. Again these skirted the moat and turned north. Here and there snow had been disturbed and brushed off the branches by the passing intruders. Sir Roger summoned Alfred and, with the dogs, they set out to follow as far as they could. Indeed, as reported, a couple of horses had been tethered, well hidden, in the woods and ridden off.

'I'm worried that this is the work of those Sons of King Arthur we've been hearing so much about,' said Sir Roger, expressing his concerns. 'I'm going to be a killjoy - no more drinking for the guards and double the watch. Whatever is going to happen will happen soon. I can feel it in my water.' It was this intangible sensation that had often kept Sir Roger alive. It was the footprints crossing the moat that made up his mind *A man made those, as Alfred pointed out, not a child skating.*

There would be complaints; he knew that - *what would Christmas be without drunkenness?* But now, when simple expediency called for it, he had his Pantler lock the cellar.

'I shall control the key.' Sir Roger held out his hand.

Mercurius looked up at the Green Boar banners, admiring the beast's exaggerated tusks. *I should tell him, then again...* Mercurius was caught between the devil and the deep blue sea and opted for the coward's way out. He'd do nothing to jeopardise his situation. The knight with the scar had told him to expect a signal, but had not been told what it would be. He assumed it would be obvious. Then all he had to do was lower the drawbridge. *That's easier said than done.* He would have to find a way of getting into the gatehouse.

Nunny found that, since the episode with Lady Alice in the graveyard, there had been a subtle change in the way Master John approached her. He bided his time, but now and then he would ask oblique questions about concoctions, herbs and potions; it was obvious to her that he was desperate to see her mother's herbal. She noticed little things. What meagre possessions she owned had been ever-so-carefully rifled through - she knew this because she was a careful woman. His one look on that awful day had alerted her.

Nunny had stood, as a child, and watched her mother being dragged out of their family home and tortured for heresy, all because she possessed that self-same volume; her agonised cries had seared themselves deep into Nunny's psyche, and unless she was very careful the same fate awaited her. *I should have taken up holy orders.* But Lady Alice now relied on her more and more, and, as her intimate confidant, she felt protected enough not to set out on a new life. So she hid the book in the tower room, where empty travel trunks and boxes were stored, and was confident that no one would ever find it, wrapped in oilcloth and tucked between the roof beams and thatch. She had made a ladder out of boxes, which she then evenly repositioned across the floor.

She sat patiently listening while Clothilde unburdened herself.

'My bleeding is late,' Clothilde said, trying but failing to hold back her tears. 'I'm two months late and I get sick in the mornings. It must be Guillaume's. I'm scared.'

Nunny offered what words of comfort she could, but the story was always the same. *The lusts of men are gross and brief.*

—m—

Master John had heard Dan's summons and followed discreetly. Putting his ear to the door he had heard enough. 'Ransom' and 'gold', followed by the unmistakeable clink of coin, quickened his pulse. All he needed to do was find a way to get his hands on it. His priority, though, was to find Nunny's book. *First I have to find where the witch has hidden it.* He'd already searched very, very thoroughly, but of it he had found no trace. *She's guilty of heresy.* That one glance had been enough to make up his mind and he'd stoop to almost anything to get his hands on that volume. He had the patience and would bide his time, stalking his prey. *The book's the key.* Without it his case would be purely circumstantial. Once he had located it, then the heretic would burn and the power contained in the book would be his. *Gold, book, amulet, gold, book, amulet.* He kept repeating this to himself.

—◊◊◊—

The prospect of a dry holiday did not unduly worry Mercurius the Magnificent as he had several small barrels of finest Rhenish wine secreted in the false bottom of his wagon. The cold night air gave the sky an inky blackness against which the pinpricks of light shone brightly. He often wondered about celestial bodies. He knew that stars twinkled and were fixed in their constellations while a few, which the Romans had named after their gods, did not.

It was because of his passion for astrology and fortune-telling that he had acquired the Rom girl. She, though, had proved ignorant - a waste of his money. She claimed she could read palms, but was slow to learn any useful language - not that this stopped her gabbling incessantly. She would never make back what he'd spent on her. *Three silver pennies for not having to listen to her shrill voice for a bit... Perhaps the Bailiff will buy her off me, and good riddance.* For Handley found the gypsy girl's charms irresistible, her dark features and oriental allure set her apart. He was not so toothsome, but his bad breath had been cured. His run-in with his mystery assailant in the autumn had done him a favour and now he was as randy as a rutting buck. They would emerge from his room for meals and retire again for another bout of love making, though he was starting to get very sore.

—✳—

'I want everyone to have weapons close by their persons,' Sir Roger instructed the armourer who had just been sent for. 'There is to be extra vigilance at the castle.'

'That's being a bit melodramatic, isn't it?'

'Better safe than sorry, I suppose.'

Mercurius watched these preparations with a rising sense of unease. *Perhaps I should tell my host.* He was so preoccupied with this dilemma that he did not hear Simon's footsteps. The hand on his shoulder made him jump and break out into a cold sweat.

'You gave me quite a start.' He tried to gather his equanimity as quickly as he could.

'I've been watching these preparations going on all day. Do you know what is going on?' Most of the castle, with the exception of Clothilde and, of course, Zuzu, ignored Simon.

Mercurius bit his tongue. Putting an arm round him he said 'No. But how about a drink? I have some good wine in my wagon.'

'I was actually after some warm clothing,' said Simon, who was on the scrounge. The second-hand suit he'd been given was thin and threadbare and he had not been able to feel the ends of his fingers or toes for some days now, so the offer of a drink, too, would help no end. For meals in the hall, he was still placed at the end of the table nearest the door, receiving scraps that would then be given as charity to the parish poor. He had hoped that, with his parole, he would be elevated in status in the dining department as well, but no, his seat remained firmly at the bottom of the food chain. The charcoal brazier in the mummers' wagon brought on a tingling sensation in his extremities and the strong sweet white wine started to produce a pleasant light-headedness. For a palate used to fine wine it was a joy, and a change from the thin, sour beer that the English all seemed to relish.

The drink loosened Mercurius's tongue. 'You must be alert tonight,' he confided. 'There might be some trouble.'

But Simon didn't really care, he hated the English more and more with each passing day, and wanted desperately to get away and back to his beloved France. He was now seriously considering breaking his parole, and aired the subject with his newfound friends. Could they sneak him and Clothilde out of the castle in their wagon when they left? Mercurius had found his unwitting ally in Simon. Giving him the other two-gallon barrel - one Sir Eustace had given him - he told him the price for his escape.

'Get the gatehouse drunk,' Mercurius said conspiratorially. *That way, if Scarface wins, I can say I did my bit.* Rummaging around in a large trunk he came up with a star-covered theatrical cloak that he placed around the shivering Simon's shoulders. 'There, you look like Merlin the Magician. Go work some magic.'

Whytethorne was away from his duty residence, at home with his family in their house in the village. Six men were on gatehouse duty. They had drawn lots and the losers were bemoaning the fact that the Steward had locked his suite of rooms. The Guardroom had no shutters on the yard-side windows or the outer facing arrow embrasures so an icy draft quite negated any heat from their brazier. Dinner had been brought to them before dusk and now they were cold and bored. So when the Frenchman sidled in and revealed his precious cargo, they set about draining it before the Ox returned from his rounds.

John Gwyn was a suspicious man by nature. He liked certainty and the present situation was one that worried him. Sir Roger's coldness towards him of recent months made him think he had gone too far. *I have to get rid of Dan, and then everything will return to the way it was - lifesaver, champion... That's the way it should be.*

The newness of the defences was such that they were untried; their weaknesses were an unknown quantity. There were too many unknowns to give him peace of mind. He saw the Frenchman heading towards the gatehouse, arousing his suspicion, but in the gloom of dusk could not see what he was carrying. As he passed the mummer's wagon, Mercurius intercepted him.

'Just the man,' Mercurius's voice was full of bonhomie. 'Can you help us get this piece of scenery into the hall for tonight's show?' He indicated towards something inside the wagon. As Gwyn lowered his head, a blow from a blackjack rendered him unconscious. Quickly, they bound his arms behind his back and, stuffing a rag in his mouth, they dragged his inert body away and hid it.

The Hall was warm; the fireplace threw out heat and the Yule Log burnt well. After the meal had been cleared, the mummers put on their performance. This play was not as good as the previous ones. Mercurius was not his usual bombastic self and some of the cast fluffed their lines as if nervous. Sir Roger put it down to sobriety. He had not seen Gwyn or Simon and it was usual for his sergeant to report on the watch before he went to bed. He called Justin over.

'Have you seen the Ox?' *Perhaps he's still avoiding me.*

'The last I saw of him he was headed for the gatehouse. I suppose he's still there.' He shrugged his shoulders. Nor had Justin seen Simon, but this was not unusual as the Frenchman had been down in the dumps recently and he assumed he had gone to his bed to keep warm.

Harry put his dagger under his pillow, clutching the hilt as Lady Alice tucked him in. 'Will bad men come tonight?'

'I don't think so,' his mother said soothingly, but she, too, was not so sure. Her husband was lying on top of the bed, quite still and straight, eyes staring up at the ceiling. He was wearing his aketon and chain mail and had his scimitar beside him, his hands in front as if in prayer. Lady Alice let out a gasp.

'You look just like a statue on a tomb.' It was fashionable for knights to be remembered by having their likeness sculpted for the tops of their sarcophaguses. 'Are we really in danger?'

'I think so, otherwise would I be dressed like this?' He got up and kissed her tenderly and then he went over to where the children were snuggled up and kissed them too. *If I'm wrong*, he thought as he returned to the hall, *then I've made a fool of myself - but better safe than sorry.*

He felt for the lead amulet in his purse, having heard Fyscher's story of the strangers he had taken the precaution of bullying the priest into handing over the evil talisman. *I think it's better that I control this cursed object… Where's Gwyn?* He had not reported in. All was quiet. Those who slept in the hall, and there were quite a few, had already made themselves comfortable, and a couple of the troop were playing dice by the light of a guttering candle. He checked all their weapons.

'Have you seen Gwyn?' Again the answer was no. Putting on his cloak, Sir Roger went into the courtyard. In the bright moonlight all was deathly still. The snow crunched under his boots. It was as nearly as bright as day yet there was no colour, he could see the mummers' wagons parked near the gate. A faint choking sound caught his ear. He found his sergeant gagged. Drawing his sword, he deftly cut Gwyn's bonds and, pulling the rag from his mouth, before Gwyn could utter more than a splutter, Sir Roger cautioned him to silence.

'Get your *falchion*, and put everyone on alert- quiet mind, we don't want our enemies to know we're awake,' he whispered. 'I'll see what's up with the gate guards.'

The guardroom was unusually silent, and when he entered he immediately saw why. The six men-at-arms and Simon de Pressi were all lying on the floor. He could not tell whether they were dead or fast asleep. He booted the nearest one and got a grunt but could not rouse him or any of the others; they had been drugged into unconsciousness.

Chapter 53

Camelot Denied

S ir Eustace's mind was made up. It was do or die, he told Falke as he torched Caxton Manor that morning before setting out for Ipers. 'We've passed the point of no return.' *And if that isn't incentive enough...*

He made them carry his grime-covered altar and his collection of black magic paraphernalia from the cellars. The latter joiners of the Sons of King Arthur looked back at the flames and felt a wave of unease; those more sanguine outlaws, who had joined his gang from the Coterels, reckoned Sir Eustace had gone bonkers and decided enough was enough.

'We're going to try and attack a castle - the man's lost his marbles,' said one.

'Sheer folly,' whispered another. Their leader's grandiose ideas were becoming too rich for their blood. 'I think it's time to go home.'

None relished a trudge across the winter-bound countryside, but they'd force themselves on a hamlet here and there, extorting food and warmth with menaces. They were prepared to take their chances elsewhere, and by the time Sir Eustace had reached Ipers, of his ten seasoned outlaws, seven had melted away.

The sun drifted to blood red as Sir Eustace set up his necromancer's altar. Falke's scepticism had waned as success had followed success over the summer months, and he'd conveniently forgotten the bloody nose they'd been given when they were last run out of Ipers. He was now a full convert to the black arts and hoped that Mercurius would fulfil his promise. He'd been given a barrel of wine spiked with a sleeping potion of valerian and poppy juice that he was to give to the gatehouse guards on the night of Holy Innocents.

The Sons had raided a smallholding on the way, stealing a couple of fowl. Beheading the cockerel, Sir Eustace summoned Beelzebub and his army of demons, and he poured powders and potions into a chalice and mixed them with the blood. In the stillness, voices and the sounds of revelry came from the castle.

'Bring the blanket of sleep,' he intoned, inflecting his voice with as much melodrama as possible. 'Sleep. Sleep.' He waved his arms theatrically towards the looming castle. The performance was as much for his men's benefit as anything, but shortly thereafter a quiet *did* descend over the castle.

'See, it works,' Sir Eustace was delighted. 'The silence tells of slumber.' He poured a flask of wine into a chalice and made each man drink, each echoing the toast, 'Camelot Restored!' as they sipped the bitter brew. An early quiet descended.

The spell is working!

'Camelot awaits the arrival of the Sons of King Arthur.' Sir Eustace addressed his men with stirring words. 'All inside will be yours except Lady Guinevere.' This was his name for Lady Alice. 'She's mine.' *I've waited long enough for the red-head.* He slipped into a daydream of the humiliation he would mete out on her before he slit her throat - *preferably in front of that hogtied pig of her husband, too.* He would abuse them and kill them one by one. His fantasies had become more elaborate and now he had them all worked out…. 'And try not to kill the squire,' he said as an afterthought. *I don't want my son's murder on my hands.*

A gibbous moon had arisen fat above the horizon and hung huge over the snowbound village. The stark outline of the castle grew clear, washed in the pale moonlight. The assault parties had several scaling ladders and would come at the castle from different sides. His ruffians were muffled and padded with heavy sheepskin jackets, They stamped their feet ready for action, keen to get into the warmth; they were all very hungry and hoped that some of the feast remained.

'And women too,' chirped Sir Lancelot, who was a runty sort.

'Remember the lady of the manor is not to be harmed.' Sir Eustace looked up at the castle; the moon had turned white. 'Don't kill the actors either- they can entertain us for the rest of winter.' The increasing brightness illuminated every detail of the snow-covered walls with its little turrets; behind he could see the main building, the new hall rising above the old. They waited until the moon was almost above them- still there was only silence. *Praise be, my magic actually works.* Sir Eustace gave the Devil his due as he waved his depleted assault force forward.

Christina sat on the edge of the bed, folded her arms across her chest, and screwed up her face. She turned towards the wall. 'She goes or I go,' she said, nursing her bleeding hand where Zuzu had bitten her. 'I don't care if it freezes to death, I'm not going to spend another night in the same room as that... as that *thing*.' Karelians didn't have a word for ape. She made her feelings clear, shouting while Dan tried desperately to calm her down.

She issued an 'it's her or me' ultimatum. So, with considerable reluctance, Dan took Zuzu out to the corner turret, where he made a nest of rags. Zuzu gave him a pitiful look and hunched up as he closed the door and went back along the snow-covered walkway to the servant's quarters. When he returned, his wife had a triumphant look on her face. She opened her arms and welcomed him into her bosom where he soon lost himself in the sweetness of her embrace.

The turret door, being new, had warped and had not shut properly on the latch. Zuzu pushed her snout into the crack.

Silently, the raiders split into two groups, each with their ladders. Sir Eustace held his trusty Normans back, unlike the outlaws, they had nowhere else to go..

'Let the dross go first,' he told Falke, 'They're expendable.'

The first group scaled the wall near the cells. They had unlit oil-soaked faggot torches with which they would try and fire the thatch.

Zuzu pushed at the turret door - she wanted to follow her master back into the warmth. Her hair had grown thick with winter's onset, making her look similar to a medium-sized shaggy dog. She hated snow; it hurt her paws. She was contemplating what to do next, resigned to the fact that any journey would involve contact with snow, when she saw a shadowy figure climb over the top of the wall, then another and another. She hissed and bared her fangs at the approaching stranger, who had a sword in his hand. Thinking she was a dog the man lunged, and was surprised when the beast leapt vertically into the air and up the wall, emitting an ear-piercing shriek.

Dan heard it and reached for his weapon. He favoured a billhook. 'Hide,' he shouted to Christina as he raced back out onto the parapet and was just in time to see the first faggot torch being placed under the thatch of the old hall. He slashed at the man trying to clamber through the crennelations and, yelling the alarm, pushed the ladder back off the wall with his weapon. The three invaders on the ladder crashed backwards onto the ice and those in the queue to climb fled. Dan turned to confront the figure on the wall. With lighting dexterity learnt from wielding his pilgrim's staff he lunged. *This is the first man I've killed.* Dan felt the blade slam through the man's guts. It was quick and easy and it felt good.

Sir Roger heard it too. Leaving the comatose men, he strode outside and started to ring the iron alarm triangle vigorously. Men grabbed their weapons and sallied into the courtyard from all directions. Chaos reigned. In the flickering firelight figures flitted in and out of buildings. Here and there more fires erupted, but they did not last. The rain of the last few months had soaked the thatch and the recent cold had frozen it solid. As the heat grew in intensity, so the ice melted and the fires fizzled out again.

Handley was so engrossed in the throes of passion that he was only faintly aware of the pandemonium outside. His raven-haired lover had mounted him again. Suddenly the door crashed open and a scythe-wielding bandit burst in. With one sweep he decapitated the gypsy girl, her head bouncing across the floor. A fountain of blood erupted from the severed neck, drenching all around. The man raised his weapon, ready to slash at the immobile Bailiff. The corpse twitched and lurched forward as Handley tried to sit up, desperately scrabbling back toward the corner. His nemesis grinned at his predicament.

'Don't you recognise me?'

It was too dark and Handley was too shocked.

'You had me thrown out of my house. William Wood, William Wood.' He kept repeating his name as he advanced on the terrified Bailiff. *I'll kill him slowly - revenge, sweet revenge.* However, his assailant had not reckoned on the slippery blood covering the floor. His feet went up from under him and he crashed unceremoniously onto his backside.

I remember Wood. He insulted me so I turned him out of his house. This Handley recalled while grabbing a three-legged stool that stood by the bed and getting to his feet. *I took his cow before having him and his wife chased out of the village.* The Bailiff resolutely smashed Wood in the face, catching him in the mouth as he struggled to regain his footing. Involuntarily he dropped his scythe as he reeled back, teeth shattered. The Bailiff found his dagger, plunging it with all his might into the man's neck; he felt the point go through gristle and bone as the body went limp. Pulling up his braes he groped around for his boots. They and he were wet with still warm blood. He sneaked into the kitchens, where he failed to dodge Max, who came up behind and felled him with a blow from a heavy frying pan.

'Oh shit,' said Max when he realised whom he had just rendered unconscious.

Those of the country bumpkins-turned-outlaw that had managed to get over the wall before Dan's timely intervention proved no match for the Castle's garrison. The shock of the cold had swept away any cobwebs of sleep as they hurriedly assembled after Gwyn's first frantic bellows. One group was soon isolated and cornered by the pigsty. The sweeping of Gwyn's *falchion* reduced their numbers as a reaper cuts into ripe corn; several severed hands flew into the air. Those that remained dropped to their knees, pleading for their lives. Dan had followed and noticed that one had evaded capture. The marauder was poised to strike the Sergeant from behind, but the Shrimp's timely shout alerted the Ox who swivelled and beheaded the bandit with a sweeping blow. He waved his acknowledgement and thanks.

Master John heard the commotion from his cell. He lit his candle and sneaked up the stairs into the solar, overcome by greed. He felt sure that Sir Roger had placed the bag with the gold coins in his strongbox near his desk. In the confusion he decided to pinch a few, enough to cover the weight of the lead amulet. *If Fyscher wants its weight in gold.* He rummaged through the papers, looking for the key. *I know it's here somewhere, I saw him putting it…*

He found it under the tattered hymnal.

—ᴡᴡ—

Sir Eustace waited on the top of the wall above Lady Alice's snow-covered rose garden; from there he could see figures trying to fire outbuildings. Here and there a blaze had caught hold, at the workshops and armoury on the compound's far side, diverting the garrison's attention. Even though the element of surprise was lost, he signalled his Normans forward. It would be do or die. Shouts and screams echoed in the crystal stillness of the night.

'We can still carry the night,' he told Falke as he joined him on the wall with his Normans, who were veterans of campaigning in Scotland and Gascony, and masters of larceny on highways and byways; nothing like the peasants he had persuaded to become the 'Sons of King Arthur'. 'We'll kidnap as many women as we can find and take them with us.'

They sidled undetected towards the lookout tower, carrying an iron-tipped log ram. *I want the red-head.* His eyes were ablaze with hatred. *She's the one I'm after.* He didn't care about the rest.

—ᴡᴡ—

Sir Roger hurried to where his Sergeant had cornered a sorry group of ill-armed raiders. A cursory glance revealed no one of consequence.

He collared his knights and raced back inside, taking stock. Candles and torches were hastily relit. By their guttering yellow light at first he could see nothing untoward. Dice were still on the table, the room seemed empty. Then a face peered out from underneath a table. Slowly, as the light dispelled the gloom, more people were revealed. In all the corners, backs to the walls, were a huddle of servants. Max, Edgar and William, scullery boys and assorted womenfolk were holding a pathetic selection of carving knives, brooms and cutlery. Frantically, he scanned their faces: his wife and children were not there.

Shouts came from the kitchen as Handley, consciousness recovered, burst in breathlessly, covered in blood, eyes rolling and yelling maniacally. He stood stock still at the sight of Sir Roger and went silent, mouthing words that would not form. He stared blankly at him for a full five seconds before racing off like a demon out of the hall, slipping on the top stair and bumping all the way down to the courtyard, where he sat immobile in his pain and anguish.

Somewhere in the distance they heard a faint thud, then another and another. Everyone held their breath.

'Tower door' shouted Sir Roger, galvanised into action, scimitar in hand.

It had taken three swings of the ram to break the hinges on the Tower door. The passage was dark but for a faint glow from the solar. Sir Eustace peered in and saw the candle on the desk and made out the kneeling figure of Master John. Falke crept by, stealthy as a cat, and grabbed the monk by the scruff of the neck. Sir Eustace struck him with a single stabbing blow with his *poignard*, through the temple, piercing the Chaplain's brain. Between him and Falke they had perfected this method of killing. It was quick, silent and for those who watched, quite shocking. He wiped the needle blade on his sleeve and listened.

Above his head, floorboards creaked. Silently, Sir Eustace pointed towards the ceiling.

'Hold the staircase,' he ordered his men quietly, voice redolent with malice. 'I have business upstairs.' He turned back into the solar; something on the desk had caught his eye. The bag of gold coins was spilled across the desk. *So you were stealing your master's money, were you?* He kicked the body on the floor and picked up the bag, scooping the rest of the coins into it before putting it into his waistband pouch.

—m—

Worrisome screams and cries percolated up into the bedchamber where Lady Alice, Nunny, Harry and Isabel had taken refuge. Isabel whimpered as, with rising horror, they heard the thuds on the Tower door. Alert to this new danger, Lady Alice whispered for Nunny to go and warn those below, but she was too late.

As she reached the top of the spiral stairs a spear point was enough to make her faint. A heavy blow from the shaft ensured continued unconsciousness.

Harry slipped away from his mother's skirts and hid under the bed. There he slid his new dagger from its sheath and gripped it tight. He should have felt scared but, remembering his father's words, he knew that he must become a knight.

Lady Alice was glad of the new coat her husband had so thoughtfully bought her for Christmas, she felt the one child leave; Isabel remained clinging to her leg. She thought about hiding but it was too late. Falke was upon her, spear point levelled at her belly. In the lamplight, he could see her red hair. This was the prize Sir Eustace wanted above all else. He grabbed the child and dragged her away from her mother.

'Be silent!' The tip of Falke's dagger drew a bead of blood from the little girl's throat. 'Now we wait.'

They searched the other rooms along the corridor, dragging out Clothilde and Beatrice, and since no one else was found he signalled to three of his men off to find Sir Eustace.

'Falke's found the bitch,' hissed one of the men as he caught up with his master. This was sweet music to Sir Eustace's ears and he left off, instructing his men to secure the hall. As he climbed the spiral staircase, he sheathed his *poignard* and licked his lips in anticipation.

'Let's take her and go,' urged Falke nervously. Already he could hear Sir Roger's men fighting their way up the stairs. But Sir Eustace was not listening. Reason had departed and he had removed his helm and gloves. *My men can hold a spiral stair for hours if need be,* he thought, mistakenly as it happened - his men were so muffled against the cold that they had misheard his order.

'I'm going to rape her first,' he said, grabbing his victim by the hair and dragging her backwards, ripping off her coat. By the light of the single lantern, held high by Falke, Lady Alice could see his hate filled face, livid scar and lopsided grin. She screamed with all her might.

'Scream and scream, I like a screamer.' Two men grabbed her hands and dragged her over to the bed, pulling her clothing over her head. Sir Eustace admired the writhing exposed triangle of her sex. He lifted his mail shirt - he would plant his seed first.

From under the bed, Harry could only see feet, booted and armoured, as they dragged his mother above him. He remembered what his father had said while they watched the corpse dangling on the rope, maggots feasting on its pecked eye sockets. *'Be brave, little soldier, fear not Death, only a coward fears death. Defend the weak and the women.'*

Holding that thought, dagger held firmly, he rolled out from under the bed. At the same time Sir Eustace, his penis pulsing and erect, advanced towards his struggling mother, pinned and vulnerable. With an upward sweep, Harry plunged his razor sharp blade up to its hilt through Sir Eustace's scrotum.

At this same moment, his father burst through the door and it was as if time stood still. Everyone froze where they stood. For Sir Eustace the pain was overwhelming and he could do no more than clutch at the dagger hilt in his blood-squirting crotch.

Falke reacted first, dropping the lantern, plunging the room into darkness. In the confusion that followed, he grabbed Lady Alice's Vair cape, which was lying on the bed, before leaping through the closed window, landing on a snow-covered lean-to roof. He slunk away, keep-ing to the shadows. He slid back over the wall and ran across the moat.

In the distance, on the other side of the compound, fire raged out of control. He reached the horses, climbed on the best and took the rest before vanishing into the night.

By the light of more candles and lamps, Sir Roger took control. Sir Eustace's life was ebbing away through the severed arteries of his groin. Sir Roger stood over his fallen enemy.

'Who betrayed me?' He reached down and hauled the dying man upright so he could look into his face. He had one final question for his enemy. 'Who told you the secret of my fortune?'

'Gwyn. It was John Gwyn,' whispered Sir Eustace with a great effort. 'I got him drunk and he told me.'

Sir Roger reached into his purse and took out the lead-encased amulet containing Godfrey's semen, waving it in front of his eyes. 'Recognise this?' It's your curse,' he growled, before pushing it into Sir Eustace's mouth with such force that his front teeth broke. 'You can give that to the Devil when you meet him.' Hatred gleamed in Sir Eustace's eyes as he flailed about, choking on the egg-sized object. Sir Roger removed Sir Eustace's head with one sweeping blow from the scimitar, leaving his corpse pumping blood from the stump of his neck. Seeing no harm had befallen Alice, who was being comforted by her maids, he picked up Harry and Isabel, who were shivering and shaking from shock. Kicking the severed head in front of him, he carried his sobbing children out of the room. The other two men surrendered without further fight.

—◊—

A brooding melancholy descended on the hall. The fire was stoked up, and the yuletide log crackled back to life. From his dais the lord of the manor, now wrapped in his vanquished foe's wolf fur cloak, was deep in thought. He had also found his gold in Sir Eustace's pouch. Before him were the remnants of the Sons of King Arthur. Half a dozen were seasoned fighters, the rest peasants and twelve corpses. They had found two at the bottom of the ladder - one with a broken back, the other with smashed legs; both were killed on the spot. Eight more had fled across the snow, got lost and had been rounded up after being discovered cowering in the Ash Store. Whytethorne had locked them in Simon's old cell.

Sir Roger had his chair moved to the fireside and he stared into the flames, taking a child onto each knee, Lady Alice by his side in her chair. Together they sat in silence, oblivious to the rest of the servants and soldiery that busied themselves tidying up the mess left by the raiders. From time to time, Whytethorne intruded into their space to whisper a further report into his master's ear.

'I want this scum to sing, like blackbirds in spring.'

The knotty problem of the sleeping guards preyed on his mind. One had died, choking on his own vomit. The others could remember nothing except for Simon coming in with the cask. Mercurius and some mummers had tried to leave at dawn, bearing the corpse of the gypsy girl, saying they needed to give her a Christian burial, but their way was barred. Sir Roger had ordered that the drawbridge was to be lowered for no one.

He knew Simon was lying, his excuse fatuous. Saying he had found the barrel and had felt it a shame if it should go to waste on such a chilly evening was flimsy. But Sir Roger had other plans for *Monsieur* de Pressi.

Eventually his children dropped off to sleep and were carried back to their beds. He took Alice in his arms and they hugged, but she felt ashamed for her nakedness and dirty, even though she had not been raped. She tore herself away. She wanted to run to the bedroom, but the memory was too raw, so she had the servants heat water for a bath – something she, too, had come to appreciate. With the last of Eccles's soap, she scrubbed herself clean.

A ragged line of prisoners were lined up in the courtyard, both alive and dead.

'You will suffer as I have suffered,' shouted Sir Roger in fury as, by the cold light of day, he strode around and surveyed the damage to his castle. 'My falcons have been burnt to death, my wife near ravaged, my sanctuary violated.' He circled Sir Eustace's headless corpse, which lay naked and white at his feet except for a brown stain between his legs. From time to time he would give it another kick as he surveyed the desperate men who had invaded his domain. He would make an example of them. They would not hang like common criminals.

'Build a fire on the moat.' He ordered a big pile of brushwood and logs soaked in pitch and lamp oil to be placed in the centre of the ice.

A table, chairs and a brazier were taken out and placed in the snow opposite the gatehouse.

'Strip them,' Sir Roger ordered as they were made to kneel. 'They can get warm in front of the fire.' All the time he watched. 'That one!' He selected one at random. The guards dragged the man, still on his knees, to the edge of the table.

'What's your name?'

'Lancelot,' came the meek reply. A guffaw echoed of the walls, for this was no paragon of manliness.

'So tell me, *Sir* Lancelot, who betrayed me?' His eyes swept the rest of the prisoners. Casually he let his gaze fall on Mercurius, and he thought he could see a slight flush come over his cheeks. 'Come closer, Lancelot of the Lake, put out your hand.' The unfortunate put out his hand with trepidation. 'Now tell me again, who betrayed us?'

'I don't know.' His voice cracked with anxiety. The Ox grabbed the outstretched hand and rapped it onto the table. The man winced with pain at the cracking of his knuckles.

'Pin it.'

With a grin widening on his face, Gwyn looked at his victim. 'You're going to enjoy this.' He chuckled as he nailed a leather belt to the table, over the wrist and nailed again so the hand was palm side up. By now the man was gibbering inconsequential rubbish.

'I swear I only joined the band recently.' He tried protesting his innocence. 'I am a decent fellow with a wife and three children.'

'Start again, from the beginning,' said Whytethorne, who was making notes. 'What is your real name?'

'John Cadnam.' He came from a village close-by. 'He made us pick the names of King Arthur's knights.' He pointed with his free hand at Sir Eustace's head, which lay in front of him. 'He said that after we had captured your castle we would all get a virgate of land.'

'So you became Sir Lancelot?'

The fellow nodded as he remembered, bitterly, and regretted heartily his decision to pick such a name.

'In that case, step forward Sir Bedevere, Sir Kay.' Sir Roger named half a dozen of King Arthur's knights at random. Three captives tried to rise and were dragged to the long table; their right hands were strapped down, leather cutting into each wrist so they could not move. Picking one, he pointed to the brazier that stood by his chair. Gwyn picked up a hot coal with a pair of tongs. The man tried to close his fist but the heat of the coal made it open involuntarily. Gwyn dropped the glowing coal onto the palm and pressed it in, where it sizzled - the smell was reminiscent of roast pork. The wretch screamed and screamed, writhing in pain, but could not move as a man-at-arms stood on his calves.

Sir Roger watched his Sergeant, who was obviously enjoying his work, oblivious of the accusation made by the dying Sir Eustace. *What am I to do with you? He got you drunk and you spilled the beans.* The betrayal weighed heavily on his mind. *Alexander wept for three days from remorse after killing Clytus.* Would he do the same? He didn't know.

The same procedure was carried out on the other four men. Again Sir Roger glanced at Mercurius, still unsure as to what his role in this fiasco had been. The bellows of pain drowned out any real confessions, but he had a shrewd idea that only the veterans knew the truth. These, he noted, did not have any concocted airs or Arthurian pseudonyms. He examined the rest of the kneeling men, separating serfs from soldiers.

For Mercurius, the pressure was becoming intolerable. He knew that it was now only a matter of time before a confession would seal his fate. He had tried to maintain his sang-froid but he cracked. He would try and bluster it out. He rushed forward and prostrated himself at Sir Roger's feet.

'By all the saints have mercy,' he whined. 'He said that he wanted to give you a surprise gift; he said he was one of your retinue. I believed him. He was supposed to contact me so I thought I should do something to help him, otherwise he would kill us along with the rest of you. I didn't know the wine was drugged. I didn't mean for any of your men to die.' And so Mercurius blabbered on, telling of the fateful meeting on the road from Nottingham, only hoping that he would not pay the ultimate penalty for his greed and folly. 'I have abused your hospitality most grievously.' There was little now to save his hide. 'He paid us ten marks to come and entertain you.' It was the mention of money that saved his life, the eternal commodity for which men bartered their soul; that, and the fact that Dan pleaded for his life.

'Forgive my rudeness Sire.' Dan knew he was speaking out of turn, but he couldn't see a man who had been friends with his father killed. It hadn't been Mercurius's fault that Sir Eustace had fooled him. Sir Roger stayed his hand.

'I will have all your money and more. Henceforth, when the hat is passed round, my man will take it all. Now dress yourself.' He would provide a pittance for their expenses and food and drink, the rest would be recompense for damages. 'Take his wagon apart,' Sir Roger ordered, 'plank by plank, we'll see what's hidden there.'

And thus Mercurius's tidy stash was revealed. It was enough fill Sir Roger's purse, but not for long.

'I do confess to having enjoyed his performances!' he told Dan later. *He makes me laugh, unlike pompous Master John.* He found the Chaplain condescending and deeply irritating to boot. 'Where is the Chaplain?' he asked, 'has anyone seen him?'

His body was found in the solar, hand still inside the strongbox.

Sir Roger had heard enough, their guilt was plain. He mounted his horse and taking Gwyn's whip, started to herd the naked men in front of him.

'This will teach you to ride under false colours,' he shouted as he cracked the rawhide mercilessly into the Norman's backs, making each one kneel down and kiss his banner before chasing them over the drawbridge. 'Now, light the brushwood,' he ordered, watching the first torch being tossed onto the oil-soaked mixture of gorse and fag-gots topped off with Sir Eustace's altar and kit, which had been found nearby. The prisoners watched in terror as the brushwood crackled. Yellow flames licked hungrily at the oil and soon there was a roaring blaze. A howling mob of villagers had gathered to see the end of the Sons of King Arthur.

The outlaws were pushed onto the ice with pikes and spears by cir-cling soldiers while the crowd hooted with derision and hurled insults. Scullery boys, with ropes tied around their waists, had been armed with whippy sticks that they wielded with dexterity, driving the naked men towards the roaring fire, their bodies blue with cold and red from flames. Some tried to draw away, but were forced back.

It did not take long for the fire's heat to weaken the ice and the combined weight of doomed men did the rest, preceded by a crack-ing sound that echoed like distant summer thunder. The skittering youths were pulled to safety as the ice broke, and as it did so the frozen men slipped inexorably to a watery grave as they and the fire plunged together under the moat's icy waters, where they were swallowed up with a hissing of steam.

'I have truly seen Hell on Earth,' said Fyscher, who had been mum-bling prayers for the sinners, holding his crucifix aloft as he watched the whole ghastly spectacle. There had been no confessions, no abso-lution, no souls saved. He looked intently at Sir Roger and shook his head from side to side. Now he'd seen it all. He'd often wondered what the Gates of Hell looked like. *Now I know. It'll be easy to keep my flock faithful; the devil has shown me, oh yes, the devil has shown me.*

No one mourned for Master John, dying with his hand in Sir Roger's strongbox, undone by his greed. Along with the gypsy girl and the drunken guard, they had been the only casualties. A few others had suffered cuts and bruises. And there was also the small matter of the one who got away. Alfred set out with dogs and a band of hobelars; it would be some time before they returned.

Chapter 54

The Price of Treachery

F alke wrapped the stolen cape around his shoulders; even though it was not made for a man of his size, the extra protection it afforded against the cold was most welcome. From his vantage point high up in a tree he shivered, watched and waited. He would still have to find shelter before nightfall or face freezing to death. Cold and frightened horses had proved harder to handle than expected, and he had abandoned them after five miles, setting them free, chasing them in different directions, hoping their aimless wandering in search of food would confuse anyone trying to follow.

He had become hopelessly lost during his flight from the castle. The snow-covered forest at night was a harsh, unforgiving place. Familiar features and landmarks were all hidden and he could only guess at where he was. He wondered what had happened to his comrades, but for now his own survival was at stake. He could hear voices as horsemen with hunting dogs spread out through the wood, hot on his trail. In the distance he could see a single plume of smoke rising high in the stillness.

He was right about dispersing the horses - his pursuers spent hours rounding them up.

'Take them back to the castle,' said Alfred loudly, wanting to signal his intentions clearly. He had a strong hunch that his quarry would head for Caxton, but the tracks in the snow told a different story.

'There are no more tracks,' one of his men reported.

It nagged Alfred that his quarry should thus elude him. *He must be hiding somewhere near about.* He had made an almost too ostentatious show of returning to the castle and now he, too, waited silently. Beast or man, his pride dictated that he did not come home empty handed. He tried to think what his prey would do: porcines were the hardest and most irrational; deer were easier to read; and men were usually predictable. He went back to the release point and studied the ground. He had made sure that his men had not returned by the same route, not wanting to obscure any sign that might aid his trap. Getting off his horse, he backtracked along the main path. Sure enough, amongst the jumble of hoof prints, one set had deliberately doubled back. He turned quickly and made a wide loop through virgin snow before cutting back into the trail. He reasoned that the other horses, when freed, had not wandered more than a few hundred yards, so his quarry would have hidden his mount close by. It took him an hour to find it. The only tell-tale sign was where snow had been dislodged from a holly bush - a cloak must have brushed the leaves, leaving them shiny and dark. He slid gently behind a snowdrift that had formed on a low branch and waited.

Falke slid back down the trunk and tried to get his bearings. The sun had gone, replaced by iron-grey clouds. His horse was tethered in a thicket some way back and he hoped that it had not been found. He had ridden one of the spares to the release point, all the time looking out for a suitable overhanging branch. This he had grabbed, hauling himself up and climbing on to safety. *In my experience, hunters rarely look upward for their quarry.*

Alfred did not have to wait long. The lone figure furtively followed the track back the way he had come. Alfred knocked a deer-killing arrow into his short hunting bow, a beautiful composite that had been traded from the East, designed for using from horseback. It was also exceptionally powerful. He believed it had belonged to an oriental nobleman from the inlaid ivory swirling that he presumed was writing - he could not read, whatever the alphabet. His master had given it to him as a gift, but where he had got it from he did not know.

Alfred contemplated whether to try and kill with the first arrow or just maim. Either way, the only trophy he sought would be the head. The man drew close now, nervously scanning the path.

Falke knew his horse was close. A whinny and a snort revealed where, and with a sense of relief that this part of his ordeal was nearly over, he straightened up. His bladder had been full for some time, so he pulled his cape back and flicked it over his shoulder. He was just taking off his gloves when he heard a faint noise, and with an expression of surprise staggered back as an arrow buried itself in him up to the fletching, piercing his heart as it did so. His knees buckled and he crumpled to the ground.

Alfred let out a hissing sigh of satisfaction. A grin played across his lips as he put the Vair cape over his shoulders. It fitted well. *No one gets the better of me,* he thought, as he used his skinning knife to remove the head. The look of surprise remained frozen on Falke's face. All attackers accounted for.

—ɯ—

Sir Roger sat on the edge of the bed, lost for words as Lady Alice fought back another bout of tears, still traumatised from the attack. She had nearly suffocated when Sir Eustace's men pulled her clothes over her head. Even though no harm had actually befallen her, she had continual nightmares and could not sleep for fear that they would return. Her husband was tongue-tied - what could he say? The ways of women were a mystery, so he gave what comfort he could and changed the subject.

'What am I going to do about my Sergeant?' He told her about the betrayal. She wiped away the last tear that had made it half way down her cheek.

'He's been your faithful sergeant for eight years now, saved your life at least once, and now you want to kill him.' She became her old fiery self, the one that talked sense. 'Even you can't do that.' *And you'll kill anyone at the drop of a hat,* she thought, *you have no compunction about consigning souls to the hereafter.* 'Even you,' she said it again. 'He was drunk for Christ's sake. How often do you say things you shouldn't when you are drunk? It sounds as if Sir Eustace did it deliberately - forced it out of him. There's been enough killing for one Christmas.' She made it clear that the conversation was over as she took out her embroidery bag and called for her ladies.

—⟋⟍—

Simon and the Ox stood nervously outside the Steward's rooms. His master and Whytethorne had been closeted together for a goodly time, and try as they might they could not hear what was being said behind the closed doors. Eventually the summons came, the Ox first. The men sat stony faced. A drawn dagger lay on the table, pointing towards an empty stool.

'Sit,' said Whytethorne, peremptorily. He drew in his breath as if waiting for a lead from Sir Roger, who sat glowering, hands together as if in prayer, fingers splayed, touching the bridge of his nose.

'You are accused of betraying your master.' He let the words sink in. 'Betrayal of your oath is punishable by death, you know that.'

Gwyn thought hard, trying to understand what had just been said.

'I would never do that,' he protested loudly, 'never, never, never.'

'But you did, when you were drunk.' Sir Roger cut in. 'You told Sir Eustace about the Jews' money.' He watched this information sink in. 'I should hang you for that.'

Gwyn went as white as a sheet, swallowing hard, trying to bring saliva into his dry throat as he waited for sentence to be passed.

'But I won't. You saved my life then, I haven't forgotten. Now I'm going to spare yours. The debt is expunged. I no longer owe you any-thing. You are dismissed from my service.' Sir Roger took out a leather bag, into which he had put eight of the marks that Sir Eustace had given Mercurius. He laid the coins on the table, pushing them across to the flabbergasted Ox. 'One for each year of service.'

'Count yourself lucky,' said Whytethorne quietly. 'I would have seen you swing.'

Simon's turn was next. He drew in his breath and approached the table. 'I can explain some. I am afraid Mercurius duped me into being

his accomplice.' He drew himself up and tried to be as disingenu-
ous as possible. 'He tricked me, he said that you had told him to give
the guards something to drink as it was so cold and I believed him.
Honestly, I did not know the drink was a sleeping draft.'

This much was true; Sir Roger had found him as fast asleep as
the rest. But he sat, stony-faced, and let the silence get uncomfortable
before rising and indicating that Simon should follow.

'Guillaume,' Sir Roger had made up his mind. 'I have something to
show you, come with me.'

They found Dan in the hall.

'Come,' he said, 'we have to talk to Monsieur de Bapaume about
his ransom.'

Simon looked surprised as Sir Roger put on the wolf fur. Dan was
already wrapped up.

'Come along, hurry, no time to waste.' He chivvied Simon, who
was still ill-equipped for the cold. 'Here, here's a blanket.'

They marched off into the snow, past the village, until they got to
the edge of the marsh before sliding down through the gully and onto
the concealed causeway. The standing stones were plastered with snow,
but the wind had kept their bloody points clear. The skulls in the trees
stood out - antlers, horns and tusks revealed in macabre relief. Simon
could not fathom the meaning of this place but felt afraid. *Is he going
to sacrifice me?*

'Guillaume's ransom has been paid,' said Sir Roger rather flatly.
'One hundred brand new golden florins stolen from the English royal
exchequer, no less.' Alarm crossed Simon's face as Sir Roger drew his
scimitar, which he had concealed under his cloak. He brought the tip
up to Simon's throat.

'So Guillaume de Bapaume is free to go. But not you.' He watched
Simon swallow nervously, his Adam's apple rising onto the sword
point. 'Take off your blanket,' he ordered sharply, 'and kneel.'

Simon sank to his knees, most fearful, his teeth chattering, his eyes
filling with tears.

'You are not Guillaume de Bapaume, are you? Your real name is
Simon.' He let the name sink in. 'Simon de Pressi, I believe.'

He nodded dumbly.

'That little cunt of Admiral Toad's able lieutenant...'

Shock and fear were in Simon's eyes as he nodded. The knight before him even knew his master's nickname.

'And there has been no ransom demand for him,' continued Sir Roger. 'Do you remember the traitor's heads? Now I'll tell you what will happen. We're going to stand here and watch as you freeze to death. It shouldn't take long. I can see you are going blue already.'

Simon was starting to feel light headed. 'Anything, I'll do anything.'

'Do you remember how you told me that you had never sworn your oath to any king? Then you will swear your Oath of Allegiance, the one you never did, on this cross.' He pointed to the rough wooden crucifix. 'To me and to King Edward of England. You will forswear your loyalty to France or freeze to death in this miserable and accursed place. There is no hallowed ground here to take your body, there is no priest to hear your confession, and you will die unshriven.' He pointed to the half-hidden boar's head. 'This place is the gateway to Satan's realm. You belong to King Edward and to England. Oh, I didn't tell you,' and now Sir Roger made it up, 'I sold you to him. He said he'll make a place for your head on Traitor's Gate if the body was not prepared to come too.'

And so a frozen Simon de Pressi put his hands under Sir Roger's mantle where he found a book he took to be a bible and swore his oaths. The matter of honour had been resolved. The two men kissed. *So help me God, I really am now a traitor to France.* It was Simon's last thought, unable to make any rational conjectures as the cold robbed him of his powers.

They dragged his half-frozen form, fingers and face blue, back to the Manor.

'Don't be so miserable,' said Sir Roger as Simon warmed up in front of the fire, a broken man. 'You will marry Clothilde, I know you bedded her.'

But Simon did not care. His world had been shattered. He would no longer see his beloved wardrobe of fine and fancy clothes, or spend his fortune, or buy back his family's lands. His first and only adventure had become his living nightmare.

Lady Alice was sitting quietly, unnoticed in the minstrel's gallery, and watched as her husband had dumped Simon by the fire. *What hideous torture has my brutish husband inflicted on his parolee?* Then she thought she heard 'marry Clothilde'. *This concerns me; Clothilde is mine, and not my husband's to give away.* She appeared out of the gloom.

'What have you done to the poor man? He's half dead.'

'I want you to meet my new vassal. Simon de Pressi.' Sir Roger told her of the King's letter. 'I know,' he said, 'I should have asked you if he could marry your lady-in-waiting, I'm sorry.'

He wasn't, and she knew it, but gave her consent anyway. Nunny had already told her that Clothilde had confided that she thought she was pregnant with Simon's child.

'I suppose I should tell Clothilde. I don't know whether she'll be pleased or not.' She, too, had been lied to. 'So what other surprises have you got for me?'

Sir Roger only nodded. No more surprises, he promised.

Later that evening, Simon found Clothilde in the maids' bedchamber. She gave him a quizzical look when he asked if she understood. She smiled at him so sweetly and said that she might have fallen in love with Guillaume but she could love Simon too. 'I understand you had to do it for France, there is no dishonour in that.'

'Yes, but now that bastard has made me a traitor,' he said angrily. 'Worse than that, he's made me an Englishman. I feel as if he has taken my manhood and chopped it off.'

They snuggled together for warmth under a pile of blankets, where she reached down, seizing his member.

'Then I'd better revive it.' Clothilde would do anything to escape from this dismal country.

'That's not what I meant. I mean I don't want to force you to marry me just because they say so.'

'No, I know what you meant. I too would be loyal to France if I had the choice. You cannot imagine how awful life has been amongst these English sheep-lovers.' And she wriggled herself onto his hard-ened shaft. *'Je t'aime.* We'll make French children. You never know, with another King as your master we might do well.'

Maybe there will be a golden future. After all I am Simon de Pressi, the peacock will rise again. No, he thought. *No more the peacock, but the Phoenix!*

Chapter 55

A Bitter Farewell

'Dead. Dead. Dead. Vanished without trace. Sent to the Tower. Dead.' The merchant Eccles sat opposite Prior Hugh as he placed a line of notched tally sticks on the refectory table. He had finally rescued them from the ruins of his house. He picked each one up and examined it in the candlelight, trying to make out the names.

'Here we are, this one's alive and well and no doubt living in luxury.' Even after all the rain, it was possible to discern the name 'de Bohun' on it. 'Can I borrow a horse? I think I'll pay him a visit and collect what's left of my money.'

Now I'll make you eat humble pie. His diligence had finally paid off. After months of scrabbling and digging he had found the proof of Sir Roger's debt. It had been a lonely Christmas without his family. He had devoted himself to praying for the souls of his murdered family and friends. *Except Mary still lives.* He thought about trying to find her. *No she is gone, my angel has been snatched away and will never return.* He wept again.

Eccles found it hard going to reach Ipers. The journey, which normally took a couple of hours, took him most of the day. His mount slipped and slid and often, on the iciest patches, he had to dismount and lead his horse. Above the gatehouse, crows and kites argued over scraps of flesh pecked off severed heads that graced spikes on the battlements. One had a strange, metallic glint in its mouth; another had a shocked expression on its frozen features.

'I've come to see Sir Roger. Is he home?' Eccles stated his business to the porter. A gaily-coloured wagon lay in bits. Here and there dark brown-red stains discoloured patches of ice. He could see scorch marks where, unsuccessfully, the raiders had tried to fire the hall. *Perhaps I was wrong about the luxury*, he thought as he surveyed the burned and blackened buildings.

'Eccles, my good fellow, how pleasant to see you.' Handley greeted him at the top of the stairs. 'Watch out, they're exceeding slippery.'

It had taken three days for Handley to recover his powers of speech. The Bailiff was much changed; the shock of his experience had altered his demeanour. He had hardly eaten and, most noticeably, had not persecuted a soul. The slightest unusual noise made him flinch.

They found Sir Roger in his solar, staring out of the window. Eccles had mulled over in his mind what he was going to say on his journey from the Priory, but now it seemed inappropriate.

'I suppose you've come for your money.' Sir Roger was forthright as the merchant produced his half stick. He told Eccles about the attack. 'It was that monkey that saved us, the one we got from the Venetian. Who'd have thought it? Sorry business this,' he said, telling him of the end of the Sons of King Arthur. He took out the leather bag of leopard florins, now augmented with the money they'd found in the mummers' wagon. 'A debt's a debt.' Sir Roger produced a handful of gold coins. Already this money had been stolen twice, and he suspected that it would be stolen several times more before its time was up. 'Haven't got much silver. What are these worth?'

The merchant had come prepared and produced a set of weighing scales and a few weights from his purse. They could only go by the weight. Eccles argued for five, the knight stuck at seven and in the end they deciding these gold florins had a nominal value equivalent to six shillings worth of sterling silver. They bargained for over an hour, or, to be precise, four beakers of mediocre wine, and settled on ten shiny coins.

They took the two halves of the tally sticks, and matched them up. They placed them with due ceremony on the brazier that warmed the solar, and watched as they crackled into flame, the debt expunged.

'How are your sheep?' asked Eccles. Business was business; he had to start again.

'Murrain has taken over half and the rest are starving to death,' Sir Roger said sadly. What sheep they had recovered had been brought in suffering from the wetness of November and, in the subsequent cold, lesions had appeared in their mouths and blisters around their hoofs. They were wasting away and dying in droves. What had seemed such a good investment, when he had talked over the whole business with William Pole, had turned into a financial disaster. Fewer than a thousand remained and he was worried that not many of these would make it to spring. *So I didn't really lie to the Sheriff.*

'I'm leaving for Flanders as soon as I can, and I don't know when I'll return.' Sir Roger summoned Edgar. 'Bring more wine, my very best!'

He and Eccles reminisced about happier times, before the arrival of the dreadful Genoese.

'They took Mary - I saw them lead her off. I'm sure she's still alive.' Eccles often tried to imagine her fate, placed on the auction block and sold into slavery or worse, thrown into a Genoese brothel. 'If only I could see her again, I'd give anything to get her back.' *How rosy life was only a few months ago.* A comfortable future that had seemed so secure had now turned into ash and death. 'Back to square one!' he said ruefully.

'And I have to go to war again,' said Sir Roger, nodding in agreement.

'I'll buy your sheep,' said Eccles. 'Five florins for the lot.'

Lady Alice heard laughter and came in to find her husband and Eccles getting seriously drunk.

'Well, someone sounds happy!' she said to Nunny as she retreated back up to her chambers. The ineffable Nunny had come up with a potion for her mistress's depression and now she was almost feeling herself again. Nunny had wept silently to herself at the loss of her book, burned in the turret; it was her last link with her mother. She consoled herself that she had memorised every page. *One day I'll get hold of some paper and try and write it all down again.*

The following morning Sir Roger was irritated. His head hurt after he and Eccles had consumed, by the Pantler's reckoning, a gallon of wine.

'I wish I'd never heard of bloody sheep. Bloody trouble, bloody sheep,' he grizzled to himself as he stomped around, quelling faction fighting that had broken out between members of his troop and the constables. He confirmed the rumour of his impending departure.

'I'm going to miss my Ox,' he told Whytethorne.

'You're better off without him,' the Steward said, trying to be conciliatory. 'Consider that chapter of your life closed.'

The Steward, too, had made up his mind. His new master didn't vacillate, was direct in his actions and spoke plainly, and was an astute leader of men, *deserving of his square pennant.* He had been unsure at the beginning, but in giving Gwyn eight marks, Sir Roger had shown his true nature. *That was the proper Christian thing to do.*

'Don't worry, I'll get the castle repaired and make sure your family is safe,' Whytethorne promised.

That's the Venetian's money spent, and the ransom's dwindled fast.

By the end of the week, Sir Roger had relented. Going to war without his Sergeant would be… *like a woman not covering her head in public.* It was unthinkable.

'I have to go, it's my duty,' Sir Roger told his wife.

'Parliament convenes again in two weeks and I have to attend.' From there, he would go straight to Flanders and sell Simon to the King. For the last week his messengers had visited all the surrounding manors, begging and borrowing equipment. De Palton lent him a campaign cot, worm-eaten but serviceable. De Bokland had an old tent, and the ladies spent many hours sewing patches over moth holes. Prior Hugh had some battered valises, salvaged from Southampton.

'I don't want Clothilde's child born out of wedlock,' said Lady Alice firmly. 'Let's get him married before you go. She's definitely having his child.' *We've got enough bastards around here.* 'It will just add one more link to his chain.' *Which is how it should be.* And so it was, on the Sunday before their departure, Simon de Pressi married Clothilde.

'I want you to have this,' said Mercurius, removing a golden chain from around his neck on which hung an exquisite rock crystal pendant containing brown powder. 'This is the blood of St. John the Baptist,' he explained in reverential tones. It was his most valuable possession. 'It was collected from the very salver that held the Baptist's head that was presented to King Herod himself.'

Sir Roger knew the power of these amulets. Sir Eustace's curse had destroyed his fortune.

'It came from St. Peter himself and has been authenticated by none other than Pope John three hundred years ago.' Mercurius allowed himself some artistic licence as he recounted its provenance. 'This hallowed and treasured object has passed through many hands; it once belonged to Bishop Odo of Bayeux.' He didn't say how it had come into his possession. 'It has kept me safe all these years and now I owe my life to you.' Mercurius continued, 'May this keep you safe as it did me. My life is now on time borrowed from your mercifulness. And I thank you for it.' *It saved me from you, too.*

Sir Roger, for once, was lost for words. *The Baptist's blood! It must be one of the holiest objects in Christendom.* 'You are welcome to stay in my castle till spring,' he said eventually, overcome with Mercurius's generosity. He was pleased, too, once Dan had told him more.

'I want you to devise a show for the King himself,' he told them. 'You'll join me in Flanders.' He knew his friend the King liked to be well entertained. 'Make sure it's good.'

Dan and Mercurius nodded their heads up and down in unison. To perform for a king was the ultimate honour; there was nowhere higher to go except the Emperor, then St. Peter.

Simon said his *au revoir* to his new wife and wondered whether he would ever see the child that would bear his name. He feared the wrath of his erstwhile boss. *So I've become a traitor now, unless I am very careful, I'm marked for an early death.*

It was with trepidation and uncertainty that the column of men and whatever equipment they could scrape together prepared to leave the castle. The Ox held their banner high. *OK Shrimp-Turd, you did me a favour, I owe you one.* He stuck his tongue out at Dan and saluted - though he'd *still* fight dirty next time they met in the ring.

Lady Alice had been most tearful, to be left amidst the ruins. Sir Roger was relieved that harmony reigned in the marital bed once more. They had both tasted forbidden fruit and had found it sour. There was something about love within marriage, both agreed, that transcended the brief pleasures of the flesh. This, though, did not stop Sir Roger's mind turning to the fact that Lady Caroline might be in Flanders.

Lady Alice climbed to the top of the tower. She was not over-enamoured with life amongst the Anglo-Saxons. As far as she was concerned they were a dismal, ugly race that spoke a guttural and incomprehensible language. She steeled herself for the task ahead. She longed for the civilised life of Court. She remained on top of the tower with the children. They waved as the procession clattered over the drawbridge and waved until the column was out of sight.

I'm going to make those pigs clean this place. She turned and went back into the Hall.

For those of you who have enjoyed **'Trouble Brewing'**,
the story continues in **Volume 2**, **"The Banneret's
Blade – Revenge is Sweet"**,
which will be published shortly. The adventures of Sir Roger
continue as he undertakes more exciting missions for his King. The
Toad, meanwhile, is busy assembling the mighty French 'Army of the
Sea' and plans to invade England. The action culminates in the great
sea-battle of Sluys in 1340. Who will win? who will die…?

Bibliography Sources and Acknowledgements.

In writing this book I have unashamedly copied, paraphrased and otherwise plagiarised, pilfered, borrowed and possibly bowdlerised many distinguished works on the subject of Edward III, the start of the Hundred Years War, how medieval people lived, ate and dressed. How they fought and farted, how they died. Some of it I got from the TV, some more from numerous sites on the Internet (thanks Wikipedia, I sent you some money) whose URLs have been swallowed and, sadly, lost.

Obviously I have dovetail and switched a few parts of real history to fit my narrative better, these are few and far between, generally I have tried to ensure as an accurate timeline as far as possible. I am sure scholars amongst my readership will note a few errors, but do I care? Of course, but... I still hope you enjoy this glimpse into a world far different from today's.

The principle book and pamphlet sources have been:

Jonathan Sumption 'Trial by Battle, *The Hundred Years War I*'
Ian Mortimer 'The Perfect King'
W.M. Ormerod 'The Reign of Edward III'
Clifford J. Rogers 'The Wars of Edward III'
Frances & Joseph Gies 'Life in a Medieval Village'
Frances & Joseph Gies 'Cathedral, Forge, and Wheel'

Geoffrey Parnell 'The Royal Menagerie at the Tower of London'
Christopher Gravett 'Medieval Siege Warfare'
Rupert Willoughby 'Life in Medieval England'
Andrew Stewart Jamieson 'Coats of Arms'
Doris Cotton 'The History of St. Michael's Church, Southampton'
Simon Thurley 'Royal Lodgings at the Tower of London 1216-1327'
Clive Bartlett 'English Bowman 1330-1515'
Peter Crisp 'The Medieval Church'
Tony McAleavy 'Life in a Medieval Castle'
Ian Lapper & Geoffry Parnell 'The Tower of London, A 2000 year history'
Nigel Smith 'Life in Medieval Britain'
Andrew Langley 'Medieval Life'
Sharon Pay 'Medieval Southampton'
Antony Mason 'If you were there: Medieval Times'
David Nicolle & Angus McBride 'French Armies of the Hundred Years War'
Terence Wise, Richard Hook & William Walker 'Medieval Heraldry'
Christopher Prothero 'The Armies of Crecy and Poitiers'
Sir Nicholas Harris Nicolas 'A History of the Royal Navy, part 1'
Steven A. Epstein 'Genoa and the Genoese 958-1528'
Richard Barber 'Life and Campaigns of the Black Prince'
Frances Gies 'The Knight in History'
History Eyewitness 'The Pastons in Medieval Britain'
Tom Tierney 'Medieval Fashions'
David Herlihy 'The Black Death'
Glyn Coppack 'Medieval Merchant's House, Southampton'
Maggie Black 'Food and Cooking in Medieval Britain'
Christopher Allmand 'The Hundred Years War'
Christopher Hibbert 'The English, A Social History'
Bridget Ann Henisch 'Fast and Feast'
Bridget Ann Henisch 'The Medieval Calender'
Scott L. Waugh 'England in the reign of Edward III'
Norman Davies 'The Isles'
Barbara Tuchman 'A Distant Mirror'

Michael Prestwich 'The Three Edwards'

Michael Prestwich 'Armies and Warfare in the Middle Ages'

Andrew McCall 'The Medieval Underworld'

Dom Frederick Hockey 'Beaulieu, King John's Abbey'

Jim Bradbury 'The Medieval Seige'

Eric Jager 'The Last Duel'

Richard Kieckhefer 'Magic in the Middle Ages'

Roger Stalley 'Early Medieval Architecture'

Judith Herrin & E.L. Ladurie 'A Medieval Miscellany'

Anne Curry & M. Hughes 'Arms, Armies and Fortifications in the 100 Years War'

Christopher Dyer 'Standards of living in the later Middle Ages'

Alison Weir 'Isabella, She-Wolf of France'

W.L. Rodgers 'Naval Warfare under Oars 4th-16th Centuries'

Donald Featherstone 'The Bowmen of England'

About the Author

Nick de Rothschild is a scion of the famous banking dynasty who never became a banker. He was one of the pioneers of the video industry before moving out of London to look after the family's estate at Exbury in the beautiful New Forest, Hampshire. His grandfather created the world-famous Exbury Gardens, about which he makes the occasional film. He likes to think of himself as 'The Man Who Lives in Paradise'. He also has a degree in Archaeology, Anthropology and Art History from Cambridge University, collects South African flowering bulbs, and is fascinated by all things.